ALSO BY STEVEN A. McKAY

The Forest Lord Series
Wolf's Head
The Wolf and the Raven
Rise of the Wolf
Blood of the Wolf

The Warrior Druid of Britain Chronicles
The Druid
Song of the Centurion

LUCIA – A Roman Slave's Tale

THE NORTHERN THRONE

By

Steven A. McKay

**Book 3 in the
WARRIOR DRUID OF BRITAIN
CHRONICLES**

Copyright © 2020 Steven A. McKay
All rights reserved. No part of this book may be reproduced,
in whole or in part, without prior written permission
from the copyright holder.

PLACES IN THE NORTHERN THRONE

As ever, some of these names are my own inventions since there's no written records of what many places were called during this period. I've tried to keep things simple, and as clear as possible. You may live in one of these areas and know a more accurate name – if so, let me know.

ALT CLOTA – Strathclyde
ARD SABHAL – Barnhill/Overtoun, West Dunbartonshire
AUCHALIC – Lower Auchalick, Argyll & Bute
BRANODUNUM – Brancaster, Norfolk
BRUACH GLEANN – Ardoch Roman Fort, Dunblane, Perthshire
DALRIADA – Argyll
DUNADD – Hillfort in Lochgilpead, Argyll & Bute
DUN BREATANN – Dumbarton Castle, West Dunbartonshire
DUNCRYNE – Gartocharn, West Dunbartonshire
DUN EDIN – Edinburgh Castle
GARRIANUM – Burgh Castle, Norfolk
HIBERNIA – Ireland
IOVA – Iona, Inner Hebrides
LOCH LAOMAINN – Loch Lomond, West Dunbartonshire
MEDIO NEMETON – Bar Hill Roman Fort, Twechar, East Dunbartonshire
SEGELOCUM – Littleborough, Greater Manchester
SMOO CAVE – Durness, Sutherland
SYDERCED – Syderstone, Norfolk
TRISANTANO – River Trent

CHAPTER ONE

**Medio Nemeton Roman Fort,
Northern Britain, AD431**

"Are you insane?"

Bellicus, Druid of Dun Breatann, crossed his arms and thought about the question for just a moment before a sardonic smile tugged at the corners of his mouth. "Probably," he admitted. "What I'm proposing, however, is anything but."

Bellicus, along with his loyal friend, the former Roman centurion, Duro, were in the campaign tent belonging to King Cunedda of the Votadini and, although their meeting appeared quite cordial, its circumstances were far from it.

Cunedda's army had been marching westwards, where they planned to meet up with a Pictish force led by King Drest. Together they would continue on and lay siege to the towering fortress of Dun Breatann, capital of Alt Clota.

With the combined might of two armies facing them, Bellicus knew Alt Clota would have been in trouble. Those lucky few gathered atop the ancient volcanic plug Dun Breatann was built upon might be lucky enough to survive, for the fortress had never been taken by invaders in all its long history, but everyone else in the surrounding towns and villages would suffer at the hands of the invading soldiers.

Livestock would be butchered, crops stolen or destroyed, wealth carted off, and, most seriously, the common folk would be raped, killed or forced into slavery by Drest and Cunedda's men.

Narina, newly crowned queen of Alt Clota following the death of her husband, Coroticus, at Bellicus's hands just a few weeks earlier, was no fool. Far from it, which was why she had been so readily accepted by her people as their new ruler. She, along with Bellicus and her other advisors, had spent many hours discussing their options before choosing the course of action that now saw the druid in this tent, surrounded by enemy soldiers in the middle of a field.

The previous Alt Clotan king had taken it badly when his and Narina's daughter, Catia, was kidnapped by a Saxon warband. Coroticus took out his frustrations on the neighbouring tribes and, eventually, this had driven them to war. It had been short-lived though, as Drest, Cunedda and their Dalriadan ally, Loarn mac Eirc's first attempt at a siege ended unsuccessfully with the onset of winter and the need to return to their homes to prepare for the coming harsh season.

On that occasion the invaders had left without doing much damage to the surrounding lands or people, purely because they expected to return soon enough and take what they wanted. It wasn't sensible to kill a farmer when you'd be needing his crops to survive in a few months.

Narina knew the next time their enemies came in force, however, they would not be so quick to leave without some form of recompense for their time and effort.

That they *would* return was a certainty. The one thing in Alt Clota's favour was the fact the Dalriadans would not be much a of threat for a while, as Bellicus and Duro had travelled west, into their lands, and somehow managed to kill King Loarn mac Eirc. No wonder it was widely believed that the giant warrior druid was beloved of the gods – to slay two kings in such a short space of time, and survive, was truly the stuff of legends.

All this meant Queen Narina and her people had only to fear the Picts in the north and the Votadini in the east. And she soon decided, with her advisors, that it would be better to strike first themselves, instead of waiting for their enemies to arrive at their gates.

So, leaving only a small force to defend Dun Breatann, Narina journeyed west to gather loyal warriors to her banner, while Bellicus led the Alt Clotan army east along the old Roman road to find the Votadini.

The druid knew this area well enough – the great earthen wall built by the Roman Emperor Antoninus still stood, although the forts and assorted support structures that once stood so proudly were now mostly gone or falling to ruin. Bellicus decided the best place to ambush Cunedda's warband was here, at Medio Nemeton.

Once, this had been a thriving fort, with granaries, barracks, a commanding officer's house in the centre, and even a bath house, all enclosed within earth and timber ramparts. Now, it was little more than mounds of grass that had grown over the demolished and burnt buildings in the past two hundred and seventy years but, crucially, it was set on a hill so afforded a view of the road along which the Votadini were sure to march. This made it ideal for Bellicus's purposes, so he'd brought the Damnonii army here and then waited for Cunedda's warband to arrive.

It was a risky strategy, for there was always a chance the Picts would turn up at Dun Breatann while the defenders were away hunting the Votadini, but Cunedda's men had walked right into the ambush Bellicus had laid for them.

The numbers on each side were similar, but the Damnonii had taken up positions that allowed them to surround the Votadini on three sides, with the ruined fort on the fourth which some of Bellicus's slingers had taken positions upon. If there was a fight, Cunedda's men would be annihilated in short order and the Votadini king knew it. When the druid had asked to discuss terms of his surrender Cunedda had little choice but to accept.

So here they were, and Bellicus wanted to get things over with as soon as possible. He stood up, causing a ripple of anxiety amongst Cunedda's half-dozen guards, for the young druid was nearly seven feet tall. Taking no notice of the consternation he'd caused, he took out a wax tablet and placed it on the table in front of the Votadini king.

"Look. You know what this is, I assume, my lord?"

Cunedda, eyed the image drawn on the wax and frowned uncertainly. "Britannia," he answered.

"Exactly. This small section here – that's your lands. This, larger part, is Drest's. And here, and here," he stabbed a finger at the north-western side of the image, "are Alt Clota and Dalriada."

"You didn't come all this way with an army just to give me a lesson on how the land lies, did you?" Cunedda demanded, brows furrowed irritably. "Why didn't you just attack us anyway? That's what I'd have done, had our roles been reversed. And will you sit down, druid? You're making me nervous, hovering around like a giant hawk."

Bellicus grinned and even Duro smiled at Cunedda's candid remark – it wasn't often a king would admit to anxiety over another warrior's mere physical presence.

"One moment," the druid said, apologetically, and pointed again at the crude depiction of Britannia on the wax tablet before the Votadini king. "You see the size of the rest of the island? Well, this whole section of the eastern shore belongs, or soon will do, to the Saxons." He paused to let his words sink in, before continuing. "Look at the size of that piece of land." It appeared even bigger than it really was, because Bellicus had purposely skewed the proportions of his drawing, making the Saxon Shore seem massive. "And look at how close it is to your lands. Here," he pointed, "is your own fortress, Dun Edin."

Cunedda eyed the drawing in silence as Bellicus took his seat once again.

"What of it?" the Votadini captain, Eburus, a broad-shouldered, surprisingly young man, demanded. "The Saxons are no threat to us – they've got their hands full trying to take over the lands in the south and, from what we hear, it's not going too well for them."

"It's going well enough that they've managed to take that whole part of the eastern coast," Duro replied. "And trust me, it's not that long a journey from there to here. I made a similar one myself just last year. To suggest the Saxons are no threat is blind stupidity."

"Who are you calling stupid, you old Roman twat?" Eburus demanded, half-rising to his feet, but Cunedda grasped his arm and, in a low growl, commanded him to be silent. Bellicus hid a smile behind his hand, pleased to see Duro rolling his eyes disdainfully at the Votadini's loss of temper. The experienced centurion was a good man to have at the bargaining table, he thought.

"What is it you really want from us, druid?" Cunedda demanded, plainly irritated himself by how his day was turning out. "That we go home and swear to leave Alt Clota in peace for…a year? Two?"

Bellicus frowned and glanced again at Duro. The Votadini king still hadn't grasped what they were saying.

"Yes, I expect you to lead your warband home," he agreed. "But I wasn't making a jest when I said I want an eighth of your men to come south with me to the Saxon Shore."

"This is a waste of time," Eburus spat, getting to his feet and slamming a hand onto the table. He was even younger than Bellicus, perhaps twenty-one or -two, and yet to learn patience, it seemed. "Come, my king. Let's send these two fools back to their comrades so we can face them like real men – on the field of battle."

Cunedda merely stared at his hot-headed young warrior, and it was Bellicus who broke the silence. "I liked your previous champion better," he said, gazing at the Votadini king who laughed mirthlessly at his comment.

"Why don't we start things off," Eburus retorted. "Me and you, druid. Come on, outside. I've heard all about how mighty you are, but I've beaten harder men than you in my time."

"By Mithras," Duro sighed, shaking his head. "Can you send this idiot away, lord king, so we can talk properly?"

Cunedda rose to his feet and grabbed the enraged Eburus by the sword-arm, shoving him back, towards the tent's entrance flap and the guards waiting there. "Get out of here you young fool, before you get us all killed. I'll speak with you later, and don't even think of saying another word to me or I'll have you stripped and flogged! Get out!"

The champion, face scarlet, looked murderously at Bellicus and Duro but turned and shoved past the guards, out into the midday sunshine. His voice could be heard as he moved away, loudly complaining about Damnonii cowards from Alt Clota who wouldn't fight like men.

"Where did you find him?" Bellicus smiled once the tent was calm again.

"He's the son of one of my chieftains," Cunedda muttered, pouring himself a cup of wine before offering the jug to his guests, neither of whom wanted any more. "A fine warrior. Well, that's an understatement – he's the best fighter in my army, to be perfectly honest. He challenged my old champion, Con, during the winter months when warriors become bored sitting around with no battles to fight." The king shook his head sadly. "Eburus beat Con quite handily, which was a surprise to us all. Apart from Eburus, of course, who's blessed with an arrogance and self-belief like you've never seen before."

"Con?"

"Dead, unfortunately," Cunedda said. "Took a nasty cut from Eburus's sword and the bleeding couldn't be stopped. Shame. Con had been with me for years and knew his place. Unlike that young fool." He brightened suddenly, grinning slyly as he contemplated the druid. "You say you want me to send warriors with you?"

"Oh no," Duro broke in, shaking his head emphatically. "He's not the type we're after."

"He's a superb fighter," Cunedda said. "Isn't *that* the type you're after?"

"Considering we want to build a warband from all the disparate tribes north of the Roman walls," the centurion growled, "I'd say it's more important that we have soldiers who know how to obey orders and can keep their mouths shut. Men with discipline, in other words."

"He's right," Bellicus said flatly. "That young man would cause all sorts of trouble between the various factions and ultimately someone—either one of us, or him—would end up dead. No. You can keep him."

The Votadini king looked forlorn, and Duro tilted his head up, eyes narrowed.

"Does that mean you're willing to send some of your men with us then?"

Sighing, Cunedda refilled his cup and nodded slowly. "Doesn't seem like I've got much choice, does it?"

"Not really," Bellicus agreed, holding out his own cup now that things were moving forward. "Let's drink to it, and we'll be off, so you can choose who should come with us."

The three men toasted their new alliance, although it was quite obvious, despite his attempt to mask it, that Cunedda was inwardly seething at being forced into this. He had expected to join up with Drest and the Picts and loot the smoking remains of Alt Clota – yet here he was agreeing to go home, while also giving up an eighth of his warband. Thirty spearmen!

It was that, however, or see the Votadini wiped out completely. As unpalatable as it was, there could be no other choice. So Cunedda smiled tightly and drained the last of his wine, which was good enough for Bellicus.

The first part of their plan was complete, and not a single life had been lost. The gods were on their side it seemed.

"We'll get back to our own lines then," the druid said, rising, as Duro followed his lead. "Thank you for your time, my lord. I truly believe this is the best thing for our peoples – the Saxons are the greatest threat facing us all right now."

Cunedda managed a grunt but little more as he ushered them outside, past the stony-faced guards.

"When do you want my men, druid?"

Bellicus replied instantly, having expected the question and being in a hurry to get back on the road – they still faced the threat of the approaching Pictish army after all. "At least an hour before sundown. That way we can get them settled in for nightfall and they can share a drink with their new brothers-in-arms."

Another sigh from the king, whose red beard was practically glowing in the pale spring sunshine. "All right. I'll bring them myself. See you then, druid. Centurion." He nodded to both, barked an order at one of the guards to bring their captain to him, then disappeared back into the tent.

Bellicus led the way towards their own waiting warband but, before they'd gone more than a dozen steps, an angry voice hailed them.

"By the gods, not this whoreson again."

It was, of course, Eburus. He wasn't alone, either, for half a dozen men around his own age trailed behind him, sneering, and giggling amongst themselves.

"Are you just going to walk away then?" the Votadini champion demanded, as his friends shouted similar questions. "Cowards, that's what you are. Afraid to test yourself against a real warrior."

"Where is this great warrior?" Duro demanded, looking about exaggeratedly. "I can't see any. Only beardless boys who probably still need their mothers to wipe their arses."

King Cunedda reappeared from his tent, but Eburus was already running towards the Alt Clotan negotiators and Duro drew his spatha from its sheath as Bellicus held up his eagle-topped staff of office defensively.

"By the gods, Eburus, I'll have your balls for this!" Cunedda roared, but the hot-tempered young warrior was past hearing even his own king.

"Try not to kill him," Bellicus muttered as they prepared to meet the oncoming young man, but Duro laughed incredulously at his statement.

"The lad isn't their champion for nothing, druid. I'll do whatever I can to survive." He brought his spatha up and set his feet, ready to fight. "I'd suggest you do the same."

Instead of following the centurion's lead though, Bellicus walked ahead and awaited their battle-crazed opponent's arrival with his arms outstretched as, behind him, Duro groaned, fearing the druid had bitten off more than even he could chew this time.

CHAPTER TWO

The ship lurched as a wave caught it but the man in the prow barely shifted his feet to compensate. Sigarr had been a sailor for most of his thirty-two years and was well used to the motions of his vessel. It would take something more than this gentle squall to tip him off balance and ruin his enjoyment of the view.

He wiped the chill spray from his brow, barely registering the numbness in his nose and cheeks, and eyed the land they were approaching. Through the smirr he could just make out a large promontory, extending out into the water in the distance. There were buildings up there, he was sure of that, although they were too far away yet for him to see them.

Dunnottar. Great fortress of a warlike tribe even the Romans couldn't tame: The Picts.

Sigarr turned and shouted to his second-in-command. "Lower the sail and bring her in the next time we have a chance, Cretta. We're here." He looked then to his crew—a dozen of them—and opened his mouth to bark an order but stopped himself and smiled wryly as he turned back to gaze again at the approaching land. The men didn't need to be told to prepare for landfall, they were already moving, bringing in the sail and taking up positions at the oars. Most of the men were as experienced as Sigarr. They knew their business, on sea and on land.

If trouble met them as they made their way towards the commanding fortress on the coast, Sigarr and his warband would face it with weapons ready in hand and Woden by their side.

Yet they weren't there for trouble. Sigarr had come as more of a diplomat than a raider, sent by his cousin Hengist—*bretwalda,* or warlord of those the people of Britannia called Saxons—in order to form an alliance between the two peoples, even if only for the coming summer. Still, they didn't know how the Picts would view their arrival, which is why they weren't sailing on and putting in at the docks their intelligence told them were situated just a little further north.

Merchants from Sigarr and Hengist's home in Jutland had, in the past, traded with the Picts and they'd told the *bretwalda* all about the layout of the land around Dunnottar. In recent years such trade had reduced drastically though; the waters were simply not as safe to sail thanks to the number of Saxons migrating here, and the Pictish raiders who regularly sailed south to attack the lands belonging to Britons. The merchants had understandably found other, safer, trade routes to exploit, where pirates and sea-wolves wouldn't steal their cargo along with their vessel and toss them overboard for the fish to devour.

Indeed, the Picts, bold and warlike as ever, had even taken to raiding the lands now controlled by Hengist's people in eastern Britannia. That was what had prompted this journey – Sigarr was to offer Drest treasure to keep his warriors away from the Saxon Shore, allowing Hengist to concentrate fully on pushing further westwards. Horsa, younger and more aggressive brother of the *bretwalda*, did not like the idea of paying someone to leave them alone, but Hengist had assured him it would be worth it.

Of course, Sigarr had not brought any treasure with him on this voyage, but he'd been given the authority to negotiate a suitable price with Drest and return later with the payment. Sigarr felt his responsibility keenly, and desperately wanted to prove himself worthy of the *bretwalda*'s trust.

The land opened up on their port side, revealing a small bay, into which Cretta steered the ship, named *Ceolgar*, deftly avoiding a handful of rocks sticking out like rotten teeth in the surf while the men expertly worked the oars, slowing their progress. The wooden hull struck the pebbled shore and slowly came to rest halfway out of the water.

"Ealdred. Hrothulf." Sigarr, who was a jarl—a nobleman, and used to giving orders—spoke directly to two of his warriors. "You wait here and guard the ship. Any sign of trouble, sail away and come back for us when it's safe, all right?"

The sailors he'd addressed nodded and sure enough, their arrival hadn't gone unnoticed – as the rest of the men gathered their gear and jumped overboard onto the beach a small figure watched them from atop the headland before sprinting northwards, towards the fortress.

"They know we're here," Cretta rumbled, sending pebbles flying as he thumped down onto the ground.

Wig, a barrel-chested young warrior, gazed up at the low cliff, watching until the running figure disappeared. "Just a child," he noted.

"A shepherd perhaps," Sigarr suggested. "He'll raise the alarm, so have your weapons ready, but remember!" He turned to face his men, a wave of pride washing over him as he looked at them. "We're not here for a fight. Only strike in self-defence and ignore any insults they might throw our way."

"We won't understand a damn word they're saying anyway," Cretta replied.

"Maybe not," Sigarr smiled. "But I'm sure you know what this means, Cretta – you've been called it often enough." He made a gesture and the others laughed as they began trudging across the loose stones towards a path leading up towards the grass of the headland.

"No idea," Cretta retorted. "And I don't know what you're laughing at, Wig. You're the biggest wanker in the whole warband."

"Wig the Wanker," someone called, raising more laughter which even the butt of their joke joined in with. Soon, however, they fell silent, becoming serious as they reached the top of the path and gazed around at the homeland of the Picts.

"Is this it?" Cretta asked, a little bemused. "I thought these lands were supposed to be full of great hills and mountains."

The ground was quite flat for as far as the eye could see, broken only by the occasional copse of trees or farmhouse. No people were visible, but there were sheep in one of the fields and the chimneys in the distant roundhouses breathed smoke from cooking fires.

Doubt struck Sigarr and he wondered if they'd somehow missed their destination and ended up in a completely different place. By Frigg, what would his cousin say when he found out? But Sigarr was confident in his abilities as a sailor, and besides, now that the light rain had stopped, he could see the Pictish stronghold not too far ahead. There was no mistaking it – there couldn't be many other fortresses perched atop a promontory like that.

The icy chill in his guts dissipated and he forced a smile onto his face as he led the way northwards. No, they were in the right place. Now all he had to do was talk with King Drest.

Despite his assertion that they wouldn't understand Pictish insults, one of their number could speak the language of the "painted ones": Eata. He'd been born in these windswept lands but travelled south five years ago, when he was seventeen, to become a mercenary. The Saxons were always happy to swell their numbers with strong fighting men and Eata had been welcomed by Sigarr and given a chance to prove his worth, which he'd done many times.

The young warrior was good with an axe and steady in the shield wall and now Sigarr hoped he would also be of use as a translator.

Their presence was noted by more of the locals as they headed for the fortress and the warriors muttered unhappily about wandering around enemy lands without their spears but, since Sigarr did not want them to appear threatening, he'd ordered the conspicuous polearms left on board the

Ceolgar. Swords, axes, and shields would have to be enough protection.

People in the nearest fields could be seen hurrying towards their homes, while the sounds of doors and windows being barred carried on the wind. Weapons – mostly crude pitchforks and wood-chopping axes – would be gathered by the labourers, and their dogs worked into a frenzy, ready to attack anyone who came near.

It was all to be expected, and little for Sigarr to worry about. The simple-folk would not attack his warband without provocation, he hoped. Not when they had their chief in his fortress nearby to look after them. Of course, if Drest decided to start a fight with his visitors the Saxons would find themselves beset on all sides. It would not be pleasant. Some men would grin and welcome the chance to bloody their axe in that situation, no matter the odds, but Sigarr was no violent savage. He wanted power and wealth as much as his cousins, but he would prefer to use guile before violence, if possible. And remaining alive was quite an important part of his plans.

As they neared Dunnottar they saw only one entrance – a long, narrow path leading down before sloping steeply up towards a wooden gatehouse. The natural walls of the fortress towered above the pathway and, most disturbingly, wooden stakes had been hammered into the ground at regular intervals. These bore the decapitated heads of the Picts' enemies – some were merely sun-bleached skulls, having been in place for a long time, but others were fresher and still had rotting flesh left on them. A carrion crow was perched atop one such head and, when it noticed their approach it took a last hasty peck at a piece of scalp before flying off with an outraged shriek.

"I don't like the look of that at all," Cretta growled, and a number of the men, in full agreement with Sigarr's second-in-command, cursed when they realised how vulnerable they would be if they were to walk to the gate along this eldritch path and seek entry.

"They won't just fill us with arrows," the jarl laughed as if their fears were baseless, although he felt as fretful as any of the grumbling warband. "Not until they know who we are, what we want, and, more importantly to them, how many of us there are."

"Don't tell them there's only one shipload of us," Wig advised. "Let them think we have a whole fleet behind us."

"Thank you for that insight, Wise One," Sigarr replied sarcastically. "I would never have thought of that myself."

"Idiot," Cretta said, shaking his head in disgust at Wig before addressing his jarl. "Unfortunately for us though, they might already know we have only a single ship."

"Perhaps," Sigarr agreed as they reached the narrow curving path that rose upwards towards the fortress. "But we're not looking for a fight, and we're no threat to these people so I'd like to think the universal rules of hospitality will keep us alive. Now." He halted and waited a moment, with Cretta by his side, until the men formed up into two ranks of five. "There's no point in us all wandering down there. I'll go with Cretta and Eata to speak to them. Drest is probably waiting at the gatehouse to greet us. You men just wait here."

"What if they...What if something happens to you?" a grizzled warrior with a large gut asked.

"You're not likely to scale the walls in order to avenge us, are you, Egil?" the jarl said with a wry smile. "So, if there's trouble and we're cut down or taken captive, you all return to the ship and carry the news back to Garrianum, all right? Good. May Woden protect us then."

"Woden protect you," Egil repeated, with others muttering their own blessings, and Sigarr gave a last reassuring nod before turning away and striding along the sloping path towards Dunnottar, Cretta and Eata following behind.

"What do you think the Picts will do when they know why we're here?" Cretta asked, glancing to Eata.

The young mercenary's brows lifted while his mouth turned down in an exaggerated frown. He clearly had no idea how this would go.

"I've never met Drest," he said. "From what I hear he's not as headstrong or vicious as many warlords. I guess he'll let Jarl Sigarr say his piece and then decide if we should live or die."

"That's a start," Sigarr chuckled mirthlessly, and then all three fell silent for the path had started to slope steeply upwards now and none of them wanted to arrive at the Pictish gatehouse while labouring for breath.

Their passage wasn't helped any by a rising breeze and, as he walked, Sigarr gazed up at the hugely impressive, even picturesque, fortress, wondering if any invading army had ever managed to capture it. It certainly wouldn't be easy. Even if the place was only garrisoned with twenty men, as long as they had enough stones for their slings, and rocks to drop on any who came close enough, this narrow walkway would soon be made impassable by the bodies of the dead and injured.

There was a shout from the gatehouse ahead and the Saxons halted. Another shout, and Sigarr turned to Eata.

"What are they saying?"

"They're telling us to stop," the younger man replied. "And asking who we are."

"Tell them who I am then," Sigarr commanded and turned back to look at the Picts atop the gatehouse as his underling shouted something in the strange tongue of the painted-folk. The jarl could see four men behind the wooden palisade, all in leather armour, wearing helmets and holding swords or spears. To his surprise, a tall woman was also there and something about her stance told Sigarr she was the one in command.

They listened to Eata and then the woman replied and, even before the mercenary had translated their words, Sigarr felt disappointment rise within him.

"They say we should go back to our ship and, well, piss off basically," Eata reported in a neutral voice, perhaps wondering if this kind of chatter was part of the usual diplomatic negotiations.

"Drest isn't here," Sigarr muttered, meeting Cretta's gaze. "Count the men on the walls and look at the girl standing there as if she's in charge. Not a king among them, and only a few guards left to defend the place." To Eata he said, "Tell them I'm a kinsman to the Saxon *bretwalda,* Hengist, and I'm here to discuss an alliance with them."

As Eata began shouting again Sigarr shrugged and said to Cretta, "Maybe the king's out hunting and will return soon."

Laughter came from above and jeers too. The Picts pointed at Sigarr with great mirth and the Saxon felt his face flush red. He couldn't speak their tongue, but he knew very well what they were saying.

"They, ah…" Eata stammered, and looked away as if unwilling to translate the Pictish words.

"They say, 'How can he be a kinsman of the mighty Hengist and Horsa', is that it? 'He's a skinny little shit, not like those great warriors at all.'"

"Something like that, my lord, aye," Eata rubbed the back of his neck with a hand and looked uncomfortably down at the surf crashing against the beach below.

Sigarr's father, Svipdagr, was the brother of Wihtgils, father to Hengist and Horsa. His cousins were tall, muscular, and impressive enough that their names and exploits were known even in this far-flung pocket of civilisation. In contrast, Sigarr was smaller than most men, wiry rather than powerfully built, and his fame had not spread much beyond the borders of his home in Jutland.

This was not to say Sigarr was a weakling or a coward in battle. On the contrary, he was as brave as any man, but the gods had not blessed him with the more obvious qualities of his cousins. He lacked the charisma of Hengist, the sheer viciousness of Horsa, and the martial prowess of both.

He had accepted all that years ago, and chosen to use their relationship however he could, to raise himself to as lofty a position within the Saxon ranks as possible.

He was no fool—in truth, intelligence was one area where the gods *had* blessed him—and, when Hengist asked him to travel here to speak with the Picts, Sigarr gladly agreed, sensing a chance to prove his worth.

Unfortunately, it didn't look like he'd be winning much renown on this trip and that was a harder draught to swallow than even the mocking laughter of the bastards in the gatehouse overhead.

"We're wasting our time here," the jarl growled, throwing a last, vicious glance at the sniggering Picts and the tall young woman who was making an obscene gesture at him. "Come on."

"Eh?" Eata was glad to move out of range of the guards' slings, but Cretta followed them more reluctantly. "Are we just going back to Hengist? He won't be pleased you know. This has been a complete waste of time."

Sigarr was too deflated to muster an angry retort. Instead he sighed and tugged at his beard. "Don't you think I know that? But there's nothing else for us to do, my friend. Drest might be anywhere and those fools in the fortress are hardly likely to tell us when he'll return."

"You never asked them." Cretta was plainly just as disappointed in their mission's failure as his jarl for he wouldn't normally question Sigarr's actions as openly as this, with one of their men in earshot.

Now, Sigarr did round on his second-in-command, eyes blazing. "Listen to yourself, Cretta! Do you think they'd tell us if their king is off fighting a battle somewhere a week's march away? Just tell us, a Saxon warband, that their king and his army are miles away and their fortress is essentially undefended?"

Cretta looked surprised. He hadn't thought of that, apparently.

"The Picts might believe we're just the vanguard of a much bigger force. For all they know, we have a dozen more ships at anchor half-a-day's sail away, ready to attack if we believe Dunnottar is ripe for it. So, I ask you again: Do you really think those arselings in the gatehouse will give us *any* information?"

He turned and strode back towards the rest of their companions again, but Cretta wasn't ready to admit defeat just yet.

"All right, what you say is true," he said. "I didn't think that far ahead. But I still think Drest may only be out hunting. Why don't we head back to the ship and stay in the bay for a day or two? The king might come home by then, and we can fulfil our mission."

Sigarr could see Eata nodding silent agreement with this suggestion and he had to admit it was a decent idea. They should be safe enough on board the *Ceolgar* – they'd maintain a watch and, if any enemies appeared, they could simply sail to safety. He was confident the *Ceolgar* would be able to outrun whatever vessels the Picts might be able to muster.

"Fine," the jarl replied. "That's what we'll do then. We've enough provisions on board to last an extra couple of days anyway."

"There's plenty sheep about too," Eata said, pointing at one large beast grazing on the hillside not far off.

"No stealing the livestock," Sigarr commanded. "By the gods! We don't want to antagonise these people; we're supposed to be making friends with them. No stealing, and we keep our distance from the natives. I don't want them attacking us because one of our lads can't keep his hands, or his cock, away from the local women. We maintain the peace and, Woden willing, when Drest returns he'll be more likely to grant us an audience, and the alliance we're here for."

The three men walked on in thoughtful silence, ignoring the gruesome trophies that had seemed so intimidating when they passed earlier, but they were still a fair distance away from the rest of the warband when Sigarr spotted something.

"Soldiers," he said, jerking his head to the west. "At least a dozen of them."

"Drest?"

The jarl shook his head. "I doubt it. They're not in formation. I'd expect a king's guard to be more disciplined as they march. Especially since they've surely seen Wig and the others. Oh, shit."

Sigarr began to walk faster but he could already see his warriors forming a shield wall, and that hadn't gone down too well with the oncoming soldiers, who brandished their own weapons and began to hurl insults and threats in their own, strange tongue.

"So much for keeping the peace," Cretta growled, and the three of them started to run towards Wig.

* * *

Cunedda had stopped shouting by now and Duro risked a quick glance at the Votadini king, seeing the beginnings of a smile playing on his lips. Of course, if Eburus managed to kill one of the Alt Clotan emissaries it would not be too disastrous for the king, who was no friend to them despite their newly agreed alliance. And he could hardly be blamed for the actions of a headstrong, and possibly drunk, young warrior, could he?

Duro looked back towards the charging Eburus, who was being cheered on by his friends. They wanted to see a fight that day, rather than simply giving in as they thought Cunedda had done in his pact with the Alt Clotans. The rest of the Votadini warband didn't seem quite so enthusiastic though, as they warily eyed the land behind Duro and the army gathered there, ready to defend the centurion and his druid companion.

The foolish actions of Eburus could be the end for dozens of men, no matter who won the fight between him and Bellicus.

"Die, druid!" Eburus screamed, raising his sword over his head, eyes wide, nostrils flaring, and everyone gathered in or around the field looked on breathlessly, waiting to see who would triumph between these two massive young combatants. Duro wished Bel's great wardog, Cai, was with them – a single thunderous bark from the animal was always enough to distract an enemy, but they had left the mastiff back at the camp with the captain, Gerallt, since their mission had been a peaceful one and the dog's presence would have been viewed, understandably, with alarm and suspicion.

Suddenly, Bellicus dropped his outstretched arms and stepped forward a single pace, then he appeared to say something to Eburus, although the words were spoken too quietly for anyone but the Votadini champion to hear.

To everyone's astonishment, Eburus stopped in his tracks, and stared, frowning at Bellicus as if he'd forgotten why he was running. "What?" he asked, bemused.

The druid spoke in a low voice again and Eburus shook his head, as if clearing it, and then, as his sword arm began to drop, the druid exploded into motion. The bronze eagle on top of his staff snaked out, smashing into Eburus's forehead, and then Bellicus swung the great length of ash around, into the back of the stunned Votadini's legs.

Crying out in agony, Eburus fell onto the grass at the druid's feet and Bellicus stood on the fallen man's neck, holding the butt of his staff over his face.

"Yield, fool, or I'll crack your skull like an egg."

For a moment the Votadini champion simply glared at his enemy, mouth a bloody mess, and then he muttered something.

"What was that?" Bellicus demanded, pressing down on the man's neck.

"I yield, you bastard!" Eburus cried and Duro made to walk forward for it was obvious what would happen as soon as Bellicus let the beaten young man back to his feet. He may have conceded the fight, but Eburus was so enraged at his loss of face he would not simply walk away meekly from the druid.

Thankfully, Cunedda recognised this too and had already commanded two of his guards to restrain Eburus. Bellicus stepped back as they hurried forward and grasped their disgraced champion roughly by the arms, holding him down so he couldn't make things worse.

Turning, Bellicus winked at Duro and they began to walk casually back towards the Alt Clotan army, with the astonished Votadini warband looking on in amazement. How could their mighty young champion, the best fighter they had in their ranks, have been beaten so easily?

"You have until sundown, Cunedda," the druid shouted over his shoulder and his tone was light. Joyous. "Thirty of your best men. Don't be late!"

When they were safely out of the Votadini slingers' range Duro laughed, shaking his head in wonder. "You never cease to amaze me, my friend. What did you say to stop him in his tracks like that? Some magical spell? A curse?"

Bellicus turned to him and smiled.

"I told him the lock on my front door was replaced three months ago, with one that matches the colour of the wood better."

The centurion's brow furrowed as he took this in and they continued to walk before, at last, he spoke up again.

"I don't get it."

"Neither did he," Bellicus replied dryly. "It confused him just as much as it's confused you. Magic doesn't always have to make sense."

They walked on, the druid's long stride eating up the ground as Duro began to laugh softly.

"You astonish me," the centurion said. "Great tales will probably be written about that fight, and how you somehow halted the mighty Votadini champion mid-attack, with nothing more than a single, earth-shattering word of power. Songs will be written proclaiming the wondrous event!"

"Aye," Bellicus agreed. "I'll write most of them myself."

Their laughter faded quickly however, at the sight of a rider, galloping towards their camp from the north. His speed suggested he had urgent news to share.

"I don't like the look of that," Bellicus muttered, breaking into a jog with Duro following his lead, although neither man moved too fast. The sight of the giant druid sprinting towards camp, robe flying behind him, might have caused even more alarm.

A tent similar to Cunedda's marked the centre of the Damnonii encampment and the guards jerked to attention when they saw the two officers approaching, offering respectful nods to both. Bellicus had long since won the respect of the people of Alt Clota, and his tales of recent adventures battling Saxons and Dalriadans made sure Duro had been embraced by them too.

"My lord." The messenger was sitting on one of the camp stools, legs outstretched, a cup of beer in his hand as he waited to deliver his information. He looked exhausted from riding but made to stand up before Bellicus waved him down again.

"What news do you bring, Cefin?" the druid asked, pouring a drink for himself before passing the jug to Duro.

"Not good," the messenger said with a frown. "Drest's army have been sighted. Three hundred strong, marching southwest."

"Towards Alt Clota," Duro said, drawing a nod from Cefin.

Bellicus sat down and drained his beer. He was an experienced warrior, but even he appreciated a good drink to calm him down and bring him back to reality after a fight.

"Oh well," he said, pragmatically, even managing a smile at the messenger. "We were expecting this – it hardly comes as a shock." He leaned back on the stool and yawned. The travelling and excitement of recent days were taking a toll on everyone in the army, including him, but it couldn't be helped. There was no time to rest.

"At least we now have more men to face him with," Duro said, then, responding to the messenger's puzzled gaze, told him what had happened that morning with the Votadini king, and champion. When he finished, a proud gleam shone in Cefin's eyes as he grinned at the druid.

"That'll give all the lads heart when they hear about it," he said, gladly accepting another cup of beer from Duro.

Footsteps approached and the tent flap was thrust aside as a craggy-faced soldier came inside, eyes searching the faces of the three men already gathered there.

"Well met, Gerallt," Bellicus smiled, gesturing the newcomer towards one of the other stools as Duro again filled a cup and handed it over. "And you too, my lad." This last to his great wardog, Cai, who pressed his muzzle into the druid's hand, licking his palm affectionately, before lying down.

Gerallt was, nominally, the commander of this portion of the Alt Clotan warband, although, in truth, Bellicus was his superior officer. After Queen Narina's coronation she had made a few changes to the structure and personnel of her army, promoting Bel to overall Warlord of her forces, although it was a rank that would only really mean anything in times of war. During peacetime, when it came, Gavo, Captain of the Queen's Guard, would remain in charge of the army, with Gerallt as his second-in-command, allowing Bellicus to concentrate fully on being the Damnonii druid.

Since Narina and Gavo were not there with them right now, that meant Gerallt and Bellicus were in charge, and the druid thought the queen had chosen her captain well.

Gerallt was in his late forties, with neatly combed silver hair and a beard to match, and he was straight-backed and broad-shouldered with decades of experience as both a lord and a soldier. He knew how to keep calm under pressure and was blessed with a fine, tactical mind, which Bellicus had been happy to defer to when it came to choosing a position to lay their ambuscade for Cunedda.

"Drest's coming, I assume," Gerallt said. "And, since the Votadini aren't attacking or even retreating, your visit to Cunedda must have been a success."

"It was," the druid confirmed, quickly repeating the tale again, with Duro embellishing things here and there.

"Nicely done, lads," Gerallt said approvingly. "With the Votadini taken care of, and the Dalriadans in disarray, all we have left to deal with are the Picts."

Bellicus nodded. If they could defeat Drest it would put Narina in a very strong position. Ultimately, the druid would like to see her crowned High Queen of all the northern lands, and it seemed that day might be close. A Damnonii High Queen would nullify the growing threat the Christians' posed to the old ways, while allowing the united tribes to face the Saxon threat at the side of Arthur and the Merlin. The druid just had to find a way to steer events towards such a favourable outcome.

"How long have we got before Drest arrives in Alt Clota?" Gerallt asked the messenger, disturbing Bellicus from his reverie.

"At the speed they were marching when I observed them," the messenger reported, "I'd say about three or four days, my lord."

"That should be more than enough," Duro said, resting his left hand on the pommel of his spatha. "If we leave here tomorrow at sun-up, we'll be able to head them off on the road before they get anywhere near Dun Breatann."

"And we're thirty men stronger now, too," Gerallt said, smiling grimly. "We'll be able to ambush the Pictish bastards just like we did the Votadini."

"Hopefully you're right, and we *do* surprise them," Bellicus muttered, gazing thoughtfully into his half-empty cup. "Because if Cefin's numbers are accurate, Drest's army still outnumbers ours."

CHAPTER THREE

Sigarr could tell soon enough that there would be no way out of this without a fight. His original estimate of the enemy's numbers proved correct but, of the twelve men approaching them, at least four of them were quite drunk, and the rest looked terrified. Not in a good way though – they wouldn't turn and run straight away. No, their fear would not overcome their need to appear brave in front of their kinsmen. But that type of foe wouldn't be reasoned with, Sigarr knew, for they'd not trust themselves to maintain their composure for long and would simply attack as soon as they were within range.

Unless, of course, they had a strong leader to bolster them and calm things down.

The man at the front and centre of their ragged line did not look like he would be such a leader. He seemed the drunkest of them all. Despite that, he was tall and broad shouldered and hefted his sword like he knew how to use it.

"Cretta," the jarl muttered. "You take out the big one. He's the main threat."

The captain nodded and hefted his axe confidently.

"The rest of you, hold the line and let them attack first. They're obviously untrained and shitting their breeches with fear, but that doesn't mean we can be complacent, you hear?" He glanced along the line and nodded at the determined faces he saw there. "Get this done without any of us being hurt, and then back to the ship in case the bastards in the fortress come out."

"Maybe it wouldn't be such a bad thing if they did," Eata said, drawing frowns from those beside him.

"How could that possibly be good for us?" Sigarr demanded, feeling sweat already beginning to make his palms slick as the Picts drew ever closer. "There might be twenty or thirty men in Dunnottar."

Eata nodded, never taking his eyes from the enemy who were now only a few yards distant, their faces flushed and fearful, their hoarse shouts little more than a babble of noise.

"True. Or there could be less than a dozen. If we beat them, the fortress would be ours."

The idea was so incredible that it hadn't even crossed Sigarr's mind. Now that he thought about it, Eata's suggestion brought a swelling of ambition to the jarl's heart, but he shook his head and ordered the warband to focus on the task at hand.

Even if they *did* somehow take control of the fortress, they were too few to hold the place once Drest returned with his own warriors. It would be foolhardy to even try, for the Picts would know all the secrets of Dunnottar – hidden ways in perhaps, that would render the high walls useless.

And yet…He could just imagine Hengist's roar of laughter when he heard the news Jarl Sigarr had captured the mighty Pictish stronghold. Even that sour-faced giant, Horsa, would have to give him some credit.

His musings were brought to an abrupt halt as the oncoming enemy line suddenly charged in a ragged formation.

"Remember!" Sigarr shouted, wishing his voice was stronger. "Hold the line. Let them strike first, and then take them down without mercy!"

The Picts' leader broke into a run, heading straight for Cretta who was, being the biggest of the Saxons, his direct counterpart and seemingly the biggest challenge. Whoever won that fight would earn great renown amongst their companions and kinfolk.

"Hold the line!" Sigarr roared, as Cretta stepped forward to meet his opponent. The Pict's sword came down with enough power to cleave halfway through a man's torso, but Cretta was sober, and well versed in the ways of war, and he used the shaft of his axe to bat the Pictish blade to the side.

The rest of the enemy reached the Saxon shield wall then and Sigarr had to turn his attention to the man trying to stick a pitchfork into his face.

Cries of rage and challenge turned to roars of pain and whimpers of fear as weapons did their bloody work but Sigarr's warband held steady. They remained calm, even those who'd been injured in the early clashes, whereas some of the Picts – mere farmers after all – looked petrified now that their initial drink-fuelled charge had been halted.

Sigarr could hear more voices from the west now and, batting another thrust of that damned fork over his shield, he was somewhat relieved to see only women and children coming to urge on their menfolk. Some of the women carried crude weapons of their own though, and he thought they might have been hardier fighters than the pitiful lot that had come to face them.

He lunged forward, slamming the boss of his shield into his opponent's face. It wasn't a particularly brutal blow, but it threw the Pict off balance and Sigarr followed it up by sliding the point of his sword into the man's guts. There was a scream, and another as the Saxon jarl repeated his attack before turning to take out another of the enemy in a similar fashion.

With those two down on the ground bleeding out the battle was as good as over. Only three Picts remained alive, but they wouldn't last long now that they were so badly outnumbered. It was a shame, Sigarr mused, as he watched his men move in to cut them down – they had fought bravely, if without skill.

The jarl looked round, a little surprised to see Cretta still battling the tall Pict who perhaps wasn't as inebriated as they'd assumed. The combatants appeared quite evenly matched in size and skill, and the Pict's ferocity seemed to be making up for the slightly slowed reflexes one would expect in a man who'd imbibed strong drink before a battle.

Sigarr had fought alongside Cretta for years, and he knew the warrior was as tough as they came, yet, as he looked on with interest, the Pict easily dodged another attack and dragged the edge of his blade along the Saxon's side. Cretta gasped in pain as the sword managed to slice through his leather cuirass, leaving a long, shallow wound in his side.

This man must have been a mighty warrior in his day, Sigarr thought in appreciation. A nobleman perhaps. He'd been left behind to lead the farmers when Drest took his army off to wherever they'd gone. Thank Frigg there was only one such hardy fighter, or the battle might have gone rather differently.

The Pict *was* drunk though, and at least twenty years older than Cretta who was only just into his thirties. It was impossible to guess who would win here, but Sigarr had no intention of letting the fight run its natural course and possibly losing his closest advisor.

He wandered around to the rear of the Pict, shaking his head ruefully as the man – either too drunk or too focused on Cretta – didn't even notice him moving, and didn't hear the watching women screaming warnings at him either. Then, when the big warrior was about to launch another attack, Sigarr simply stepped in and pushed the tip of his sword into the Pict's back. It wasn't a powerful thrust, but it was in just the right place, and the enemy warrior fell to his knees, open-mouthed in surprise, before Cretta's axe thudded home in his skull.

The native women had ceased their shouting by now and were running away as fast as they could without leaving the children behind.

"Don't even think about it," Sigarr growled as Wig, leering at the retreating forms, began to walk after them. "We're done here. Strip these fools of any valuables, if they have any, and then we head for the ship. Quickly now, move!"

Wig scowled at him, angered at not being allowed to claim his reward for winning the battle, but he didn't question

Sigarr's orders. Instead, he spat on the grass and began to rifle through the dead enemies' clothes for anything of worth, the rest of the warband following suit with an efficiency born of experience.

The jarl looked at his men as they went about their business, noting bloodstains on three of them, some damaged armour on others, and Eata was limping, but all were alive and seemed in decent shape, thank Woden.

"I might have lost if you hadn't stepped in, Sigarr," Cretta muttered, staring down at his fallen opponent with great respect in his eyes. "He knew what he was doing – must have had some training in his younger days. Hard bastard too."

"He was," Sigarr agreed, grasping his captain's arm encouragingly. "But so are you, my friend, and we'll all learn from this day's work."

They quickly took the fallen giant's sword and other goods, including a neat little comb which Cretta thought would do a good job of taming his own thick beard, and some of the Pictish armour which proved to be very well made, reinforcing Sigarr's belief that the veteran warrior had been someone of importance in these lands.

When the bodies were looted, Sigarr led the way back towards the beach. They eyed the fortress as they went, all the time half expecting another, stronger, force of Picts to come striding out to avenge their slaughtered countrymen, but no-one came. They could see the soldiers on the walls, including the tall woman, watching them as they left, and Sigarr guessed their orders had been to hold Dunnottar at all costs. That meant not opening the gate unless there was no other option.

"Those poor bastards must be itching to come out here and give us a good kicking," Egil grinned, raising his arm in the air and making a vulgar gesture towards the watching Picts.

"You're probably right," Sigarr replied irritably. "So don't provoke them any more than we already have, idiot! We won't be safe until the deck of the *Ceolgar* is beneath our feet and this place is a rapidly fading memory."

The men talked of the battle as they headed back towards the beach, laughing and joking now that the danger was over, describing their kills and showing their wounds or chipped weapons to prove a point.

"Who do you think he was?" Cretta asked, glancing over his shoulder as they began the somewhat precarious descent back down the hillside towards the anchored *Ceolgar*. "The warrior I fought, I mean. He was no farmer."

Sigarr shrugged. "Probably one of Drest's closest companions, in his youth. Then he fell foul of the drink, as so many men do, and became more of a liability than an asset, so the king placed him in charge of the farmers here. I've no doubt," the jarl said, grabbing at a tuft of grass as his foot almost slipped out beneath him, "that the Picts didn't expect any real trouble to turn up in Drest's absence."

"It's a pity," Cretta said, somewhat sorrowfully. "I'd have liked to fight alongside him, rather than against him."

Sigarr nodded. It wasn't uncommon for men to feel a strange affinity for their vanquished foes after a skirmish, especially if they had fought as well as the big Pict had done. "We'll be back on board the ship and on our way soon enough," the jarl said. "You can pray that he finds a place at the feasting tables in Walhalla and you meet him again one day."

He raised his arm in the air and made a circular motion. Ealdred and Hrothulf on board the *Ceolgar* were watching their comrades return and immediately set to work preparing the ship for departure.

It didn't take long before the warband were on board once again, pulling off their wet trousers and boots that they might dry off in the weak sunshine while those with injuries set about binding them. There were smiles all round for, although they hadn't completed their mission, that was Sigarr's worry. The rest of them had fought and won a battle and taken booty, however meagre, as their reward. The tale of this journey would at least earn them all a few drinks from the rest of Hengist's army on the Saxon Shore, for most of those warriors had never visited these lands and would be interested to hear what Dunnottar was like.

To that end, Sigarr ordered his helmsman to take them north before they headed home, so they could scout the docks and any other defensive structures that might have been erected recently. The jarl knew they would be unmolested, for if the Picts had any ships ready to attack them, they'd have already done so. No, they were safe enough to complete a quick trip along the Pictish coast and it gave Sigarr at least some new intelligence to report back to Hengist although, in truth, there was little to note. Drest apparently felt quite safe from sea-borne invaders for there were few walls or other defences.

This was nothing like the Saxon Shore, with its great stone buildings and walls which had failed to keep out Hengist's army anyway. The *bretwalda* would hopefully find this information useful.

They completed their quick scouting trip along the coast and then the jarl stood in the stern, feeling the spray on the back of his head and neck as the *Ceolgar's* sail was unfurled and they began the long journey back south. As the land receded though, Sigarr couldn't help imagining what it would have been like had they been able to wrest control of the hill fort from the skeleton force left to defend it. And who was that young warrior-woman anyway?

A sigh escaped his lips and he turned to find Cretta watching him.

Sigarr shrugged. "We leave not as victors, since we didn't successfully complete the task Hengist gave us, but at least we're still alive, and another day will bring us another chance to prove our worth."

Cretta nodded and even managed a smile. "Come on, lord. My feet are freezing. Let's get some mead and warm ourselves beside the brazier."

CHAPTER FOUR

Bellicus stood in the tiny settlement of Duncryne, not far from the low hill known locally as the Dumpling, and took in the sight of the Pictish army on the road to the east. Once there had been a fort atop the Dumpling but, although it was long gone, the mound still afforded excellent views of the surrounding lands so it was here the druid had brought his army once their business with Cunedda and the Votadini was concluded at Medio Nemeton. They'd made it there before Drest's Picts but the ambush Bellicus had hoped to lure the enemy into hadn't worked out as well as he'd hoped.

The first, initial, charge down the hill by the Damnonii soldiers had taken out a few Picts and evened up the numbers of the two opposing forces somewhat, but after that both sides had formed into defensive lines across the road and been unwilling to commit to a full-blown assault on their opponents. There had been skirmishes over the past two days, but it seemed as if the standoff might last forever for the messengers Bellicus sent to Drest had been chased away by the Pict's archers.

Even with the addition of the warband Cunedda had sent with Bellicus, the Pictish army was too big to meet head on without an unacceptable number of casualties and no guarantee of victory.

The druid frowned as he thought of the men Cunedda had loaned them. The king's own youngest son, Ysfael, led the Votadini warband and he was an impressive enough man if rather arrogant. The warriors that came with him were quite formidable too, and they at least owned decent weapons and armour. The only problem Bellicus had with these new allies was one man: Eburus, the hot-headed champion who liked a drink too much and had a score to settle with the druid after their short but violent tussle.

To be fair to Eburus, he didn't seem the vindictive sort, but his presence was already beginning to grate on the men around him and Bellicus wished Cunedda hadn't insisted on sending the brash young man with them, even if he would be useful when the fighting resumed.

Beside him there was an excited exclamation and, train of thought broken, he glanced at Duro, who was staring up at the Dumpling. The druid watched in wonder and relief as he realised it was the Alt Clotan queen on top of the hill, and what that might mean.

"By Mithras, isn't she magnificent?"

Duro spoke in low tones and Bellicus could only agree with his friend's statement, although he didn't reply out loud. There were enough—false—rumours going around regarding the druid and Narina as it was, without him adding to them by expressing open admiration for her. It was impossible to argue with the centurion though, for the queen held every warrior's attention as she appeared on the summit of the Dumpling in her great war chariot.

Strictly speaking, Alastor and Helios were the first ones to come into view and, from this distance, framed in the sunlight as they were, they appeared every bit as impressive as the queen.

Alastor was a huge black stallion, with a coat so glossy it seemed to shimmer in the early afternoon sunshine, while Helios was a similarly sized grey whose lighter colour showed off the enormous, rippling muscles in his legs as the horses brought Narina into view. The stablemaster, Uven, had chosen the two beasts well, for they looked like something from legend as they slowly drew the chariot over the crest of the hill.

Narina was surely the centrepiece though. As the horses came to a halt on the summit the queen was momentarily caught by the sun behind her, and her brown hair appeared like a magnificent halo as she gazed out upon the men below.

Of course, the spell couldn't last forever, but, as the Pictish army began to stir once more, ready to take up the fight again, a column of a dozen men led by her captain, Gavo, followed Narina over the hill to her left. And then another group followed to the right. And behind those, a line stretched out across the hill in single file, standing in silence, spears in hand, the sun casting long shadows before them that made them seem almost like giants.

Bellicus counted quickly. Although the sight was hugely impressive – so impressive he wished he'd choreographed it himself for it was truly a remarkable piece of magical theatre – Narina's new force only numbered around forty men.

Probably not enough to destroy Drest's army.

But, flanking the Picts as they were, it was enough to make them nervous, and enough to make Drest realise he could not win this battle without losing most of his own men.

"What do you think he'll do?" Duro asked, peering into the enemy forces, trying to see their king although from this distance it was impossible to gauge Drest's reaction to the Alt Clotan queen's arrival.

Bellicus shook his head uncertainly. "Hard to say. Drest isn't as headstrong or reckless as, say, Loarn mac Eirc. But I can't see him giving up as easily as Cunedda did – the Picts have put in a lot of effort to gather such a large army, and travelled a long distance to get here."

"They can't win though," the centurion said. "Well, I suppose they could, since they still outnumber us, but it would be a bloodbath on both sides. Certainly not the kind of victory I'd have wanted when I was in the legions. What's the point in winning when you've got no-one left to help you maintain control of the territory you've just won?"

"Exactly what I hope Drest is wondering himself right now," Bellicus agreed. "Losing so many soldiers would also leave his lands terribly weakened. News like that has a way of travelling fast – Cunedda, or even some of the Dalriadan warlords, might take the opportunity to lay siege to Dunnottar." He beckoned to Gerallt, who was a little way behind, where he could direct his men better, and the captain started moving towards them. "But, like I say, Drest has put a lot into this campaign. He won't just roll over. We'll have to offer him something in return for his giving up the fight…"

Gerallt appeared beside them, a wry smile on his lined face. "Offer him? What have we got to offer, Bel?"

"Probably nothing Drest actually wants," the druid replied, watching as the Pictish army moved slowly into a different, looser formation, as if their commanders feared a missile attack from Narina's newly arrived followers. "But maybe it'll be enough for him to save face and head back home without us all killing one another. Duro, have our horses brought over, will you?"

The centurion moved away to carry out the request, and Gerallt watched him go, lips drawn down almost disapprovingly.

"I don't know why he has to wear that Roman armour," the captain muttered. "And the helmet? The legions are long gone, Bel. Someone should tell your friend he isn't a centurion anymore."

"Have you seen him fighting over the past couple of days? Aye? Well you must have noticed the fear in the Picts' eyes as they realised how dangerous he was. Duro's armour makes him stand out. Any good army needs heroes, Gerallt, and that's why the centurion continues to wear that helmet, and that armour."

The captain harrumphed. "I don't believe we need tricks like that, druid. Our warriors' actions speak for themselves, without any fancy outfits or magic."

And that's why you'll never be anything more than a captain, the druid thought to himself. *No imagination.* But he remained silent. Gerallt's simplicity was one of his assets, and the reason he'd been promoted to his current position.

Other people could supply the flashes of inspiration – the captain would do as he was told, without deviating from his orders, and not be found wanting. True, an army needed heroes who would rally men to them with their ferocity or charisma, but it also needed a backbone of unimaginative, competent soldiers like Gerallt.

Duro reappeared, riding his own speckled-grey mount, leading Bellicus's own horse by the reins.

The druid smiled, as he usually did when he saw Darac, who was just as impressive an animal as the queen's own Alastor. He quickly mounted with a grace that belied his prodigious size, and, with a final nod of salute to Gerallt, cantered up the Dumpling towards Narina's chariot.

They took the long way around, to avoid riding too close to the Pictish army. Bellicus could tell much of the fight had been knocked out of their enemy by the appearance of Narina's reinforcements, but they would still make short, bloody work of the talismanic druid and his deadly centurion companion if they came within range of their slings or hunting bows.

Soon enough, the riders reached Gavo and the queen and she smiled warmly at both men. She had loved her husband Coroticus, and she'd been happy to live in his shadow, but now that she was the one in charge, Narina had come into her own.

She was born to rule, and Bellicus could not remember ever seeing her quite as vibrant as she appeared now. Her eyes blazed as she looked from the druid to the resting armies on the plain just a short distance below.

"Well met, Gavo." Bellicus said to the dour, faithful captain who nodded in reply and even managed a wink. Then the druid bowed his head respectfully as they rode up close to the chariot. "My queen, you and your warriors are a sight for sore eyes."

She smiled, first at the druid, and then at Duro who also dipped his head and grinned at Narina.

"It seems we arrived just in time," she said. "Your messenger reached us on our way back to Dun Breatann and told us you were going to attack the Picts here, so we changed our course."

"Aye," Bellicus admitted. "We've been fairly evenly matched but Drest has the upper hand in numbers. If you hadn't turned up, lady, we'd have been beaten, or forced to retreat once he ordered his warriors to attack again."

"The Dalriadans accepted you as their queen then?"

Narina turned to Duro and nodded, although the light in her eyes dimmed just a little, as did her smile. "Some of them," she replied. "Not as many as I'd have liked, but…" She gestured towards the warband assembled on the hillside behind her. "Enough to give Drest pause, eh?"

"I've had word from my protégé, Koriosis," Bellicus told the queen, whose interest was immediately piqued. Koriosis, an eighteen-year-old lad, had recently come from Iova, where he'd been training to be a druid, just as Bellicus had done before him. He would serve Alt Clota going forward, learning his craft in the real world and, for now, he'd been given the job of taking care of all druid duties in Dun Breatann while Bel was away. "He's most excited about his new bee-hives, which he tells me will provide honey for our mead in time and—"

"Never mind that," Narina cut in, frowning. "How's Catia?"

Bellicus smiled and she realised he'd been teasing her on purpose.

"The princess is doing well," he said. "In your absence she's taken it upon herself to become the lady of the fortress and, according to Koriosis, the servants and guards do her bidding with smiles on their faces and a spring in their step."

"Well, send word back to him," Narina said imperiously, although the pride in her ten-year-old daughter was evident, "that I want him teaching her more than just how to run a household. Letters, numbers, languages. And make sure Beda is showing her how to use a sword – she should be able to defend herself if she's ever attacked by raiders again."

Bellicus nodded and they gazed down the slope at the Pictish army ranged against them. Their commanders had formed the various units into a great defensive circle, with the valued noblemen in the centre.

"Speaking of attack," Duro said. "Now would probably be the best time to charge the Picts, when they're gathered before us like that."

Narina shook her head. "I think not, centurion. Look."

Drest was walking through his army towards them, with two other figures beside him, and a dozen spearmen.

"They seek to parley now," Bellicus muttered, although his voice betrayed his doubts about enemy motives and sincerity. "They haven't wanted to speak with us before," he told the queen. "Your appearance has at least drawn this from them."

"Best bring some of your warriors in close, my lady," Duro said, glancing around at the Dalriadan soldiers Narina had brought with her. They looked fresh, and eager to do their bit for this woman who promised to be a better ruler for them than Loarn mac Eirc had been. The centurion grinned and waved as he spotted Galchobhar, headman of Auchalic, a settlement not too far to the east which had shown him and Bellicus hospitality not so long ago, after their mission to kill the former Dalriadan king.

Narina noticed their friendly gestures and smiled herself. "Aye, you two made a good impression on the people you visited last year. It certainly made my task of bringing them onto our side a little easier." She turned back to Gavo. "Have my personal guard line up behind us. We'll meet the Picts from a position of strength; let's not show them any weakness. These are *our* lands, and he has no place here."

"Are we meeting them on the hilltop like this?" Bellicus asked. "I mean, if we want them to be in a decent mood, I think we'd be better going down to meet them, rather than expecting them to walk up to us."

Narina thought about it for a moment and then shook her head. "Taranis take them," she growled, lip curling. "They wanted to come here and steal our lands. I'm not going to make things easy for them. Besides, it's only a little hill."

From the corner of his eye Bellicus could see Duro and Gavo sharing an approving look and the druid shared their sentiments. The new queen was going to be no pushover.

So, they stood and watched as Drest led his small band of followers up the slope towards them and Bellicus found his eyes drawn to the slightest figure among the Pictish group.

Ria. The young woman who'd been a student on Iova alongside Bellicus, learning the Old Ways, and the lore of the druids. They had once been friends of a sort, as children, although Ria's blossoming womanhood had inspired confusing emotions within her fellow pupil, and then she'd gone off somewhere to learn new things and Bellicus hadn't really seen her since.

Some druids liked to smear their hair with shit before a battle, and caper and dance like madmen before the gathered enemy. As Bellicus gazed at Ria's lithe figure he suspected that, even if her hair had been encrusted in faeces, she'd find no shortage of suitors among the warriors on that day's battlefield.

Green-eyed, yet with dark hair that contrasted starkly against her smooth white skin, she was quite beautiful.

He was suddenly aware of a sensation of being watched himself and glanced sideways to see Narina staring at him with a frosty expression.

"Watch what you say to them, my lady," he said quietly, as if he hadn't noticed her disapproving frown. "Drest is bringing two druids with him. Qunavo and—"

"Ria," the queen broke in. "I see her. I'm sure one as powerful as you will be capable of dealing with an old man and a little girl."

Bellicus opened his mouth to remind Narina that the 'little girl' was in her late twenties, around the same age as she was herself, but he sensed any further discussion of Ria's merits would not be met with approval and, instead of speaking, simply poked at a tooth with his tongue.

Narina turned away and Bellicus found his eyes drawn once more to the druidess striding easily up the slope towards them.

She might have found the climb straightforward, but Drest's face was red, and old Qunavo was visibly labouring for breath although he had a knowing look on his face. He, at least, understood Narina's decision to make them come to her.

At last the Picts stood before them, Drest's guards forming an impressive line at the rear. If any violence was offered to the three Pictish nobles the perpetrators would find themselves cut down instantly, even if the guards would die themselves in the melee that would surely follow.

Drest gazed at Narina and his expression was a mixture of approval and irritation as he allowed himself time to regain his breath, eyes moving from her to Duro, Gavo and finally Bellicus before he bowed to the new Damnonii ruler.

"Well met, Queen Narina," he said. "That was an impressive entry. I couldn't have ever imagined your dead husband appearing over the hill on a chariot like that."

"No," Narina replied coolly. "That wasn't Coroticus's style. He'd have just ran down the hill at the head of his warband and charged into your ranks, killing all who stood in his way."

Drest nodded. "True. So why didn't you attack us?"

"This war was started by my husband," Narina said. "And I mean to clean up his mess one way or another. But slaughtering a generation of young warriors does neither of us any favours."

The Pictish king shrugged. "That's what happens in war. We all die eventually – those who fall in battle earn their reward in the next life."

Narina sighed. "That may be true. But why die fighting Damnonii warriors, when there are others who pose more of a threat to you?"

Drest looked at Qunavo who frowned and cocked his head, as surprised as his king.

Bellicus spoke up, his powerful voice seeming to carry all across the countryside with its silent, watching armies. "The Saxons."

For a moment, the Picts merely looked at him, and then Ria smiled, revealing straight white teeth that made her appear even more beautiful.

"The Saxons are no threat to us," she said, in a low voice that somehow seemed to carry just as much weight as Bellicus's had. "They have their hands full dealing with the warlord, Arthur, and his Britons in the south."

"She's right," Drest agreed. "We've never had any trouble from the Saxons, Jutes, Angles, whatever they're called, other than a few raids here and there."

"Maybe not," Narina said. "But their attention will turn to us in the north eventually, for their numbers are continually swelling and the southern folk can't withstand them forever. They'll come for us soon enough, I fear."

"Either Hengist's Saxons will defeat Arthur's Britons in battle," Bellicus said. "Or the two peoples will assimilate and become one."

Drest shook his head, frowning in exaggerated confusion. "So what?"

"Much of your wealth comes from raids on the other tribes that share this island with us, Drest," Narina said. "Your warriors are despised and feared by the men of the south, perhaps even more than the Saxons."

"That's true," Drest admitted, smiling proudly.

"Hengist will bring peace to the lands south of the Roman walls eventually," Bellicus said. "And, with no more battles to fight, his warriors will grow bored."

"Then they will come for us," Narina said. "And for you."

Drest's smile fell away as he thought about that suggestion.

"If it happens," Qunavo finally spoke up, "it won't be for years. We've plenty of time to prepare for them coming."

Drest nodded and his voice became hard. "Exactly. You speak of a war that *might* happen, Narina, but you seem to have forgotten that we are in the middle of a battle right here and now."

"A battle you can't win," the queen stated flatly, gesturing with the sweep of an arm to her army. "We have you penned in like cattle ready to be slaughtered, Drest. Make no mistake, my lord – I mean to end this here. Either by defeating you, or forging an alliance with you."

"You're overestimating your strength," the Pict countered, but Bellicus could see the Damnonii queen had greatly impressed the king during this short meeting. He masked it, poorly, by smiling condescendingly. "We still outnumber you, Narina."

"And yet," she replied levelly, looking around the battlefield and off into the distance. "You seem to have fewer men with you than I expected. Where is King Cunedda?"

Drest didn't reply immediately, and Bellicus could guess what was going through the Pict's mind at that moment. Would he bluff, and claim Cunedda was on his way? Or would he say nothing and hope Narina would set aside a sizeable portion of her army just in case Cunedda's Votadini did arrive in time to join the battle?

Qunavo spoke though, saving his king from making a decision. "Who knows? Perhaps the Saxons sailed north and besieged Dun Edin."

Drest and Ria both laughed at that, but their mirth was short-lived, when they noticed Bellicus and Duro also laughing and shaking their heads at one another.

"Dun Edin is not under siege," the giant druid attested. "But Cunedda's men—some of them at least—are already here. Look." He pointed down the hill, to a group of warriors, one of whom towered a head taller than his companions.

"Eburus. Cunedda's champion. And Ysfael. His youngest son."

Drest's eyes narrowed but he kept the surprise from his face as he turned to gaze at the distant figures Bellicus had marked out.

"Is it truly Ysfael," the king muttered to Ria, who nodded.

"Looks like it," she confirmed.

"That turncoat bastard!" Drest exploded, finally betraying some emotion after giving little away for so long. His eyes blazed and spittle flecked his lips as he turned back towards Narina, shaking his head as if this piece of news was a mere setback. "I'll deal with Cunedda once I'm finished with you," he promised.

The Queen of Alt Clota smiled, and it was the same expression Bellicus had seen her bestow on princess Catia when the little girl asked a naïve, childish question. Delivered to a king as proud as Drest, it was more powerful than mere words might have been.

"You can't win," Gavo said, sounding bored by this whole conversation. "Aye, you'll take a fair number of us with you as your army is destroyed. But we *will* destroy you, my lord, you have my word on that."

Drest had regained control of his fury but his earlier jocularity was gone now. "I didn't bring all these warriors here merely to walk away empty-handed," he said.

Narina nodded, realising the king was, at last, giving her a chance to offer terms for peace.

"I am prepared to make…reparations, for the things my husband did. The things that started all the trouble between our peoples in the first place."

Drest remained silent. A good sign.

"The lives of our young men are worth more to me than any material goods," the queen went on. "So, we can talk things over properly, and come to an agreement that suits us both. An alliance. Yes?"

Before the Pict could reply, Bellicus broke in. "Before that, though," he said. "You should think on what we said about the Saxons. You know how they think, Qunavo. Their gods are bloodthirsty, and they're a warlike people who will not be content until they take control of the entire island, and everyone on it."

"Again with this, boy?" Drest waved a hand dismissively. "I remember when you were a child, Bel – don't try and pull the wool over my eyes with your fancy words. Qunavo taught you everything you know. I'll listen to his counsel before yours."

"That may be," Narina said, drawing all attention back to her. "But Cunedda saw the truth of it, which is why he gave up the war against us and, instead, sent many of his warband to join us."

"Once this is settled here, we're taking the fight to the Saxons," Bellicus said, and strode forward, towards the Picts. Drest shrank back instinctively, while his men raised their spears threateningly, but the druid ignored them all, striding past to gaze down the hill at the warriors gathered there. "Look at them, my lord," he said, nodding at the Pictish horde. "You said yourself they came for a fight." He turned to stare directly into Drest's eyes.

The king returned the look in silence, as if captivated by Bellicus.

"Let them fight," growled the druid, a small smile tugging at the corners of his mouth. "But not us, your neighbours. No, let them fight Hengist's sea-wolves!"

The Pict seemed to have shrunk as he stood before the towering druid, and the guards shifted nervously, not appreciating the sight of their king appearing so weak.

Qunavo broke the spell, striding in between Bellicus and Drest and heading down the hill towards the Pictish army, Ria falling into step at his back with a final, long look at the Alt Clotan men.

"The light is failing," Qunavo called over his shoulder. "Come, my lord. We can discuss the Damnonii's words over meat and drink."

Drest nodded, and it was telling that he didn't appear irritated by his druid taking charge of the situation. Bellicus already knew Qunavo wielded immense power amongst the Picts, and now it was clear for Narina and the rest to see. If there was to be peace, the old druid would need to be persuaded just as much as the king.

"All right, my lady," Drest said, addressing Narina, and his composure was back again. "I'll think over your proposal and meet you on the morrow to discuss terms. I have your word that you'll not attack us during the night? Good, then you also have mine."

"Enjoy your meat and drink, my lord," Narina said. "But have a clear head in the morning, for, by the gods, what happens then will set the course of our peoples' lives for years to come."

Drest bowed his head one final time and, with a final, almost condescending wink towards Bellicus, headed after Qunavo and Ria, his guards following suit with stony faces, weapons still held ready for anything.

Bellicus and the others watched the Picts until they were out of earshot and then Narina said, to no-one in particular, "Do you think they'll accept our terms?"

"No," Gavo said, sourly. "They've come here for a fight, and they won't leave without one."

Duro nodded at that. "Drest and his chiefs have spent the winter working their men up into a frenzy of righteous hatred after what happened over the past year. I'm not sure they'll just walk away, even if their king commands them."

"And if Drest knows that, he won't even ask them," Narina mused. "In case they rise up and overthrow him in favour of a leader who wants to destroy us now that they have us gathered around them." She glanced at Bellicus. "You're quiet, for once. What do you think, druid?"

He looked down at her and sighed heavily. "I'm not sure. Drest is no fool, and must know engaging with us in battle will go badly for him. In saying that" – he gripped his staff and watched the distant figures of Drest and his advisors disappearing into a large, colourful tent in the centre of the Pictish army – "I wouldn't trust him to keep the peace tonight. Qunavo in particular might see this evening's truce as their best chance to sneak victory, and advise Drest to strike in the small hours, while we're napping. I suggest we maintain the usual watches."

Narina nodded and spoke to Gavo. "Take word of what's been happening to Gerallt, please. The two of you can have the commanders sort the watches and discuss how you want our forces to set up in the morning. Best to be ready for the worst, eh?"

The captain dipped his head. "I'll see to it, my queen. The bastards won't catch us unawares, you can be certain of that."

He left, ordering half-a-dozen of the guardsmen to keep watch over Narina at all times, although there was little chance an enemy assassin would be able to strike so deeply behind Damnonii lines.

For a time, Bellicus and Duro stood in silence as the queen stared out into the rapidly darkening lands around them. At last she shook her head, as if waking from a daydream, and turned to them with a somewhat forced smile. The druid could tell the pressures of ruling were taking their toll already but felt sure she had enough about her to come through this current trial stronger than ever.

"Join me for a drink, you two," she said. "My men should have set up my pavilion by now, and we have much to talk about."

Bellicus nodded assent. Duro was already moving, never needing a second invitation to fill his belly with the finest provisions in the camp.

CHAPTER FIVE

Bellicus came awake, opening his eyes reluctantly for he'd been in the middle of a pleasant dream that involved himself and Narina… Instantly, he remembered where he was and sat up, staring at the pool of light cast by the flickering torch his visitor held at the entrance to his tent.

"My lady," he said in confusion. "What's happening? Is Drest attacking?"

The queen stroked Cai's head then turned and pulled back the flap covering the doorway. "Get dressed, quickly, Bel," she replied, in the soft tone of voice one naturally uses in the dead of night. "You need to see this. I'll wait outside."

"Shit," the druid muttered, rising and hurriedly pulling his mail vest over his tunic before throwing his long, dark robe around himself and lacing on his boots. He had warned Narina that the Picts might break their pact, but he hadn't really believed it. It was one thing for a small force to sneak into an enemy's territory at night in order to take out a specific target, but no man enjoyed the chaos of fighting a full-scale battle in the dark.

He buckled on his sword and lifted his staff of office. "Come on, boy," he said, and Cai needed no second telling, loping ahead of the druid, out through the flap. Bellicus and Duro had spent a couple of hours with their friend Galchobhar earlier, sharing food and drink and tales and jokes with the likeable headman of Auchalic. Now Bellicus wished he'd indulged a little less, but then he hadn't expected to be woken in the middle of the night like this.

"Will Cai keep up with us?" Narina asked, as Bellicus came outside and breathed deeply of the freezing night air, trying to clear his head of the dream images that yet lingered maddeningly in his memory.

The queen must have ordered the druid's horse be made ready to ride and he nodded a silent greeting to the two guards by his tent before walking over to strap his staff onto Darac's saddle and then mounting.

"Of course. Cai, here," he said in answer and the dog, bladder emptied onto the frost-rimed grass, ran across, gazing up at him eagerly. "Good lad."

Narina nodded grimly, not sharing the druid's smile, which said more than words to him. Normally the queen found Cai's behaviour quite endearing, but her stony face was testament to how worried she must be feeling.

She kicked her heels in and her mount, Helios from the colour of the beast's coat, obediently walked forward, followed by Darac. Their hooves thumped softly on the hard ground and Bellicus felt somewhat annoyed that he hadn't woken up until Narina was right inside his tent. It was just as well she hadn't been a Pictish warrior, sent to sneak through their lines and slit his throat as he slept.

Lit torches were placed around the camp, and cooking fires burned low, but brightly enough to offer some illumination as Narina carefully led them past sleeping warriors, Cai moving silently at their side. Once they were past the camp perimeter they were able to pick up speed, despite the lack of torches to light their path, thanks to the bright moon which hung high overhead like a sparkling gem.

As they rode, the druid wondered why the queen wasn't ordering the army to rise from their slumber and prepare for the Picts' oncoming attack. He assumed he'd read the situation wrong however, and Drest's army was not about to charge into their ranks after all, although he was at a loss to explain Narina's strange, tight-lipped expression and their night-time ride any other way.

He thought about asking her where they were going but it soon became clear – they were heading up the Dumpling. If she'd wanted to tell him why, she'd have done so already – she was the queen and he would let her do things her way. He'd find out soon enough what was going on.

Cai ran at their side, keeping pace without apparent effort, although Bellicus could see the dog's breath misting in the moonlight and couldn't help smiling. They'd been through so much together over the past year or so and the druid could not have wished for a more loyal companion.

Before his thoughts could turn to Eolas, his other dog, which had sadly been killed in a fight with the Saxons, Narina held up a hand and reined in her mount. Bellicus was relieved, for he always became maudlin when he remembered Eolas who had been with him for even longer than Cai. That bastard Horsa! The Saxon jarl had ambushed the druid and brought about the death of brave Eolas…

One day Bellicus would make Horsa pay, and take more than just a few toes like he had during their last meeting.

"Look."

They'd reached a spot on the hill where the Pictish army could be seen on the plain below and Bellicus frowned before dismounting smoothly. The queen followed suit and dismissed a pair of lookouts who'd been keeping watch there on the summit, one of whom, the druid guessed, had alerted Narina to whatever was happening now. When the men had gone the queen and Bellicus stood side-by-side, silently watching the enemy activity beneath them.

"What are they doing?" the druid finally asked, having satisfied himself he hadn't misread the situation. "Did they send a messenger to tell you of their plans?"

Narina stared at the dozens of Pictish torches which lit the scene well enough to make it clear the entire enemy army was working together towards one purpose. Like a swarm of bees busily tending to their hive, the shadowy warriors below were making ready for…something.

"No messengers," the queen replied. "I've no idea what they're up to, but the fact they're doing it quite openly suggests to me that they're not about to attack us."

Bellicus nodded, straining his eyes to try and see if there was any sign of movement on the unlit fringes of Drest's army. Were they making a show of breaking camp to divert the Alt Clotans' attention? Were small parties of the Picts' best-trained warriors even now moving through the darkness, up the hill, on a mission to…what? Kill the queen? Kill Bellicus and the other Damnonii noblemen?

He shook his head. Such a ruse was highly unlikely to succeed and what would it gain? No, something else was at play here. Some factor that Narina and her druid didn't know about.

Something warm touched his hand and he moved his fingers to stroke Cai's soft coat, then stopped and glanced down from the corner of his eye, surprised, for the dog lay by his feet and whatever had touched him felt smooth.

It was the queen's hand, grasping at his, almost like little Catia's had done so many times on their long road back from the Hanging Stones.

He stood without saying a word, not really sure how he should react to this unexpected show of affection. Or was Narina simply anxious and in need of reassurance and companionship from her closest advisor? She had been thrust into her lofty position of power without any real preparation after all, and recent events would test even the strongest, most ambitious person's resolve.

No, Bellicus knew what the queen wanted. He'd been trained to read people after all – that was one of a druid's most important skills. To tell how a person really felt from the look in their eyes, or the way they stood, or the words they spoke and the true meaning that lay hidden behinds those words.

In another time, another place, he would have been content to live a simple life with Narina and Catia. But fate was never that simple, and such an existence was not to be for them; not now and perhaps never.

"You know the people miss Coroticus," he said, holding the queen's hand and allowing her to rest her head against his arm. "As strange as it seems, I've heard them telling stories about what a good king he was."

She looked up at him, puzzled. "Well, for most of his rule, he *was* a good king to them."

"Aye," he nodded. "But at the end they wanted him replaced. They knew how destructive his behaviour had become, and they were glad when we…supplanted him."

He could feel her body tense against him, as if irritated by his words, which was understandable. She would always feel guilty for her part in Coroticus's death, even if she did know it had been the only option open to them at the time. She did not pull away though, clearly savouring their closeness more than any annoyance at the druid's words.

"The people didn't know him," she said. "They weren't around him like we were. Is it really surprising that they remember only the good times now that he's gone? Isn't it the same for all of us when someone, or even just a certain time, passes?"

"You're right," he squeezed her hand gently. "It's a natural process. Our minds hide the darkest memories, leaving mostly the good. It's how we cope with life without going mad."

As Coroticus had done. The words went unspoken, but both knew it was true.

"Why are you bringing him up just now, Bel?"

The druid gathered his thoughts, framing them carefully so as not to offend Narina by being too blunt. "The people have been thrust into a war which, aye, they always knew was coming, but you are now the figurehead for these current troubles." They looked on as the Pictish army began to move, slowly but unmistakably north. "Rumours have been going on about us, about our relationship, for months. Since before Coroticus died, in fact. At this time, when nostalgia is making the people see their dead king as some kind of folk hero, it would be a mistake to give the gossipmongers more to talk about. The last thing we want is the truth about Catia coming out..."

For a time they remained in the same position, holding hands, but then the queen let go and stepped forward, arms folded across her chest, and Bellicus wished he could see her face.

"If the people believed we got rid of Coroticus just so we could be together, they would—rightly—see it as morally wrong. Such an act would be frowned on by the gods and affect all of Alt Clota. If the crops fail, or cattle get sick, or fish disappear from the estuaries, or the bees stop producing honey, we'll be blamed."

The queen still didn't reply. There was no point in railing against fate after all, and it had certainly weaved a tangled web about Narina and Bellicus in the past few months.

"In time," the druid said earnestly. "We might—"

"What are the bastards doing now?" A familiar voice suddenly broke in from close behind, and the druid glanced back to see Gavo riding towards them, with Duro and Gerallt a little way behind him. "By Taranis, are they leaving?"

Neither Bellicus nor Narina answered. The queen didn't even turn to greet the captain, making the druid suspect there might be tears on her cheeks. He felt a hollow pit in his stomach, as if an opportunity had been lost forever.

Duro, oblivious to his friend's silence, crouched down beside Cai, stroking the dog's great head and allowing it to lick his cheek affectionately. Gerallt and Gavo walked ahead to flank their queen as all eyes continued watching the enemy force slowly moving away into the northern gloom, their torches lighting the way and leaving a strange, dark emptiness behind.

At length the queen turned and stared at Bellicus. Her face was set in a neutral expression, whether for his benefit or the other men he couldn't say, but there were no tears on her cheeks or in her light green eyes. "Do you have any ideas then? What's Drest up to? Anyone?" She looked around for answers but was met with only bemused looks.

The Picts had done something totally unexpected, and it made them all uncomfortable.

"No? Well then, Gerallt, send riders after the Pictish army. Make sure they do actually leave and aren't just trying to lull us into a false sense of security. Gavo – wake the army. I know it's not yet dawn, but we'd better be ready for anything."

The captains bowed, and hurried off to carry out their orders, the queen calling after them to come to her pavilion as soon as possible that they might advise her what to do next.

"You two follow me," she said to Bellicus and Duro. "We'll get something to eat and start thinking about our plans from here on, whether Drest has gone for good or not."

As they mounted and made their way back down the Dumpling towards the centre of the camp, the sounds of trumpets and the roars of noblemen rousing their subordinates could be heard as the army was brought to readiness.

Narina moved purposefully and appeared lost in thought, passing easily through the scrambling men. Indeed, she might not even have been noticed were it not for the presence of the giant druid and his dog. Bellicus watched with amusement any time a young, beardless warrior observed the queen's passing and stood, open-mouthed, having never been so close to royalty before.

"I don't like this," Duro growled, oblivious to the slack-jawed looks their passing had engendered. "Drest leaving, I mean."

Bellicus frowned. "What's not to like? I don't think this is a trick. He's really leaving, and that's surely a good thing. It saves us a battle, doesn't it? And that means we can take a stronger force south, to stand against Hengist."

"True," Duro granted. "But we wanted some of Drest's men with us when we made that journey, did we not? I'd hoped he would see sense and leave without a fight while also granting us some of his warriors."

The druid continued walking, pondering his friend's words. "You have a point," he admitted. "And by leaving like this, Drest still has that army behind him. When we go to join Arthur we'll have to leave extra men in Alt Clota in case the Picts return again in the summer." He shrugged. "Still, if there had been a battle today, we'd have lost dozens of our warriors and been terribly weakened. It's always a good outcome when your people don't die."

They reached the pavilion and the guards stood to attention, as straight as the spears they held in their right hands. Preoccupied, Narina, Bellicus and Duro filed past the warriors with hardly a glance and the queen quickly grabbed a pair of tallow candles for the leather tent was nearly pitch-black inside. Only the guttering torches beside the guards outside allowed her to see what she was doing and she was able to light the candles quickly from those same torches, bringing the brightness back inside and making the place instantly more welcoming, even cosy.

"Sit," Narina said, peering up at the two men who, as protocol demanded, had remained standing. "Does a druid really need my permission to take a seat?"

She smiled and so did Bellicus, and then, compounding her lack of queenly etiquette, Narina poured three cups of water and handed them out herself.

"Gerallt would be shocked to see your behaviour," the druid said, emptying his cup in one quick pull as Cai lay down by his side. "You should have a slave to serve guests."

Duro grunted agreement but Narina shook her head. "Gerallt is a good soldier, but the day I can't even pour a drink for a couple of friends is the day I give up the throne. Here. Help yourself."

She placed a loaf on the table between the two men and Duro grinned as he tore off a piece of the bread, feeling its texture and squinting in the candlelight at its colour. "This is fresh," he said, with all the authority of a former baker. "Well, as fresh as you can get in the middle of a battle."

"I *am* the queen, Duro," Narina said, laughing. "It has its perks. There's butter too."

"By Mithras, I wish the legates and prefects had been as nice as you when I was a legionary, my lady," the centurion said, happily taking the proffered butter and smearing it thickly onto his bread. He made a small groaning noise as he began to chew.

Bellicus shook his head at the little performance and grabbed the bread. "I'll have some of that before you finish the lot, if you don't mind." Rather than eating it himself, as his friend had done, he buttered a piece and handed it to Narina. She hesitated, apparently having little appetite, but Bellicus thrust it towards her again.

"Take it," he said. "It'll do you good. Trust me – I know about these things. I'm a druid."

She met his eyes and her lips twitched in a small smile. "I suppose I should since it's fresh. Would be a waste not to enjoy it before it starts to go bad."

"Oh, it won't go to waste," Duro said. "I'll—"

"Shut up," Bellicus said, rolling his eyes in amusement. "And finish what you've got." Then he tore off a piece for himself – a large piece, which didn't go unnoticed by Duro who looked on with a hurt expression – and the three of them ate quietly, listening to the sounds of the army preparing outside.

Soon enough Gavo appeared, gladly helping himself to the rapidly dwindling loaf, and then Gerallt arrived as well. He looked rather forlorn at the meagre amount of bread left but buttered it and washed it down with some water just as the others had done before him.

"Now that we're all wide awake and refreshed," Narina said, looking around the table at them. "What the hell is Drest doing, and what do we do about it?"

"Our scouts haven't returned yet," Gerallt reported. "If Drest had stopped marching, our riders would have come back to let us know; the more time passes, the further away the Picts are."

Gavo leaned back on his stool and folded his arms, a thoughtful, pensive look on his bearded face. "So, they are actually going home."

"So it seems," Narina agreed. "But why?"

"Has Cunedda broken our pact already?" Duro wondered, eyeing Bellicus. "Perhaps the Votadini decided not to go back home to Dun Edin after all, and sent word to Drest. Could be they're meeting somewhere to join forces, and then they'll come back here to meet us in battle, on a better footing than the one the Picts found themselves on yesterday."

Narina looked at the druid, plainly alarmed by the centurion's suggestion, but Bellicus shook his head.

"No, I don't think so," he said reassuringly. "We have dozens of Votadini warriors within our ranks now, including his own son and his champion too. Cunedda knows we'd slaughter them in an instant if he attacked us with Drest." He peered down at Cai who was, rather incongruously, making soft whimpers as he'd fallen fast asleep and was now dreaming. His hind leg jerked and Bellicus shook his head as he returned his attention to the queen. "Something else has happened to make Drest leave the battle empty-handed."

"What, though?" Narina demanded in exasperation.

"Only one way to find out," Bellicus said, since no-one else had an answer. "Ask him."

Everyone turned to look at the druid, and then Duro groaned. "Oh, not again. By Mithras, why do you always have to do this?"

CHAPTER SIX

Arthur frowned as he watched a group of men struggling to lift a long wooden beam into position on the front of the gatehouse, wincing when one of them almost dropped the thing. It seemed the people in too many of these settlements, located in the central part of the country, had lost the knowledge and will to build proper defences around their homes.

This particular village, Segelocum, had once been a Roman fort and it was easy to see why the legionaries had chosen to setup a camp here, for the River Trisantano curved around the settlement on three sides, making it much easier to defend. There was one road in from the west, along with a ford across the river to the east, and the Romans had built two impressive gatehouses to protect those points.

Unfortunately, when the legions abandoned the place the fortifications fell to ruins and when people began living here again they didn't think it important to renew the walls and gatehouses. Arthur had come to see that the current occupants made sure Hengist's Saxons, or indeed any other enemies, couldn't just walk in unopposed and take whatever they pleased.

"Now, you!" Arthur called out, pointing to the man on top of the framework the new western gatehouse was being built around. "Tie it in place, that's right. Good job!" He smiled encouragingly, but here, like many other towns and villages the warlord had visited during the spring, he feared for the inhabitants if the Saxons did turn up any time soon. "Budic," he said quietly, turning to one of his own warriors. "You continue to oversee the building works. Don't let them take a rest until noon or they'll never be finished."

The man nodded and wiped sweat from his brow for it was warm day. "Trust me, lord, the gates'll be ready to go on by tomorrow morning."

Arthur smiled at Budic's confidence, not really sharing the feeling but trusting Budic would do his best to make sure the lazy workers completed their task as soon as possible. He clapped the man on the arm and wandered into the settlement, eyeing the newly raised post warily, but it had been safely lashed in position and looked solid enough.

Many of the people he passed lowered their eyes, seeing him either as some great king although he claimed no throne, or as something of a nuisance. A few, mostly older folk, smiled warmly at him, happy that someone was finally seeing to their safety. There hadn't been much trouble in these parts for decades, as raiders from across the seas tended to strike hardest at coastal settlements or those further north. It made the younger men and women complacent but, perhaps now, Arthur would make them understand the danger posed by this new Saxon *bretwalda* and his followers.

Tall and wiry, with a neatly trimmed brown beard and long, wavy hair, Arthur had an air of command about him that inspired confidence and loyalty despite the fact he wasn't yet thirty.

"How's the rebuilding going?"

He smiled ruefully at the white-bearded figure seated on a barrel in the centre of the village and sat down on one of the many others which had, until recently, been filled with locally brewed ale. "We'll get there, Merlin," he said. "Just like we did in Venonis, and Calcaria, and Rigodunum, and the rest. This place is easier to fortify than those others since we only really need one high wall and a pair of gatehouses." His face grew dark. "Gates and walls are only one part of the problem though. It's *warriors* we need. What use are fortifications if there's no-one to defend them?"

The druid, whose real name was Nemias but was universally known by his title, Merlin, High Druid of all Britannia, shrugged resignedly. "I've sent more messengers out, requesting men. To King Vortigern in the west, Constans, Lewdwn, and Cador in the south, and Queen

Narina in the North..." He shrugged. "And, obviously, Lancelot has gone to ask King Urien of the Carvetii for his help. We'll see if anyone comes."

"Narina will have her hands full," Arthur noted. "Trying to clear up the mess her husband made."

"That's true," Merlin agreed, spotting a dandelion clock in his beard and plucking it out irritably. "But Bellicus saw for himself how much of a threat the Saxons are. He'll persuade the Damnonii to send us at least a few spearmen, you'll see."

Arthur smiled again, thinking back to his first meeting with the giant young druid. "If he stays alive for long enough," said the warlord. "I think our friend Bel has a habit of getting himself into trouble."

"Rather like you," Merlin retorted. "Two peas in a pod."

Suddenly there came a sound of screaming from outside the new village wall and the pair looked at one another.

"We should go and see what's happening," Merlin suggested, standing up nimbly for, despite his flowing white beard he was well under sixty. He lifted his staff as the woman drew closer to the settlement, her wailing growing louder with every passing moment.

Arthur muttered agreement and they hurried towards the gatehouse alongside a handful of curious, chattering locals. The warlord noticed that most of the people didn't even think to bring weapons with them and he shook his head. If this were an enemy attack, Segelocum would not last very long.

"What's happening?"

"Who's that shouting? She'll wake my baby."

"What's all the noise? By the gods, shut up, woman!"

When they reached the half-built gatehouse Arthur nimbly climbed up the scaffolding and stood on the narrow platform the builders were using. From up here he had a good view of the surrounding lands and he watched as the source of the screaming came into view, running painfully slowly towards the village.

When she saw the towering new structure, her cries became more coherent. Less of a breathless, disjointed wailing, her words were understandable now, and the effect on the gathered locals was immediate.

"Saxons! Saxons are coming!"

Some of the villagers ran towards their homes and Arthur hoped they were going to fetch whatever weapons they owned. Others stood rooted to the spot though, unsure what to do.

"Budic!" The warlord shouted, his powerful voice ringing out over the frightened babble below. "Form the men into a line."

"Get inside the wall," Merlin commanded, shepherding the confused locals back into the village, telling the older folk to tend to their children and the younger to find swords, hunting bows, slings, spears or even hayforks and shovels. "You were warned the sea-wolves would come one day," he called as the people milled about as if too panicked to think straight. "Just thank the gods we were here to stand beside you when it finally happened!"

"Aye," Arthur grinned, jumping lightly down from the scaffolding and drawing his sword. "That was lucky, eh?"

Together they met up with Budic and the rest of their warband outside the gates and waited for the woman to reach them. As yet, there was no sign of whatever had frightened her so much but, when she saw Arthur's men—more than twenty of them—lined up ready for battle, her face split wide in a grin of utter relief.

"Saxons," she gasped, running directly to Arthur and falling on her knees before him. "Lots of them, my lord."

Immediately he bent down and raised her up with his left hand, holding her arm firmly, comfortingly. "You've nothing to fear now, lady," he said, meeting her anxious gaze. "The Saxons know us. They'll not come into Segelocum while we stand against them. Now go." He gently guided her towards the gatehouse. "Find your family and let them know you're safe."

"Thank you, my lord," she replied, running off tearfully.

Some of the locals came to stand with them, and Arthur nodded a greeting at each one. Almost all of them looked terrified, but they'd found the courage to face the approaching enemy and that was all Arthur wanted, for now.

"I don't expect the Saxons to attack us," he said, loudly enough for everyone to hear. "But if they do, you *must* stop them. If they get inside the village…" He trailed off, not wanting to put into words what the raiders would do.

Merlin did it for him. "They'll rape your women and slaughter your children," he said, and the villagers cried out in rage and alarm as the white-bearded druid shrugged. "Well, they might let some survive," he admitted. "They'll enslave them of course but…Better than dying, eh?"

Arthur listened to the anguished voices behind him but didn't seek to reassure them this time. It was better that they knew what they were facing.

"There they are!"

All eyes followed Budic's pointing spear and now the villagers saw what they were up against.

Twelve tall, broadly built warriors, each with spears, shields and other accoutrements of war were heading towards them. To most of those looking on they looked like any other group of soldiers, but any questions about their origin disappeared when one called out, "Who are you?"

"Shit," someone groaned near the back of the gathered villagers. "They really are Saxons."

The man who'd shouted to them had a thick accent that clearly marked him as belonging to one of the Germanic tribes.

"I am Arthur," the warlord shouted confidently in return. "And these lands belong to the Britons."

The Saxons muttered amongst themselves for a moment before their leader addressed Arthur again. "What if we decide to come and take your land here, Arthur, along with all your belongings, and your women?" His companions grinned like feral wolves and moved ahead, into a line that, although not quite as wide as Arthur's, was still extremely intimidating to the simple folk of Segelocum.

Arthur grinned as widely as any of their enemies and held his arms out wide, as if to embrace them. "You're welcome to try," he said.

The Saxons started to bang the shafts of their spears against their shields, creating a terrible noise much louder than seemed natural and, at the same time, they began edging forward again, towards the settlement.

"My lord," Budic shouted, and his eyes were wide. "We might be able to beat them, but a lot of us are going to die. I say we run while we can. Leave Segelocum to take care of itself."

The villagers heard his words and cried out at them.

"No, you can't leave us to die!"

"We can't beat them by ourselves!"

"Gods, save us from the Saxons!"

At last, Merlin silenced them with a curt chopping motion and then he stared towards, first, Budic, and then the people gathered before their new gatehouse. "Of course we're not running away," he yelled. "Arthur, Bear of Britain, does not leave his people undefended, and never will." This brought cheers and even sobs of relief from the villagers before the druid turned back to Arthur and surreptitiously winked at him.

The Saxons had mercifully halted their advance as they realised the Britons were not willing to back down, and Arthur shouted to them once again. "Come, fools. Let our spears taste your blood and send you to your feasting hall in the afterlife. You can tell your forefathers there how Arthur and his warriors slaughtered you, like foxes let loose in a chicken coop."

For a time the two sides faced one another in grim silence and the air became heavy with the threat of impending brutality but, at last, the Saxon chief barked something in his own, strange tongue, and his men started to move slowly backwards. "You may live, for now," he shouted to Arthur. "But these lands—all of these lands that belong to you Britons—shall be ours soon enough. I'll be back to reclaim this village and when I do, I'll make a terrible example of it. The smoke from the burning buildings and the screams of our mutilated victims will even reach Woden and Thunor in Asgard!"

With that, the Saxons turned and disappeared into the woods, leaving the people of Segelocum tight-lipped and pale-faced with fear.

Not a word was spoken for a long time, until it seemed the enemy really had gone, and then Arthur turned and looked at the villagers. "You did well," he told them, but there was no triumph in his voice and his expression was grim. "But you see now what you're up against. Next time we won't be here to help you."

"We need to get those gatehouses finished," one man said. "Fast."

"Aye," another agreed. "And get some better weapons for ourselves."

"And armour!" someone else shouted, and then they all started to talk amongst themselves about what they had to do to prepare for the Saxons' next visit.

"People!" Arthur shouted eventually, drawing their attention back to him. "Standing here isn't going to get anything done, is it?"

They took his meaning and hurried away, some returning to the building works, while others headed for the little beer hall to make plans, and yet others went to the same place simply to calm their nerves with strong drink.

Arthur's men watched them go, stony-faced until they stood by themselves, and then they smiled at one another.

"Well played, Budic," Merlin said quietly. "Your performance gets more convincing every time we do this."

"So does Bedwyr's Germanic accent," one of the men noted. "I'd swear he really was a Saxon if I hadn't grown up beside him in Powys."

"Aye," Arthur agreed. "Our ruse worked perfectly again, lads. Well done, all of you. The villagers were really shitting themselves, but hopefully now they understand the importance of strong defences. Come on, we'll help them get the gates sorted, and then we can move onto the next village and do it all over again."

As they returned to Segelocum, Arthur thought about what they'd just done. He couldn't help feel a little ashamed by their ruse—Merlin's idea, of course, a classic druid trick—but he knew it was the best way to make the people in these quiet places sit up and take notice of the threat facing them.

"I told you this would work, didn't I?" Merlin said as he headed back to his barrel seat in the centre of the village.

"Aye," Arthur replied. "Although I'm dreading the day when we try it, and the villagers get brave and decide to go after the 'Saxons'."

Merlin laughed. "Don't worry about that," he said. "Bedwyr's a fast runner."

* * *

Narina frowned and then shook her head. "You can't go after them," she said firmly. "What's to stop them killing you? No, let me finish, Bel."

"Aye, let her finish, Bel," Duro groused. "Maybe she can talk you out of another suicidal mission which I'll no doubt be invited to take part in."

The druid smiled but remained silent, allowing the queen to continue.

"Drest and his men came here for a fight and to take whatever booty they could carry back home. For some reason they've been thwarted and are leaving with nothing to show for their trouble. Do you think they're just going to welcome you, the Damnonii Druid and near-mythical warrior champion, if you ride after them? Don't be naïve, Bellicus."

"What you say is true," the druid said, noting the nods of agreement from Gerallt and Gavo. "But you forget I know Drest – I spent much of my youth around him and his people. I don't believe he'd just cut me down because he's upset at not winning this battle. Besides," he said, taking his staff in his hand and tapping the oak shaft. "Qunavo was my tutor for years. He won't allow a fellow druid to be senselessly cut down."

"What about me?" Duro demanded. "I'm not a druid. In fact, I'm a former Roman legionary, and the Picts bloody *hated* the Romans."

Bellicus shrugged. "You don't have to come," he said, watching Duro's sour expression quickly change to one of outrage.

"Not come?" he demanded. "Who'll look after you when you get into trouble then? Oh no," shaking his head as if scolding a naughty child. "I'm coming all right."

"Well that's settled then," Bellicus said, getting to his feet and facing Narina. "We'll be on our way. No point in delaying, that just means further to ride until we catch up with them."

Narina stared at him, bemused at this turn in the conversation. She'd just told the druid he couldn't go on this mission, yet now he was preparing to leave. She said nothing, pondering her options, wondering if she should command Bellicus to do her bidding, or let him go.

In the end, as kings and queens were wont to do, she bowed to her druid's wisdom. She didn't do so with particularly good grace though. "Fine," she muttered, irritably. "You go and let Drest's warriors take your heads back to the north as a trophy. The rest of us," a nod to Gavo and Gerallt, "will deal with things in Alt Clota without you."

"Don't worry, I'll be back soon enough," the giant mystic replied. "Come on then, Duro." Cai was already on his feet and following at Bellicus's heels but the druid stopped, stroking the dog's head sorrowfully. "Sorry, boy, you'll have to wait here. I don't want you scaring the Picts."

Cai's head tilted to the side, but he seemed to know what was being said and sat down as Narina came and put an arm around his neck affectionately.

"We'll look after him until you return," said the queen, and Bellicus waved in salute to her and the others as he went out to be welcomed by the sight of a glorious pink sunrise.

"Looks like rain," the centurion said, gazing at the sky's beauty. "Or snow, knowing our luck."

"'Red sky at morning, shepherd's warning,'" the druid recited, leading the way towards their horses which were tethered just a few paces away, happily munching on a patch of grass, an island in the mud that hadn't yet been trampled by the booted feet of dozens of warriors. "Let's move fast then, in case the old saying proves correct. First, though, we need to go back to our tents and gather our things."

"I thought you said this mission wouldn't take long," Duro said as they walked their mounts through the camp. "What do we need to get from the tents?"

Bellicus looked back over his shoulder reprovingly. "Well, provisions for a start. What if it does rain heavily and we're caught on the road? Say a bridge collapses or one of the horses injures itself. You want to be stuck in the middle of nowhere with nothing to eat and no shelter? I'm surprised at you, centurion. You should know better."

Duro harrumphed. "I knew you were downplaying the difficulty of this whole thing. Was that even true, what you were saying about Drest and Qunavo respecting your position too much to cut us down? Or were you exaggerating that relationship too?"

"We'll find out soon enough," the druid replied, and they continued on to their tents in silence.

Both men were experienced, old hands at packing for a journey and it wasn't long before they'd gathered what they would need and were on the same road the Picts had taken during the night.

Of course, this might not be deemed a 'necessary' mission by some, but Bellicus wanted to know what had made Drest give up a decent position and head for home. And, on top of that, both he and Duro desperately wanted Pictish spearmen for the warband they were putting together to help Arthur and the Merlin win back the Saxon Shore. Drest *had* to be convinced to see sense, and turn his attentions towards Hengist, or it would mean the end of life as all the disparate cultures of Britannia knew it. Pict, Votadini, Damnonii, Briton, Scotti, Dalriadan…whatever names they gave themselves, or to one another, they'd be wiped from history eventually if the Saxons weren't stopped within this generation.

Bellicus was a druid, but he needed no gift of foresight to know it to be true, and he had no intention of sitting idly by waiting for it to happen.

Drest would see sense, as Cunedda had done.

He had to.

CHAPTER SEVEN

As predicted, it took hardly any time at all for Bellicus and Duro to catch sight of the retreating Pictish army, although they'd travelled further than either man expected.

"They're not hanging around, are they?" the centurion said, allowing his horse to slow from a canter to an easy walk as they took in the sight of Drest's spearmen striding through Alt Clotan lands as if they couldn't wait to return home.

"No," Bellicus agreed with a frown. "It's almost as if they fear they're being chased by someone, or they're chasing someone themselves. Oh well," he patted Darac's neck absent-mindedly. "We'll know soon enough what's going on."

"What makes you think Drest will tell you?" Duro asked as they closed in on the stragglers in the Picts' rearguard. "He's hardly likely to admit any weakness, is he?"

The druid cursed as a wet spot, either rain or sleet, settled on the tip of his nose and he looked up at the sky, fearing the snowfall they'd spoken of earlier. "You're probably right," he conceded. "But it's not really important anyway. They're leaving Alt Clota peacefully, and the main thing is that we somehow persuade him to let thirty or so of his warriors join us."

"Which won't be easy. Cunedda had little choice but to give in to our demands," Duro said, warily scanning the enemy soldiers who had noticed their pursuit by now and were holding their weapons as if eager to use them. "But Drest will have the upper hand in this negotiation. We have nothing to force him to comply with our demands."

"Well, the queen offered to pay Drest to give up the fight. She never had to make that payment, so it's still in our hands. We can use that to barter with the Picts, if need be."

"Do you know what I think?" the centurion asked, turning to look at his friend with a suggestive smile on his face. "I think you just wanted to come and speak to these bastards so you could see the black-haired girl again."

Bellicus returned his gaze in surprise. "Ria?"

"Aye," Duro nodded, grinning and turning back to watch the enemy soldiers who were now almost within touching distance but, thankfully, hadn't shown any signs of aggression. Yet. "I saw the way you looked at her as she walked up the hill to meet us. Extremely pretty woman."

"She always was," Bellicus agreed. "But there was never anything between us." *As much as I'd have liked there to be,* he thought wryly, remembering his younger self and the confusing feelings his fellow student had inspired in him in those days.

Any further talk had to be put aside for now though, as they were upon the Picts and a dozen of the enemy warriors had turned and formed a line, spears held out towards the riders point first.

Bellicus and Duro reined in their mounts at the same moment, moving with the precision that came naturally to two experienced warriors who understood their companion's ways. They both looked at the stocky Pict with the scarred forehead and straggly grey beard in the middle of the enemy line, for he was clearly the leader. His comrades held spears and wore hatchets or daggers in their belts, but the man in the centre held a sword, marking him as one of high status.

"Well met, friend," Bellicus said, raising his head in salute to the man who stared back, stony-faced, managing only a grunt in reply. "I am Bellicus, Druid of Dun Breatann, and this is Duro of Luguvalium."

"I know who you are," the Pict said grimly. "I remember you, boy."

Duro let out a low groan that only Bellicus could hear and looked at the ground. Addressing the druid as 'boy' said much for the respect these men held for the Damnonii envoys.

"You remember me?" Bellicus eyed the man for a moment, then shook his head. "I'm afraid I don't recall meeting you before this."

"Ha," the Pict let out a gravelly laugh that didn't hold much humour. "I thought you druids could remember everything. You were training for long enough, by the gods. Years! Well, to be fair, I didn't have this at the time." He pointed to the wide, poorly healed scar across his brow, and then shook his head in apparent disgust. "I'll remind you: You spilled my drink during the Imbolc feasting one year, when you were smaller, and thinner."

Suddenly a night two decades ago flashed into the druid's mind. He could hear again the overwhelming babble of drunk men's' voices, and the flash of the serving girls' bare skin as they were pawed at, and the thick, greasy smell of roasting meat, and the warmth of the packed feasting hall.

And he could feel again the blow from the warrior whose ale-mug he accidentally knocked over while serving drinks to the gathered nobles.

He had been seven years old, and he hadn't been able to hear in that ear for three days afterwards.

"I remember you," Bellicus said and Duro's hand instinctually fell to his side, ready to draw his spatha from its sheath for he recognised the cold anger in his friend's voice.

"You were a clumsy little shit," the Pictish chieftain snorted, looking along the line of his spearmen, drawing nervous laughs from them.

"I was a boy," Bellicus replied softly, and he stared at the Pict unblinkingly for a long moment, until the man began to turn red. "I'm not clumsy anymore, Gartnaith, as I'll be happy to show you once I've finished my business here with your king."

"We've come," Duro spoke up, before the Pict could respond to the druid's threat, "on behalf of Queen Narina."

Gartnaith looked from Bellicus to the centurion who spoke in the same commanding tone of voice as the druid. It clearly rankled him to be spoken down to by these men and emotions warred across his features as he pondered his next move.

"Drest and Qunavo will want to hear what we have to say as soon as possible," Bellicus said. "I suggest you either take word of our arrival to them, or move aside and let us pass through your ranks so we can find them ourselves."

The line of spearmen eyed Gartnaith nervously, undoubtedly fearful of angering Drest should they deal with this situation poorly. The chief noticed their glances and seemed to be struggling within himself to decide what to do next. Bellicus could tell the man would like nothing better than to cut them down and be done with it, but his fear of angering the king, and wariness over killing a druid, held his sword arm firm.

At last, the Pict muttered an oath and nodded.

"All right, but you can both dismount. I'll not lead you past my own kinsmen with you lording it over me." He saw Bellicus's disapproving frown and shook his head. "Don't argue with me, druid. My men will look after your horses until—if—you return."

Bellicus watched him snigger at his own implied threat and dismounted, motioning for Duro to follow his lead. Conceding to this small demand at least allowed Gartnaith to believe he was in charge of the situation although, by the look on the Pict's face he'd not realised the druid had continued growing since he was seven years old.

"Lead on then," Bellicus smiled, staring down at Gartnaith who was still forced to crane his neck in order to meet the druid's gaze.

With another vicious oath, the lordling turned away and hurried after the rest of the army. The main body of men was some distance ahead of them now and it took a while to catch them up. By the time they started to push through the ranks Gartnaith was sweating heavily despite the cold, and the scar on his forehead was a livid red. He might have pictured himself leading the Alt Clotan emissaries through his kinsmen like a conquering hero, with his charges wandering along at his back like beaten puppies, but the reality was rather different. If anything, it looked more like Gartnaith had been captured by the imposing druid and the centurion, and was now forced to lead them on.

Only the fact that the Pict still carried his sword told the rest of the warriors that Gartnaith was, apparently, in control of the situation and the marching men parted to allow them through although one or two, recognising the giant druid, shouted insults.

He ignored them, and even smiled at the more imaginative ones. If being called names was the worst he had to suffer, that was fine by him.

Of course, their progress was hampered by the throng around them, and, when they finally neared the front of the army, Gartnaith had taken to snarling and forcibly pushing people out of their way. Bellicus noticed he always chose younger men, boys almost, to shove, rather than any of the taller, more experienced warriors or those who, like him, carried a sword to mark them as men of status.

By the time Drest came into view Gartnaith was having more insults hurled at him than Bellicus, which only served to make the bald chieftain even more flustered and he had to make a visible effort to pull himself together before calling on the king to wait.

"Watch where you're going, you baldy bastard," a tall young man spat, as Gartnaith roughly nudged him aside once Drest had reined in his mount and the entire column started the long process of halting in their tracks behind them. The chief turned to glare at the warrior, but the youngster returned his look boldly and Gartnaith decided it wouldn't look good to start a brawl in front of the king. Instead, he muttered a promise to teach the man a lesson if they ever crossed paths again and continued on to stand by Drest's horse.

The king didn't bother looking at Gartnaith for he'd already noticed Bellicus and Duro. Drest's hand fell to his sword and he half drew it from its sheath before he mastered his instincts and paused, watching as the newcomers approached.

"That's far enough." Lutrin, the Pictish king's one-eyed captain jumped down nimbly from his mount and stepped in front of Bellicus, raising a warning hand to emphasise his command. Without needing to be told, Drest's personal guards, six of the hardest-looking men Duro had ever seen, suddenly appeared and the centurion knew they would not hesitate. If any sign of aggression was shown, these blue-painted warriors would cut them down like farmers reaping wheat.

"Have you come to kill me, Bel?" Drest asked, grinning widely. "Like you did to Loarn mac Eirc?"

Bellicus smiled in return but shook his head. "No, my lord. We've merely come to talk. And I can't take credit for killing Loarn either – it was Duro here who landed the blow that eventually saw him off to the Otherworld."

Drest nodded thoughtfully at Duro, who bowed his head respectfully. He had chosen not to wear his legionary armour or helmet for this mission, fearing it would only antagonise the Picts and he was glad of it now as all eyes turned towards him.

"Ah, the centurion from the south," said the king. "Aye, we've heard about your adventures together, Bel. Word travels fast."

"Especially when the tales are so entertaining," said another voice, and Qunavo rode up with Ria following at his back. "No doubt you were the one who started the stories about your quest to rescue Princess Catia, eh Bel?"

"You know how it works," Bellicus admitted. "It was you, my mentor, who taught me the power of tales, after all."

"My lord," Gartnaith interjected. "I captured these two and thought I should bring them—"

"Captured?" Drest demanded, instantly silencing the red-faced chieftain. "You say you captured them, yet both these men still carry their weapons. Can you imagine what that staff of his would do to your scarred forehead, Gartnaith? It would shatter it like a hen's egg. And yet you've escorted him, and a Roman centurion wearing a spatha, into my presence?"

Gartnaith looked around at the army watching them in silence.

"You don't think I'm in any danger, because I have my guards, and all these fine warriors with me?" Drest shook his head in disgust then, when the chieftain opened his mouth to speak, the king chopped his hand down in the air for silence. "Enough." Turning back to Bellicus he rested an elbow on his horse's neck and cupped his chin. "What do you want then, druid? Speak up, and let's get this done with, for I'm in a hurry to get home in case you hadn't already noticed."

The Damnonii druid frowned and so did Duro. They hadn't expected this. It was customary for a discussion such as this to be conducted in private, not in front of the entire army. Was Drest really in so much of a rush?

"My lord." Bellicus began slowly, gesturing with his hand at their rapt, if unfriendly, audience. "Shouldn't we speak in private?" He moved his hand upwards, to stave off the king's sharp retort. "I won't take up much of your time, you have my word. But there are important events to be discussed – events that will affect all our lands, not just Alt Clota. Everyone, including you and your people."

Drest had been fidgeting with his horse's reins the whole time Bellicus was talking and he shook his head now in annoyance. "Whatever you have to say, druid, will be said here and now. I have no time to waste following the usual courtesies. Besides, you two are enemies and we are still at war, despite the fact my army is leaving."

"Why *are* you leaving?" Bellicus asked, and he spoke sharply, using his most persuasive voice. Often this tactic worked, and its target would blurt out the information he needed before they realised what they were doing, but Qunavo had been the one who taught Bellicus this trick. He had shown his young student how to pitch his voice just so, and spent hours training the boy to perfect the technique, for this was a skill the druids had found very useful over the generations.

Qunavo broke in, before Drest had a chance to say a word. "You don't need to know, Bel," the old druid said, using the same, sharp, commanding tone as Bellicus. "None of your tricks now, lad. I know them all, remember? Now – speak your piece or begone."

Duro shifted restlessly, hands at his side, but open, ready to draw his sword at any moment for this meeting was going rather differently to how he'd expected and the Pictish army's hostility suffused the air with an invisible, stifling pall.

"Fair enough," Bellicus said, clasping his hands and returning his gaze to the king. "We've come to ask you to form an alliance. My lord, times are changing. The old ways are passing, and we must adapt if we're to survive."

The king was smiling but it wasn't a pleasant expression, and Duro felt a shiver run down his spine. This had been a mistake. Bel expected his former mentor, and his previous relationship with Drest, to soften their stance towards him, but the Picts were in no mood for this. They'd been forced to leave a battle they had a chance of winning for some reason the centurion was not privy to, but whatever it was, it had not put the enemy king in an accommodating frame of mind.

"What are you talking about?" Drest demanded. "An alliance? Bel, we're leaving because we have to. I can tell you right now, I was going to command my men to attack your forces this morning. We came all this way for a damn fight, and…" He trailed off then raised his voice and drew his arm out, encompassing his entire army. "Look at them, druid!

Each one of my warriors is worth two, three, four of your Damnonii cowards!"

A loud cheer rose up and Duro allowed his hand to grasp the handle of his spatha for there was naked aggression in their enemies' eyes now.

"But, go on," Drest said, smiling condescendingly at Bellicus as the cheers and shouts began to subside. "Tell us what you want, exactly. Why have you so unwisely wandered into the middle of my army like this? What's so important that you would place yourself in such a dangerous position? I thought Qunavo had taught you not to be a fool but…apparently not."

Even the king's personal guards, stony faced up until now, were smirking at Bellicus and Duro, enjoying Drest's performance for even a small victory was better than nothing on a day when they'd been forced to retreat, something every Pict viewed as cowardly. None of them had moved, or even drawn their weapons, but they eyed Duro's hand as if daring him to take out his sword so they could put him down.

"I hope you're going to say something clever," the centurion muttered. "Because this doesn't seem to be going very well." A crow cawed loudly from somewhere high above and, to Duro, it was a bad omen, but he held his face impassive, not giving anything away, as Bellicus spoke again.

"The Saxons *are* coming, Drest." As he said the words there was an almost imperceptible flicker in the king's eyes which Bellicus only noticed because he'd been staring hard at the man's face. "They will destroy us all unless we stop them now." He turned his attention to Qunavo. "You must realise this, old friend. The likes of Horsa hold no respect for our gods, or our ways. The Saxons will come in their ships, aye even to your far northern outposts, and they will smash everything and everyone in their way." Now he spoke louder, so everyone gathered there could hear his words. "I've seen them – seen their fanatical ways. They will stop at nothing to take control of these lands even if it means killing every man, woman and child living here."

"The Romans already tried defeating us," someone shouted dismissively. "And they were a lot more powerful than any ragged band of foreign sea-wolves."

Cries of agreement rose up, and more jeers, and some of the enemy warriors moved forward, as if they could barely restrain their hostility towards druid and centurion. Bellicus looked to Drest but his face was drawn, pensive, and the king remained silent.

Qunavo nodded his head almost imperceptibly however, and Duro cried out, jerking to one side just in time to avoid a blow from an enemy soldier who had somehow managed to get close enough to launch an attack without being spotted.

The centurion had his sword in his hand instantly and used it to parry another blow from the assailant, before bringing it around and slicing deeply into the Pict's arm. With a scream, the man fell back but this was apparently how Duro was to die, for there was no command from Drest to halt the attack on the Damnonii emissaries and he saw Bellicus also fighting for his life against the oncoming tide of enemy warriors.

His head rocked sideways and he almost blacked out, swinging his blade wildly and desperately trying to clear the dancing spots of light in his vision, but then something slammed into his kidneys and, winded, he collapsed onto the sodden grass, spatha falling uselessly from his fingers.

He tried to curl into a ball and would have sobbed with rage if only he could catch a breath, as he saw Bellicus, face down on the grass with his eagle topped staff by his side, unmoving and silent as the Pictish troopers continued their assault with dreadful glee.

CHAPTER EIGHT

There were voices somewhere nearby, but he couldn't quite make sense of them; couldn't quite follow the words, and his mind refused to form them into coherent sentences that he could understand. It was merely a noise from some unknown space around him which told him he was alive. Probably.

Then the voices faded away into the distance and he became aware of other things.

A crackling sound or, perhaps…He tried to focus his hearing, straining to make some sense of things and…Yes, there were at least two torches burning nearby – one close, the other further away.

And the smell! What was that mixing with the tallow from the torches, by Taranis? Piss and shit, and the damp, musty smell of wet, cold stone and…death? Decay, certainly. Perhaps some animal had died close to where he was lying, or perhaps he was dead himself and he could smell his own rotting flesh before he departed this lifeless shell and moved onto another body and rebirth in another life…

Should a dead person feel such a pounding in their head though?

The pain suddenly hit him, bringing him to full wakefulness although his training meant he gave little outward signs of his return to consciousness. He gritted his teeth and held in the groan that wanted to burst from his lips, and that made him aware of the dryness of his mouth and the tight feeling on the surface of his skin. Dried blood, he guessed, caking around his chin and neck.

A sound came from beside him and, keeping his eyes closed, he focused on the space, drawing everything he could from his senses. Ah…There was a different smell he noticed now – not like the stench of filth and decay, or the greasy scent of the burning torches. No, this was soft, delicate, and unmistakably female.

She didn't have to speak for Bellicus to know who was in the room with him. The girl, or woman, was maintaining almost total silence which most normal people would have found impossible.

"Ria," he croaked, and the name was almost unintelligible for his chapped lips were sticky and his throat dry.

"You're awake," the druidess replied softly and Bellicus fancied he could detect an almost imperceptible relief in her tone, as if she was glad he'd survived the beating the Pictish warriors had given him.

"Is Duro alive?" he demanded, opening his eyes but closing them instantly as even the dim light in the cell, for that's where he was, sent pain and nausea flooding through him.

He waited for her response, but she remained silent and he forced his eyes open again and squinted at her angrily. "Is he alive, damn you?"

"Keep your voice down," Ria hissed, returning his vicious look before peering out through the barred gate towards the corridor. "Drest has commanded the guards to tell him as soon as you wake. Your shouting will have sent them running to get him, fool."

"So?" He tried to stand up but found his legs wouldn't co-operate so settled instead for sitting with his back against the cold stone wall and checking over himself for broken bones or other injuries. "Why are you even in here with me?"

"I…" She hesitated and then turned away from him almost sheepishly. "They were going to kill you," she said, gazing at the damp floor. "Until I told them you were worth more alive, and they brought you here to Dunnottar instead."

"I hope you told them the same thing about Duro, because if Drest had him killed…"

"Don't be so dramatic," Ria scolded, although she smiled just a little and came over to him with a cup of water. "Here. Drink some of this."

Kneeling, she held the cup of water to his mouth and allowed him to sip, with only a little spilling down his chin, which he was glad of, as it eased the tightness from the caked-in blood there.

"You're a prisoner, Bel," the young druidess told him, taking the cup away from his mouth and touching him gently above the eye. He winced, for there was a lump there which he'd not even been aware of until now, but he remained sitting as Ria traced her hand down his face, inspecting every cut and bruise until their eyes met again.

"You'll heal," she said, and her voice was low, and breathy, just as Bellicus remembered it from when he'd been so taken with her as a young boy growing into manhood. As they stared at one another he felt a stirring in his loins which he guessed she sensed, as her smile widened and her tongue brushed her teeth playfully.

She got to her feet though, just as the sound of footsteps came to them from the far end of the corridor outside.

"That'll be Drest come to question you," she said, and the warmth had gone from her tone as she looked down at him. "Do not play with him, Bel. Qunavo isn't here, but the king understands much about our druid ways and he'll guess if you're not being truthful. Tell him what he wants to know, and you might get out of the fortress alive."

The light grew outside the cell and a guard appeared carrying another flaming brand. Drest strode into view still clad in his leather cuirass as if expecting to be in a battle, or perhaps having just come from one. The king looked through the cell gate, his face hidden in shadows as the guard moved behind him with the torch. Bellicus could see another three burly warriors in the corridor, all heavily armed.

"I told you to let me know the instant he awoke, Ria," Drest growled, and even in the gloom the displeasure on his face was obvious.

"You're here, aren't you?" the druidess replied curtly, slipping past the guard as he unlocked the gate and opened it inwards. "Remember what I told you, Bel," she said over her shoulder, walking away towards the stairs leading up to the castle proper. "Tell the king what he wants to know. It'll be best for you."

Drest turned and watched Ria with a frown until she'd gone, then he shook his head and muttered something Bellicus couldn't make out, but it brought a snigger from at least one of the guards.

Apparently Ria had the power to make other men feel uncomfortable, not just the battered druid.

Drest came inside the cell and stood with his back against the wall opposite Bellicus. They eyed one another in silence until the king finally turned to one of his guards and ordered the man to bring him a chair.

A folding camp stool was quickly produced, and the king sat down with a small grunt which reminded the druid that he must be approaching his fortieth year by now. Not exactly a young man anymore, which perhaps explained the recent desire to expand his borders into Alt Clota. Drest had let his youth pass him by before finally realising the power that could be his if he just reached out and took it.

Again, the pair glared at one another as the Pictish guards stood watching, trying to make no noise but their armour creaked distractingly with every small movement such was the dead quiet in the cell.

Drest knew it was a fool's game trying to outstare a druid though and he soon grew tired of the silence.

"What—"

"Is my friend alive?" Bellicus broke in before the king could even start his sentence properly.

Drest's face turned dark with rage and he stood up, crossing the floor and striking down with his open palm at the druid's head. Bellicus saw the blow coming but he didn't even attempt to move for he knew jerking out of the way, in his current condition, would cause him just as much pain as the king's strike.

"Be silent, druid, until I speak to you!"

Something had angered the king—something beyond Bellicus's perceived insolence—yet it didn't stop the druid asking again.

"Is my friend alive?"

The guards moved in a step, ready to aid the king in beating their Damnonii enemy into submission again, but Bellicus spoke again as Drest raised his hand to strike once more.

"Whatever you want from me, you'll get nothing until I know Duro's fate."

Drest paused but his eyes still shone and Bellicus wondered just what it was that had caused such fury within the man. His rage seemed personally targeted against the beaten mystic, as if Bellicus had done something to him, or played a part in someone else doing him some evil.

"Just tell me, my lord," he muttered, closing his eyes as another wave of nausea coursed through him, threatening to make him vomit. "Then I'll co-operate as best I can."

"You'll 'co-operate', eh?" Drest repeated sarcastically, slapping Bellicus on the side of the head again, although without quite as much vigour this time. He moved away and sat back down on the camp stool, jaw clenched as he watched the druid retch although there was nothing in the giant's stomach to bring up for he'd been unconscious for days. "Oh, you'll co-operate all right you big bastard, one way or another. You know my methods when it comes to making prisoners talk. I'm sure you remember."

Bellicus drew himself back up on one arm and wiped spittle from his lips with the back of his hand. He felt utterly filthy and humiliated too, but he remained calm, just as Qunavo had taught him all those years before and, at last, the sick feeling passed.

"I remember well enough," he admitted. "Now – is Duro alive or not?"

Angrily, Drest stood up, knocking his stool aside, and he glared murderously at the sickly druid who returned his look calmly. The Pictish king laughed and shook his head, but this time there was admiration in his expression as he retrieved the stool and dropped onto it once more.

"Aye, your friend is alive. Actually, he's in a better state than you, truth be told. For now."

Bellicus searched the king's face for a lie but found none. With a sigh of relief, he slumped down and gazed at the dripping ceiling, exhausted by his enforced show of calm. He thought of making some flippant or threatening remark about how it was just as well Duro yet lived, then thought better of it. There seemed no point in aggravating Drest even more than he already was.

If he was going to find a way out of this prison Bellicus would need to heal as quickly as possible. Enraging the king and his guards would not be conducive to that end.

"Now," Drest said. "You will tell me what I want to know."

Bellicus made an attempt at a shrug, only to find his shoulder flaring with pain. He gritted his teeth and grasped the injury with a hand. By the gods, the Picts really had worked him over properly, for it seemed like every part of his body was bruised. "What exactly *do* you want to know?" he asked.

"I want to know," Drest replied, pulling his stool forward so he was closer to the druid. "I want to know what you're planning, Bel."

"Planning?"

"It was no mere coincidence that sent you along the road after me," Drest said. "To warn us of the threat from the Saxons, just after one of Hengist's kinsmen had launched a murderous assault on Dunnottar."

It took a long moment for the king's words to sink in and then the implications struck him like one of mighty Taranis's thunderbolts. His first instinct was to laugh, for surely now

Drest would understand the danger, and send men to meet this new threat directly at its source on the Saxon Shore. Yet he held his face impassive as he realised Drest might not take too kindly to a show of amusement. Certainly, the Pictish king didn't look like he was about to laugh any time soon.

He stared at the floor and took in every nuance of the cold, damp stone, noting every crack and every patch of white, furry mould, simply to occupy himself as he pondered how best to react to Drest's statement.

So, the Saxons had come this far north, even attacking some of the Pictish warriors left behind to guard the land while the army marched on Alt Clota to wage war. It surprised Bellicus for, although he'd always expected Hengist to send his men ranging far and wide across the length and breadth of Britannia, he hadn't expected the Saxon warlord to begin hostilities with the Picts so soon. Hengist still had a war to win against the Britons further south after all and it would be no simple task, what with Arthur marshalling the people into a more cohesive fighting unit than had been seen in those lands for generations.

"Well?" Drest barked, bringing Bellicus rudely back to the present. "Do you, and your new Queen Narina, think we Picts are all fools, druid?" The king stood up, shaking his head, brow furrowed. "The Saxons killed Galan – one of my oldest, most loyal friends. A mighty warrior in his day, mercilessly cut down and robbed by the sea-wolves, and it was all witnessed from the fortress walls by Aife and her guards. You obviously knew the bastards had attacked Dunnottar, but you didn't expect me to see through your little ruse, did you?"

"Ruse?" Bellicus's thoughts were spinning. He had no idea who Galan or Aife were, but they were clearly important people to the Picts.

"Don't play games with me!" Drest stepped forward and lashed out, striking Bellicus on the side of the face again. The blow was a powerful one that rocked the druid's head sideways and, from the stinging pain he could feel in his cheek, Bellicus knew the skin had been broken.

Yet another bloody wound to add to all the others.

"You asked me to send some of my men away with you, didn't you? To fight the Saxons, or at least that's what you said to Cunedda, although the only battle you used his warriors in was against me!" He jerked his hand back as if he would strike Bellicus once more, but he changed his mind and shook his head in disgust, spitting on the ground next to the druid instead. "You wanted me to send a large part of my army with you, while I returned home. Then your friends—the Saxons—would attack Dunnottar, knowing my army was much smaller than it had been originally."

Bellicus closed his eyes and rubbed a hand across his brow, bemused, and more than a little amazed.

"None of that makes sense," he said at length. What was it with kings making wild, baseless accusations against him recently? First Coroticus suggesting Bellicus was trying to steal his family, and now Drest blaming him for…what, exactly? "You say a Saxon force attacked Dunnottar. But your entire army was miles away in Alt Clota at the time! Why would the Saxons need you to split your army by sending men away with me? Dunnottar was practically defenceless as it was!"

Drest gazed at him, fists balling and un-balling repeatedly, as if the king was filled with a nervous tension that might explode at any moment into extreme violence. Then, in a low growl, he said, "I know you're up to something, druid. I know how you people work – always plotting, sly and cunning like a fox, you think the rest of us are fools you can manipulate. But," he smiled grimly, "you forget Qunavo is my chief advisor. We *will* have the truth from you, Bel. One way or another."

Bellicus shook his head in exasperation. "There is no truth, Drest, other than that which I've already told you. If you can't see it, then you really are a fool, and a bigger one than

I'd ever have thought possible." He groaned as a spasm of pain ran through his cracked ribs, then forced himself to look up at the king again, just in time to see the fist as it smashed into his mouth.

Then Drest was on his knees beside him and the king had his hands around his throat, squeezing, eyes bulging maniacally as the guards formed a tight circle around them. Bellicus instinctively raised his own hands up to break his attacker's grip, but he was too exhausted, too agonized, to prise Drest's fingers off. The pressure on his throat became unbearable and he started to pass out, almost welcoming the sensation as a relief from the pain that wracked his entire body and mind. What a pitiful way to die he thought, wishing he had the strength left in him to take down at least one of the enemies within the shit-stained cell.

Then the king's hands fell away and Bellicus was able to suck in breath after burning breath, coughing and spluttering weakly as Drest rose to his feet and walked back out through the iron gate, his guards following in silence, although their looks were pure malevolence as one of their number threw the bolt across and locked the druid in again.

Bellicus rarely made threats – he knew actions spoke much louder than any words and silence could be far more intimidating than promising to kill someone. Even so, as he lay in his own filth watching King Drest, the giant druid wished he had enough strength to curse the Pict, and swear vengeance against him. As it was, he could barely catch a breath and he was forced to hold his tongue as he wheezed, trying to gulp in great draughts of air, and his attacker turned, face shrouded in darkness, to look back at him.

"You may not value your own life very much, boy, but what of your friend? The centurion?"

With that, Drest disappeared along the corridor with his guards, their heavy boots pounding into the distance until only the sound of the guttering torches outside his cell could be heard and the druid closed off his mind to the pain wracking his body.

Something was going on here. Something that hadn't been said by the Pictish king, but, in his state, Bellicus could not begin to figure out what it was. Perhaps when he regained consciousness he'd be able to make some sense of everything.

If he regained consciousness, he thought bitterly, as even the flickering torches couldn't keep the darkness at bay any longer.

CHAPTER NINE

Bellicus didn't remember this cell from the time he'd spent in Dunnottar as a student of Qunavo. It was probable that he had been down here before, as watching prisoners being questioned was an important part of a druid's training, but he had no recollection of it. If it had happened, it had either been a fleeting visit, or it occurred when he was too young for it to have made a lasting impression on him.

As a result, he had no real idea whereabouts in the castle he'd been placed. Obviously, he was somewhere below the main building, for it was dark and cold and he could hear the muffled sounds of everyday life going on above him. Cells, dungeons, they were generally in the darkest, dampest, most unpleasant parts of a fortress, but he wished he had some idea of where on the actual rock he was. Thoughts of escape occupied much of his waking hours and, if he were ever to manage such a feat, it would be useful to know which direction he should go in once he was out of the cell.

He had his suspicions, of course.

Dunnottar was essentially a large rock on the coast, quite like Dun Breatann in fact, although with only one, flat, peak rather than two steeper, more rounded ones. As a result, there were more structures in Dunnottar for it was better suited to building a community upon. In truth, only its location made Dun Breatann the more important of the two strongholds, for in almost every other way Dunnottar was a superior fortress.

He could feel the cold breeze forcing its way through the myriad gaps in the wooden wall on the left of his cell, and he could hear the gulls and the cries of sailors coming from the same area, so he knew that side was where the sea was located. He suspected that, if he could somehow smash his way through the wall there, he would be looking out east, across the water, and the ships that could carry him to freedom. Of course, it was a sheer drop of over one hundred and fifty feet, so he didn't see much hope in that direction. Unless he could find a rope.

An extremely long one.

For the first time in a while he smiled, but instantly regretted it as the scabs on his battered face cracked painfully and he closed his eyes, head dropping down as he tried to marshal his thoughts.

He was only in his late twenties, still relatively young, but he did not fear death. That did not mean he welcomed it however, for he still had much he wanted to do in this present life.

Killing Drest being very near the top of the list.

An image of Dun Breatann in springtime came to him then, the grass and trees green and lush, buttercups and daisies carpeting the ground while baby birds squabbled over scraps of food and the Clota sparkled in the warm sunshine. The contrast with his gloomy cell was stark and he felt a great sense of loss. Would he ever see his home again?

Suddenly a feral roar of pain came to him from somewhere nearby and he opened his eyes, listening, trying to figure out what he was hearing. A moment later it came again, and this time it was followed by what could only be an oath, as the unfortunate recipient of the mistreatment cursed his tormentor. The words were not discernible, but the tone—the timbre of the man's cry—was clear enough.

Bellicus's blood ran cold then, for he knew whom the voice belonged to: Duro. It sounded like his friend was in a room directly overhead and the knowledge that the centurion was being tortured mere feet away enraged Bellicus, who got to his feet, glaring impotently at the ceiling which, given his height, was easily within reach.

Another roar of pain filtered down through the floorboards and the druid thumped back with his fist. "Drest!" he shouted, no longer noticing his own aches and pains. "I'll kill you for this, Drest! By Taranis, I swear it!"

There was silence from above, although what that meant Bellicus could not say. The boards beneath the floors were clearly very thick since this was the first time he'd really heard any halfway perceptible sounds filtering through in the days he'd been incarcerated here. For all he knew, Duro had passed out, or even been killed, and now the Picts were marching along the corridors and down the stairs to come for him.

He balled his fists and prepared to dole out as much violence as possible in his weakened state. If he could just get his hands on Drest, he might be able to—

But then another noise came from above, a scream this time, which tailed off into a keening cry that told of a long-drawn-out, lingering pain and, with that, Bellicus allowed himself to slump down onto the floor of his cell and close his eyes. He withdrew into himself, focusing inwards, shutting out the hateful sounds in the room overhead, using the techniques he'd honed over many years to find peace.

He felt no guilt, for there was nothing he could do for his friend. Not now, and perhaps not ever, but if the chance did come, the druid's retribution would be all the more brutal for what Duro had been forced to endure this day.

* * *

The merchants' carts could obviously not make it up the steps within Dun Breatann so they'd set up their wares for inspection on the grass outside the fortress. The men hired as guards did go inside though, to the great hall, where they enjoyed a well-earned drink while the traders hawked their wares: spices, salt, expensive dyed fabrics, ceramic and glassware and more. Most of the simple folk in Alt Clota didn't have the means to pay for these goods but before the merchants moved on again local nobles heard of their arrival and came on foot, by horse, or along the Clota in boats. People always loved bartering or spending some of their old

Roman coins if they still had any. Eventually, there would be none left, since no more were being minted, but that didn't stop women using them to buy material for a new dress or men looking for well-crafted drinking glasses to show off their high status.

Gavo wasn't interested in such fancy nonsense but he went out to speak with the merchants anyway, for men like these were always a great source of information from far-off towns and settlements.

"You look like a man of taste." One of the traders, a short fellow with a prodigious moustache, smiled when he saw the guard captain approaching his cart. "Can I interest you in this exquisite figurine? It depicts the Roman god—"

Gavo waved the man to silence with a frown. "No, I don't need any of that. I just wanted to hear any news you might have from the south. Where have you travelled through on your way here, friend?"

The merchant's smile never wavered, for his information would fetch a price just like any of his other commodities, and he listed off a number of towns, some of which Gavo had never even heard of.

"Are you a chieftain?" the man asked, eyeing Gavo's sword and proud bearing. "My name is Cadwethen and I may have some news you'd be interested in hearing."

"For a price, no doubt," the captain smiled. "Fair enough. Aye, I'm a chieftain of sorts – I'm one of Queen Narina's advisors so if you can tell me anything interesting, I'm sure she'd be grateful."

"Ah!" Cadwethen's eyes lit up. "Well then, you're in luck, for I've a message for the queen, or her druid, Bellicus."

"You do?" Gavo asked. "Who from?"

"The famous warlord," Cadwethen replied. "Arthur, Bear of the Britons!"

"All right, I'll make sure your paid for your message, so what is it?"

The merchant spread his hands out apologetically. "I was told to deliver it only to the queen or the druid, my lord. Can you fetch one of them? Ah! What a happy coincidence, that must be Queen Narina herself!"

Gavo turned to look at the gatehouse and, sure enough, the queen was walking towards them with her maidservant, Brixta on one arm and nine-year-old Catia on the other. He smiled, for this saved him climbing the stairs himself or sending one of the guards as a messenger.

"My lady," he said, nodding respectfully as the women approached but the middle-aged guard captain was of little interest to the queen or her maid when there were carts laden with such interesting items behind him and Catia had already ran past him excitedly. The queen's eyes sparkled with delight and Gavo was pleased for, since Bellicus and Duro vanished Narina had been quiet and introspective. It was good to see her happy again, even if only for a short time. "My lady," he repeated, this time drawing the queen's attention. "This trader, Cadwethen was it? Aye, he has a message for you, from Arthur."

Narina frowned, clearly irritated at being drawn away from the wares she wanted to explore. "Arthur? The warrior Bellicus met? The one who rides with the Merlin?"

"The very same, my lady," Cadwethen agreed, smiling charmingly.

Narina's happy expression had faded now and Gavo felt irritated at the merchant although it was hardly Cadwethen's fault.

"Is it important, this message?" the queen asked, then checked herself. "Of course it is. Why else would the warlord be sending it?" She sighed and held out her hand. "I assume it's written down and not in your head."

There was only the slightest hesitation as the merchant wondered about his payment, but he was an experienced man and knew better than to offend a queen. He smiled and lifted his hand to signify she should give him a moment then he went around to the back of his cart and rummaged beneath a pile of light blue fabric. When he returned he had a folded parchment which he handed over to the queen with a deep bow.

Narina inspected it, seeing the beeswax seal was still intact although she had no idea what the little image impressed into the wax was supposed to be. A bear perhaps, given Arthur's well-known epithet. She eyed Cadwethen, wondering if he'd broken the seal, read the document and then resealed it with his own but there was no way to tell and he returned her look quite innocently.

"My lady," Gavo said. "The message has taken weeks to reach us. I think it can wait a little longer, if you'd like to browse the merchants' wares."

Narina smiled at him gratefully. "No, I'll read it first. It might be vitally important." That was unlikely, or Arthur would have sent a rider directly there with his message, but she broke the seal and unfolded the parchment, eyes scanning the few lines that were written there in Latin. The merchant watched her, plainly surprised that she was able to read herself, but Narina's father had appreciated many 'civilised' Roman traditions and made sure she learned her letters as a child. When she was finished, she folded the parchment again and handed it to Gavo. The captain could not read but he tucked it into his belt for safe-keeping, watching her curiously.

"Now, I will look at what these traders have to sell," she said, taking her maidservant's arm in hers and smiling once more.

This was the cue Cadwethen had been waiting for and he grinned, nodding and rubbing his hands as he began laying out little trinkets which he thought might catch the queen's eye.

Gavo narrowed his eyes and, as Narina moved past him she patted his folded arms and told him, "Arthur sends word that the Saxons have added even more men to their army and are pushing out further west with each passing month, burning towns and killing everyone that stands in their path," she said. "He wants us to give him men to force them back before it's too late."

"And will we?" the captain asked.

Narina shook her head. "Until Bellicus returns to lead the warband he was gathering for Arthur, our men will be going nowhere. We've enough to deal with as it is, without worrying about an enemy hundreds of miles away." She passed him and lifted the corner of the blue fabric Cadwethen had hidden the parchment beneath. "Oh, and Gavo, please see the trader is paid for bringing his message to us."

Gavo didn't think it possible, but the merchant's grin became even wider and he launched into a well-practiced sales pitch extolling the quality of his wares.

I don't know what you're so happy about, the guard captain thought gloomily. *Soon enough the Saxons will put you out of business. Gods, they're going to put us* all *out of business!*

* * *

Most men would have lost track of the passage of time within just a few days and, eventually, even Bellicus with all his druid's training couldn't tell how long he'd been in the filthy cell for it had gone well past a week with no sign of sun or moon or stars.

The only things that broke up his days were the terrible sounds from the room above and the occasional appearance of his guards who placed bread and water outside his gate where he could reach them. It never crossed his mind to refuse the food and drink – although he felt despair almost overcome him at times the desire to live, to free Duro and wreak vengeance on their captors, burned fiercer within Bellicus with every passing meal.

Twice, the druid awoke during what he assumed was the night, with a sense of being watched. The first time, he could see no-one for the torches hadn't been lit and it was pitch black. That suggested to him that his unseen companion had senses beyond any human, for what would be the point in a man watching him in the dark? He thought that perhaps the gods had come to inspect his prison for themselves. The second time, though, a rushlight or torch had been lit outside his cell, offering just enough light to let him recognise who watched him: Ria.

He said nothing and gave no indication that he'd noticed her and she remained in silence until he dozed off again. When he awoke, it was dark once more and the druidess was gone, although her faint, evocative scent had lingered for a long time afterwards. Or perhaps he just imagined that – his sense of smell had been inevitably, and mercifully, dulled after spending so long living in his own waste and he wondered if his mind was fooling him. Creating the pleasant odour to try and somehow calm him. If so, it didn't work. He longed for the girl to come to him, to offer some kind of companionship in this nest of vipers.

Which was ludicrous, he knew, for Ria was a Pict as much as he was one of the Damnonii. They may share a spiritual calling, but their earthly loyalties lay poles apart at this moment.

The sounds of Duro's beatings in the room overhead became less frequent as the days wore on and, eventually, seemed to stop altogether. Of course, Bellicus had no idea if that was good news or bad – had the centurion been so badly used his body had given out? Certainly, he could not have told Drest what he wanted to hear, since Duro did not know anything.

The druid could only pray to the gods that Drest had finally realised as much.

If that was the case, Bellicus could expect the king's attention to turn back in his direction.

Sure enough, a short time later the sound of footsteps approaching reached the druid and, judging by the number of men he could hear, this was not the lone guard delivering his daily 'meal'.

"Are you enjoying my hospitality, Bel?"

The druid rose to his feet and gazed at the grinning, bearded figure on the other side of the iron gate. "Have you killed Duro?" he growled, and his voice was laced with a terrible threat although it was wasted, given his position.

"You could hear us chatting, could you?" Drest smiled. "Aye, we've had quite a few good…talks."

His expression was infuriating, and it took a force of will for Bellicus not to try and tear the gate from its fixings so he could kill the Pictish scum.

"No. He's not dead."

The druid examined Drest's face and, with a great feeling of relief, decided the king spoke the truth. His next words dashed Bellicus's brief flare of hope though.

"For now, he lives. I came down to see if you wanted to talk to me yet, druid." Drest nodded to the guard on his right and the gate was quickly unlocked, four of the men filing into the cramped cell, led by the king and every one of them stepping gingerly to avoid stepping in faeces, puke or urine. "Tell me what you know about the Saxons' raid on Dunnottar, Bel." He smiled again, a look that was intended to invite trust but simply made the captured druid wish he had his sword, Melltgwyn, in his hand that he might take Drest's head and toss it out into the sea far below.

"Where is Qunavo?"

"What has he to do with anything?" Drest asked, surprised by the question.

"He can watch as I tell you I know nothing about any Saxon raid, and he will be able to tell you whether I lie or not. It would save us all a lot of trouble."

Drest shrugged. "You are right, lad. It would make things easier for me if I had him here, but he is still away on one of his frequent errands. You know what he's like. He would have made your friend talk soon enough though, you're right, rather than me having to resort to more…brutal tactics."

"You are an old fool," Bellicus hissed, and, although much of his bulk had fallen away during his time in confinement, his presence suddenly seemed to fill the little cell and Drest's guards moved in close as one, drawing short, stout clubs threateningly as they gazed at the druid who had not even taken a single step forward. "Duro told you nothing because he knows nothing."

"Maybe," the king retorted, and he was angry now. Angry and ashen-faced at the thrill of fear he'd felt simply being on the end of the Damnonii druid's unnerving gaze. "But *you* do. And if you don't tell me what I want to know, I'll simply keep beating your friend, Duro, to bloody ribbons." He stood up and shrugged. "Your choice, Bellicus. If you won't talk now, you are responsible for what befalls the centurion."

From the far corner of the cell there came a sudden, low growl. It was loud, and unmistakeably that of a dog. Everyone turned in shock, even Bellicus who felt sure he recognised it. *Cai?*

"What was that, by Taranis?" Drest demanded, shrinking back, away from where the noise had come from.

As the men listened, trying to make sense of what they'd heard, the sound of mocking laughter filled the air and Drest stared at Bellicus in a fury.

"Was that some trick of yours, druid?" the king demanded. "Throwing your voice, eh?"

Tears rolled down Bellicus's face as he laughed but he shook his head. "It wasn't me. Perhaps it was the gods warning you, Drest." He became serious and his voice was low, feral, almost like the dog they'd apparently heard. "I'll kill you Drest. Somehow, I will—"

The guard nearest to him lashed out with his club, aiming for the side of Bellicus's face, but the druid was expecting the attack and grabbed hold of the man's arm, twisting him around and kicking him forward into another guard. Then the druid dropped to one knee and punched outwards, straight into another Pict's midriff.

At another time, Bellicus would have moved on from this position of strength and at least got out of the cell, but today, weakened as he was, it didn't even take an enemy soldier to stop him.

As he turned to take on the next opponent stars flashed before his eyes and a wave of pain engulfed his head. He collapsed in agony on the floor and knew his escape attempt was over before it had even begun, as kicks and clubs hammered into his legs and torso.

CHAPTER TEN

Drest had been telling the truth: Duro was still alive. Bellicus knew this because the sounds of pain and torment overhead resumed in the following days, or nights, or whatever it was. A strange part of the druid admired the Picts' tactics – any normal man would have folded beneath this kind of pressure and given up the information Drest demanded. Of course, Bellicus was not a normal man, and, crucially, he didn't have the information required anyway. He pondered making up a lie, something that would give the king what he was looking for, but soon discarded the idea.

He had no way of knowing what had happened to bring Drest's ire, and any story Bellicus came up with would inevitably have holes in it. That would only mean even more pain for both he and the centurion who must, by now, be nearing his physical limits. Duro was a strong man, and he'd seen much brutality and violence in his life—indeed, he'd suffered a significant head injury as a younger man that had almost seen him invalided out of the legions—but he'd never had to face a situation like this before.

The druid could see no way out for either of them. If they couldn't satisfy Drest, he would continue to punish them and eventually their weakened bodies would simply not be able to take any more.

Bellicus wished he could see his friend, even just for a moment, to check on his condition. Images of a bloodied, bruised Duro haunted him in the dark. Had the Picts resorted to even more vicious techniques than mere beatings? Had they broken the centurion's limbs? Torn out his teeth, or his fingernails? And that growl he'd heard! Was it truly Cai, watching over him? Oh, how he missed the loyal hound…

Bellicus forced his mind to calm, halting his imagination which was rapidly moving onto vile tortures that would leave Duro maimed for life and unable to move even if they somehow did manage to find a way out of this nightmare.

That was another problem for the druid, although it seemed a small one at that moment – if Bellicus could get out of the cell and leave the fortress, what about Duro? He couldn't leave his closest friend behind, could he? Yet wasn't it more important for at least one of them to survive, that they might then avenge the other's tortured death?

He had been doing push-ups, trying to retain as much of his muscle-mass as possible in readiness for any chance to bring violence to his captors, but he stopped now, breathless and dizzy, and lay down on the floor.

His mind moved on from Duro and thoughts of escape, to previous days, when the pair of them had faithful Cai alongside, and they were strong and bright-eyed. And well fed. What a team, he thought with a smile. They had shown the Saxons and the Dalriadans what it meant to be in a fight with Britons, by Taranis!

That took his thoughts in another direction, to Catia, princess of Alt Clota and his own unacknowledged daughter. She suspected he was her father, but it was still a secret and, sitting here in this foetid cell, Bellicus wished he could give her a hug and tell her the truth before he died. Tell her how proud he was of her.

A tear rolled down his cheek and, unusually for Bellicus, he allowed himself to sink into melancholy, knowing it would do him no good, but not caring any more. Self-pity was a sure sign that he was close to breaking, but even druids had limits of endurance.

Suddenly he caught a scent in the air and he froze, breathing slowly, giving no indication that he was aware someone was watching him. He realised with a start that Ria had come along the corridor holding a rushlight and he'd only become aware of her presence when she was standing directly outside his cell looking in.

"Drest's sent you in his place today?" His lip curled in disdain and he would have spat if he hadn't been loath to waste his precious bodily fluids. Water was hard enough to come by after all.

"No," the young woman hissed, glancing back along the corridor and unlocking the gate. "The king has no idea I'm here." She shut the gate at her back and slipped across to him, the light in her hand dancing gracefully as she approached and knelt beside him. "How are you?" she asked, and there was genuine concern in her voice.

Surprised, he met her eyes and looked for some sign of duplicity, or even mockery, but there was none. "I've been better," he admitted.

She held something out to him and he squinted in the gloom. His mouth was watering before his dulled conscious mind had even realised what it was. "An apple!" He grabbed it from her, fearful that she might be teasing him and steal it away again, but she simply smiled and watched as he set about the small fruit.

Bellicus groaned as he bit into its flesh and the sweet juice filled his mouth, so unused to such tastes after days and weeks of nothing but bread, water, and the occasional small cup of ale. It was delicious, like it had been grown in the gods' own orchard.

"You're not Ria, are you?" he asked, only half-joking. "You're Sulis herself. Come to see me into the Otherworld."

"No," she replied, but her eyes constantly moved to the door and the corridor beyond, as if fearing someone would appear at any moment and find her there. "It's not your time to die yet, Bel. But it will be, if you don't tell Drest what he wants to hear."

"By the gods," the druid muttered in exasperation. "How many times must I repeat myself? I do not know anything about the Saxons' raid on Dunnottar. It was probably just a random attack, or maybe they wanted to hire mercenaries to fight Arthur or…" He shook his head and tossed the tiny remnants of apple core into the corner where he usually emptied his bowels. "I *hate* the Saxons, Ria. We came after your army to ask for men to go and *kill* Hengist and Horsa – I'm not working with the whoresons and neither is Duro— the bastards murdered his wife!"

Again, the druidess searched his face and Bellicus stared back defiantly, knowing her skill at reading people was at least equal to his. She'd always been a good student and really should have gone out into the world by now, to take up a position in another land, for the old ways needed to be tended and cared for if they were to flourish once again. Ria had always loved old Qunavo though, and it seemed she would remain by his side until the day he passed onto the Otherworld.

What a waste of her talents, Bellicus thought.

"Then you will die here," she said, sighing heavily.

"Speak on my behalf then. We're druids, we have a responsibility to help one another."

Ria shook her head and got to her feet. She paced up and down the small cell as Bellicus looked on, struck by her beauty which stirred his loins and made him curse the death that seemed fated to be his. The druidess would make a fine companion.

"Drest doesn't heed my counsel the way he listens to Qunavo," she muttered. "I'd be wasting my time, although I agree we share a bond, Bel. That's why I came to see you." She stopped pacing and knelt beside him again, placing a hand on his bruised cheek.

It took a monumental effort of will for him not to lean forward and kiss her, but he suspected it would be a mistake. He was encrusted with filth after all, and rutting on a shit-stained cell floor was not likely to stir Ria's sense of romance. Yet, even so, her dark eyes seemed to penetrate his soul and a part of him was certain that, in other circumstances, she would not refuse his advances.

A sudden image of Queen Narina, dressed in a dazzling white tunic, came to him, contrasting sharply with the gloomy cell and Ria's own dark features. He looked away, shaking his head in exasperation. Why did life have to be so damned complicated?

"I must go," the druidess said, stroking her palm down Bellicus's cheek before getting to her feet again. "I slipped a henbane mixture into the guard's ale, but only a small amount. He'll come to soon enough."

"What am I to do now then?" Bellicus demanded. "Simply wait here until Drest tires of torturing my friend in the room above, and then comes down to finish me off as well?"

They remained in silence for long moments, the sound of waves crashing against the stones far below an unceasing, constant reminder of where the druid was, and then Ria's small shoulders lifted in a shrug.

"I don't know," she admitted. "I had hoped you were merely being stubborn and might give up your information to the king if I could persuade you but…" She shook her head and walked over to the door, pulling it shut and throwing the heavy bolt back into place just as she'd found it. "Qunavo is away on some mystical quest he didn't see fit to share with me, so I believe Drest will keep you both alive until his return. That might be tomorrow, or it could be a month from now." She raised her hand and made the druid's sign of farewell then walked away, trailing darkness behind her. "The gods be with you, Bel, but I fear you'll be making that trip into the Otherworld before much longer."

When she had gone a feeling of despair almost overwhelmed him. Her presence, as much as the rushlight, had brought some desperately needed brightness into his day, but its passing left a gaping void that seemed even darker than before.

So, he sat, and he willed his mind, his emotions, to silence and then, perhaps it was the apple working its way through his body, elation came over him, incongruously but unmistakeably, and he began to sing. He sang the words of the lament he and Duro had written together, in honour of the centurion's wife who'd been murdered by Horsa's Saxons in

Luguvalium. It was only a short song, with a mere few lines of lyrics so, when he came to the end, he started again, and his voice grew in power as he allowed the music to fill his soul.

"A flock of geese fly overhead,
And I see you.
The sun sets on the water,
And I feel you near.
The smell of roses fills the air,
And you're with me again,
My wife, please don't leave me."

On the third repetition he realised he was not singing alone—a second voice was joining in, harmonizing, in the room above.

Tears streamed down his face, but a sudden sense of joy filled him as they sang together, for they both still lived and that meant there was still hope.

He had no idea how they were going to get out of Dunnottar, but by Taranis, he was not about to give up trying just yet and, from the sounds of it, neither was Duro!

CHAPTER ELEVEN

King Drest didn't come to see Bellicus again over the next few days, or months, or years – however long it was, the druid could not tell any more, for time had become fluid to him. His existence was now one, long bland routine—occasionally broken by vivid memories of past lived events—and he stopped caring about how many days were passing and focussed instead on retaining his mental and physical health as best he could.

Duro suffered another beating in the cell overhead during that period, and Bellicus sat, fists clenched, listening to the muffled grunts and cries of pain but it seemed even Drest was growing tired, for the torture didn't go on as long as it usually did before there was silence once more.

That was not a good sign, the druid knew. If Drest thought his captives were not worth questioning, they wouldn't be worth keeping alive either. Yet what could he do? There had been no chance to plan an escape attempt, and nothing to work with either. The walls of his cell were thick and he had no tools to even attempt to weaken them. The guards who delivered his food and drink would have spotted such destruction anyway.

So, although it infuriated him, Bellicus had been forced to merely sit and wait for the gods to decide what his fate should be. He hadn't wasted the time completely though, spending much of the days in darkness exercising, or practising his concentration techniques, forcing his mind to still for, he was certain, much longer periods than he'd ever managed before.

Qunavo would have been proud of him, he thought wryly, but it mattered little if he was soon to die.

The sound of a key turning in the lock at the end of the short corridor reached him and he focused his attention on it. He knew it was Ria before he saw her pretty face wreathed in those raven-black locks, for she had a much lighter touch than the guards who would rattle their keys and throw back the lock with no care for the noise they made.

She came to him, again holding a rushlight which gave off an acrid stench he was glad of, for it at least temporarily masked the other smells he'd been forced to live amongst.

"Is Qunavo back yet?"

Her face seemed drawn, more gaunt than usual, although that might have simply been a result of the gloom. Her manner was surely more furtive than it had been on her previous visits though, and Bellicus felt dread begin to form like a stone in his guts.

"No, he's not returned," she said, and her voice was as calm and measured as ever. Bellicus wouldn't expect any less though – she was a druidess after all, and control of one's voice was one of their most basic teachings. "It would be better for you if he had."

She unlocked the gate and came to him quickly, drawing something from beneath her dark tunic. He frowned and hurriedly got to his feet, ready to defend himself when he saw the rushlight's flame reflected from the steel and realised she carried a short sword.

"Don't be stupid," she growled, shaking her head and holding the weapon out to him. He didn't need a second invitation and grasped the hilt almost gleefully.

At last he had some means of killing the bastards who'd been making his life a waking nightmare for the gods knew how long! But this didn't make sense. He tore his gaze away from the blade, having examined its quality and finding it a decent enough weapon, and looked at Ria. What was happening now? She was a Pict, yet here the druidess stood, offering him a chance to kill her own people.

"Drest has decided you're no longer worth keeping alive."

A chill ran down Bellicus's spine and he grasped the sword tighter, but his anger paled in comparison to his outrage. "He would murder a druid?" The thought was almost inconceivable, for Drest yet followed the old ways, and

Bellicus saw now why Qunavo's absence was no good thing for him.

Ria nodded and there was fury in her eyes too. "If you remember, your previous king, Coroticus, also killed a druid not so long ago."[1]

"That was in the midst of a battle!" Bellicus hissed. "One in which the druid was part of an invading warband."

The girl shrugged. "I'm sure we can agree it should not have happened, though?"

"Of course," Bellicus said. "Does that make it right for Drest to imprison me, torture me, then slaughter me? A representative of the gods?" He truly felt little fear, his disgust at this erosion of the Old Ways' power was all he could think about for the moment.

"No, and that's why I've given you the sword." Ria grasped his arms, her small fingers seeming almost like a child's against his great biceps. "They are feasting tonight. Tomorrow will be your trial and execution. Qunavo wouldn't allow it if he was here, and neither will I. You escape tonight."

"Not without Duro."

"I'm not a miracle worker, Bel," Ria said, eyes flashing impatiently.

"Are you not?" he said, a small smile pulling the edge of his mouth. "I thought that was exactly what we druids were supposed to be."

She did not share his humour. "It'll be hard enough getting you out alive, without somehow helping the centurion as well. You're mostly in one piece," she sighed and shook her head sorrowfully. "Your friend has been ill-used, Bel. It would be a tough proposition for him to walk out of the fortress, even if I could get him out of his cell without the alarm being raised."

---

[1] See *The Druid*

"He lives, doesn't he?" the druid demanded, instantly regretting his harsh tone. Ria was trying to save his life after all.

"He does," she confirmed.

"Well he comes with us then," he said in a softer voice. "I'm not leaving him behind. He wouldn't leave me."

"Us?" Ria asked, confused. "I'm not going with you, Bel."

He stared at her. "You can't stay behind. Drest will kill you when he finds out me and Duro are gone. Don't be foolish, Ria."

She returned his gaze and now it was her turn to allow a smile to play on her pale features. "He'll have no idea who let you out," she said. "I know what I'm doing. I had the same training as you, and I've spent many years around these people. I can handle Drest well enough, at least until Qunavo's return." She let go of his arms and began to move towards the cell gate. "If I left with you they'd know it was me who helped you. Besides, I'm not changing sides, Bel. I'm still a Pict, and you're still Druid of the Damnonii. I merely refuse to allow one of my Order to be murdered on the whim of a king. Besides," her eyes sparkled mischievously now. "I don't think your queen would appreciate me turning up in Alt Clota on your arm. From the way she looked at you, I think she wants you for herself."

The gate was pulled shut and bolted, the rushlight making her eyes appear huge in the gloom as she peered in at him. "Be ready to move when I come for you. And I've left something for you to keep your strength up." With a last, almost sad smile, she turned and walked away, leaving Bellicus alone in his cell. Before her light disappeared he looked down, frowning, wondering what she meant.

A small bundle lay on the floor, wrapped in leaves. He opened it and, although the meagre light flickered out of view, the smell made his mouth water. Inside the package was a large piece of buttered bread and a lump of cheese.

After just a few, wonderful mouthfuls, he felt stronger than he had in days. In fact, a short time later, as he moved around the cell practising with the sword, getting a feel for its weight and working the muscles that hadn't been used in so long, he felt a rush of joy, almost like the feeling he got when performing a ritual to the gods.

He was tempted to force himself to calm down, not to get carried away, but instead he embraced the feeling, allowing it to fill his soul, so, soon enough he was thrusting and parrying, dodging and hacking apart invisible foes with Drest's face.

Before long, however, he regretted his burst of enthusiasm as a wave of dizziness came over him and he had to sit down, back against the wall, to try and steady himself once more. The grim smile never left his face though, for he had a sword, and food in his belly, and the blessing of the gods to do whatever he needed to escape the Picts' clutches and return home to Dun Breatann. To Cai, and Catia, and Narina…

He slowed his breathing and closed his eyes, forcing his mind to calm, making a mental note to dull the sword's blade with muck before Ria returned for him so it didn't catch the torchlight and betray his presence.

He would be ready when she came, and Taranis protect any who tried to stand in his way.

* * *

"What's wrong with him?" The young druid, Koriosis eyed the massive dog warily as it growled for no apparent reason, and Princess Catia shrugged, a worried expression on her face.

"I don't know," she admitted. "It's nothing to do with you though, you don't have to be frightened. He's been doing this for the past few days – growling and whining." She reached out and stroked Cai's head and the hound pressed against her, seeking comfort or perhaps offering some to the concerned girl. "It's all right, boy, shh."

Koriosis looked down at the pair who were lying side-by-side on the grassy eastern summit of Dun Breatann, gazing out at the River Clota which stretched into the distance, a sparkling ribbon of blue on this sunny morning.

When he'd first come to Alt Clota and met Bellicus he'd been impressed by the giant warrior-druid who cut such an imposing, confident figure with his great eagle-topped staff and muscular war-dog by his side. He'd soon come to realise Bel was as friendly a man as any he'd ever met and happy to pass on his knowledge and lore to the younger druid while also showing an interest in the bee-hives Koriosis was setting up. Honey and bees were a great passion of Koriosis's, who believed the insects and their sweet, valuable produce were a great resource that should be nurtured and made more of.

He'd never quite grown to trust the hound though, despite the fact everyone in Dun Breatann treated Cai like a big pet, lavishing treats and cuddles on him whenever he passed by. Koriosis didn't have much experience with dogs, especially one as big as Cai who, although he seemed friendly, had, if the stories told about him were true, killed more than one enemy warrior over the years.

"Do you think he can sense his master? Is he whining because he knows Bel's in trouble?"

Koriosis sat down and replied without hesitation. "Of course. Animals can form strong magical bonds with their human companions and, from what I've seen and heard, Cai and his master were very close."

When the druid and Duro first disappeared it caused much consternation for there had been no clues to their whereabouts, as if they'd simply dropped off the face of the world. Of course, it seemed obvious that Drest or his followers had done some harm to the missing pair, but there'd been no torn clothing, no bodies…Nothing found to suggest foul play. Cai had been taken along the road to try and find his master's scent, but he'd only been able to follow so far and then became as lost as the humans.

Koriosis could see the anxiety on Catia's face as she thought of the vanished men and said, "If Cai is sensing bad things happening to Bel, it suggests to me that Bel must still be alive."

The princess's face lit up but only momentarily. "Where *is* he then? Has he been stolen away to the Otherworld? And Duro as well? It would take a lot to beat those two, I think." She smiled slightly, recalling her recent adventures with the druid and his centurion companion. "I wouldn't want to fight them, even if I was one of the faerie folk."

Koriosis didn't reply. Did he believe people could be stolen away to another world? Of course. There were many tales of just such a thing happening, where a child was taken by some sprite, only to return years later having aged not at all, for time flowed differently in the Other World. Did he believe Bellicus and Duro had been taken in such a fashion? No – he'd heard Gavo and the other soldiers talking and he sided with their idea: That the men had been abducted by the Picts for some reason. Of course, there should have been a ransom demand by now if that was the case, but what else could have happened?

Cai growled again and Koriosis edged away slightly but the dog took no notice of him. The young druid looked about, trying to see if there was some mundane reason for the hound's behaviour—an irritating fly, or some unpleasant smell, or a threatening sound carried on the east wind—but he could sense nothing and the three of them lapsed into silence.

"If Bellicus doesn't come back that'll mean you're Druid of Dun Breatann, won't it? At least until they send someone else with more experience."

Koriosis swallowed. Of course, that thought had crossed his mind already. He'd trained for over a decade on Iova and other places, learning many of the things Bellicus would have learned before him so, in theory he should be able to step into the older druid's shoes. If it came to it, he would have no choice, but he truly hoped it wouldn't come to that. Not quite yet. Alt Clota was a large place and he was still just finding his way around. He prayed to the gods that Bellicus would return and reclaim his rightful place.

"If that happens, I'll be ready," he said to the princess, but his promise sounded weak even to his own ears.

Cai stood up suddenly, staring towards the north-east but making no sound, simply looking at something Koriosis and Catia couldn't see before, at last, sitting down and, somehow, appearing more content than before.

"I think Bellicus is still alive, and in this world," Koriosis said as he watched the dog. "I suggest we make an offering to the gods, to help him come through whatever trials he faces right now, for Cai is surely sensing *something,* and it's wise to take heed of such signs."

Catia immediately got to her feet, happy to have something to do at last. "Come on then," she shouted, hurrying down the slope towards Dun Breatann's great hall. "We'll ask my mother for a chicken, and you can offer it tonight, when the moon rises!"

There seemed nothing else to do, so Cai and Koriosis made their way after the precocious girl. She was right, the druid thought. Tonight was a good time for a sacrifice and he felt sure Bellicus could do with all the help he could get right then.

"A sheep," he called after the princess. "A sheep would be even better than a chicken. I've always found it easier to read the entrails of larger animals."

"A sheep then!" Catia shouted over her shoulder, grinning. "Come on, keep up, we'll have to choose the best ones and get everything ready in time for nightfall."

As they neared the hall Cai barked excitedly and it almost seemed to the young druid like the dog approved of their plan and could hardly wait for night to fall.

"Don't worry, lad," Koriosis said, finally finding the courage to stroke the animal's head as they reached the hall doors. "Wherever your master is, he'll have the gods' help tonight. I hope he can make the most of it…"

* * *

Bellicus opened his eyes, and shoved himself up on one hand, startled to realise he'd fallen asleep. Grasping the sword with its filth-coated blade he stood up, wiping the drool from the side of his mouth and listening for what had awakened him. He didn't have to wait long, and his heart began to pound as the familiar dim glow of a rushlight approached from the opposite end of the short corridor.

Ria was there, her glossy black hair almost forming a halo around her head, like a dark version of one of the Christians' so-called saints. With unwavering hands she undid the lock on the door and shoved the gate open, gesturing for him to follow.

Without a backward glance at the stinking room that had been his home for what seemed an eternity, the druid slipped silently into the corridor behind Ria who was already moving towards the exit. As they walked, Bellicus glanced from side to side, surprised to realise his was the only cell, and the corridor was shorter than he'd believed, so before long they were out and into a wider, slightly more open area.

A guard snored right next to them and Bellicus jerked, bringing his sword up, ready to attack. Ria smiled and shook her head at his reaction.

"You'd better calm your nerves," she admonished in a low voice. "This is just the beginning, and he'll be sleeping for the rest of the night. Try not to seem so anxious if we meet anyone else. You're not as strong as usual, Bel, so don't waste energy jumping at shadows."

"Are you expecting to meet anyone else?" he muttered, falling into step behind her as she moved on, this time to the left where a narrow staircase wound upwards.

"No," she said, holding the rushlight a little higher as they ascended, its weak light throwing strange shadows on the wooden walls. "But if we do, they're bound to recognise you instantly. You're pretty distinctive, in case you hadn't noticed."

He didn't reply. There was no point in asking what he should do if they were seen. She hadn't given him the sword merely as decoration after all. Yet her warning not to be too eager to fight was a sensible one, for he *was* a shadow of his former self after weeks of near starvation. It would be much better to avoid confrontation if possible.

Ria held up a hand and he paused as she climbed the rest of the stairs alone. Moments later she whispered for him to follow and, when he reached the landing he saw another guard sleeping off the effects of whatever the druidess had slipped into his ale skin. Poppy resin probably, although he half-hoped it was something more deadly, or at least something that would give the guard a severe dose of the shits when he came to.

"Your friend is in here," Ria said, nodding towards the thick, oak door the dozing warrior had been guarding and Bellicus took it in, forming a mental map of the building with the knowledge that his own empty cell was located beneath where they stood. "I haven't seen him recently," the girl went on, grasping the giant druid's sleeve in her free hand. "You should prepare for the worst and *remain calm*, all right?"

Her words did little to ease his state of mind—they merely heightened his sense of anxiety. He would rather face half-a-dozen Pictish axemen charging up the stairs than walk into the locked room and face Duro at that moment.

Even if the centurion was alive and in one piece, the brutality he'd suffered at Drest's hands would leave mental scars that might fade over time, but they'd likely never heal completely.

"Sulis," the druid intoned, calling on the goddess almost silently. "Give Duro the strength to get through the next few hours." He looked at the sleeping guard and had the idea of slitting his throat, offering the Pict's lifeblood as an offering to the gods in return for the centurion's well-being, but he discarded it immediately. He had killed sleeping men in the past, but only ones that were a threat. Killing this defenceless warrior would not please any gods Bellicus wished to serve.

"Just open it," he growled. "Let's get this over with and get out of this shit-hole before we're discovered, and people have to die."

Without another word she unbolted the door and pushed it open. Bellicus lifted the torch that was in the iron holder on the wall beside the guard and stepped into the room.

Strangely, in the short distance they'd walked from the cell on the floor below—through the walkways with fresher air, untainted by the stench of shit and piss and sweat—Bellicus's sense of smell had somewhat returned. He gagged now as the odour of Duro's recent captivity hit him almost like a blow.

He cursed and breathed through his mouth, wincing as he hurried across to his friend who lay unmoving on the floor.

"Watch the door," he commanded, and Ria quickly moved to comply as the druid knelt and examined his friend. He stared at Duro's back, letting out a sigh of relief as he saw the shoulders rise and fall and knew the centurion still lived. "Wake up," he murmured, shaking his friend gently while simultaneously checking for broken limbs. All appeared intact, praise Sulis, and he muttered, "Wake up," again, more insistently now.

"Do you have any water, Ria?" he asked, placing the torch into an iron sconce on the cell wall.

The girl moved around outside and returned with a skin of water which she found beside the unconscious guard.

Bellicus took it while she went back to keep watch. He pulled out the stopper, sniffed to make sure it really was water, and took a sip himself. It was good—better than he'd been given anyway—and he upended it over Duro's open mouth.

A few drops went in and the centurion's eyes flickered. His mouth worked as he licked his lips and then groaned, but still he didn't wake. "Come on, man, get up!" Bellicus poured more water over Duro's lips and chin and this time, with a deep breath of shock and fear, the centurion came to, jerking backwards, away from the druid.

"What is it?" Duro whispered and his voice was whining and pitiful and that, more than anything Drest had done to him, almost broke Bellicus.

"You're safe," the druid said in a firm, but calm voice. "It's me, Bel." He forced a smile onto his face and moved his head into the light so Duro could see his features. "I've come to get you out. We're going home, my friend." He got up on one knee and held out a hand. "Get up, soldier. The Picts are drinking themselves into a stupor in the great hall, and we have to move before someone discovers us."

Duro frowned in confusion and mistrust, as if he couldn't quite believe he was really seeing Bel before him. As though the druid was some trick of his tortured mind.

"It's really me, Duro," Bellicus said, nodding, hand still outstretched as he retrieved the torch and Ria came to take it from him. "Did you think I'd let Drest kill you, old friend? Never. But you have to get up now, come on." He moved forward and, gods be praised, Duro stretched out his left hand to him, allowing the druid to help him onto his feet.

"You took your time," the centurion muttered, but his forced attempt at humour didn't raise his spirits and Bellicus could see tears forming in the man's blackened eyes.

"Sorry, I was a bit tied up myself," the druid replied, placing the centurion's arm across his shoulders and feeling almost the full weight of Duro settle upon him. "Come on, let's go. And, here, while we walk…" He took out a small parcel wrapped in leaves and put it into his friend's right hand. It was half of the buttered bread and cheese that Ria had given him earlier. "I saved this for you."

"Thank you," Duro whispered, and his gratitude was so pitiful as he started eating the little meal that Bellicus felt like weeping to see him in such a state.

As they moved forward, closer to the druidess and the torchlight, Bellicus noticed something from the corner of his eye and glanced down at the centurion's left hand, which was resting on his shoulder. It took everything in him not to cry out, but his training held him in check and he kept moving, taking even more of Duro's weight on his own tired legs.

Drest had taken two fingers from the centurion, leaving unbandaged, bloody stumps which had presumably been cauterized with fire. Every one of his nails had been torn out as well. No wonder the poor devil had been screaming so loudly.

"Bastards have been playing with me, Bel. I thought they'd have killed me ages ago – I must be stronger than I thought."

Bellicus squeezed his friend's arm and replied through gritted teeth. "You are. And when we get out of here we'll enjoy a good meal, a good drink, and then set about finding the scum that did this to you."

They passed out into the hallway with its dozing guard and Ria eyed them up and down. Her eyes passed over Duro's bloody hand dispassionately and Bellicus wondered if severing fingers was a common tactic employed by Dunnottar's king when he took prisoners.

Bellicus had seen worse, gods, had *done worse* himself to enemies he needed information from – he recalled the Saxon madman who they thought had originally kidnapped Princess Catia what, two years ago? The druid had made the Saxon's last hour on life a horrific, agonizing experience, and left the mangled body to be devoured by the crows and foxes.

But it was different when one of your own friends was on the receiving end of such brutal treatment.

"Wait." The druidess pushed open a door and went into what Bellicus could see was a simple storeroom. His heart soared suddenly, as she passed something out to him and he realised what it was.

"Melltgwyn!" He dropped the weapon Ria had given him in the cell, then reached out to grasp his sword, feeling almost as if he'd been reunited with a lost lover. "Can you stand by yourself yet, Duro? Just for a moment?"

There was a grunt of assent and Bellicus let go of the centurion to buckle his swordbelt around his waist. But there was more, as Ria hurriedly thrust his brown robe towards him, although he noted sadly that all the pouches sewn inside it had been emptied of their contents. No doubt Qunavo had helped himself to the valuable herbs and other ingredients he'd collected. Oh well, he could collect more in time.

As he quickly threw the thick robe about his shoulders, Ria came out with another swordbelt, which she placed around the centurion's waist and buckled it safely in place.

"Sorry, Roman," she shrugged. "Your clothes were taken by one of our noblemen, as was your spatha. The only reason Bel's things are still here is because Drest wanted to execute the pair of you with the druid's own sword, in a public ceremony."

With his hood pulled up, Melltgwyn on his left side and Duro on the other, Bellicus truly started to feel like his old self again. He could sense the strength flowing through him and knew the gods were with them, no matter what happened this night.

"What about my staff of office?" he asked, and Ria, to his delight, smiled.

"You'll see that soon enough. Are you ready to move?"

Bellicus turned to Duro, whose hand was resting naturally on the pommel of his borrowed sword, and then nodded at the druidess. She smiled and strode ahead, urging them to move as quietly as possible.

As they walked, Bellicus could see outside and he began to remember the layout of Dunnottar from his childhood visits. It wasn't a huge place, after all, and he'd always had a good memory, even before the druid training honed and sharpened it. To their left stood the largest building, a sturdy wooden tower that was comprised of four individual levels. Lights shone out from all the floors, and the maddeningly delicious smell of roasting meat wafted from the lowest of them, which Bellicus knew to be the kitchen. Loud, drunken laughter and male voices drifted out of the topmost level, although the windows were closed over against the chill spring air.

Bellicus stopped in his tracks as he heard one voice rise above the others and burst into a bawdy song. It was Drest, and he completed the first verse alone, cheered on by his companions, and then everyone in the lofty room joined in.

"Maybe we could set alight to the building," the druid growled, eyes searching the darkness outside for some means of ignition. "The kitchen, perhaps? All it would take would be—"

"Enough foolishness," Ria snapped, grabbing his hand and pulling him, and the limping Duro, along once again. "Our main objective is to get you out of here. I'm not letting you murder my people, Bel. By the gods, your time in that cell has addled your mind." She shook her head in exasperation as they reached a door leading out to the main path that would take them away from the fortress if they could just get through the gates.

Instead of running towards those gates, though, Ria plunged her torch into a bucket of sand to extinguish it, and then led them to the left.

"Where now?" Duro asked, and his voice was overly loud, despite the ale-fuelled carousing in the building beside them.

His question was answered by the sound of whinnying, and the unmistakeable smell of horses.

"Darac!" The druid broke into a grin as he caught sight of the big black who'd shared so many adventures with him, standing eyeing their approach in one of the stalls. His joyful expression fell away, however, when a man's voice called out from behind them.

"Ria? Is that you, lady? Who's that with you?"

Bellicus muttered an oath as he heard at least two men approaching, but he let go of Duro, hoping the centurion would be able to remain standing without support, and grasped Melltgwyn's hilt as Ria turned to face the newcomers.

Her smile was wide and engaging, and it must have set the men at ease for the one who had addressed her spoke again and his tone was more jovial now.

"What's happening?" he asked, and his accent was so thick even Bellicus had to focus to make out the words. "Who are these two lads? I don't recognise them. Gods, that one looks ill."

The warriors were right behind them now, and Bellicus knew the alarm would be raised as soon as the Picts realised who accompanied Ria. Even if she had some cover story, one of the guards would run to ask Drest if the prisoners were supposed to be wandering about the fortress with only the druidess for company.

The druid spun, drawing his sword at the same time, and slammed the point home into the nearest Pict's heart. The man was wearing a leather breastplate but it offered little resistance against the powerful thrust, and Bellicus felt the blade slide deeply into the man's chest. He twisted it, then dragged it free, but the second guard was no fool and had already drawn his own weapon, a square-headed axe, from its loop on his belt.

"Invaders!" the Pict screamed, aiming a blow at Bellicus's midriff, but the druid saw it coming and batted it aside with his sword. He stepped in close to the enemy soldier and hammered his knee between the man's legs. The cries of alarm were cut off with an agonised groan, but that too was silenced when the pommel of the druid's sword smashed down onto the back of his head.

Ria had not waited to watch the outcome of the fight. She was already opening the stall where Darac stood, watching his master dispatch the enemy guards.

The massive horse had already been saddled, presumably by the druidess, earlier in the evening, and she gestured impatiently to Bellicus who had spotted a small crossbow on the first Pict he'd killed and was bending to unhook it, along with some bolts, from the man's back.

"Get on the fucking horse, man!" Ria hissed, glancing up at the top room in the tower, but the merriment there continued undisturbed by events outside. "Move!"

She let go of Darac's bridle and the beast ambled over to the druid, who pressed his head against the horse's affectionately before he noticed his staff buckled onto the saddle and grinned in relief. Now he felt like he had everything he needed to escape this foul place.

Next, Ria led another animal out, and Duro shambled across to it. Bellicus knelt and cupped his hands for the centurion to step on and then, with much grunting and even a wretched whimper, Duro managed to climb into the saddle. He held the reins with white knuckles and allowed his head to rest on the horse's neck. He even forced a smile, which Bellicus returned before hauling himself onto Darac.

"There's food, drink, and medical supplies in the saddlebags," Ria said, still eyeing the tower uneasily. "Now, walk the horses behind me. I'll see about getting the gates opened."

She hurried along the path that led to the main entrance. Thankfully it was downhill a short way, so the fight hadn't been seen by the men there. Bellicus guessed there would be at least two, possibly three or four, men within the gatehouse – too many for him to kill on his own without *someone* raising the alarm and bringing the rest of the Picts down upon them anyway. Even if he'd been in full health, which was certainly not the case now he mused, as his whole body felt shaky and if he hadn't been on Darac's broad back he'd probably have had to sit down and wait for the weakness to pass.

The gatehouse stood within a natural gap in the rock, and it was quite narrow. There were actually two gatehouses, one at either end of the path so, if the first was taken by an enemy, they Picts could fall back and defend the second without the fortress being compromised. Only the outer, main gates were barred though, and a brazier burned on the top of the wall there. One man could be seen silhouetted beside the flames, but Bellicus was certain at least one more guard was inside the gatehouse, awake, and ready to help if any threat was sighted.

The druid reached out and hauled on Duro's bridle, as well as his own, stopping both horses while Ria's lithe form disappeared inside the gatehouse.

"How in Mithras's name is she going to get us out of here?" Duro asked, still resting his head against the horse's brown mane but staring bright-eyed at the guard atop the gatehouse wall. "Those bastards surely won't just throw the gates open and let us ride through in the middle of the night."

"Maybe she's going to kill them all and open the gates herself," Bellicus suggested, and realised he wouldn't be surprised if that's exactly what Ria planned on doing. She obviously cared for him more than the Pictish guards he'd just dispatched.

"Why?" The centurion muttered, not taking his eyes from the shadowy figure by the brazier for a moment. "Why is she helping us? Was she your lover when you were younger?"

"If only," Bellicus replied without thinking, but Duro merely grunted in apparent agreement of his friend's appreciation.

"By Mithras!" The battered centurion's oath was little more than a whisper but the emotion in his voice was as clear as if he'd been directing new legion recruits on the parade ground. "Look, Bel."

The druid was looking already, and he shared Duro's surprise, for Ria had crept up behind the guard on the wall and then he'd fallen down without so much as a cry. From the way his shadowy form had buckled it was obvious he'd been stabbed or otherwise expertly, brutally, incapacitated.

"Isn't she a Pict herself?" Duro asked, turning to look feebly across at his companion.

Bellicus nodded. "I don't know where she was born or who her original kinfolk were," he said. "But she's lived here since she was a child so, she's as much a Pict as any of them I suppose."

"Yet she's helping us escape this place, and murdering the guards to ensure we succeed. It must be those rugged good looks of yours."

They watched and waited in anxious silence, glancing backwards or upwards at the tower beside them, fearing more warriors would appear and try to stop their bid for freedom. Ria soon reappeared from the gatehouse though, and they could just make her out as she hurried towards the gates and hastily lifted away the bar that held them shut.

There must have been more mechanisms sealing them in place but it was too dark to see her as she moved around although, at last, the narrow gates were opened and the foaming waves could just be seen sparkling in the moonlight on the other side.

The girl came back to them, a grim look on her face which, Bellicus noted, also had a smear of blood along it.

"Are you all right?" he asked, and she nodded.

"I am. The way is clear. The rest is up to you now."

They stared at one another but then a sudden cry from the drunken gathering brought them back to reality and the druid nodded. "Thank you, Ria. I won't forget this. If you ever have need of my help, just send word, or come to Dun Breatann. The gods know, I—we—owe you our lives."

"Make no promises you might regret," the druidess replied but Bellicus merely reiterated his gratitude and pledge of future assistance and she smiled before walking to the back of Darac and slapping the big black on the rump. "Go!" she hissed, and the horses began moving through the gates.

Another cry came from the tower, but this time it was uttered by a fat, red-faced man in the lower storey. He was staring out at them, and Bellicus could see the beads of sweat on his face from the heat in the kitchen.

"Shit," he swore. "Cook's seen us, Duro. We need to move, fast. Hold on!"

He kicked his heels in and allowed Darac to speed up, hoping the centurion's mount would follow his lead. He was pleased to see no sign of Ria – she must have disappeared inside one of the buildings, and he prayed she'd managed to get away safely before the cook realised she'd been with the escaping prisoners.

The dark and the steep, uneven path meant the horses couldn't build up too much speed or they'd end up tumbling down onto the rock-strewn beach below, or slip and break a leg, either of which would mean the end of their escape attempt for Duro was in no state to run.

Neither am I, Bellicus thought, pulling Melltgwyn a little way from its sheath just in case he had to use it. Which seemed more likely with every passing moment, for now, when he turned and looked back he could see the shutters had been thrown open on the topmost floor of Dunnottar's tower, and angry, confused men were watching them ride towards the mainland. Their outraged voices carried clearly on the wind although there was no need to hear the words to understand what was being said.

"Can you hold on, Duro?" Bellicus demanded, looking over his shoulder at the pale-faced centurion. "When we get off this path I mean, and we can let the horses gallop."

Through gritted teeth, the centurion replied, but his voice was too weak and whatever he said was swept away behind them.

"I'll take that as a 'yes'," Bellicus muttered, and prayed to the gods that they'd soon be off this rough, uneven path and on hard, even grass. He assumed the Picts kept this approach to the fortress in poor condition to make it even harder for an attacking army to make it up to the walls. The slower the enemy moved, the more time Drest's garrison would have to attack with arrows, slingshot, rocks and whatever else was to hand.

Pursuit had already been mobilised, judging by the hollow thuds Bellicus could hear now, of hooves pounding on the ground behind them. At least the Pictish horsemen would face the same problem as their prey and have to hold their mounts in check until they were safely off the worn path.

Or maybe not.

"Damn!" The druid risked another look back, trusting Darac to hold a safe line without his guidance, and noticed one Pict in particular seemed to care little about the danger of tumbling down onto the shore beneath them. "Drest must have promised them a huge reward if they could catch up with us," he said, more to himself than Duro, who was concentrating too hard on simply remaining in his mount's saddle to engage in conversation.

They were almost at the end of the narrow path but Bellicus knew they would not reach it, and be able to urge their horses into a gallop, before the crazed berserker coming after them caught up.

Quickly looking backwards again, the druid saw their foe clearer now that he was closer. He gave no concern whatsoever to the uneven ground, driving his horse as fast as it could run while he himself was holding a long-handled battle-axe aloft, bearded face twisted in triumph as he grew ever nearer to his quarry.

"Get in front!" Bellicus yelled, slowing Darac just enough to let the centurion pass him. "Faster, Duro, ride faster!"

There was no reply, or at least none the druid could hear over the wind, and he drew Melltgwyn, praying to Taranis to give him the strength to wield the weapon effectively. He felt dizzy and nauseous, and the thought of trying to fight the pursuing warrior from horseback was not a pleasant one, but there was no other choice for, although he had the stolen crossbow, there was no way to load it while galloping at this speed, even if he could shoot accurately.

He had to stop the Pict somehow though, or their escape would be over before it had even begun.

To his dismay, Duro's horse was slowing, and Darac was following its lead, so the screaming berserker behind them was closing in faster than ever, and so were his fellows.

"Fight, you whoresons!" the Pict shouted, and there was no problem hearing his booming voice over the whipping wind. "Cowards! Let my axe taste your blood, druid, it's time for you to die!"

Bellicus turned to gauge the distance between them and was shocked to realise their enemy was almost upon them. Without thinking, the druid pulled back on the reins and, as the Pict came alongside, swung Melltgwyn. There was a clatter as both weapons came together, and a terrible, dull pain shot through Bellicus's arm.

I can't beat him.

The truth was unavoidable. That first coming together had almost thrown the druid from the saddle, and his whole right side was ringing with pain. The Pict was facing him, allowing his horse to match Darac's pace, and he swung once more.

This time the horses moved apart to avoid a stone on the path and the blade missed Bellicus by a wide margin, which was just as well as he hadn't even been able to lift his own weapon to parry.

Duro's face was still pressed against his horse's mane but he was staring back, wide-eyed and despairing, as he watched the one-sided fight behind him. If Bellicus had any hope of somehow beating the crazed warrior, the centurion's expression would quickly have disabused him of the notion.

"Time to die, you Damnonii bastard." The Pict's mouth opened in a grin of triumph and he nudged his galloping horse sideways, bringing his axe back and laughing as the druid tried without success to raise Melltgwyn up one last time. "For King Drest!"

With that deafening war cry, the Pict swung his weapon back, and Bellicus, sickened by his inability to save himself, closed his eyes, praying that Duro would somehow make it back to Alt Clota safely.

CHAPTER TWELVE

Koriosis, lean frame resplendent in a pure white robe that almost seemed to glow in the light of the moon, raised his hands and closed his eyes. He did not feel nervous despite his inexperience and the dozen or so people gathered to watch this ceremony; he did feel a great responsibility to complete the ritual properly however, for he truly believed Bellicus and Duro needed the gods' aid if they were ever to return safely to Dun Breatann.

The stars glittered in a sky made cloudless by a chill north wind but Koriosis felt no discomfort, only a deep sense of peace and growing joy. Some of that could be attributed to the draught he'd brewed earlier, a mixture of strong wine, sacred herbs and other ingredients only the druids knew the secrets of, but Koriosis understood the veil between the worlds was parting. He could feel it deep within his being, and he knew, somehow, that Queen Narina, Princess Catia, and all the other folk taking part in this magical event felt it too.

When Catia had asked her mother about the possibility of Koriosis performing a sacrifice in order to help Bellicus and his centurion companion the queen had agreed straight away, thinking it an excellent idea. Gavo had suggested performing the ritual in this place, on a low hilltop on the road between the nearby villages of Dun Buic and Credigone. There had once been a fort here, many generations ago, and it was said the land retained some of its power. Bellicus himself often came here to commune with the gods and so it seemed the ideal place for this ceremony.

Koriosis could only agree when they'd arrived and he looked out across the sunlit Clota. Not only was the view pleasant, but the ancient remains of the fort gave the hilltop a sense of the Otherworld which he knew would only be heightened when the sun went down.

Torches had been prepared, spices burned in censers and, when night fell, everything was ready.

The druid spoke the words to invoke the great god Lug and then lowered his arms and sat cross-legged before a flat, weather-beaten stone that must have lain on the hill for many hundreds of years. It had been carved with some unknown script which, although it could not now be deciphered, held a potent magic within it. Even with his eyes closed, Koriosis could sense the power emanating from the stone – it seemed to pulse within him, growing stronger and stronger as the moments passed until even that sensation was forgotten and he knew the gods had come.

He raised his right hand slowly, as if in a dream, and the sheep that had been chosen for the sacrifice was brought forward. It came quietly enough, not suspecting for a moment why it was there, and the calm, meditative atmosphere soothed it just as it soothed the people around it. The men who brought it gently lifted it onto its side and applied gentle pressure to hold it there. For a moment the beast struggled but soon went limp and still no fear touched its eyes.

The young druid felt a momentary panic when he tried to raise himself up onto his knees, for his body was so relaxed that, at first, it refused to respond to his commands. Before he was forced to ask for help though, his eyes opened and he was able to move, taking up the sharpened stone knife that he'd brought with him.

He began to sing, softly at first. He had not memorised the song—indeed, he'd never even heard it before—but the words came into his head as he sang, and his voice grew louder and more powerful as he went.

"Chill is the wind,
Winding is the path.
Mighty is the stag,
That leads us on.

Storm in the mountains,
Rivers in turmoil,
Lofty is the eagle,
That heeds our call.
The ice has cracked,
The Way draws near,
Lug take this gift,
Make your wishes clear."

The sheep had still not tried to move and Koriosis reached out now with his left hand, covering the animal's eyes while, with the knife in his other hand, he cut its throat. The men held it down until its struggles stopped, and then the druid cut its belly open and reached in to draw out its insides.

The people looked on in reverential silence as the mystic arranged the entrails in a certain way and inspected the sheep's organs, particularly the liver. It was common for the druid in this situation to smile and pronounce great fortune on its way for his people, but Koriosis remained silent, his face grim for a long time as he moved the innards this way and that, his hands slick with blood.

At last, he muttered a prayer thanking the animal for its life, and then a little shakily, he got to his feet and turned to face his audience.

"What is it?" Narina asked, frowning. Some rulers might have guided the druid to make the expected, positive prediction simply to keep the people happy, but Narina was not that sort of queen. If trouble was coming, she wanted the Damnonii to be ready for it.

"Darkness," Koriosis replied in a strange, monotonous voice. "I see darkness approaching for Bellicus, and for Alt Clota." He stared at Narina and it was as if he looked right through her. "Do not eat this animal's flesh."

There were unhappy murmurs at that for succulent, roasted meat was the part of these ceremonies that many of them looked forward to the most. But the druid went on in in the same emotionless voice. "Burn it. Every part. And pray that Lug accepts it in return for his favour."

With that, the druid turned and sat down before the sacrificed sheep, closed his eyes, and remained motionless while his commands were carried out.

It was sunset before he awakened from his trance and he looked around groggily, trying to get his bearings. The two men who'd handled the sheep had remained with him through the night, to make sure no harm befell him from earthly dangers, but Narina, Catia, Gavo and all the others were gone.

All that remained from the druid's ritual was a pile of ashes, a few charred bones, and the blood on his hands.

* * *

Darac pounded on, and on, and the druid opened his eyes again, wondering why the Pict's axe hadn't yet smashed his skull open, but he appeared to be alone, with only the centurion in sight.

Confused, he looked back to see the rapidly dwindling form of the bearded Pict, lying unmoving on the path. There was no sign of his horse.

It took a moment for Bellicus to understand what had happened and then he kicked in his heels, pushing Darac to an even faster pace for they were now onto the flat grass of the mainland. As he reached Duro he slapped the centurion's mount on the rump with the flat of his blade and shouted as loudly as he could, making both horses run harder.

"The fool's horse must have turned its hoof on a hole in the ground, or slipped," Bellicus shouted breathlessly. "It went over the edge, and I think the rider's broken his neck!"

They both managed to turn for another look back and felt relief as they were outstripping the remaining pursuers who were riding more cautiously now, no doubt in response to their comrade's apparent death.

"The gods have given us a chance," Bellicus said. "We can't waste it. Hold on for all your worth, Duro, ride harder than you've ever ridden before, and pray Ria chose the fastest horse in Dunnottar's stables for you!"

High on the wall of the fortress the druidess watched them ride away into the darkness as Drest's soldiers gave up the chase. A smile flickered on her pale features, and then she turned away. It was time for her to rest now. In the morning she would be expected to perform the funeral rites for the men killed during Bellicus and Duro's escape and it had been a long night.

A long, satisfying night.

* * *

Horsa was tired, and when he was tired, he became even more irritable than usual. His men had come ashore at Branodunum, an old Roman coastal town which had capitulated to the Saxons months ago. What chance did they have? the jarl mused happily. The soft folk that lived and worked on the docks and surrounding industries had been protected by the legions for too long, and it had left them weak.

They'd been easy pickings, although Hengist had not wanted everyone killed off, for that would leave no-one to load and unload the ships that kept the valuable trading routes working. The Saxons wanted those resources, and Hengist was no fool. So the people of Branodunum swore allegiance to Hengist, in return for his protection against other Saxon pirates or raiding Picts.

Now, though, the Saxons sought to expand, to take control of more settlements in these lands that once belonged to the warrior-queen of the Iceni tribe, Boudica. So Horsa had been sent with thirty men to Branodunum. Docking there that morning, he had requisitioned provisions for his warband from the sullen locals, and then marched south, with the intention of battering the towns and villages thereabouts into submission. Of course, Hengist had warned him not to wipe out entire settlements, for what was the point in ruling a country with no-one to work the land? But, of course, Horsa had his own ideas and, since he was leading the mission, he would complete it as he thought necessary.

The first place they came to had been little more than a collection of ramshackle farmhouses and the warband didn't spend long there. Horsa roughed up the headman, assaulted the man's wife, and then left them with instructions to send tribute to Garrianum every six months or face a return visit that would be even more unpleasant.

Then they moved onto the next village along the road and basically repeated the same thing. The men in these lands were sturdy enough, with weather-beaten faces and calloused hands, but when faced with so many well-armed and armoured invaders there was little point in putting up a fight. It would mean certain death, in a most unpleasant fashion. Everyone in these lands had heard about the coming of the Saxons, and they knew what it meant to stand up to them. Better to do what they asked, and hope to be left in peace.

"Look over there," said Seaver, a small man with red hair and a scarred nose. "That must have been some place in the old days."

Horsa followed the man's pointing finger and grunted. "Another bloody villa," he said. "Not worth our time even visiting. The farmers will have picked it clean long ago."

"Imagine it, though," Seaver persisted, eyes wide with wonder. All that remained of the place now were some crumbling walls that had almost been reclaimed already by the undergrowth, but it seemed to have fired the little warrior's interest. "Whitewashed walls, orange tiles, and slave-women rushing about doing whatever you told them." He grinned, and so did the men closest to him. His vision was certainly more entertaining than the bland road that stretched ahead of them.

Horsa didn't answer. He had no interest in the past. He cared only for the future and what he could make of it for himself.

"You know," Seaver mused, still gazing across at the ruined villa. "The people that lived in those villas buried their treasure when they knew they were leaving, or if they knew enemies were coming for them. I bet if we dug around the grounds of some of those old ruins we'd find gold and all sorts."

"On you go then," Horsa replied, shaking his head at the man's foolishness. "We'll meet you here on our way back to the ship."

"Aye," another man joined in, nodding at their leader's cynicism. "You could search for years and not find a thing. There's just too much ground to cover."

"Maybe," Seaver admitted irritably, before his eyes lit up again. "It would be nice to find a hoard like that though."

"It would belong to Hengist," Horsa growled. "Since these are now his lands. So, if you ever do find buried Roman gold, Seaver, be sure to hand it all over to my brother."

The red-haired warrior didn't reply, he merely walked on, stroking his beard and looking around as if he could see into the past and the people that had once lived and worked here.

"Night will fall soon," Horsa said, noting the position of the sun and guessing they only had a couple of hours of daylight left at most. "The next place we find will be our last for the day. Pray to Thunor that it's big enough to provide us with fresh bread and beer."

"Hopefully they put up a bit of a fight," a man with a bulbous red nose muttered. "I'm fed up with all this walking. I want a good fight and a good drink after it."

"What about a good woman to roll about with?" someone asked, before continuing before the man could reply. "Oh, I forgot how ugly you are, Cynestan. Never mind – there's plenty of sheep around here that you can rut with!"

The men laughed and jeered and demanded to know if Cynestan was going to take such an insult, but he grinned good-naturedly and eyed the blond warrior who'd insulted him. "Iceni women. Sheep. Your mother," he said, and the nostrils flared in his bulbous nose. "I've done them all, but your mother was the worst, Froda. She smelled like a pig and ate like one too, even when I was humping her!"

"Enough!" Horsa said, raising his hand and silencing the hoots of laughter aimed at young Froda, whose handsome face was flushing red with embarrassment. "There's the next settlement, and it looks like it's bigger than the others we've seen today. Have your weapons ready."

"It must be Syderced," Seaver told them. "This is the largest village in the area, according to the alehouse keeper in Branodunum."

The smoke from cooking fires could be seen rising above the settlement, and the scent of meat and pottage carried to the Saxons on the wind, making them walk faster, eager to try some of the tribespeople's fare.

Their approach had been noticed, however, and shrill, frightened voices could be heard passing word of their coming about the place. Horsa was not surprised to see a welcoming party gathering on the road to greet them, but he was amused to see the men holding weapons.

"It looks like you might get that fight you wanted, Cynestan," the jarl snorted, shaking his head in amusement. "These fools surely don't think to stand against us, do they?"

Indeed, it seemed like even the other villagers thought it was a bad idea to defy the Saxons, for women and even some men had come to remonstrate with their armed kinfolk, presumably pleading with them not to try and defeat the oncoming warband.

It was too late now, though. Horsa and his men were too close, and he walked to within a couple of spear lengths before halting and staring at those who barred their way into the village.

The sound of doors slamming, and children crying, could be heard, but the Iceni farmers' faces were grim and determined, despite the fact there were only about twenty of them. Their leader stared at Horsa, who was tall and powerfully built, with a dark beard that was impressive for his young age. His only apparent weakness was a slight limp, thanks to having toes chopped off by the Damnonii druid, Bellicus, but that wasn't evident just now as he stood, sinister yet oddly serene, sizing up Syderced's inhabitants.

"What do you want?"

Horsa continued to look around at the village for a while, before finally deigning to look at the villager who'd spoken. The man's voice was unexpectedly calm and it made the Saxon wary. The Iceni had been a warrior, and did not, apparently, fear death. He might be hard to beat, and possibly even take down some of Horsa's men before he expired himself. A handful of his compatriots looked similarly dangerous, but only a handful. The rest were mere farmers, and only the shame of being branded cowards held them rooted in place. They wanted no part of any fight with the Saxons.

Too bad, Horsa thought, eyes glittering with amusement that didn't reach his mouth.

"We want food and drink," he said to the Iceni leader. "Perhaps some entertainment for the night – a story, songs, dancing women, that sort of thing." The Saxons beside him grinned and nodded as he went on. "And then you will swear loyalty to my brother, Horsa, *bretwalda* of Britannia. And if you don't, well…I think you know what will happen."

"Let them pass, Antedrig," a woman cried, clutching a baby to her breast. "Please!"

"Aye," Cynestan grinned, revealing a near-toothless mouth to go with his swollen nose. "Let us pass, Antedrig."

"There's no food or drink for you here," the Iceni warrior replied evenly. "There's nothing for you, so turn around, and go back to your ship or wherever you came from."

Horsa turned to look at Cynestan as if offended by the lack of hospitality. He shrugged, and said, "Kill them."

As if they'd been waiting for the command, the Saxon warband charged forward, screaming warcries, and the speed and ferocity of the attack caught the Iceni by surprise. As expected, the few experienced warriors amongst the defenders fought brutally but they were no match for Horsa's sea-wolves. Antedrig was one of the first to find a spear ripping into his guts and the rest of the men barring the road soon shared his fate.

Horsa didn't try to stop his men when the short battle was over. They had earned their entertainment after all, and it would be bad for their morale if he was to rein them in. Besides, he liked the look of Antedrig's pretty wife.

When morning came, the Saxons looked for whatever ale or mead they hadn't consumed after their debauchery of the previous evening and drank away their hangovers. Horsa always found it remarkable how powerful mead could be, turning the worst mood into the best in such a short space of time – it was almost magical, and certainly a gift of the gods.

"Ready lads," he called, eager to be on his way again. There was nothing to stay in Syderced for now anyway.

"Did we really kill everyone?" Froda asked, looking pale and sickly, as if his hangover hadn't been cured as nicely as Horsa's.

"Nah," Seaver replied. "Some of them ran away."

"That's good," Horsa said. "They'll tell the rest of the bastards about here what happens if they fight back. Hengist will be pleased. Come on, by Thunor!" He roared at a couple of men who weren't quite ready to leave yet. "It's time to make the journey back to Brandonum, and our ship. We'll go a different route this time, take that road there, to the north-east, and stop off in the settlements we find, just like yesterday."

He breathed deeply, feeling like he could take on any man and best him, and looked around at the village that, just a day before had been a busy place full of families and hard-working folk. He glanced at Seaver, who was watching him, ready to receive the jarl's orders. "You're sure the place has been properly looted? Yes? Good, then burn it to the ground."

Seaver's flint and steel were already in his hand, for he'd been expecting this command, and he hurried away to do Horsa's bidding. By the time the jarl reached the north-eastern road out of the village he could hear flames crackling behind him and wondered if any more of the Iceni farmers in the settlements they came across that day would try to fight back, like the fools here in Syderced.

A fresh morning breeze carried the sweet smell of woodsmoke to him, reminding him strangely of the camp in Garrianum—his home, for now—and he smiled. He was a powerful young warrior, and life was good. He hoped more Britons *would* fight back, for he greatly enjoyed killing them.

Indeed, he planned to go on killing them, all through the summer, as he and Hengist led their army further west, claiming more and more lives and more and more land, until the winter frosts halted their expansion.

CHAPTER THIRTEEN

"I can't go on any further, Bel, I'm sorry."

The druid could hear the anguish in his friend's voice and knew the centurion was already at breaking point. Indeed, he probably had been from the moment they took him from his cell – it was a miracle he'd made it this far.

"I could do with some rest too," Bellicus replied, looking all around at the land which was only partially lit by the crescent moon. He'd been searching for a safe place to stop and rest for a while now but hadn't yet found anywhere suitably hidden from their pursuers. Drest's men might bring hunting dogs, and the first places they'd search would be the abandoned farmhouses or small, crudely built shelters for weary travellers that dotted the landscape.

They'd passed a couple of streams, shallow even at this time of year when summer still hadn't fully burst into bloom, and walked their horses in the water to try and hide the scent of their passing, but even that would only hold up the dogs temporarily.

There was a sudden thump, and Bellicus, startled, grasped his sword. It was no enemy though, it was Duro, sliding off his horse's back onto the dew-rimed grass.

"Gods!" The druid jumped down from Darac's saddle and ran to his injured, exhausted companion, muttering soft, reassuring words, but Duro was unconscious and couldn't hear a thing.

It wasn't ideal, but they'd have to spend at least a few hours right there. To push the centurion any further would only bring about his death. The man's skin was already grey and sickly looking, and Bellicus took off his own robe and lay it on the damp ground before rolling Duro onto it with some difficulty. Then he pulled the edge up around his friend and hoped it would be enough to keep him warm.

They couldn't build a fire, even if Bellicus had fuel and something to start one with, so, to stave off the cold in this deepest part of the night the druid decided to peg the horses reins to the ground and give them a quick rubdown before making camp. The Picts had taken good care of Darac at least, for he looked as strong and healthy as ever.

Then Bellicus looked in their saddlebags to see what Ria had packed for them. The druidess had been thorough in her preparations for the escape, for the bags were filled with useful items. The first of them was a leather tent – Bellicus didn't set it up, but he did use it as an extra blanket to cover Duro. Then he found two proper woollen blankets and placed one around his own shoulders as he continued to delve into the packs.

Dried, salted meat; a loaf; two ale skins; two more, empty skins that could be filled with water when available; strips of cloth that could be used as bandages; dried mushrooms that would catch a spark when it was safe enough to start a campfire; and finally a small amphora.

When Bellicus pulled the clay stopper from the vessel he knew instantly what was in it, from the pungent smell that made him wince: vinegar.

He took it, along with the bandages, and knelt beside Duro, wondering where to start. The centurion seemed to have so many injuries that needed tending.

"I suppose I should begin with the worst of them," he muttered, lifting the sleeping patient's left hand and peering at it in the weak moonlight. The pinkie and ring fingers had been hacked off and the wounds cauterized with fire, but that had been the extent of the Picts' medical aid and the stumps were not healing well. "Forgive me," Bellicus whispered, as he poured some of the vinegar onto Duro's hand, half-expecting the centurion to cry out in agony, but there was no reaction which, although useful for the operation, wasn't a particularly good sign.

He cleaned the wounds and bandaged them expertly, before moving onto the torn-out nails and other visible injuries on Duro's body. Then, since he didn't feel tired, and the centurion was still unconscious, Bellicus took his knife and used it to trim his friend's hair and shave his face.

Although Bellicus did not really mind having stubble or even a beard himself—most druids had one after all, it was almost expected of them—Duro preferred to be clean shaven. It had been a rule within his Roman army unit, and he'd continued the practice even all these years after the legions had disappeared.

Hopefully when he woke up the centurion would feel like a new man after his days and weeks in captivity.

When the job was done Bellicus shaved his own face and head. He used a little of the vinegar to clean the tiny spots of blood that sprang up on his scalp, gritting his teeth and wincing at the pain. If only there had been a stream nearby, he would have washed himself more thoroughly, despite the chill in the air, but even without bathing he felt cleaner than he had in weeks.

More like himself again.

He gathered up all the hair he'd cut from himself and Duro and took it with them for burning later, so Qunavo wouldn't find it and use it in some harmful ritual against them.

Then he crossed his legs and closed his eyes, slowing his breathing and offering prayers of thanks to the gods for their escape, and asking for aid in making it safely back to Dun Breatann. In his weakened state he moved easily into a trance and it felt like the spirits of the land were all around them, watching and wondering who they were, yet offering no harm to them as they recognised Bellicus as a friend.

When he was finished, the druid lay down and planned their next move. Or at least that's what he intended. As it was, he soon fell fast asleep, completely exhausted by his night's work.

The sun was up when Bellicus awoke, and he squinted, wondering what the great yellow glow was at first, as it had been so long since he'd seen it. Then the memories from the night before came rushing back and, panicking, he reached for his sword which lay on the grass by his side. It was slick with morning dew but it didn't matter. His eyes adjusted to the brightness and he saw Duro staring at him while hastily packing their equipment into the horses' saddlebags.

"Good morning," the centurion said. "Feels good to be free, eh?"

Bellicus slumped onto his back again, grinning, staring up at the sky with its white clouds drifting lazily past. He could smell things, wonderful things, that told of rebirth and nature awakening, and it was so different to the stench of Dunnottar's cells that he felt his chest swelling with joy.

"Aye," he agreed. "It feels good."

He simply lay there for a time, enjoying the scents and the sounds of a spring morning, doing his best not to worry about what the future held for them over the next few hours and days. He heard Duro moving around and realised his friend was anxious to be on the move again and he regretfully rose to his feet to help prepare for the day's ride.

"Your friend, the druidess, packed us some food," Duro said, tossing Bellicus a chunk of bread and gesturing to one of the ale skins which lay next to the druid's sword. "You can eat and drink as we ride. And," he held up his bandaged hand. "Thank you for this, my friend. You must have been as exhausted as I was last night, yet you made sure I was patched up before you rested."

Bellicus bit into the bread and chewed it quickly, almost as if fearing one of his guards from Dunnottar might appear and take it away again. "You'd have done the same for me," he said, moving across to Darac, who stood cropping the grass quite happily, looking fresh and fit for the coming journey.

"Maybe," Duro grunted, and Bellicus could see more of the bandages had been used. He guessed the centurion had tended to the wounds hidden underneath his clothes which the druid hadn't seen to the night before. That was good –

they were both on the mend, their cuts were cleaned, and they had food and drink enough to begin rebuilding their strength. Of course, they'd be no match for the Pictish warriors who were undoubtedly coming after them, but, gods willing, there would be no need for a fight. Darac and the other horse would carry them away from Drest's lands soon enough.

"What are you going to call that beast of yours?"

Duro shrugged. "I hadn't thought about it," he said. "I've had other things to worry about."

They were finished packing up the tent, food and medical supplies at last, so they unpegged the horses and, with groans of pain and irritation at their injured, weak bodies, mounted up.

"It's always easier when a horse has a name," Bellicus said as they headed south west, scanning all around for signs of pursuit but, for now, seeing none. "Besides, the animal saved your life. He," the druid leaned down and checked between Duro's mount's back legs, "deserves a good name."

Duro shook his head as if it really didn't matter to him. "If you insist. What about…" He trailed off, frowning, mind utterly blank, which might have been a symptom of their recent harsh treatment, or merely a sign of the centurion's lack of creativity. He was, generally, a man of action—blunt and direct—not one given to flights of fancy or imagination.

"What about Pryderi," suggested the druid, and Duro shrugged carelessly.

"All right," said the centurion. "Good enough, eh, Pryderi?" He patted the animal on the neck and it warmed Bellicus to see his friend in a much better state, physically, than he'd been the night before. It would take weeks for them both to fill out and regain their normal weight, and the mental scars would stay with them for much longer than that, especially in the centurion's case. But they were on the right path.

"Pryderi was the son of the horse goddess, Rhiannon," Bellicus said. "There are many tales about their adventures, quite exciting stuff too. I'll tell you some of them when we're back in Dun Breatann with mugs of ale in our hands and trenchers of roast meat before us."

"Oh, gods," Duro groaned. "That sounds good. Let's hope we make it there, for I'll hold you to that promise!"

Every so often one or other of them would turn and look back for signs of pursuers, but they saw nothing all through the morning. They allowed the horses to move at an easy canter, not pushing them too hard in case they would need to urge them into a gallop at some point, but even so they covered a lot of ground and, when they came to a stream a short time after midday, Bellicus felt it safe to call a halt although Duro didn't seem too happy about it. He was clearly frightened by the prospect of being recaptured but there was no sense in pushing their mounts, or themselves, too hard.

They filled their waterskins and allowed the horses to drink, before sharing some of the bread and salted meat. Their bellies had shrunk, so they didn't eat too much, knowing it would merely make them sick, but both men felt better for the food and all of them were refreshed by the time they moved on again.

"D'you think they've even bothered coming after us?" Duro asked as the sun began to dip into the western horizon and still there were no signs of Drest's men chasing them. Of course, the land was hilly and uneven, and there were many groves of trees and bushes to conceal even a decent sized warband, but still, it seemed like they'd escaped easier than the centurion would have expected.

"Oh, I'm sure of it," Bellicus growled. "The bastards had big plans for our execution." He glanced over his shoulder for the hundredth time. "They'll turn up soon enough. They'll exchange horses at the settlements along the way and push them much harder than we can." He was about to tell Duro to prepare for the inevitable fight, but it was pointless.

The centurion was in no state to fend off half-a-dozen blue-inked warriors and, in fact, Bellicus realised his honesty was doing the nervous centurion no favours.

They would simply have to hope the gods would protect them, as they had when they escaped Dalriada and Loarn mac Eirc's hunters just a few months earlier. The thought made him snort with sardonic laughter and shake his head.

"What's funny?" Duro asked. "Tell me. I could do with cheering up."

"I was just thinking," the druid replied, still smiling. "How we manage to keep finding ourselves in these situations. Chased all across the lands by mad warlords and kings."

"Aye," Duro said, frowning. "It's hilarious, isn't it?"

"We're still alive, aren't we?" Bellicus said, letting go of Darac's reins so he could spread his arms wide, as if asking the world to embrace him. "The bards are going to enjoy this tale when we get back to Alt Clota, mark my words."

"Unfortunately for me," Duro retorted, not joining in with the druid's hopeful outburst and instead raising his left hand to display his missing digits, "I won't be helping them write their songs, since I can't play the damn flute anymore!"

That dampened Bellicus's mood and he nodded sympathetically, understanding his friend's sorrow. It was a terrible thing for anyone to lose fingers, but especially so for a man who had to hold a sword and shield during battle. Still, losing body parts was an occupational hazard for a centurion or a warrior and Duro would eventually grow used to his loss.

"We're still alive," the druid repeated, although his earlier grin was now a sympathetic smile. "And I once saw a man with missing fingers play a flute, so it can be done. You just need to learn the different fingerings. Besides, we'll make Drest pay for those stolen fingers, just like we're going to make Horsa and Hengist sorry for what they did in Luguvalium."

Mention of Duro's former home brought more sadness, for the centurion's wife, Alatucca, had been murdered by the Saxons there not so long ago and that pain was still very raw for him.

They rode on in silence again, Duro anxiously fingering his sword hilt and checking over his shoulder every so often.

In these lands, like Alt Clota, there were crude shelters dotted around for hunters and other travellers to use. They were usually wooden constructions with thatched roofs, built next to a water source such as a spring or stream and, although far from the height of luxury, they were much better places to spend the night than outside beneath the stars. Only in summer was it pleasant to sleep outdoors, but that season sometimes seemed to last for only a couple of days this far north of the Roman walls, as Duro often joked.

Bellicus spotted one of these shelters just as the sun was beginning to set and they headed straight for it.

"Is this wise?" Duro asked as they rubbed down the horses and made sure the animals were comfortable and safely tethered for the night, before seeing to their own needs.

"You mean the Picts will notice this building and come to see if we're here?" Bellicus asked. "It'll be pitch black soon, look," he jerked his head upwards to the sky. "Heavy clouds. It'll pour down, and there'll be no moon. No-one will be able to see this place in the dark since we won't risk a fire."

"They might have an idea it's here though," Duro said, checking the road behind them for the hundredth time. "The men that live in these lands will know where these shelters are located. And that's not to mention the dogs they might have tracking us."

Bellicus waved away the centurion's concerns but he worried now that Duro's constant state of fear was becoming infectious. "You could be right, but we'll take turns on watch, and," he held out a palm and frowned. "It's starting to rain. Would you rather we move on and try to sleep in that little tent Ria packed for us?"

The drizzle very quickly turned into a tremendous downpour and the men hurried inside the windowless shelter, pulling the leather curtain that was nailed over the door into place. It wouldn't keep out the cold wind that was brewing, but they would at least remain dry while they rested.

"Drest's men won't ride in the dark," the druid said sitting on one of the two wooden pallets provided by the shelter's builders and pulling out a piece of tough salted meat from his pack. "Not with that going on."

"I suppose not," Duro conceded, pulling back the edge of the curtain and peering out into the gloom. "Shame there wasn't a stable for the horses, eh? Poor bastards are getting drenched out there."

Bellicus smiled and bit off a piece of the meat, wincing as he did so at the taste, and its toughness. "They don't mind," he said, chewing slowly. "They keep warm by eating, so they'll just crop the grass. Besides, they're beneath those trees and the leaves are starting to come out. Darac and his new friend, Pryderi, will be fine. Come away from the doorway and have something to eat. You need to build yourself back up again."

The centurion remained, staring out at the land in the direction they'd just come from until, satisfied at last, he sat down on the other pallet and helped himself to a long drink of ale from the skin that had been packed for him by Ria. Then he ate some bread and a little cheese, which was more than enough to fill his shrivelled belly and took off his cloak. He used his pack as a pillow and drew the cloak over himself like a blanket but his eyes never left the doorway.

It was utterly black inside the shelter by now but, although the wind was howling outside and the rain was hammering against the roof, the two travellers were quite cosy. Despite the wet weather, the temperature was mild and the leather curtain did a surprisingly efficient job at keeping out the wind and dampness.

"I'll take first watch," Bellicus said, standing up and going across to the doorway.

"All right. Although you'd probably be as well sleeping," Duro noted regretfully. "With no fire, and the pissing rain, you'll have to just sit in this little room, in the pitch black, doing nothing. It's too dark to even see your sword, if you had a stone to sharpen it."

"A fair point," the druid admitted.

"Like you said earlier—no one is sneaking up on us this night," Duro went on although he sounded as if he was trying to convince himself more than anything. "Only a madman would be out in that, surely."

"You mean like us?"

"Aye, exactly," the centurion replied, mirthlessly. "Now keep your ears open. If anyone approaches the shelter that horse of yours will hopefully let us know. It's almost as good a guard as Cai."

"That's true," Bellicus agreed and felt his way along the wall in the darkness, back to his pallet, where he sat down. "That's why I left my staff beside him – I know it'll be safe. Sleep well my friend, but not too deeply."

"My sword is unsheathed and beside me," Duro said. "Now stay alert and wake me for my turn on watch. We'll have another hard ride in the morning, and I want to be alive when the sun comes up."

Bellicus sat in silence until he heard the centurion's low snore, and then he simply allowed his mind to be still. He meditated on recent experiences, allowing the stress of their escape to pass away into a dark cloud he conjured in his mind and, at the end of it, felt much calmer.

It was a long night though and, after a while he jerked upright, cursing himself for almost falling asleep. The rain had stopped and it was silent outside, although the leather curtain let in no light so he couldn't tell how long he'd been sitting on watch. It might be the mid-morning for all he could tell, although there were no sounds of birds or insects. Duro's soft, even breathing continued in the pallet beside him however, so the druid got up silently and moved towards the doorway, intending to empty his bladder and make sure the horses were still comfortable.

As he reached the curtain, Darac whinnied and Bellicus froze. Although the centurion had been joking when he said the big black horse was as good at keeping watch as Cai, there had been some truth to it. Darac was a clever animal and had been trained in the ways of war. He would feel anxious if there was an enemy nearby. That whinny the druid had heard might well have been the equivalent of one of Cai's growls.

Yet it might just be the horse enjoying a dream. Should Bellicus waken Duro, when the centurion needed as much healing sleep as he could get? He pulled back the door curtain just a fraction, and a dim light illuminated the interior of the shelter, telling the druid it was almost sunrise.

Darac made another noise outside and Bellicus drew his sword while simultaneously leaning down and placing a hand over Duro's mouth.

"Quiet," he muttered, pressing his mouth to the centurion's ear. "There's someone outside."

He could easily see the whites of Duro's eyes from the dim light that came in where the curtain had been pulled slightly back. It was a wrench to see as much fear as determination in the usually stolid centurion's expression.

They both stood up, weapons at the ready and took positions on either side of the doorway.

Then Bellicus had an idea. Raising a hand to tell his friend to remain where he was, the druid lay down on the bed again, but drew out the small crossbow he'd taken from the guard in Dunnottar. Hurriedly, he drew it back and fitted a bolt in place, and then he let out a soft snore.

Duro's teeth flashed in the dull light and the two men waited, centurion with sword drawn back, ready to thrust, druid lying on the pallet with the crossbow hidden beneath his dark robe.

The sound of footsteps came to them then, and it was clear there was more than one person outside the shelter. Bellicus could hear at least four different people moving around and, given the fact they were attempting to approach the shelter silently, it was obvious they weren't simple travellers seeking solace from the weather.

The Picts had found them.

CHAPTER FOURTEEN

Two of the enemy came right up to the doorway of the shelter, hesitated for a moment, and then the curtain was drawn back slightly, and an eye appeared in the opening. Bellicus watched from hooded lids and made another low snoring sound, reassuring the man who stepped inside the small structure and immediately confirmed his intent, for there was a naked sword in his hand.

The druid held his nerve and allowed the would-be killer to take another step towards him, glad to see a second man slipping inside the shelter. At that moment, Bellicus raised the crossbow above his blanket and released the bolt with a click that seemed deafening within the cramped building.

At such close range there was no way the missile could miss its target and it thumped home in the Pict's chest. The man wore a thick woollen cloak and a leather breastplate which took some of the energy from the bolt, but it struck deeply enough to stagger the man, who had no idea what had happened to him. Before he could react, Bellicus jumped up and slammed the crossbow stock up into his chin, sending a terrible *clack* through the air as the Pict's teeth slammed together. As he collapsed, the druid smashed the crossbow down onto his skull.

When Duro heard the druid's weapon release he had attacked as well, plunging the tip of his sword into the second Pictish night prowler. The man reacted by throwing his elbow back instinctively and, weakened as he was, the centurion couldn't react quickly enough to avoid it. Stars exploded in his vision as the Pict's blow struck his nose, but Duro's sword had done its work and the enemy warrior collapsed onto his knees, only for Bellicus's crossbow to hammer against the side of his head.

Instantly, the druid was fitting another bolt to the weapon but Duro sat down on the bed, holding his head in his hands and cursing, close to panic.

"Are you all right?" Bellicus asked, concern in his voice at the sight of his friend for he had no idea how badly injured he was.

"The bastard got me a good one, right on the damn nose," Duro replied. "I'll be fine, it's nothing serious. Should have seen it coming though, by Mithras! Shit, now what do we do?" He looked up, squinting at the pain in his head, blood running down from both nostrils. "There's still at least two more of them out there!"

"And we're stuck in here," Bellicus growled, looking at his stolen crossbow and wondering if the Picts outside had them too, or bows. If they did…

"They won't have long-range weapons," Duro said, guessing his friend's thoughts. "The crossbow is for hunting – these lunatics like to fight their human enemies face to face. They'll want to kill us like real men, with swords or axes."

Bellicus nodded. The centurion was probably right – the Picts were renowned for their courage, even taking it so far as often not bothering to wear any armour during battles. It was unlikely that the warriors outside would be content to just pick them off with arrows or crossbow bolts, not when the druid and centurion were trapped and at their mercy.

"You out there!" Duro had suffered weeks of torture and starvation and just had his nose bloodied, and, although the words were confident, his voice betrayed his anxiety as he addressed the besieging Picts. "Your comrades are dead. You should leave now, before you join them."

There was a muttering before one of the men outside responded. "You come out, Roman, and face us like true warriors. Or stay in your hole, cowering as frightened children, it makes no difference to us." A mirthless laugh. "More of our folk will be along soon enough, and then we'll make short work of you."

"Wouldn't you like to take our heads to Drest yourselves?" Bellicus called before Duro could say anything else.

"Imagine the fame you'd earn if you killed the Druid of Dun Breatann."

There was more muttering outside, no doubt as the Picts debated the merits of attacking now and winning eternal glory, or taking the safe option and waiting for reinforcements. Soon there came the sounds of someone approaching again, but this time the footsteps went to the back of shelter. Moments later there the familiar noise of a twig being rotated furiously came through the walls and Duro cursed again. One of the Picts was trying to light a fire.

"The whoresons are going to force us out," the centurion whispered. "And we're not even sure if there's only two of them left. There might be more!" He met Bellicus's gaze and shook his head. "We don't have much choice. We have to go down fighting."

The druid nodded and passed the crossbow to his friend. "You'll be better taking this. If you can manage to hit one, even in the leg or something, it'll give you an advantage when the swordplay starts." Then he raised his voice so the Picts could hear him clearly. "You men out there, know this: I am Bellicus the Druid, beloved of the gods. I call on Lug, and Taranis, and Cernunnos, to protect me and guide my blade." The man behind the shelter stopped his scratching but only for a few heartbeats before his quest to start a fire began again, and now there was a smell of smoke which Bellicus and Duro both knew heralded the onset of a flame. "Furthermore," the druid roared, making Duro wince, "I call on Dis Pater to accept the cursed souls of the fools who would stand against me this night!"

Outside, there was a gasp of relief and a soft crackling as whatever the Pict had used as kindling finally started to burn. "Our own druid cast spells of protection over us," the man shouted through the wall. "The only souls meeting Dis Pater tonight will be yours!"

Bellicus nodded to the door, tapped himself on the chest to let Duro know he'd take the lead, then he drew Melltgwyn and bent down to lift the smaller of the dead men on the floor. Although much leaner than he'd been just a month ago, the druid was still prodigiously strong and he was able to hold the corpse up around the chest. Then, with one final look at his friend, Bellicus burst outside, letting go of the dead man just as a sword hammered into the body.

"What in the name of the gods?" The warrior who'd just slashed his own kinsman's cadaver stumbled in surprise, allowing Bellicus the opportunity to land a blow of his own. Melltgwyn sang out, slicing forward and cutting a huge, red wound in the Pict's neck. Blood pumped as the man dropped his sword and tried to stem the crimson flow, but Bellicus knew it was a mortal wound so he stepped past that enemy and looked to the rear of the shelter, for the man setting it ablaze.

Seeing another of his companions downed by the druid, the firestarter came screaming around the side of the smouldering structure, sword held aloft, eyes flaming with righteous fury. He faltered, a look of pained confusion appearing on his face as a crossbow bolt thudded home in his ribs, and one of the horses behind them reared with an alarmed whinny as Bellicus lunged forward and swung his sword into the Pict's legs.

Astonishingly, despite his injury, the enemy warrior was able to bring his own weapon around in time to parry Melltgwyn, and Bellicus cried out as the blades clattered together. The Pict's mouth parted in a hideous lupine grin as the druid dropped onto one knee, too weak to continue the fight.

"'Beloved of the gods', eh?" The warrior roared as he lashed out, kicking Bellicus in the shoulder and sending the giant crashing onto the grass. "Looks like they've deserted you, druid!"

The Pict's sword rose, and then a crossbow sailed through the air to slam into his forehead and he collapsed, groaning, beside the fallen Damnonii druid. Duro hobbled across and thrust his sword into the Pict's heart, before he too dropped onto the ground.

"I hope there's no-one else out there to fight," the centurion gasped, and then he passed out as the shelter came down behind them in a flaming orange mass of sparks and smoke.

* * *

"Mithras's balls, druid, this is no way to treat a man in my condition!"

Bellicus looked across from Darac's saddle and smiled in relief. When Duro passed out the druid had barely had the strength to drag the fallen centurion away from the burning shelter. He'd managed it though, and then sat with his back against a tree beside the horses, sipping ale and chewing bread to try and regain some of his old vitality as the fire burned itself out on the sodden ground.

When Duro had shown no signs of awakening, and with the threat of more enemy hunters coming for them, Bellicus took the decision to lift the centurion onto the gelding's back and lash him in place using clothes harvested from the dead Picts.

They had ridden for many miles and the druid feared his friend might slip out of the makeshift harness and injure himself even more in the fall or, worse, simply never wake up again. They had been through an awful lot after all, and even a centurion had his limits.

So, as Duro complained now about his rather embarrassing position, Bellicus couldn't help but smile. He was glad his friend was somewhat recovered, as confirmed by Duro's next muttered complaint.

"All I can see is the horse's cock. Let me up, Bel, the beast is so well-endowed it's practically slapping me in the face!"

"Best not to stop, old friend," Bellicus replied grimly, glad the centurion couldn't see his broad grin. "More Picts will surely be after us. Every moment counts. Just tap the horse on the belly, that should make him less…relaxed. You should be flattered though – he likes you!"

"Let me up you bastard!" Duro demanded, trying ineffectually to pull himself up. "A Roman officer deserves better than this."

"Calm yourself," the druid said, openly laughing now as he slowed Darac and slid onto the ground to free Duro. "I'm sure you've been through similar trials when you were initiated in the Rites of Mithras." He undid the makeshift strap holding his companion onto Pryderi's back and grabbed him by the arms as he began slipping off. Even when Duro's feet were firmly planted on the grass the druid didn't let go, as the weakened centurion was shaky, and his muscles had mostly gone to sleep during their ride.

"Take it easy," Bellicus advised, supporting Duro as he sat down on the grass and rubbed his limbs to try and wake them up again. "It's mid-morning and we've been on the move for," he glanced up at the sun which was partially hidden by light grey clouds, "two hours or so. We'll stop here and have something to eat, all right?"

Duro nodded gratefully and continued stretching his arms and legs, rolling his head around and grumbling about getting too old for all this nonsense, as Bellicus pegged the horses in place and brought bread, salted beef and water for them.

They ate in silence for a time, eyes constantly scanning the uneven heathland for signs of pursuers, before Duro spoke again, and, although the colour had come back to his face, he sounded tired and dejected. "How much longer until we're safely back in Damnonii lands?"

Bellicus replied instantly, for the question had been bearing heavily on his own mind. He hated feeling so physically weak and, out here amongst farms and villages that were loyal to Drest, the fugitives were constantly at risk of being accosted and either recaptured or, more likely, simply killed. "Four or five days, I think. It'll seem like an eternity, but we'll get through it. Our strength will return as the time passes and the more dangerous we appear, the less likely Pictish farmers will be to cause us trouble." He nodded at Duro's hand. "How's the dressing holding up?"

The centurion shoved a piece of meat into his mouth and eyed his injured hand ruefully. "Looks fine," he said. "You did a good job."

Bellicus nodded. "We'll take if off and rebind the wounds later on, when we stop for the night," he said. "As long as we keep it clean no poison will set in and you'll be back to normal by the time we reach Dun Breatann."

"Your magic can regrow my fingers?"

Although it was supposed to be a joke, there was an element of hope in the centurion's voice and the druid merely shook his head sorrowfully as they returned to their meal in silence.

As predicted, the days passed slowly for the riders. The land they were moving through was bland and held little to draw the eye. It seemed to be little more than an endless line of orange, green and grey and they saw few people or even animals. Sometimes there would be the cry of some bird of prey high overhead and the men would watch as it circled around, searching for a mouse or hare to swoop down upon. It provided a small measure of excitement in otherwise boring hours.

Of course, the uniformity of the journey was, ultimately, a good thing, for they were not being tracked, as far as they could tell. There had been no signs of pursuing riders since the fight at the immolated shelter—no silhouettes on the horizon, no sounds of thundering hooves behind them, no hunting dogs howling and baying.

Which didn't stop both men *imagining* they heard such things. In the near-silence it was hard not to let one's imagination run away with itself and more than once Bellicus or Duro would turn in their saddle and gaze at the low hills behind, only to mutter sheepishly when there was nothing there. To make their flight even more nerve-shredding, there were hardly any trees to cover their passage, as the Romans had cut so many down to use in their building works.

Although they avoided the well-travelled roads and stuck to the fields and plains, it was necessary at times to come close to settlements if there was no other way past thanks to the presence of woods or rivers. On such occasions the signs of a large number of people passing ahead of them were unmistakeable – footprints of men and pack-animals had churned the ground to mud while trees had been felled carelessly to provide fuel for cooking fires and running repairs to what could only be the Pictish army's wagons.

It was not a comforting sight.

"What do you think it means?" Duro asked as they skirted another vacated campsite. The remnants of slaughtered, cooked animals and other detritus left for nature to eventually clear away.

"Obviously a sizeable warband is moving ahead of us," he said. "Perhaps they're heading for Dunadd, since they know the Dalriadans are weak right now. Drest may have sent soldiers to take control of the hill fortress before some local warlord brings the tribes together again and takes Loarn mac Eirc's place."

Neither man wanted to suggest another reason for the Pictish army's journey: that they might be returning to Alt Clota, to renew the siege of Dun Breatann. After all, Drest had only broken it off because he feared a Saxon invasion, but now that he knew those fears were unfounded, it might seem logical for the king to march back south to try once again to take control of Queen Narina's lands.

Especially since the Damnonii's fabled druid, Bellicus, was safely imprisoned within Dunnottar and unable to inspire the Alt Clotan warriors, or take any other part in the war. Or at least, he had been when the Pictish army had set out again. Why wasn't Drest travelling with them though, if that was the case?

A man waved to them from a nearby field, a cattle herder probably, and Bellicus raised an arm in a cheery return greeting.

"He thinks we're stragglers from the warband," Duro said, offering his own sardonic salute to the Pict with his injured hand while touching the hilt of his sword with the other. "But if he tells those chasing us that he saw two riders, they'll know we were here, and when. Maybe we should kill him."

The druid frowned, surprised by his companion's outburst. "Calm down, Duro. They'll know anyway. Where else could we go? Leave him to be about his business."

So they continued on, feeling a little more secure with every passing day and every passing mile. No more pursuers had been sighted and it seemed the only thing they would have to worry about was running into stragglers from the Pictish army marching towards Alt Clota.

"I know this place," Duro said one afternoon as they rode past a ruined old fort. "We must be almost back at Dun Breatann."

Bellicus eyed the overgrown remains of the structure on the nearby slope and chewed his lip. "Not quite. We still have a couple of days to go. That's Bruach Gleann. The Romans built it a long time ago, even before the two great walls, as part of a defensive line of forts and smaller camps all along the road here. But they eventually abandoned them and even went to the trouble of demolishing Bruach Gleann themselves when they left. Anyway, this fort lies about two days ride from Dun Breatann."

"Two days."

Duro sounded quite upset by the revelation and Bellicus watched him closely. Physically, the centurion's wounds were healing cleanly and his gaunt features were filling out again. His spirit had been almost crushed by Drest's treatment and this subsequent escape though, so the druid decided to set a faster pace. The sooner they were home the better. Like Catia after her terrifying abduction by the Saxons the year before, time would set things right for Duro.

"Well, a day and a half," he said, smiling and urging Darac into a slightly faster walk. "Then we can get drunk and tell everyone about our miraculous escape from impregnable fortress of Dunnottar, and what a collection of arseholes the Picts are."

The centurion merely grunted, and the druid resigned himself to a nervy few hours of silent riding before they caught a few hours' sleep. Duro surprised him, however, by asking why the Romans had taken down their fort here.

"Seems a lot of effort for no reward," the centurion noted. "I can't imagine the legionaries were very happy at being ordered to complete such a task."

In truth, Bellicus had no idea why the Romans had demolished their own fort, but he saw a chance to take their minds off things for a while. "It was haunted," he said seriously, nodding at his friend's questioning glance. "Aye, so the stories went. There were accidents during the original building works—so many, and all seemingly without cause—that the soldiers came to believe the spirits of the land did not want them here."

Duro glanced back over his shoulder and shivered. "Aye, I can believe that. I served in some places that seemed to be against us."

"The prefect in charge of the construction consulted a haruspex who inspected the entrails of a sheep and commanded the bodies of four dead virgins be brought to him. They buried these corpses at each corner of the fort's walls, to drive away the attacks by evil spirits."

"I don't want to ask where they got the virgins from," Duro muttered. "Did the magic work?"

"No," Bellicus replied in a low voice. "Sentries would report hearing voices whispering in their ears on the walls at night, when no-one else was beside them and strange lights would be seen hovering in the sky over the place, always accompanied by terrible screams. When soldiers were ordered to find the source of the lights and the noises they'd disappear, never to be seen again. So they abandoned the fort and pulled it down to try and appease the vengeful spirits."

They rode in silence after the story's completion and Bellicus wondered if it had been wise to tell a ghost story to the already frightened centurion. Matters were made even worse not long after, when the druid frowned and looked back over his shoulder at Bruach Gleann which was now far in the distance. "Did you hear that?" he asked.

Duro glanced across at the druid, the expression on his face now one of panic. "Hear what?" he demanded, apparently thinking this was another part of the druid's supernatural tale. "All I hear is the sound of our horses' hooves."

But there *had* been a sound carried on the wind, faint as it was. Bellicus felt sure of it, and its source wasn't anything from the Otherworld. They were being pursued again, and their hunters were almost upon them.

CHAPTER FIFTEEN

Sigarr was tired and wanted nothing more than some mead and freshly baked bread, but he knew Hengist would need to hear his report as soon as possible. Sigarr was not relishing the meeting, for the return voyage from Dunnottar had taken almost double the time it should have thanks to some unfavourable winds and then a storm that damaged the *Ceolgar*'s sail. The men had been forced to put in at the first safe place and perform crude repairs.

The length of time it had taken for the journey, along with the ultimate failure of his mission, meant Sigarr dreaded meeting the *bretwalda*, and even more so if Hengist's boorish brother, Horsa, was around. It had to be done though, and the sooner the better. Then Sigarr could make his way to his own tent, find some refreshments, and enjoy a night's sleep on solid ground.

He passed warriors, some even with their women and children having brought them here to settle in Britannia with them, and nodded greetings to those he recognised. They sharpened weapons and mended damaged armour but also told one another stories, prepared meals together and lived a somewhat 'normal' life. What had once been very much a military encampment here in Garrianum had become more of a normal settlement to these newcomers from across the sea, and why not? Apart from the warriors, this place boasted massive stone walls built by the now-departed Romans. Garrianum was a safe haven to the people it had originally been intended to keep out.

In the centre of it all was the stone building that housed the Saxon *bretwalda*.

"Ah, Sigarr," Hengist said, smiling as the little jarl came through the doorway into the spacious room the Saxon warleader used as a meeting point. "It's good to see you, cousin. I thought you'd be back days ago, and started to think the Picts had killed you."

Although Hengist's greeting was as cordial as ever, Sigarr's heart sank when he heard a snort of laughter from his right and glanced across to see Horsa sitting on a stool scraping dirt from his fingernails with a dagger.

"I've taken control of half a dozen settlements in the time it took you to sail to Pictland and back in your rotten old ship, Sigarr," Horsa said and there was no levity in his expression, only mockery. "What took you so long?"

"And," Hengist put in, "more to the point: Was your mission a success? Here." The *bretwalda* shoved a stool across to Sigarr and filled a cup with ale for him before gesturing that he might get on with his report.

"No," the jarl replied bluntly, seeing no reason to soften his words. "King Drest was not in Dunnottar when we arrived, and the folk he'd left to guard the fortress were in no mood to let us in to talk or even rest." He sipped the ale, finding it warm and not very pleasant but it did its job well enough, moistening his lips as he looked at Horsa. "A storm hit us on the way back here, which is why we took so long."

"Where's Drest?" Hengist asked although he didn't seem surprised when Sigarr shook his head and admitted no knowledge of the Pictish ruler's whereabouts.

"I knew it was a waste of time sending him," Horsa muttered, staring at Sigarr as if hoping the smaller man would take umbrage. Horsa was always in the mood for an argument.

Sigarr knew his ways well enough though, and simply ignored the jibe, turning back to Hengist again as the warlord was speaking although to himself as much as the others.

"We heard rumours of unrest in the north last year, maybe they're all at war with one another now that spring's come. That's good." He looked from Sigarr to Horsa, a satisfied gleam in his eyes. "If the Picts are fighting the other tribes around them, that means they won't be troubling us with their raids this summer and there's no need for an alliance anyway."

"So we can move forward with our plans for expansion in the coming months," Sigarr said.

"Or you could give me a few men and I'll sail north to take Dunnottar," Horsa suggested, as if it would be a simple task for him to complete. "If there's only a few guards left to defend it, as our cousin claims, it shouldn't be too hard to take."

Sigarr shook his head and threw a disparaging look in Horsa's direction. "If you'd seen the place you wouldn't be thinking of trying to attack it. You'd need Roman war engines to take the place without losing hundreds of men. The fortress is built on top of a sheer cliff, with multiple gates and a narrow approach that would see your men slaughtered by the stones and arrows of the defenders. Even a handful of men would be able to hold the place while exacting a terrible price on any attacking army, trust me."

"Maybe if you were in charge," Horsa retorted.

"Peace, brother," Hengist said. "Sigarr's right. Taking Dunnottar is not a priority. What would be the point, when we hold none of the lands that surround it?"

"We could use it as a base, just as we've done here at Garrianum," Horsa replied. "Bring more of our kinsmen across from Jutland and expand outwards, taking Pictland piece by piece."

Hengist thought about it for a moment. It was a tempting plan, mirroring their tactics here in the south of Britannia, but eventually he shook his head again. "We'll need all the warriors we can muster if we hope to take the fight to Arthur this coming summer," he said, stroking his beard thoughtfully. "Once we've consolidated our position in this eastern part of the country we can start to think of moving further north. Ultimately, I want all Britannia under our rule, but we must do it methodically. Let the Picts fight the Damnonii and whoever else – they'll weaken each other while we're down here bringing our people together."

Horsa stood up, towering over the seated Sigarr who felt tiny next to his cousin's great bulk. "I'm away to my tent," he said to Hengist. "I assume we'll be marching soon and drawing out Arthur? I grow bored sitting about the place all day." He glowered at Sigarr as if it was all his fault. "Some of us prefer fighting to sailing about in boats."

Hengist smiled and clapped his brother on the back as he walked past towards the door. "Aye, in the morning we'll make ready to leave. You go and enjoy your evening."

"Oh, I will," Horsa replied with a leer. "That serving girl, Myrgjol, has been keeping me company these past few nights." Rolling his eyes, he leaned back and groaned as he thought about the red-haired slave who was more than ten years older than him. "You should see the things she does, brother. What a woman!"

Sigarr suppressed a shiver at the mental image of a naked Horsa while Hengist laughed and ushered the tall young warrior through the door. When he was gone the room seemed lighter, airier, and less oppressive to Sigarr.

"Ignore his jibes," Hengist said, walking across to the hearth and poking at the sullen embers, making them flare into life before he added another log to the fire, making the atmosphere seem even more companionable. "If Drest wasn't in his fortress there's not much you could do about it. You've gathered intelligence we can use in future so you've done all you could." He refilled Sigarr's cup, smiling warmly at him and Sigarr was struck again by the contrast in the two brothers. Where Horsa was brash and obnoxious, Hengist was companionable and clever. Both were great warriors but it was obvious why men followed Hengist. Sigarr knew he was being manipulated by the *bretwalda* and for a brief moment felt a grudging respect for Horsa – at least the younger brother didn't try to win loyalty by pretending to be something he wasn't.

Even knowing all this however, Sigarr liked Hengist more than Horsa and was happy to follow the older brother.

"Drink up, cousin," Hengist urged. "And then enjoy what's left of the evening with your feet up and the company of a slave or two. You can tell me the whole story of your voyage to Dunnottar on the morrow."

Sigarr threw back his drink and swallowed it gladly for, as much as he appreciated Hengist's company, he truly did just want to relax on his own for a time, with no distractions and a chance to mull over everything that had occurred over the past few weeks. And then, perhaps, a slave girl to help him get to sleep...

He stood up and placed his empty cup on the table. "Thank you, my lord. Good night."

When he was gone, a door opened from an adjoining chamber and an attractive, middle-aged woman walked into join Hengist. The *volva*, or wise-woman, Thorbjorg, who was the Saxons' most powerful sorceress, had been listening in secret, as she commonly did, to the warriors' meeting.

"What do you make of him?" the bretwalda asked, nodding in the direction of the departed Sigarr.

"I think he's clever," she replied thoughtfully. "But not as clever as he believes himself to be. He'll be useful when we capture more lands, for he's an ideal administrator. Men like Horsa will win us the country, but the likes of Sigarr will allow us to hold it in peace."

"Peace," Hengist grunted. "Not for a time. First, we must destroy those who would stand in our way. This summer we take the fight to Arthur and his Britons!"

* * *

"Halt," Bellicus commanded and Darac obeyed without hesitation, the second horse following their lead. "Listen, Duro." They looked all around them, staring into the distance until a voice reached them and they stared at one other. It was a woman's voice, and she was calling the druid's name.

"What now?" Duro demanded, drawing his sword with the air of a condemned man. "Are we to almost reach safety only to be overtaken by our pursuers?"

Bellicus didn't answer, for his mind was whirling. The voice could only belong to one person, he was sure: Ria. Why would she be behind them though? Or had she somehow, using some magical trick he himself hadn't been taught, sent her voice across the miles while her corporeal form remained safely in Dunnottar? Was that possible? It was one thing to throw one's voice a few feet across a room, but across half a country?

He soon realised this was no feat of magic, however, as a lone rider came into view, thundering past abandoned Bruach Gleann.

"It's the druidess," Duro said after a moment, his vision not being as keen as the druid's. "What in Mithras's name is she doing here?"

"I don't know," Bellicus replied, eyes now searching the rest of the horizon in every direction, wondering if they were about to be attacked by the Pictish army they'd been shadowing. Something was wrong here, clearly. Had Ria been involved in some elaborate Pictish trick? Was their escape merely another part of their ongoing torture – an attempt to break their already weakened spirit? He took in the sight of Duro, sword drawn and held in a white-knuckled grip, and knew if they were recaptured now the centurion would not cope at all well.

Neither would Bellicus.

"What do we do, druid?" Duro asked, staring intently at the approaching druidess. "Kill her?"

"No, of course not," Bellicus retorted. "By the gods, man, she saved our lives. We wait and hear what she has to say, and then we'll continue our journey home." His curiosity was piqued now, and he waited impatiently for Ria to reach them, relieved to see no sign of warriors, or anyone else, following her.

"She's not come all this way to bring us another pack of food and ale," Duro grumbled, still not sheathing his sword as the druidess, dark hair flowing behind her, finally rode up to them. She slowed a little but did not smile.

"Ride!" she shouted, offering no other greeting and continuing past them without stopping.

"What the—"

"Come on." Bellicus turned Darac and they did as Ria commanded, urging their mounts into a moderate canter that allowed them to flank the druidess and keep pace beside her as they quickly left behind the haunted old fort.

"Qunavo returned the morning after you escaped," she called out and her words were clear and carried easily enough over the pounding hooves and rushing wind. "He tasted the wine I'd used to render the guards unconscious and detected my herbs."

"He blamed you for our escape?" Bellicus asked somewhat incredulously.

"I was also seen with you at the gates," she nodded. "And I'd made no secret of the fact I was against killing you, Bel – it was an obvious conclusion for him to reach. I overheard Qunavo explaining all this to Drest as I was about to go in and greet him. I immediately went to the stables, saddled my horse, and rode for my life."

"So now we have even more Picts chasing us," Duro laughed and what the sound lacked in humour it made up in volume. "Mad painted bastards in front and behind, druid. Maybe we should change our course and head south. At least there's only Saxons down there."

"Might not be a bad idea," Ria said. "There's a dozen men only an hour or so behind me."

Bellicus didn't reply, but they remained on the road towards Dun Breatann. What they would find when—if—they reached the towering fortress however… He dreaded to imagine. He also didn't care to think of Narina's reaction when she saw Ria within her fortress.

* * *

They continued riding hard for the rest of the day, seeing no evidence of Drest's men behind them. When it came time to rest, they travelled off the main road for a time and found a place to camp within a grove of trees. A stream ran beside the spot and the ruins of some long-forgotten building would keep the worst of the wind, which had begun to build up, off their tent.

As they went about the business of setting up for the night, Duro eyed Bellicus and Ria suspiciously. To him, the druid seemed to have accepted the girl's defection rather easily and, as he watched them, he thought he knew why.

"Be careful, my friend," the centurion muttered to Bellicus when Ria wandered off to collect some herbs she said she needed. "She's a beauty, but I'm not entirely convinced by her story." He shook his head to stem the angry reply. "I've noticed the way you look at her. The way your hand lingers when you pass her something. All I'm saying is," tapping the side of his head, "use what's in there, rather than what's between your legs."

"You think I can be taken in that easily?" Bellicus asked, smiling now. "Are you forgetting all the years of training I was given in order to read, and manipulate people?"

"Are you forgetting she had the same training?" Duro retorted. "And by the same person too."

The druidess returned then, a satisfied look on her pale face and she sat down on a lichen covered boulder, setting to work with whatever plants she'd been gathering and a cup of water freshly filled from the burbling stream. They had allowed themselves a small fire for, although they knew they were being hunted, the spot they'd found to camp in was enclosed and would hide the light from anyone on the road.

Of course, the wind would carry the scent of woodsmoke for miles but that would be hard to track in the darkness. Ria heated a small amount of her water and steeped the green leaves she'd collected in it, adding something of her own from pouches similar to Bellicus's, sewn inside her cloak.

Duro chewed a hard piece of bread and watched her nimble fingers, and looked up in surprise as the girl stood, and stepped around the fire to stand before him.

"Let's take a look at that hand of yours," she said. "I remember Bel's skills at bandaging wounds from the old days."

"I've got better since then," the giant druid replied in a hurt tone.

"I hope so," Ria said. "But I'm sure the centurion's injuries will benefit from a woman's touch. Come on, Duro, hurry up, I'm not going to hurt you."

Uncertainly, Duro looked at Bellicus who grinned and nodded reassuringly. "She was always much better at healing than me. My fingers aren't as deft as hers."

"Nothing to do with that," Ria snorted, using a small, wickedly sharp knife to cut away the bandage around Duro's hand. "You're just impatient. Always in too much of a hurry to finish a task." She smiled lasciviously at the druid and Duro guessed there was some hidden meaning behind her words as Bellicus looked away sheepishly.

Ria pulled Duro's hand forward so the light from the fire illuminated the wounds where his fingers had been. Then she took the pan and cleaned away the caked in blood with some of the warm water. She tilted the hand this way and that, eyeing it critically, before nodding. "It's healing well. Bel's dressing wasn't the neatest, but it was clean and did its job. This," she held her cup so the centurion could see the watery paste inside it, "might sting a little, but it'll make sure infection doesn't set in." With that she spooned some of the mixture out with her fingers and spread it on the wounds.

Duro winced, expecting it to sting but there was only a tingling sensation. The smell from it was not unpleasant although, at the sight of his mutilated hand, he felt nauseous and angry and wished he could spend a few moments alone in a room with Drest again.

The druidess prepared a strip of cloth, cutting it to size with an eye-catching white bone-handled knife, and she wound the material around Duro's hand expertly, making a far tidier job of the bandage than Bellicus had done.

"That's practically a work of art," the centurion said, gazing at the dressing appreciatively. "I've never seen a better job, even when I was in the army, and the medicus in my legion really knew his business." He looked at Ria who was smiling with pleasure at his compliment. "Thank you, lady."

She got up and wandered over to her horse, pulling what looked like a small piece of dried fruit from another of her many pockets and holding it up. As the horse drew its lips back, revealing a mouthful of large white teeth, and gently ate the proffered food, Ria said, "We'll clean and dress it again tomorrow, but I've no fears of infection. You'll be fine soon enough."

"Tomorrow," Bellicus said, lying down within the tent for they'd drawn lots earlier and it was his turn to sleep first. "We'll be safely back in Dun Breatann. I'm looking forward to seeing Cai, and Catia."

The druid and Duro had decided one of them should remain on watch all night, mainly thanks to Duro's mistrust of Ria. He did not want to fall asleep with only the Pictish druidess standing guard. They'd not said any of that to the girl of course, but she was no fool. She understood and made no fuss over it.

So, as Bellicus's soft snoring filled the campsite, centurion and druidess sat opposite one another by the fire. Somewhere in the distance there was an eerie cry, but it was too indistinct to be sure what made it. A woman in distress, perhaps, but far more likely it was a fox or even an owl. Duro was reassured by Ria's calm demeanour, for surely the druidess would know if the noise meant danger.

"You don't trust me, do you?"

"No."

Ria gave a crooked smiled at his blunt reply. "I appreciate your honesty," she said, poking the fire and bringing it back to life again.

The light played across her features and Duro was struck again by the druidess's beauty. Her skin was smooth and unlined, and her eyes were large and dark while her lips were full and moist and...With an effort he looked away into the darkness, knowing she was watching him as he drank in the sight of her. She would be used to men's appreciative stares of course, but the centurion didn't like his emotions to be so easily swayed. He'd seen too many strong men undone by their base desires.

"I don't blame you," she said, leaning back on her elbows. "Why would one of King Drest's closest advisors free two of his prisoners, and then run off herself? If they capture me, they will kill me, after all, and Qunavo has been my...mentor...for my whole life."

Duro caught the hesitation as she described her relationship with the Pictish druid and wondered if they had been lovers. He could not entirely suppress a pang of jealousy at the idea of the old greybeard bedding such an attractive young woman.

"So why are you here?" he asked gruffly. "Bellicus seems to trust you, but what you've told us isn't enough for me."

"I've hardly told you anything," she admitted. "But riding hard across country is not the best place for a tale, is it? We have hours to kill now though, so let me explain."

The time passed quickly for Duro, for the girl spoke as engagingly as Bellicus. She told him how, although she had been a loyal pupil of Qunavo's for years, she disagreed with his focus on Drest's quest for Pictish expansion. Ria saw

Drest as a weak king – he'd had decades in power when he should have used his strength to expand his borders, but he'd been content to remain where he was. The druidess often advised Qunavo that they should remove Drest and replace him with someone younger, stronger and more pliable to the druids' goals.

"What are those goals, as you see them?" Duro asked, wondering if she shared the same desires for their Order as Bellicus.

"First and foremost, we must crush the Christians," Ria said. "And the Saxons too, although I believe their religion may be somewhat compatible with our own beliefs. No," she used a stick to draw a cross in a patch of soft loam beside the fire, then viciously scored it out. "The Christ-followers are the biggest threat. They seek to destroy our way of life and replace it with their own weak philosophy."

Duro didn't know much about the new religion, but her words seemed paradoxical. "If they're weak, why do you fear them so much?"

"You don't understand," she replied. "Their teachings are designed to keep their followers pliable and in their place, without questioning things. But their leaders are single-minded, and utterly intent, on expanding until only their 'one true God' is allowed to be worshipped. It's truly a religion designed to control the populace. If they take over, we'll lose so much freedom and individuality."

And you will lose any power you have, Duro mused cynically.

"This isn't about me," she said, as if reading his thoughts, something Bellicus often seemed able to do as well. "This affects every one of us, including you. I saw the tattoo on your arm."

Duro reached up and touched his bicep where the bull had been emblazoned on his skin when he first became a follower of Mithras.

"You'll not be allowed to pray to your god when the Christians take over. They're not like the Romans, they'll not let people continue to worship their own deities. They will destroy our old holy places and build their own accursed churches over the ruins. This and more they'll do. They're a plague."

"You seem to forget the Romans tried their best to destroy the druids," Duro noted.

"That was a political thing," Ria replied. "The Romans didn't want a powerful, native priesthood controlling the people of Britannia – so they tried to wipe us out. The Christians will do the same, but they'll also wipe out all other gods or spiritual beliefs, forcing everyone to believe what they believe."

Her tone was venomous but Duro found himself unmoved. He wasn't particularly invested in Mithraism, especially since his wife Alatucca's murder, and his recent ordeal didn't speak much on his god's behalf either. To someone like Ria, however, whose entire outlook and place in life was shaped by her beliefs, it was understandable that she should fear the advent of a new, aggressive religion.

It did not really explain why Ria was there, in their camp that night, though.

"I had nowhere else to go," the druidess admitted in reply to his question. "Drest planned to sacrifice Bellicus—a great druid—to beg the gods' blessing on his war with Alt Clota. I deprived him of that opportunity. What do you think he would have done instead? Who else could he offer to the gods as a blood sacrifice? Who else would be as powerful an offering?"

"You." Duro shook his head in disgust. "I thought human sacrifices had been done away with generations ago. Isn't this one reason why we're fighting the Saxons? Because they're brutal savages who offer the blood of innocents to their terrible gods? Yet your people seem to be happy doing the same thing."

She let out a breath and gazed into the fire before replying softly. "It's not a common occurrence. Qunavo and Drest are putting everything they can into this push to seize control of all the lands north of the Roman walls. The blood of a druid was too powerful a gift to ignore."

"What about the blood of a former Roman legionary?"

She met his gaze frankly. "I had no qualms over that. As Bellicus represents the gods here on Earth, so you are a symbol of the once all-conquering Roman civilisation. You would have been a powerful offering and truthfully," she shrugged, "I wouldn't have had a problem with your death."

"I appreciate your honesty," he grunted, repeating her own earlier comment and absent-mindedly grasping the hilt of his sword.

"I'm here because I couldn't allow them to slaughter one of my Order simply to strengthen a weak king. It's not personal, Duro. I would have attempted to free any druid, not just Bellicus. You were rescued because Bel wouldn't leave without you." She stood up and pulled her cloak tighter around her shoulders as she looked down at him. "I don't know you, and I'm glad you're alive, but your death would have meant nothing to me, as I'm certain mine would mean nothing to you." She stepped across to the tent and bent low, crawling inside and lying next to the sleeping Bellicus. "I hope we can be friends however, centurion," she said quietly, before laying her head down on her arm and closing her eyes.

Duro sat in silence for a long time, staring out into the starry sky, immersed in its majesty, pondering the druidess's words and what the future might hold.

When he turned back towards the tent he noticed the flap had been drawn down, hiding the occupants from his sight and he knew at least one of Ria's claims was false. Her rescuing Bellicus *was* personal. He just hoped the druid could handle the impressive young woman. Being her friend was one thing—being her lover seemed another matter altogether and, despite her undeniable beauty and sharp mind, Duro did not envy his friend.

Much.

CHAPTER SIXTEEN

The morning brought sunshine to clear the dew, but the three fugitives were on their way long before then, fearful Drest's pursuing warriors would come upon them at their campsite. The horses were well rested, even if the humans were not particularly. Duro shook his head ruefully at the small, self-satisfied smile on Bellicus's face as they broke camp and resumed their journey home.

"We should be safely within Dun Breatann's walls by midday," the druid said, almost fully at ease once again since they'd returned to the Damnonii lands he knew so well.

"You hope," Ria muttered, as if she wasn't quite sure. Indeed, they'd passed a couple of burnt out farmhouses since rejoining the main road and the only conclusion was that the Pictish army ahead of them was to blame. There would be no point in destroying everything in their path, for Drest wanted to take control of a fully functional, productive Alt Clota. Burning every settlement in the land, and putting the inhabitants to the sword, would be a pointless waste of the very resources he coveted.

Soldiers would be soldiers though, and it was no surprise there would be casualties amongst the Damnonii civilians along the way. It was possible the three companions would find slaughtered farmers and their families a short distance away from the burning ruins of their former homes, but no-one had an appetite to search.

The fact the Picts had destroyed the buildings at all was proof the warband marching ahead of Bellicus and the others was not on a peaceful, diplomatic mission though. They were back, again, for war and conquest.

"How long were we actually imprisoned?" the druid asked Ria. "I lost track of time eventually."

He was shocked when she told him they'd been held within Dunnottar for almost three weeks. He'd hoped it was less than two. Poor Duro was even more flabbergasted.

"I'd thought we were there for months," he admitted unhappily. "It felt like it." He clenched his left fist, a new habit Bellicus had noticed he'd acquired since their escape, as if the centurion still wasn't convinced what he was feeling, with two missing fingers, was real.

"How are we supposed to get inside the fortress?" Ria asked, noting Duro's discomfort and changing the subject. "It seems clear we're going to arrive at Dun Breatann to find an army besieging it again. That was certainly Drest's command to them anyway so, unless your warriors stop them before they reach the fortress and defeat them…We'll have to make our way, unseen, through a hostile force. And let's be honest," she flashed that crooked grin which Bellicus found so alluring. "We're pretty recognisable."

Bellicus returned her smile with an equally charming one of his own while Duro rolled his eyes. "Don't worry," the druid said. "Unless Drest has somehow got hold of ships, the river-side of Dun Breatann should be accessible to us. If there's no way in on foot, we'll find a boat and row along the Clota tonight when it's dark. We can signal to the guards on the wall to let down a rope for us to be pulled up. Simple."

"I'm not so sure about that," Duro mumbled, eyeing the Pictish druidess with a frown, but his remark wasn't heard, or perhaps it was simply ignored. Bellicus's plan seemed sound, and that was all that mattered for now. Once they were safely inside Dun Breatann things would take care of themselves.

"We'll want higher ground to see what's happening," the druid said at mid-morning when they didn't have much further to travel. Duro remembered the terrain they were riding through, recognising it as the land just before a village known as Dun Buic. Bellicus led them up a hill, using a narrow road which, although well maintained, was hidden from plain sight and thus unlikely to have been used by the Picts. Drest's army would have no reason to travel up this hill anyway, since it led north, rather than west, towards Dun Breatann.

"Where are we going?" The centurion looked all around, seeing nothing but trees all the way up the slope which seemed to run as far as the eye could see. The river sparkled behind them in the spring sunshine, making Duro wonder why they were riding away from it, since its course led directly to their destination.

"This leads up behind and above Dun Buic, and along towards a place called Ard Sabhal. There's only a few dwellings there but it affords fine, unimpeded views of the fortress and the land around it. We'll be able to see what we're up against from there, with little danger of being captured."

Duro pictured the area in his head and realised they must be very close to the hidden tunnel entrance which allowed them into Dun Breatann when they returned from Dalriada the previous winter. He glanced towards Ria, wondering if she was aware of that secret way inside the Damnonii's most important fortress, since she was a druidess and members of that ancient Order shared such hidden knowledge. Then he realised it wasn't possible—if the Pictish druids knew of the tunnel Drest's army would have used it before now to take Dun Breatann with ease.

The look Bellicus was giving him confirmed Ria's ignorance and made it very clear to Duro that he should keep his mouth shut. The location of that tunnel entrance was known only to two people in the world and was only to be used in the direst emergency. They would not be travelling its inky darkness any time soon, and Duro was glad. He'd not enjoyed their previous walk through its time-haunted gloom and much preferred the idea of slipping along the Clota in a boat and being pulled up into Dun Breatann by the guards' ropes.

That was, of course, if there was no way to simply walk up to the fortress's front doors and proclaim their return.

When they reached the summit of the hill, all three realised the impossibility of that idea. They could clearly see the twin peaks of the Alt Clotan fortress, and the lands all around it basking in the warm sunshine, coming to full bloom again with the approach of summer. But, along with the cattle and sheep grazing in the fields below them, the dark mass of an army camped before the gates of Dun Breatann was unmistakeable. At this distance it was even possible to make out individual figures moving here and there.

Bellicus looked at his home and his heart soared despite the enemy presence. Dun Breatann was just as he'd imagined it back in the hated cell: green and vibrant and somehow *magical*. Perhaps it just felt like that because, for a time, he truly feared he'd never see the place again but...There was something of the Otherlands about the fortress that lay by the Clota, it wasn't simply his imagination.

"How many Picts are there do you think?" he asked, his voice resigned to the fact his people would have to try and fend off invaders yet again. "I'd say there's about forty or fifty."

Duro nodded, eyes moving from side to side, taking in the ground all along the river as their vantage point allowed them to see a fair way up- and downstream. "Fifty or so, aye, but remember Drest is bringing more with him. And there might be other bands of raiders out gathering—stealing—supplies from the locals." He stared at the giant druid dejectedly. "I think we can safely assume there's at least a hundred of the bastards, or there will be within a day or two."

"Double that," Ria said, drawing curses from the other two.

"And we've no idea how many of our own men are within the fortress," Bellicus mused, chewing his lip thoughtfully. "Are the men Cunedda gave us still there? Gods, they might even turn against Narina and open the gates! It wasn't so long ago they were on Drest's side after all. Shit, we need to get inside and find out what's happening."

Ria placed a hand on Darac's bridle before Bellicus could ride off.

"Calm down, Bel," she said. "The army won't just stand aside because they see you charging towards them. Think."

Duro said nothing, just continued to stare at the depressing scene before him as the druids conversed.

"Your original plan still stands," Ria said. "We simply wait for night to fall then make our way to the river and find a boat."

"What about Darac?" Bellicus muttered. "I'll have to leave him behind."

"It's just a horse," the druidess replied carelessly, shaking her head at Bel's sentimentality. "You can get another. Or leave him at one of the houses here on the hill. There must be someone with a stable nearby."

The druid sighed and a sheepish look came over his still-youthful face. "You're right. Our time at Dunnottar has taken its toll on me almost as much as Duro." He forced a smile and looked at the centurion. "We'll leave the horses with a nobleman who lives a short distance from here. He has a stable and, although his sons and the men he employs to protect his land will likely already be inside Dun Breatann as part of the garrison, Darac should be safe enough."

"You don't think Pictish foraging parties will come up here?"

Bellicus shook his head, noting the uncharacteristic anxiety in his friend's tone. "Not really. There's only a handful of dwellings scattered about. There are more densely populated areas nearby that'll better provide them with the supplies they'll be after. We'll be safe, don't worry."

Duro's eyes flashed briefly, as if he might take exception to the druid's suggestion that he was afraid, but then he looked away and rode on in silence.

Smoke from a cooking fire drifted lazily up into the sky a short distance ahead so Bellicus led them towards it, through the trees, riding carefully as a steep drop opened up on the left. A fast-flowing stream rushed past down below, occasional small waterfalls cascading down in white sprays, sparkling with rainbow colours in the bright sunshine wherever it could make its way through the canopy of foliage overhead.

"It's good to be back in my own lands," Bellicus smiled as a low dwelling came in sight. The main building, the one with the smoke emanating from it, had a well-maintained thatched roof, and the whole complex covered a large area of ground, to house the family who lived there as well as their animals.

"You know these people?" Ria asked, spotting a man moving around within the pig pen. From this distance she could see his iron-grey hair and broad shoulders as he tossed food to the snorting beasts with practised ease.

"I do," Bellicus confirmed, waving to the farmer as he turned and spotted their approach. "Hail, Boduoc!" he shouted, before smiling to his companions. "Boduoc is a good man, he'll take care of Darac and the other horses."

"Who'll take care of us?" Duro asked. "I could do with a mug of freshly brewed ale and some different cheese. No offence," he said to Ria. "I'm not too keen on that stuff you packed us. It's too bitter for my tastes."

The corner of the druidess's mouth twitched. "My apologies, centurion. Next time I'm planning your escape I'll try and find you something tastier."

"Boduoc's wife will feed us I'm sure," Bellicus interrupted, saving Duro from digging himself a deeper hole as the burly farmer strode across to them. The man was smiling, but it wasn't exactly the cheery grin of someone pleased to see his visitors. Understandable, given the circumstances, and who the riders were.

"My lord," Boduoc said, removing the felt cap, allowing his straggly long hair to spill out around his shoulders. "It's nice to see you. An unexpected pleasure."

Bellicus laughed and jumped down from his saddle to grasp the farmer's forearm in greeting. "Fear not, my friend, we won't be hanging around long." He unbuckled his staff from the horse's belt and stood with it in his hand, smiling reassuringly.

The relief in the farmer's face was almost comical but he masked it quickly and moved on, playing his part as host to travellers with good grace. "Let me take your horses to the stables, and we'll see about finding some refreshments, eh?"

Duro and Ria also dismounted and led their horses after Boduoc who was walking with Darac towards the building on the eastern side of the farm complex.

"Veloriga!" The farmer's voice was incredibly loud and carried across the land like a peal of thunder, making Bellicus wince and look about warily. If there *were* any Picts out foraging for supplies, they'd be drawn to the farm like moths to a flame after that. Much to the druid's chagrin, a door opened in the house straight ahead and a large woman looked out.

"What?" she roared, in almost as loud a voice as her husband's.

By now, Duro was warning the farmer of the army camped at nearby Dun Breatann so, mercifully, Boduoc held his peace as he led Darac into the stables. Bellicus hurried towards Veloriga who repeated her earlier throaty cry of, "What?"

She saw the druid coming towards her, and frowned at the finger he placed against his lips, but she got the message. Her eyesight was perhaps fading with the passing of her youth, but she knew very well who the giant, shaven-headed man with the eagle-topped staff was. Everyone in Alt Clota knew the druid.

"My lord," she bowed her head respectfully as he reached the doorway, beaming happily at her. She did not mirror the expression. "You'll be wanting meat and ale I expect." With a final glance across towards the stables to see how many were in the visitors' party, she went into the house, gesturing for Bellicus to follow.

He knew the farmer's wife of old and liked her immensely. She did not appear friendly to those who didn't know her ways, but the druid knew her outward bluster was an act. Her sharp tongue, razor sharp wit and impeccable timing could reduce a strong man to red-faced embarrassment if they got on the wrong side of her, but she had a heart of purest gold. He followed her into a spacious room with a large table and sat down on the stool she nodded towards.

A short time later Duro and Ria came in with Boduoc, who saw his wife was taking good care of their guests and left once again to finish taking care of the three horses.

"You have a lovely home," Ria said brightly as Veloriga thumped a tray bearing a jug of ale and three wooden mugs onto the table. The farmer's wife ignored the compliment then wandered back to the fire, muttering to herself as she stirred the great iron pot hanging over the flames.

Bellicus grinned at the druidess from behind his mug then the companions waited in silence, revelling in the warmth imparted by the drink, and the delicious scent of whatever broth Veloriga was cooking up. When she ladled it into bowls and carried them over it soon became clear the farmer's wife knew how to make the most of the relatively meagre ingredients available at that time of year, for the broth was both tasty and filling.

"You want more?"

Duro stared at Veloriga as she lifted the bowl he'd emptied within moments and it seemed like the centurion was a naughty child as he peered up at her uncertainly. Smirking, the farmer's wife bustled away without waiting for an answer then returned with the refilled bowl. Duro murmured his thanks, and, again, Bellicus grinned. He'd been through a very similar scenario twice before over the years, when out on hunting trips with King Coroticus and his men. Veloriga could be a terror, but no-one ever left her home with an empty belly.

When Boduoc came in he too was furnished with food and drink which he took with a word of thanks and a kiss for his wife. This show of affection seemed to surprise both Ria and Duro, but the farmer sat on his stool, oblivious to the visitors' bemusement.

"So, er… my lord. What brings you here?" Boduoc asked as he spooned broth into his mouth. Veloriga placed some salted meat on the table for them and continued working away in the background, cleaning bowls and tidying any mess, but she was listening too.

"We'd like to ask you to stable our horses here for," Bellicus waved a hand uncertainly, "a week. Two. I'm not sure yet. You'll be paid for it though, if you're—"

Boduoc broke in. "Of course, that's no problem. I'll see they're looked after. The big black, what d'you call him? Darac, is that it? Aye, I remember him, stunning animal." He upended the last of the liquid in his bowl into his mouth and handed it across to Veloriga who took it away without a word to be rinsed.

"Is there trouble we should be aware of, druid?" the farmer's wife asked.

"If you call an army besieging your queen's fortress 'trouble'," Ria answered, using her bone-handled knife to skewer a piece of meat. "Then, aye. You should be aware of it."

"Another one?" Boduoc said, rolling his eyes. "Who is it this time? Drest again, really? Do those damn Picts have nothing better to do with their time than throw men against Dun Breatann's walls?" He lifted the ale mug and refilled his cup before doing the same for the guests. "I suppose we should be on the lookout for raiders then."

"Your sons…?"

"Still part of Queen Narina's garrison," Boduoc replied. "Both of them. It's just me, Veloriga and the grandchildren. Thankfully they're old enough now that they can wipe their own arses and help out around the place." He shook his head sadly. "We could really do with our sons back here though, Bel."

"Aye," Veloriga agreed. "You lot in charge need to get things sorted so folk can get their fields sown and their damn livestock taken care of."

"Are you always this forward?" Ria asked, and it seemed she was more curious than angry or irritated by their hosts' talk. "You do know who Bellicus is?"

For the first time ever, Bellicus saw Veloriga flustered and the farmer himself looked mortified, as if they were only just realising who their guest was. But the druid shook his head and leaned forward to pat Boduoc on the arm, telling his hosts not to worry.

"Should we get moving?" Duro wondered, peering up through the hole in the roof. "If we've a fair way to walk yet, we'd be better doing it while it's still light."

"Aye," Bellicus rose to his feet, towering over everyone else as he thanked Veloriga for a wonderful meal. "We'll be on our way." He moved to take a ring from his finger as payment for both their repast and the horses' upkeep, then remembered that all his belongings had been taken by the Picts.

Ria noticed his embarrassment and took off one of her own small trinkets, handing it to the woman. Veloriga gazed at it in pleasure, as if wondering what she'd be like with such a fancy bauble on her own hand, but they all knew such things were ultimately not important to the farmer's wife. The ring would be bartered, and the goods received in return put to good use.

Bellicus looked from Veloriga to Boduoc, seeing the bonds of love and friendship clearly between them, and a part of him wished he could live such a simple life with Catia and…

"Come on then," Ria said, surreptitiously grabbing the druid's backside as she headed for the door, that familiar crooked smile making him lose his train of thought completely. He followed, as Cai would have followed him, ignoring Duro's frown.

Veloriga thrust a wheel of cheese and three skins at the centurion as he made to leave. He was surprised to see they were the ale skins from the horses—Boduoc must have brought them in and had his lady refill them. Duro took the supplies gratefully then went after his companions. At least they were well fortified for the coming boat journey along the Clota.

"I liked them," Ria said as they headed off towards the trees again, Bellicus leading since he knew where they were going from times past. "This place is like an island of calm in the middle of a storm."

"It is," Bellicus agreed, shoving aside some briars to let the druidess pass. "But the likes of you and me would soon be bored living here."

"Not me," Duro muttered, drawing his sword and hacking at the same briars Bellicus had been holding back. "I'm about ready to leave war, and killing, and kings and queens, behind forever."

"You say that now, my friend," the druid laughed. "But you're the same as us. You'd miss the thrill of battle."

"You forget I lived quite happily as a baker in Luguvalium for years," Duro replied, sheathing his sword without bothering to wipe off the green mess left by the chopped foliage, a sign of his disdain for the borrowed weapon. He missed his old spatha, which suggested to the druid Duro's assertion that he tired of fighting was not quite true.

Or perhaps he just missed the sword as it was one of the few possessions he'd owned that formed a link to his past. It was gone now, Bellicus knew, stolen by some unknown Pictish lord. Duro would never see it again, but they'd find him another, even nicer one, eventually.

The trio walked on in thoughtful, almost melancholic silence, as if Boduoc's farm truly had been an island of tranquillity and now that they'd left it behind the storm was closing in on them once again. Certainly, Duro was constantly on edge and the feeling was beginning to infect Bellicus too, although Ria seemed quite cheerful. That chirpy talkativeness was irritating Duro even further though, and Bellicus pushed through the undergrowth faster as the hill began sloping downwards again.

The trees gave way at last to a clearer, flatter section of ground but, as they walked the silence seemed strangely oppressive. Even Ria had stopped talking, sensing the change in the atmosphere around them. They saw no wildlife other than the occasional jackdaw, watching them almost malevolently from atop boulders and rocks, and once they saw a pair of magpies noisily harassing a feral cat who'd strayed too close to their nest.

"What are you doing?" Bellicus asked in a low voice as he saw Duro draw his sword for no apparent reason. "What's wrong?"

"I don't know," the centurion replied, eyes searching all around for whatever had made him so nervous. "Maybe I'm just anxious because of everything that's happened, but I feel like something's watching us."

The druid felt an icy shiver run down his back and, although he could see no enemies, he nodded to Ria who grasped her own staff tightly, ready for whatever Duro had sensed.

"Maybe we should find some cover," the druidess suggested, although Bellicus felt sure her concern was more for Duro's state of mind than any actual enemy stalking them.

Before he could answer, Bellicus heard the sharp crack of a dry twig snapping somewhere to their right. He looked up at the bulk of the hill—known locally as the Sleeping Giant—which flanked the path they were following, but saw nothing and guessed it must have been a fox, or perhaps another wildcat trying to avoid the territorial magpies.

Then there was a second crack and Duro cursed under his breath. If it was an animal within the undergrowth, it was an uncommonly clumsy one.

Bellicus knew that wasn't likely. "Come on," he hissed. "Ria's right – we should find cover to hide us as we walk. It'll take us longer to reach the river but there'll be less chance of being spotted by Pictish outriders." He stopped in his tracks and stared into the trees a short way up the slope at the rear. Movement. And not of a fox or other small animal. The closest cover was a clump of briars and, wordlessly, the druid dropped behind them on his stomach, gesturing for the others to follow suit.

"Where?" Duro asked, wiping sweat from his brow as he stared at the hill where Bellicus's gaze was aimed.

"There."

Their eyes followed his pointing staff, but nothing was visible now, other than the expected spring foliage.

"I see nothing," Ria said after a time. "Let's get moving again. Do you know a less open path to the river, Bel?"

"Mithras protect us." They frowned at Duro then noticed what he'd seen. A man in armour, wearing a shining helm and gazing down upon them from halfway up the hill. "It's a Pict."

Bellicus wasn't sure how the centurion could be so sure of the warrior's identity—at this distance it could be a Saxon or a Dalriadan, or, well, anyone—but Duro was already moving fast, south, towards the river, in the opposite direction from the watcher on the hill.

* * *

Duro couldn't remember everything that had happened to him in Dunnottar's dungeons. Mercifully, his memory had blocked much of it out although he feared that some future event, something apparently innocuous like a door banging shut in the wind, might bring it all back in a flash for he'd known such things to happen before.

Ever since Bellicus and Ria had rescued him he'd felt a lurking fear however, that they would be quickly recaptured and taken back to continue the nightmare.

The cell Drest had thrown him in at first had been tiny – so small that, if his hands hadn't been tied together he could have reached out and touched every wall without taking a step. Eventually he was moved to a slightly bigger room where the beatings were administered, but those first few days or weeks in the pitch black were what had sent him halfmad. In the pitch black, starved of food and drink, in the beginning it hadn't been too bad. He'd undergone similar trials during his initiations into the cult of Mithras after all.

That religion demanded followers who were physically strong and capable of feats of endurance, like the god himself when he'd wrestled and defeated a great bull.

One of the cult's seven initiations involved being placed in an underground trench which was then covered with a flagstone lid. Only those who could endure the dark, claustrophobic test for a certain length of time would progress within the cult. Duro had managed it comfortably enough, but Dunnottar's cell was quite different. He had no idea when, or if, he would ever be released and suspected something even worse was to come eventually. He'd been stoic enough at first but eventually the lack of sensory stimulation started to play tricks with his mind.

He imagined he could hear malevolent voices and feel things, loathsome things, crawling and flopping across his skin.

After a time even that seemed mundane and the sensations passed, replaced by visions. A man had started to appear in his cell – a blind man who played the harp for him. They never spoke to one another, but the harpist's music gave Duro strength and stopped him from going completely insane. Despite their lack of verbal communication the centurion knew the musician was called Teàrlach and hailed from Dalriada, strangely enough.

Was Teàrlach real, or a spirit, or merely a product of Duro's mind? It didn't matter. The man and his harp had seen the centurion through his ordeal and as a result Duro thought of him as a friend.

When Drest moved him to the other, slightly larger, cell, and taken his fingers amongst other vile tortures, Teàrlach had been there to soothe him and calm his fears until that day when he'd heard Bellicus singing in the cell below. At that point Duro had found a new resolve and began to think about the possibility of living again.

Now though, with the appearance of the Pictish soldiers on the hill behind them, his terror was mounting and there seemed little he could do to stop it.

Whatever happened, and despite their apparent friendship, Duro never wanted to meet Teàrlach again. He would die by his own hand rather than be taken back to Dunnottar to hear the Dalriadan harpist's sweet music once more.

CHAPTER SEVENTEEN

Ria and Bellicus hurried after the anxious centurion. Even if the unknown warrior was an enemy and part of a larger force, they had a good head start and Bellicus could think of at least two places nearby that they might hide in until night fell. Unless they were pursued by men with dogs of course. He put such fatalistic thoughts from his mind and jogged ahead. He turned back once to see half a dozen men coming down the hill alongside the helmeted soldier but didn't tell the others. It was clear now—they were being hunted again.

A cry came from the left and the three runners turned, hoping to see a friendly Damnonii patrol as unlikely as that was given Queen Narina's army were under siege within Dun Breatann at that moment. No, Bellicus knew before he even looked across the rough grassland who he'd see.

"Gods, there's more of them, Bel," Duro cried out, still running but breathless already. He was stronger than a few days ago, but still far from the condition he'd been in before their brutal captivity. "What do we do?"

"They're in front of us as well," Ria gasped, grabbing both men by their cloaks and dragging them to a halt. "Bel, these are your lands. Is there a way we can escape?"

The druid saw another party of Pictish raiders in the distance ahead and growled an oath. "The only way open, for now, is west," he said. "The bastards have every other direction covered." If he had Cai with him, and Duro had been at full strength, they might have chosen to plough ahead, towards the river as they'd intended, fighting their way through. But, given their weakened state and the absence of the powerful mastiff, all they could do was run to the west and hope more of the invaders didn't appear there too.

"We're coming for you!" The heavily accented cry rang out behind them as they changed course and began jogging once more. "Our king has unfinished business with the three of you." The man's laugh was raucous and full of hateful promise.

"We can't..." Duro gasped, sucking in breaths as if he was at the very edge of his endurance. "We can't let them take us again, druid. I'd rather die than be captured for...for that whoreson to torture me again."

Bellicus looked around at the three groups of soldiers converging on them and took some solace in the fact they weren't mounted, and didn't appear to be expending too much effort in catching them. The gap between them and their Pictish pursuers remained the same as it had been when the chase began, although there seemed little chance of escape, barring some intervention by the gods.

"He can't run much further," Ria muttered, moving to Bellicus's other side, away from the centurion. "We're going to be caught soon enough. We should make a stand now, before all three of us are too exhausted to raise our weapons. I've no more desire to be captured than the centurion. Drest has long wanted to bed me and there's no doubt he'll do that and worse if we're taken."

The druid glanced over his shoulder and muttered an oath that came out as more of a tired whimper—two of the groups trailing them were closer already. His mind whirled as he wondered what to do, wishing the gods would give him some sign.

"We must use the tunnel," Duro wheezed. "We're travelling *away* from the river."

"What tunnel?" The druidess eyed Bellicus curiously, the light of hope flaring in her expression. "What's he talking about?"

The druid ignored her. "You were told never to mention that again," he shouted angrily.

"And you said it was for use in emergencies," Duro retorted, slowing so much he practically stopped, holding his side and blowing hard. "I'd say this is a fucking emergency, Bel!"

"What tunnel?" Ria demanded again. "If there's an escape route nearby, in the name of Taranis, why are we not using it?"

"For use in emergencies that threaten Alt Clota, Duro, not the lives of a few insignificant people."

The centurion did come to a halt now, bent over, hands on his thighs, drawing in and gasping out air like the bellows in a blacksmith's forge. "What difference does it make?" he asked, almost pleading. "I already know of its existence, and Ria is one of your own Order. A druidess." He waved his sword exhaustedly at the oncoming Picts who were laughing openly at them now. "The entrance isn't far," Duro went on, beginning to move in the direction he believed the tunnel opening to be. "It's our only chance."

There seemed little other choice than to go where the centurion asked, so Bellicus jogged after his friend, slightly modifying their heading so they would reach the place quicker. No one spoke now, and the druid pondered the ramifications of using the secret tunnel simply to save their own skin. He'd been gifted the knowledge of the subterranean passage into Dun Breatann by his predecessor, Alt Clota's wise woman, Abrexta, and made to swear he'd not share its existence with any other unless the land faced a dire threat.

Dun Breatann did face a threat at that moment, but not one that their using the tunnel would alleviate. All it would do would save his and his friends' lives. But at what cost? If the Picts found the hidden entrance and used it themselves, especially if they brought more men…

"Hey, Roman," one of the men running after them called, and Duro turned with a snarl although he never stopped moving. "Drest says he's going to slice off the rest of your fingers, one by one, and then move onto the rest of you."

"Piece by piece, until there's nothing left!" another of the Pictish pursuers hollered, and many of them laughed viciously.

Bellicus could see his friend's fear and made his mind up. He could not allow Drest to take them. They would have to reach the place well ahead of the chasing warriors though, to allow the druid time to make sure evidence of their passage was covered up again. The entrance *must* be concealed.

"Fine," he said, lengthening his stride. As he passed Duro and Ria he called out, "Faster, you two. We'll use the tunnel, but we must hurry." Then, and he wasn't proud of it when he thought about it later, he added to the centurion, knowing how much the man had disliked their previous trip through the oppressively dark tunnel, "And don't forget we have no oil lamp with us this time."

Immediately the centurion fired back, "That's fine. I'd rather face the dark than another day in Drest's cells!"

They ran then, Bellicus thanking Cernunnos that this had happened so close to the tunnel entrance. If they'd been just half a mile further away Duro wouldn't have had the energy, or breath, to make it. Despite the danger they were in the druid managed a smile, glad to know the gods had not forgotten him yet.

Suddenly, a figure reared up before them from behind a low bank of grass. Without pausing to see who, or what, it was, Duro let out a horrific shriek and hacked down. The man, for man it was, hadn't expected the instantaneous attack and was unprepared for the blade that shattered his forearm and left it a mangled ruin.

A second man, who Bellicus could tell now was a Pict by his style of armour and the blue whorls painted on his bare legs, lunged at them, but the druid batted the attack aside and slammed the top of his staff into the man's face. The bronze eagle shattered the soldier's eye socket and downed him instantly, unconscious, or perhaps dead from the savage blow.

They ran on, blood pumping in their veins, thundering in their ears even harder now, if that was possible.

"I can see," Ria gasped, wide-eyed in appreciation, "why you two have so many stories and songs told about you. I thought they'd all been made up, but now…"

Neither man responded to her oddly out of place compliment. Their flight, and instinctive slaughter of the two would-be attackers, did not feel at all glorious right then.

"Are we almost there?" the druidess asked, turning to see the Picts had slowed, apparently wary after their kinsmen had been dispatched so easily. They were not in any great hurry to catch up with the escapees from Dunnottar, knowing they would tire very soon and, vastly outnumbered as they were, make a simple target.

"Aye," Bellicus replied, also risking a look back and nodding grimly as he noticed they'd opened a wider gap between themselves and the Picts. "See that tree ahead? The dead one?"

Ria muttered agreement as her eyes locked on the blasted remains of an ancient birch that must have been struck by lightning years before.

"We go uphill at that point. Get on the other side of the bushes, there, and keep going until we reach level ground." He sucked in a long breath and watched Duro do the same, almost stumbling over a hidden boulder before catching himself and continuing on with a pained expression. "We'll be safely hidden very soon," the druid finished, hoping to spur his friend on for this last, final push.

"There's no escape, you bastards," came that hateful voice from behind again, although it was further away this time. "We'll catch up with you soon enough, and then…" The threat was left unfinished but Bellicus had no doubt they'd be treated even more harshly if they were caught now.

"Here," he grunted, running to the right, behind the bushes he'd indicated moments before. "Come on, Duro, this is the final stretch, up here."

They were hidden from their pursuers' view now, and it seemed to give them all a second wind, as they powered uphill, towards the flat section that housed the hidden trapdoor. Bellicus used his long stride to move ahead of his companions, running directly towards the patch of grass which he'd marked with a particular rock that looked, to all but him, like any other. Silently, he dropped his staff, gritted his teeth and hauled upwards, peeling back a section of turf to reveal a stone block covered in skittering wood lice. A rope handle allowed the giant druid to lift the block without much apparent effort, and the entrance opened up like the black, gaping maw of some eldritch beast.

Ria reached him before Duro and her eyes were shining, from the run and amazement. "That's incredible," she said. "I'd never have found that, it was practically invisible."

"Hurry up and get in," Bellicus barked, irritated by her chatter when he so desperately wanted to drop the trapdoor and hide the secret tunnel again. She followed his command, but her admiring gaze took in every aspect of the entrance's construction, as she marvelled at the skill with which it had been built.

Duro arrived a moment later, blowing hard, and weaving from side to side as if he was about to collapse at any moment. Which he probably was.

"Have you got the dried mushrooms?" Bellicus asked, as he helped the centurion down the wooden steps into the musty gloom of the tunnel.

"Eh?" Momentarily baffled, Duro shook his head, then, touching down on the hard rock floor below, he fell onto his knees.

"Tinder!" the druid said as he lifted his staff and jumped down into the hole himself, forgetting that both of their supply packs had been taken from them back in Dunnottar and they'd left the rest in the horses' saddlebags. "Find it, quickly."

At last, the centurion understood and, using the small amount of light that came in through the trapdoor, looked at himself in bemusement.

"I have some," Ria broke in. "Close the door, by Taranis, before they catch us up and see it!"

Bellicus pulled the stone down, knowing the turf would fall back, forming the seal as it had been before they entered and thanking whoever had built this incredible engineering feat. It was possible the Picts would find the doorway and come down after them, but the druid doubted it. Even if someone knew what they were looking for, the turf blended so naturally into its surroundings that it was, as Ria had noted, as good as invisible.

People in Alt Clota had heard rumours of the secret tunnels leading to and from Dun Breatann, and many had searched for the entrances. No one had ever found them, and Bellicus was confident the Picts would have no better luck. Hopefully their pursuers would believe the druid's magic had spirited them away.

They listened, but no sound penetrated the earth above—nothing that could be heard over Duro's laboured breathing at least—and Bellicus stepped carefully in the darkness to where Ria had been standing when the light was shut off so completely.

"Ria? You have the tinder?" he asked quietly, although his voice was quite effectively muffled by the tons of damp earth surrounding them anyway.

"I have," she replied, her voice coming from right beside his ear, and he jumped involuntarily as he felt her nimble fingers running up the inside of his thigh and touching his manhood. Her tongue licked the side of his face and, thrilled despite their plight, he tried to locate her other hand, the one which presumably held the stuff they needed to start a fire.

"Shit," he muttered, finally remembering that he'd lost his fire striker. "How are we—"

"Do you think I brought tinder, but nothing to create a spark, Bel?" The druidess's voice moved away from him and a moment later a tiny flicker of light appeared within the darkness.

"You're a marvel, Ria," Bellicus said, looking on in admiration as the spark appeared again, and again, and after a few more attempts caught whatever material the girl had brought along as tinder.

"Thank Mithras," Duro said, his grimy face appearing paler than ever in the dim glow. "I was dreading walking all that way in the dark. But…wait! We don't have an oil lamp, or any torches, or anything."

A stronger light suddenly bloomed into existence, showing Bellicus's teeth as he grinned at the centurion.

"After our last visit here," the druid said, rising to his feet, casting an enormous shadow on the wall behind him, "I left this lamp down here with a small supply of oil."

Duro closed his eyes and sagged back in relief. He'd thankfully regained his breath during Ria's attempts to create a flame and now the three of them sat, or stood, looking at one another. They knew they still had a way to go before they could truly think of themselves as safe, but they now wore expressions of people who'd faced death and escaped its grasp. For a time at least.

"All right," Bellicus said when he thought they'd rested long enough and still there had been no sounds of their escape route's discovery overhead. "We'd best get moving. We're almost home and I'm looking forward to spending the night in my own house, in my own bed, after drinking the queen's stock of ale dry. Let's move."

And with that, they walked into the near-impenetrable blackness ahead.

CHAPTER EIGHTEEN

"My lady." Gavo's gruff voice and heavy knock sounded at the door of Queen Narina's chamber and she frowned, brought back to the current unpleasant reality. She'd been gazing out onto the glittering waters of the River Clota, lost in the familiar view, admiring the blossoming, green land on the opposite bank and watching as the occasional boat, unhindered by the Picts' siege of Dun Breatann, sailed slowly past. She sometimes wished she could take a boat like one of those lazily floating along, load Catia on board, and just let the current take them away to a land where there were no wars and no politics.

Truly that was a faery land though and, smiling sadly, she crossed the room, opening the door to her guard captain and, in the still-unexplained absence of Bellicus, her closest advisor. "Come in, old friend," she said, and Gavo, bowing his head respectfully, walked inside.

His eyes lingered on the serene view outside Narina's window and then he turned to face her and she was roused to curiosity by the gleam in his eyes.

"Something's happened," she said, and it was more of a statement than a question.

Smiling now, he nodded. "Come with me, lady," he replied. "We may be under siege, but, well, there's some good news at last." He led the way out of the house, standing on the gently sloping crown of the hill on which the royal dwelling stood as he waited on Narina to follow.

She did so but, shaking her head good-naturedly, slapped Gavo on the arm. "I'm not a child," she said. "I'm your queen, and you can damn well explain to me what's going on."

"You'll see soon enough," he replied and Narina was amazed at how pleased the captain appeared to be.

Catia was lying on the grass nearby, making a chain from daisies, and she eyed them with interest until Gavo said,

"You can come too, Princess, come on! Where's the dog, Cai?"

The girl stood up and shared a bemused look with her mother, but the guard captain was already moving, not waiting to see if they were following.

"I don't know where Cai is," the princess said. "He ran off a while ago and I haven't seen him since. What's happening?"

"No idea," Narina admitted, taking Catia by the hand and hurrying to catch up as the captain made his way down the winding path towards the gap between the twin peaks that formed Dun Breatann. "Gavo, what's going on? Tell me, I command it!"

"It'll be quicker to just show you," he shouted over his shoulder, and his grin was infectious so that, by the time they reached the bottom of the hill both queen and princess's eyes were glittering with excitement. When Narina realised which house Gavo was heading towards a chill ran through her and she slowed.

The guard captain, still smiling, inclined his head and opened the door to Bellicus's compact roundhouse, holding his arm up to invite them inside.

"He's home?" The queen's voice was little more than a whisper and Gavo didn't reply but she was there now and stepping out of the glorious spring sunshine into the shadowy interior of Bellicus's house. Her eyes quickly adjusted to the gloom and settled first on the centurion, Duro, who looked rather ill if truth be told, then, fearing the druid might be similarly malnourished and sickly, her gaze moved on. "You *are* home," the queen said, and, from the tone of her voice it was clear she'd never expected to see either of these men again. It had been widely rumoured that King Drest had either taken them prisoner or killed them and, after so many days without their return, Narina's hopes had faded.

Yet here they were, and Bellicus appeared unharmed, if rather slimmer than before, and her heart soared with joy.

She stepped forward to embrace him, not caring whether etiquette precluded such a show of emotion towards a man that wasn't her husband, but then the smile dropped from her face and her voice was cold as she demanded, "What's *she* doing here?"

Ria was more than a full head shorter than Bellicus and had been standing a little behind the druid, in the shadow cast behind him by the sunlight streaming through the open door. She moved forward now though, standing right beside Bellicus so their arms were touching. The edge of the druidess's mouth twitched in a small smile and she took Bellicus's hand in hers as she bowed her head towards the Queen of Alt Clota. "My lady," was all she said, and the atmosphere grew tense within the roundhouse as the women stared at one another.

Princess Catia was not as reticent as her mother, and ran to Bellicus, throwing her arms around his waist, almost tripping over faithful Cai who was already by his master's side, having sensed his return long before anyone else within the fortress.

"Ria saved our lives," Duro said, breaking the silence. "Drest would have killed us if she hadn't helped us escape his clutches."

Narina looked at the centurion, glad for the excuse to break off the staring competition—if Ria was anything like Bel, she'd have no chance of winning such a contest anyway. "It seems I owe the Pictish druidess my thanks, then," she said. Then, with a last frosty look at Bellicus, she turned and walked out of the building.

Gavo still stood there, looking somewhat sheepish now although he wasn't really sure why, or what in Lug's name was going on.

"See they're given food and drink, and water for washing," Narina said to him as she swept past, heading back up towards her own house. "Then take them to the Great Hall.

I'll meet them there in one hour, and we can hear everything that's happened."

* * *

The queen sat on Dun Breatann's throne, essentially just a slightly larger, more ornate chair than all the others in the Great Hall, in the middle of the raised dais. To her left sat Gavo while the seat to her right, normally reserved for Bellicus, was occupied by Gerallt, silver hair immaculately combed as always. The druid hadn't been replaced out of spite, he sat at a table in front of the royal one—with Ria and Duro on either side, Cai back in his usual place on the floor at his feet—recounting the story of their recent adventures in Pictland.

When he finished, the three faces on the dais looked at him with interest, and no little concern.

Gavo was shaking his head at the revelation there was a secret tunnel running from the fortress to Dun Buic, a fact Bellicus could no longer conceal since he and his companions had been seen coming out of the well by two guards.

Gerallt didn't appear excited unduly by any part of the druid's tale.

Narina, however, had been outraged when she heard of Drest taking two of Duro's fingers and starving both him and Bellicus. If Ria hadn't been there, Bellicus suspected Narina might have shown more emotion, but, as it was, she kept herself in check, only betraying how she felt by a narrowing of her eyes and a tightening of her jaw as the most brutal parts of the tale were described.

"It seems we're doomed to fight against our neighbours for evermore," Gerallt said into the thoughtful, angry silence that followed the druid's story. "So much for uniting all the people and taking an army south to destroy the Saxons."

"Why didn't you mention this damn tunnel before?" Gavo demanded, slamming his hand onto the table. "It could have saved us a lot of trouble. Now, for example! If I'd known there was a way to leave the fortress unseen, I'd have taken half the men, come around at the back of the Picts' encampment and—"

Bellicus met the guard captain's eyes coolly and broke in, halting Gavo's rant. "The tunnel's existence was a secret entrusted to me by my predecessor. It is for me, as druid of Dun Breatann, to use such sacred knowledge as I choose." His voice grew harsh as his gaze bored into the captain's. "Do not question me further on it. Not now, at least. We have other, more pressing matters to discuss."

Narina laid her hand on Gavo's arm. "He's right. I don't understand why it was so important to save his own skin today, rather than helping us break the previous siege with this knowledge, but he can explain himself later, if he chooses." She turned back to the druid who she half-expected to be flushing with embarrassment at her veiled accusation of cowardice. She should have known better, for he returned her look calmly. There might even have been a hint of amusement in his brown eyes, the queen thought. "What should be our next move?" she asked the room in general, steering the conversation in a different direction.

"We use the tunnel just as I described," Gavo replied. "Take men outside and attack the rear of Drest's army, while the rest come out of the gates and smash him from the front."

"Classic pincer movement," Gerallt mused, nodding thoughtfully at first before his expression became uncertain. "Have we enough men for it to work though?"

"Do we still have Cunedda's warriors?" Bellicus asked. "The ones led by his son?"

"They're still with us," Narina confirmed. "And it'll be good to give them someone to fight – that champion of theirs, Erebus, has been nothing but a pain in the arse since he came here. Too much aggression in him."

"And usually too much wine," Gavo agreed sourly.

"How many soldiers has Drest brought with him this time?" Gerallt asked, his eyes moving from Bellicus to Ria.

The druidess didn't hesitate. "In total? Two hundred."

Narina frowned. "That many? How do you know?"

"I know because I was with Drest and his other—" she caught herself, thinking it prudent not to remind everyone that she'd been one the Pict's advisors just a few days ago. "I was with them," she continued, "when they made their plans to come here. One hundred men travelled here while you two," she gestured to the centurion and Bellicus, "were locked up in Dunnottar's dungeons. The rest of the army, the other hundred spears, were coming after us with Drest. They'll be here by now."

"Shit," Gavo muttered. "That's a lot of men considering we sent most of our soldiers home when the last siege was lifted."

"We did?" Bellicus asked.

"Didn't seem like there was much point in having them hang around eating our supplies," Narina said. "When they should have been with their families, preparing for the summer harvest. Remember, some of them were Dalriadans as well." She sighed heavily. "I was supposed to be forming an alliance with those people and helping them crown a new ruler. That was a chance to make a lasting peace with them, but it's probably dust in the wind now."

"So how many warriors *do* we have here?" the druid asked, drawing her back to the current, more pressing issue.

"The usual garrison," Gavo said. "Plus Cunedda's warband."

Bellicus rolled his eyes. "Fifty, sixty men?"

"It's not enough is it?" Gerallt said blandly, and no-one bothered to answer him. There was no way they could split their force and encircle The Pictish army; their only option was to wait out the besiegers. Again.

"Drest won't just go away this time," Ria warned, guessing what Queen Narina and the others were thinking. "Not with so many men at his disposal. Either he'll build ladders and storm the walls, or he'll destroy and loot all the towns and villages in Alt Clota. Assuming he's not already doing that."

The hall fell silent again, the only sound coming from a serving girl who went between the tables with a jug of ale, refilling all the cups before returning to a place in the shadows.

"What now then?" Duro asked. "Can we send messengers to your other allies? Ask the Dalriadan spearmen to return? Ask Cunedda to send more reinforcements? His own son is trapped here with us after all. If Dun Breatann's taken, Drest will kill or enslave everyone."

"Cunedda won't send more men," Gavo said. "He doesn't have them to spare. And it would take too long to go from village to village in Dalriadan lands trying to gather a warband again. We don't have time to waste."

All eyes turned to Bellicus, as if he might magically provide a solution to their problems, but it was Narina who spoke.

"For now, the gods have blessed us," she said, drawing amazed looks from Gavo and Gerallt. "Our druid has returned, alive and well." Her words were joyful, but her delivery of them was flat and cold as she looked now at the Pictish druidess. "He's even brought another of his Order to help him guide us."

The corner of Ria's mouth twitched, and she squeezed Bellicus's thigh beneath the table, forcing him to stifle a yelp.

"We'll have a feast tonight," the queen announced, getting to her feet. "A feast with ale and dancing and song. Drest will hear us and think we've not a care in the world. The preparations will give me something to take my mind off this whole mess. The rest of you," she looked around at them all, even Ria. "Try and come up with a way we can smash Drest once and for all, or, at the very least, drive him back to Dunnottar."

She emptied what was left in her cup and strode from the room, leaving the others to think of a way they might save Alt Clota from possibly its darkest hour.

"Come on," Ria said, winking at Bellicus and swinging her slim legs around on the seat to stand up. "You can show me around Dun Breatann while there's still some sunlight left, and we'll see if we can come up with a plan to send Drest home again."

The druid couldn't help noticing the frosty stares Gavo and Gerallt gave him as the druidess led him by the hand from the hall, but he didn't reject her plan. There would be time to explain himself to the guard captains later, during the feast. Cai padded along at their rear as they went out into the sunshine.

"What's got into him, centurion?" Gerallt demanded when only the three men were left within the hall.

"Isn't it obvious?" Duro replied quietly, gazing at the open doorway his friend had just disappeared through. "I think he's in love."

CHAPTER NINETEEN

"Love doesn't matter!" It was a statement she'd repeated to herself many times over recent days yet, while she knew it to be true, that didn't make it any more palatable.

Catia wasn't convinced either and it showed plainly on her face.

Narina looked at her daughter and felt pride swell within her. The princess had lost the puppy fat on her face over the winter months and grown taller. She looked regal, Narina thought, and she thanked the gods that Bellicus had brought her back from those vile Saxon abductors.

Bellicus…

"Are you even listening to me, mother?"

Narina pushed the distracting thoughts to one side and walked over to her unshuttered window, resting her forearms on the sill and looking out on the Clota so far below. Catia joined her and they enjoyed the view in silence for a while until, eventually, the princess spoke again.

"I know about the importance of alliances, but…Is Cunedda really so powerful that marrying his son will strengthen Alt Clota? It seems to me like the only people who'll really get anything from it are the Votadini."

Narina glanced at her daughter, a little surprised by her perceptiveness. Was there also a hint of reproach in the girl's voice? As if she suspected Narina was merely entertaining the idea of wedding Ysfael because Bellicus had found another woman to be his companion? Was it true? Perhaps, if the queen was honest, she might accept the accusation that jealousy was driving her rather than a desire to consolidate Alt Clota's position, and yet…Bellicus and her were never to be. Too much had happened, and too many people knew the rumours – if the queen was to marry the druid it would be said that they had conspired to remove Coroticus after all. That was not the foundation Narina wanted her throne built upon.

There had to be a clean slate, and that might mean finding a suitable partner from outside her own Damnonii people.

Besides, Bellicus was obviously happy with the dark-haired little druidess who smiled so charmingly and touched him playfully, intimately, when she thought no-one was looking. He was welcome to her and her uncouth, Pictish ways.

"There must be someone better you could marry," Catia said. "One of the Dalriadan warlords perhaps? Their lands are right beside us, and there's always more of them coming over from Hibernia. If you found one of them to wed…"

Narina nodded. "It's a good idea," she admitted. "But I would have to choose the right man, and I simply don't know enough about the Dalriadans to do that. There're a number of competing noblemen, many of them with only a handful of men in their 'army'. What if I married some weakling? It would be pointless. No, at least the Votadini—Cunneda—is not an unknown quantity. And I already know his son, Ysfael. He's not bad looking."

Catia frowned and Narina laughed, a rare sound lately that echoed back from the walls and parapets below. "Well? I'd rather share my life with a handsome young man than some hairy-arsed, grizzled old warrior with the evidence of a hundred battles written all across his body."

"You said 'love doesn't matter'," Catia scolded, but there was a glint in her eyes too. "Neither should looks!" It pleased her to see her mother smiling again.

"I don't know why you're so amused," Narina shot back without thinking. "Your turn will come soon enough."

It was a joke, spoken in haste, in the moment, but as soon as it was said, the queen's face fell and they both returned their gazes thoughtfully, and a little sadly, towards the ever-flowing river they spent most of their lives beside. It had been there when Narina was born, and it would be there long after she was gone—all they could do was make the most of the days they were given and try not to let time's currents pull them in directions they didn't want to go.

"I'm sorry," Narina said to her daughter. "I shouldn't have said that. I'll never force you to marry someone you don't want to be with. Alliances be damned."

Catia smiled and put her arm around Narina's waist, cuddling her tightly. The hug was returned and the queen closed her eyes, feeling great joy in the embrace and fearing that, in just a couple of years, her little daughter might be too big for such open shows of emotion.

Gods, if she took after her father, Catia would soon be taller than any of the women in Dun Breatann, and then the gossips really would have something to talk about.

"You're the queen," Catia said. "If you want to marry...someone else, you can. You can do anything you like."

"That's exactly what Coroticus thought," Narina sighed. "And look where it got him. No, I'm afraid the needs of Alt Clota must come before anything else. That's what it means to be queen, and that's why I must marry a man who'll bring us stability and power."

"It's not fair," the princess replied softly, gazing fixedly, as if in a daydream, at the shining river. "Women should be just as free as men, to choose whoever they'd like to be with."

"Oh, trust me," Narina said caustically. "Some women do."

* * *

Ria held Bellicus's hand in hers as they strolled around the walkway on top of Dun Breatann's western wall. Although it was situated much lower down on the rock than the main living area on top of the eastern peak, their walk was a pleasant one, as this side of the fortress afforded fine views all along the Clota for miles, right down to Graenag on the opposite bank. The cries of gulls searching for mussels on the shore, which they would lift up high then smash open by dropping them again, carried on the breeze along with the scents of spring flowers, and woodsmoke from a fire somewhere on the other side of the river.

"By Sulis, it's lovely here," Ria said, and she was positively glowing as she dragged Bellicus along, beaming from ear to ear and gazing about her at everything as Cai, glad to have his master back, walked close by his heels.

"Aye, just now it is," the druid agreed, smiling at his companion's girlish enthusiasm. "But it's not quite as nice in winter. Gods, even in summer it's pissing with rain as often as it is sunny."

"Well it's sunny now," Ria replied, stopping to watch in wonder as a great black bird soared overhead, riding the air currents before calling raucously then sailing out of sight around the peak. "A raven?"

"Uchaf," the druid said. "That's his name."

"He's yours?"

Bellicus shook his head. "No, just a friend. I taught him to speak."

"Really?" the druidess appeared delighted by this news and Bellicus shrugged.

"Well, he can say a few words—"

"Curse words no doubt," Ria asked tartly but wandered ahead before Bellicus could answer. He walked after her, basking in the warm sun and the other sensations that assailed him. By Lug, it felt so good to be here, home again, and with Ria, after his captivity in Dunnottar.

That thought reminded him of Duro and his smile faded, but only for a moment as the druidess came back to him and, looking around to make sure they were alone, pulled him down onto the grass so she could kiss him.

As their lips met, Bellicus felt the familiar stirring in his loins which intensified maddeningly as Ria's hand moved down to touch him there through his cloak.

Cai, perhaps a little jealous, licked the druid's face, and, laughing, he shoved the dog away.

"Take that off," Ria urged between kisses. "It's much too warm a day for a heavy cloak."

The druid felt like a young man, enjoying a woman's touch for the first time and, as Ria slipped her hand inside his breeches he moaned and kissed her harder, allowing her to do whatever she pleased, caring little that a guard might come patrolling along that section of wall at any moment.

When they were finished they looked out on the view together and Bellicus wondered how the next few days would go. Would Drest's great army storm the walls and take Dun Breatann for the first time in its known history? Or would the gods come to Alt Clota's aid once again, and lift the siege somehow, allowing Bellicus and Ria to, perhaps, create a child together?

He smiled and shook his head, thinking ruefully how his life was never dull.

"Why's that section of the wall higher than the rest?"

Bellicus turned to where the druidess was pointing. "Oh, that. If you look down" – they walked the short distance to the area Ria had noticed, stopping just beside it and peering over towards the shore below – "you can see the rock isn't quite as steep here. A good climber could make it up, and into the fortress so" – he placed a hand on the wall, which was taller than he was at just at this one, short section – "this makes sure it doesn't happen again."

"It's happened before?"

"Aye, some enemy warriors, Dalriadans, once made it up and caused a lot of trouble before they were stopped."[2] His eyes traced the route the climbers must have taken and there was admiration in his voice when he went on. "They were all cut down eventually but when we figured out how they'd got in, this higher wall was erected. Gods, they must have been

---

[2] See the novelette, "Over The Wall".

like spiders. I wish I'd have seen them climbing up the rock. What a feat!"

Ria stared down and then turned back to Bellicus, putting her arm inside his as he led her back towards the centre of the fortress again, Cai happily loping ahead of them. "In Dunnottar we have a rope that leads down to the water. Men and goods can be hauled up or down."

"There's nothing like that here," the druid said. "The only way in or out, generally, is through the main gates. Well," he smiled, a little sadly. "There's the secret tunnel, but that will need to be filled in now I suppose, since it's no longer a secret."

"What do you think Queen Narina will do about Drest?" Ria asked as they came once more to the main stairway leading up to the twin peaks. "Can you see a way out of this?"

Bellicus squeezed her hand. "I don't know. It feels like I've exchanged one prison for another. Drest was your king – you advised him for years. What would your advice be now for Narina?"

As they began to climb, the druidess's expression was solemn. "Pray to the gods," she replied, and Bellicus, worryingly, could think of nothing better.

CHAPTER TWENTY

Gavo was standing outside the great hall when Bellicus and Ria returned to main living area of the fortress. He nodded politely, if not exactly warmly, to the druidess and then jerked his head sideways.

"Can I have a word with you, Bel?"

"Of course. Ria, you could head back to my house if you like. Duro might be there and he'll probably appreciate help preparing our evening meal."

The young woman arched her brow as if she didn't believe him, but murmured agreement then reached up on tiptoes to kiss him on the cheek. Even so, she was still far too small and he had to lean down awkwardly, not used to these public displays of affection that Ria seemed intent on performing so often.

"Should I take Cai?" she asked, but the druid shook his head. The dog rarely left his side, and even less so in the hours since they'd returned to Dun Breatann.

Ria walked away, pouting at Cai, who merely eyed her balefully, and Bellicus looked at the bluff guard captain, expecting to see amusement in the older man's eyes. Instead, Gavo's demeanour was cool, perhaps even bordering on cold, but he turned away and walked over to the wall which afforded views of the land to the north-west, including Alt Clota's shipyards which were unusually quiet just now, thanks to the Picts' siege. Only the half-built hull of a medium-sized fishing vessel lay out in the sun, abandoned until the workers could safely return and finish it off.

"What's wrong?" Bellicus asked, a little irritated by his old friend's behaviour since he'd returned. "Is this about that tunnel? Look, I'm sorry, we were running for our lives and Duro..." He shook his head as if admonishing himself. "Ach, I can't blame him. *I* wanted to escape. To rescue my friends and see my home again..."

"It's nothing to do with that," Gavo interrupted, shaking his head and sighing. "I assume you had your reasons for keeping it secret from us, and they made sense to you at the time. And perhaps you were right." His tone became less harsh and he met the druid's stony gaze at last. "You've generally guided us well over the years, Bel. But, like you said in the hall earlier, we can talk about that later, if you want. For now…"

The captain turned to gaze out at the rolling fields of Alt Clota, topped in the distance by the towering, snow-topped peak of Ben Laomainn and Bellicus wondered at his apparent reticence. In matters of war, or tactics, or even politics, Gavo was as forthright a man as he'd ever known. If he had something to say, he would normally just say it.

"Spit it out, man," the druid said, frowning. "We're friends, aren't we? That ship down there will be built by the time we're done here if you don't get on with it."

"It's about the queen," Gavo muttered, and then he lapsed into silence again as his eyes swept the realm he was sworn to protect.

Bellicus waited, understanding now why Gavo was so reluctant to speak. This was to be no mere discussion on Narina's running of Dun Breatann or anything as…mundane, as that. There was something deeper behind this, and the druid allowed the captain time to marshal his thoughts. In truth, he wasn't sure he wanted to hear what Gavo had to say—they had enough trouble to deal with thanks to Drest, without adding to it.

"She's planning to wed Cunedda's son."

The words were so unexpected that Bellicus had to think about them for a long moment before the full implications sank in. He was silent too now, trying to make sense of his emotions.

"I don't know how…you and Narina really feel about one another," Gavo said awkwardly, as if he'd rather be somewhere else, talking about fighting or battle strategy, but he forged on regardless. "And it's none of my business, really. But" – he looked at the druid seriously, and he seemed to be playing the part of the father Bellicus had never known – "I thought that, after Coroticus died, you and the queen had grown close."

"We never—"

Again, Gavo broke in before the druid's defensive retort could be completed.

"As I say, that's none of my business, and I didn't mean to imply any impropriety, Bel. You were a loyal friend to Coroticus, and no blame can be laid at your door for what happened. But…I came to believe you and Narina would end up together. It seemed like the natural way of things, especially with Catia."

They stared at one another and Bellicus remembered the day the massive bear had attacked their hunting party. Gavo had watched as the terrified princess cried to her father for help—only the girl hadn't been looking at Coroticus, she'd wanted Bellicus.

That had been mentioned once, with the druid denying any knowledge of why Catia should have acted as she did, putting it down as a reaction to her terror, and Gavo had let it go. But Bellicus knew the captain had suspected the truth ever since.

It seemed strangely idealistic, sweet almost, to hear him now talking about Alt Clota's queen and druid forming a happy family together with their daughter.

Had Bellicus wanted that too? Certainly, when Coroticus was alive, the thought never crossed his mind. Yet, when Catia was abducted by the Saxons, and Narina told Bellicus he was really the girl's father, it had set his feelings on a strange, new path which he wasn't really equipped to deal with, despite all his years of druid training. Even now, he wasn't sure what he wanted from life, and his recent reacquaintance with Ria merely served to confuse him even further.

The very thought of the beautiful young druidess made him excited, as if being with her made him feel somehow more alive. When he was with Ria he felt free, even when they were besieged within this fortress. Her presence made the future appear less bleak.

Yet he was in his late twenties now—most men his age would be married and Narina was certainly a woman whose company he enjoyed.

He wasn't most men, though. He was a druid, and druids were not bound by the usual societal conventions. Qunavo came to mind instantly. The old man had been Bellicus's tutor for much of his years on the isle of Iova. Qunavo had never married, as far as Bel knew, but he was never short of a bed-mate. Women were always happy to spend their nights with him, and he'd fathered numerous children which he rarely bothered to acknowledge.

No-one batted an eyelid at his behaviour. The women were glad to have babies fathered by one who was close to the gods after all—Qunavo never forced himself on anyone. And the people of Iova, and Pictland as a whole, were used to powerful men fathering bastards. They did not expect the druid to settle down and live a comfortable, cosy life—that would have been a restriction of his powers, of his ability to do the gods work. Druids were *supposed* to spread their knowledge and influence amongst the people.

"Why Cunedda's son?" Bellicus finally asked, forcing himself to focus on Gavo's statement as his thoughts threatened to spin-off on any number of tangents. "Why Ysfael?"

The captain shrugged. "To solidify our new alliance with the Votadini of course. He seems a decent man, if a touch arrogant. Narina could have picked a worse husband."

They lapsed into silence again and Bellicus considered the benefits of such a union. It seemed a strange choice, all things considered, but what should he do about it? He could just imagine her reaction if he went to her now and advised her to reconsider the marriage. Ria's presence by his side had certainly made things more awkward, as if they hadn't been confused enough already.

"If she's just after an alliance, one of the Dalriadans would be more suitable. The Votadini's star is fading, I think." Bellicus rubbed a hand across his stubbled head and shrugged. "She's the queen though. It's up to her to do what she thinks best for Alt Clota."

"Agreed," Gavo rumbled, clapping Bellicus on the arm. "I just wanted to let you know how things stood, so it doesn't come as a surprise to you when Narina mentions it. I don't suppose any plans will be laid for the wedding until this whole thing with Drest is sorted."

"That's a good point," the druid said with a wry smile. "If Drest storms the walls and kills us all, none of this will matter."

"Maybe we should use your tunnel," Gavo suggested. "To sneak Narina and Catia out. Gods, we could all sneak out and…" He trailed off, realising how ridiculous his idea was. Just surrender Dun Breatann, and by extension, all of Alt Clota?

"We can't abandon our home," Bellicus said, shaking his head. "And taking Narina and the princess to safety would only make the people think her a coward. No, she has to stay here and lead from the front. Besides, she'd never agree to it, she's much too strong a leader."

Gavo's shoulders appeared to slump, as if the stress of their situation was finally proving too much of a burden to bear, and now it was the druid's turn to act the wise father figure, despite being twelve years the captain's junior.

"Listen to me," Bellicus commanded, pointing to the sword that hung from a baldric on Gavo's left side. "As long as you have that, there is hope. This fortress has never fallen to a besieging army and, no matter how large Drest's army is – they're outside, and breaking in will prove harder than they realise. Our defences are strong, our garrison well drilled.

Until that Pictish bastard is standing in the hall there," he pointed to the great building next to them, "Dun Breatann is ours. Have faith, old friend. The gods have not forsaken us just yet."

With that, the druid walked away, glad to have rekindled the fire in Gavo's eyes but feeling weak himself now, and entirely unsure how he felt about Narina marrying again. He didn't want to think about it right then though – recent weeks had taken a toll on his body and he felt dizzy and nauseous and knew he should rest, so he headed straight for his house.

When he went inside he expected it to be cool for the thatched roof kept out the sun's warming rays very efficiently, but Duro was hard at work preparing what looked like a meat broth that would feed them for the next day or two. As a result, the house was humid, and smoky from the cooking fire, but the delicious smell was enough to make anyone's mouth water.

The centurion smiled distractedly as the druid came in, but Ria, sorting through her stores of herbs and spices and other ingredients, was more welcoming. She came across and took his hand, but, seeing the fatigue on his face, shook her head and ordered him to lie down for a rest. Since that had been his intention all along, he allowed her to shepherd him over to the sleeping pallet without argument, then lay down, Cai curling up on the floor next to him which drew a laugh from the druidess.

"Does that silly big lump ever leave your side?"

Bellicus's hand reached out, despite his closed eyes, and stroked Cai's back. "Not if he can help it. He's my protector."

"I thought that was Duro's job," she said, winking at the centurion who snorted derisively but didn't otherwise reply.

"Aye, Duro and Cai look after me," Bellicus agreed.

"Well, you can get some sleep for a time," Ria said firmly. "And I'll help those two take care of you. If it's alright for me to go about the fortress without an escort, I'll see if I can get some more herbs and such from the kitchens?"

Bellicus wasn't sure how pleased Narina would be if she saw Ria wandering around Dun Breatann on her own, given the fact she'd been part of the Pictish king's household just a few days ago, but he was too tired to care so merely grunted assent.

"Do you want to come a walk with me?" the druidess said, leaning down and eyeing Cai. To everyone's surprise, the dog growled. "Maybe not then," Ria said, standing up and backing away somewhat nervously

"Hey! That's enough," Bellicus said, wagging an admonishing finger at Cai who merely stared at Ria, not even having the grace to look upset by his scolding.

"I think your dog's jealous of the time I'm spending with you, Bel," Ria laughed, and the druid could only apologise and scold Cai again.

"Before you go," Duro said, as Ria opened the door, letting sunlight in and cooking smoke out. "Can I borrow that knife of yours? The one with the white handle? Drest took mine and I need something to cut this meat with."

Ria stopped in the doorway, then looked down at her belt. "Oh," she said, touching the place where it would usually be. "I must have lost it somewhere. Shit! I've had that knife for years, it was a lovely piece of work. I'm sorry, centurion."

"Never mind," Duro said, waving her away. "There must be something lying around in here that'll do the job. You go and collect whatever you need from the stores. Leave the door open." She disappeared into the sunshine as Duro called, loudly so she'd hear him. "And get some parsley if there's any!"

* * *

The blades clattered together with a crack that seemed to carry all across Alt Clota and Catia grunted, drawing her sword back, ready to defend herself once again. She was sweating a lot, considering she was young and very fit, but her opponent didn't stop to let her wipe her brow or catch a breath, coming in hard again, probing for an opening.

The weapons might be wooden, but Ria watched with interest, knowing from personal experience just how much even a practice sword could hurt.

Catia was nimble, and batted aside the older boy's attacks, but her own strikes were coming with less frequency now as her stamina waned and she was forced to spend more time defending. She was doing well though, as Ria judged there was at least a couple of years between the sparring children, and the boy was tall and rangy for his age.

He was also over-confident however and, sensing victory was near, began to swipe at the princess with more ferocity and less control, seeking to batter her into submission. He too was perspiring freely but his desire to end the contest as quickly as possible made him reckless.

Catia stumbled backwards, trying to maintain the gap between them and the boy grinned savagely, seeing the girl wince with every attack she parried. To his surprise, she suddenly halted her backwards motion and lunged forward, grasping his sword arm with both hands, her own short blade still firmly grasped between her thumb and first finger. Then she kicked him as hard as she could in the shin.

It wasn't a powerful blow, certainly not one that would do any damage, especially given the soft shoes Catia was wearing, but it was enough to sting and make the boy cry out, thrown off balance. Sweeping her wooden sword up, she knocked the boy's aside and thrust the point of her blade at his stomach, stopping and holding it just before it dug in and really hurt.

"Yield," the princess said, the skin on her face glistening with sweat, eyes sparkling with the joy of a victory well won.

Frustration and disappointment, perhaps even shame at being bested by a much smaller opponent, flashed across the lad's face, but he held his temper in check and, at last, grinned and cried out, "All right, all right. I yield!"

"Yes!" Catia's screech of delight brought amused looks from many of the people working or just standing around Dun Breatann gossiping and Ria guessed this must be the first time she'd ever beaten the boy.

"Well done, princess," a lean warrior said, nodding but not smiling as he walked into the fighting circle and clapped both young fighters on their shoulders. "You too, Cadhan. You would have won if you'd just taken your time, like I keep telling you. Impatience is your biggest weakness. Off you go now, son, and be about your chores."

The man took the practice swords from the youngsters and placed them on a rack beside a nearby building before following the boy as he jogged down towards the hall.

Catia watched them go, looking rather disappointed until the warrior glanced back over his shoulder, smiling, and said, "You're getting better, princess. We'll move onto new skills tomorrow. I think you're ready."

Ria could see how much his gentle praise meant to the girl, who sat down on the grass, tired but elated. Very soon, Catia sensed she was being watched and her eyes came up, meeting the druidess's gaze confidently. Ria went over and took a place on the grass next to her, without asking permission.

"Hello."

Catia narrowed her eyes and remained silent for a moment, before saying, "You're the Pictish woman."

The Pictish woman. Ria could tell by the way it was said that the girl had heard someone else saying that, and it hadn't been in a pleasant, friendly way. Her mouth twitched. No doubt Queen Narina had been complaining about the druidess's presence here in the fortress. Still, child or not, Catia was a princess and should have better manners.

"I'm the Pictish druidess," Ria said. "The one who saved your friends, Bellicus and Duro."

Catia didn't seem to notice the rebuke within the woman's cold tone.

"What do you want?"

"You're rather a rude child," Ria said, bringing only a shrug from Catia.

"So my mother tells me."

"I watched you sparring with the boy," the druidess told her, moving the conversation on from its impasse. "You did well, but you need to learn how to absorb attacks better. Let them slide off your blade, rather than trying to hold them back all the time. Especially when the opponent is bigger and stronger."

The princess eyed her thoughtfully. The Pictish woman had clear skin, smooth, dark hair and lips that seemed like they'd part in a winning smile at any moment. It was obvious why Bellicus had taken up with her, and similarly obvious why her mother the queen wasn't greatly enamoured with her presence here.

Despite believing Narina's judgement of the druidess was clouded by jealousy, Catia couldn't help but take her mother's side which meant that, naturally, she should not be friends with Ria.

"What makes you such an expert in sword fighting?" the girl asked, dismissively. "You're not much bigger than me, even if you are a lot older."

"If you think size matters so much, you've either had a terrible teacher, or you're too dense to take in his lessons, girl."

Catia bridled at that, her eyes flashing angrily, the excitement of her victory still coursing through her and, perhaps, giving her confidence she might not have usually felt. Certainly, she was usually a friendly, polite girl with no arrogance or great sense of entitlement despite her lofty position within Damnonii society.

"Why don't you find out how bad my teacher is for yourself?" she spat, hurrying across to the rack with the practice swords. She selected the one she always used for herself, then hesitated, looking at the others stacked there, before choosing another and walking back to hand it to the druidess.

Ria took the proffered weapon, and grudgingly admitted to herself that Catia had at least been fair in selecting this one. Although it was adult sized and slightly longer than the one the princess wielded it was not one of the double-weighted ones that Ria had noted on the rack.

The Pictish woman rose to her feet, and an older, more experienced opponent might have noticed the grace with which she moved, expecting that to carry into her swordplay. Catia merely saw a woman she knew her mother didn't like. A woman who, just a few days before, had been part of the army that was now besieging Dun Breatann. Yet she was wandering about the fortress as if she belonged there, and even had the temerity to advise the princess on her fighting technique, just after she'd finally beaten Cadhan!

Without another word, Catia took up an attacking stance and moved towards Ria, who brought up her own wooden sword and prepared to meet the oncoming threat. The princess was young and foolhardy and over-confident from her earlier victory, but she was also starting to think this might not have been the best idea. It was too late to back out now though.

Rather than attacking with a flurry of lunges and slashes as she'd planned just a few moments earlier when her blood was up, Catia instead started the bout patiently, probing and searching for an obvious weakness in Ria's posture or technique. Unfortunately, there appeared to be none.

Bellicus had sometimes told Catia about his younger days learning to be a druid. She knew his tutor, Qunavo, had taught him how to use a sword, at least before his skill outstripped the old man's. Bel had never mentioned Ria learning how to fight. The way she stepped around the fighting circle, confident and sure, suggested the Pictish woman had more than a passing knowledge of this type of combat, however.

"Hurry up then, child. You wanted to teach me a lesson, so get on with it."

As Ria finished speaking, she suddenly darted forward. Catia was staring into her opponent's eyes, but the move was not foreshadowed there at all and, before she could react, the druidess's sword slapped her on the outside of the thigh.

The blow hurt but Catia gritted her teeth and came forward again, more warily this time. Part of her was wishing her mother, or anyone, would come and stop the contest, but that thought made her feel ashamed. Ria would not badly injure her she was sure, but defeat at the outsider's hands would be both painful and embarrassing. She'd been so happy when she beat Cadhan too! Why had this bitch come along to ruin everything?

Ria was clearly enjoying herself, but her expression changed from one of cold amusement to jocularity, surprising Catia. And then a shout came from behind them, "Go on, Princess! Show her how we fight in Dun Breatann!" and the girl realised what was happening. She didn't turn, fearful of another strike from her rival's sword, but she knew an audience had formed. Whether it was large or small made no difference – the druidess was now playing the part of a friendly sparring partner.

Relief flooded through her and she launched a fast, but short attack, wondering at her thoughts. Did she really fear Ria would harm her before there was an audience to witness their bout?

She knocked aside the druidess's blade and kicked out, but Ria was too fast and, laughing as if this was all a gloriously fun way to spend a few moments, she grabbed the princess's arm, twisting it around her back and placing the dull blade of the practice sword against the girl's throat.

"Yield, you silly little brat." The words were harsh, but Catia could see Ria's face out of the corner of her eye and the woman's smile was wide and utterly convincing.

"Bellicus will never love you," the princess whispered, hoping her voice would not betray the humiliation she felt.

"He already does," Ria replied, still grinning widely and speaking in a low voice. "So your mother can forget him. I've won." With that, she let go of the child and tossed the wooden sword onto the grass before bowing gracefully towards Catia and walking away towards the watching audience. "Your princess fights well. I'm impressed." She squeezed one of the watching soldiers on the bicep as she passed him, flashing that crooked smile. "If you're all as tough as her, Drest will find it more difficult than he expects to take this fortress!"

To Catia's bemusement, the warrior's face lit up, like a happy puppy, and it seemed everyone thought the Pictish druidess was wonderful. She even noticed Gavo, standing at the door of the great hall, a look of admiration on his face as Ria approached him.

"Well done, Princess!"

"You almost had her."

The shouts of consolation came from the crowd now and Catia was forced to put on a smile of her own. She waved to the people, who finally started to disperse and be back about their business as she took the practise swords and placed them safely, neatly, into their rack again as her tutor, Beda, had taught. Feeling confused and a little numb inside, not sure what to make of the past few minutes' events, she started to walk up the slope towards her home. When she came to the summit of the eastern peak she wanted nothing more than to lie down on her bed and try to make sense of everything that was happening.

Someone was standing at the door of the house though, beside the two guards who were always stationed there, and she felt a stab of irritation for the man was apparently waiting for her return. Hadn't she had enough dealings with adults for one day?

Forcing herself to calm down, and feeling yet more shame at her reaction to his presence, she smiled and walked to meet her visitor. The man deserved her time and more, for he'd saved her life without care for his own, and, as she came closer, she could see he looked just as apprehensive as she did. He also appeared thin and malnourished and her heart went out to him.

"Hello, Duro," she said. "It's good to see you again."

"You too, Catia," the centurion replied, smiling broadly as the girl hugged him. "Can I talk with you for a little while?" They had spent a lot of time together, along with Bellicus, on the long road back from the Hanging Stones when she'd been abducted by the Saxons but, still, the princess wanted nothing more than to be left alone for a little while.

"I saw you fighting Ria."

At once, Catia's face fell.

"Do you like her?" he asked.

The girl looked at him warily. She hadn't expected a question like that, but she was always honest and saw no reason not to tell the centurion the truth now.

"No," she said viciously. Some adults would have said *petulantly*, but Duro merely waited, expression neutral, until she went on. "The woman is vain, and I'm sure she'd have hurt me with the wooden sword if an audience hadn't formed around us."

"What did she say to you?" Duro asked. "At the end?"

Catia had to think back, not sure which particular part of the conversation he was asking about. When it came to her, a sense of loyalty to Queen Narina stopped her from telling him. How could she admit that Ria knew her mother wanted Bellicus and was jealous of the Pictish druidess's hold over him?

"Be honest with me, please," Duro said gently. "I saw your face when she was speaking to you."

As she looked at him, all the stress and upset of her recent life seemed to crowd in upon her and her face screwed up as she tried desperately not to cry in front of Duro and the guards. At last, she mastered herself, or at least managed to suppress her emotions, and then, leading the centurion around the summit to a quiet spot overlooking the Clota, night began to fall and she told him everything.

CHAPTER TWENTY-ONE

"Ow! Bastard!"

The warrior-woman, Aife, shook her head and rolled her eyes at the man leading their party through the stifling, dark tunnel. "I told you to wear at least a tunic, since we had no idea what we'd be coming into here. But no…You had to show how manly you are by travelling naked."

"Shut your mouth, woman," Brude mac Uradech hissed, still rubbing at the shallow cut on the end of his manhood. "You should be naked too. We all should – that's the way a real warrior fights."

Aife snorted. "And have all these dirty beggars crawling along at the back of my bare arse? I don't think so. One of them would end up losing their fingers. And I mean I'd cut them off, before anyone makes any smart remarks."

The men in the tunnel behind them, twenty of them, might have made a joke but they knew better than to anger Aife. She was a match for most of the men in Drest's army in aggression and her tongue was sharper than any. Her decision to wear a woollen, knee-length tunic, not to mention a coat of mail, had been proved sensible, but Brude was moving on again, leading them ever closer to their goal: Dun Breatann's interior.

When Bellicus, Duro and Ria had disappeared at the end of the previous day's chase, it seemed as if the earth had simply swallowed them whole. No trace of where they'd gone could be seen, until Brude had found Ria's white-handled knife sticking out of the grass and, on closer inspection of that area, the trapdoor leading down into this tunnel was discovered.

This had been Qunavo's plan all along, ever since the gods had dropped Bellicus and Duro into the Picts' laps. Qunavo had heard rumours of a secret tunnel leading directly into the apparently impregnable fortress of Dun Breatann, and he had an idea of where the entrance must be, but no-one had ever been able to find it.

Everything Bellicus and his centurion friend had been subjected to in Dunnottar's dungeons was designed to lead to this point: the torture, the mutilation of Duro's hand and the fear it would inspire in him at the thought of recapture, and the chase by the invading Pictish warriors in this general area.

Bellicus had been manipulated by his old tutor rather easier than Qunavo expected. Ria must have played her part as the besotted, beautiful young maiden very convincingly.

Now, this group of Pictish warriors led by Brude mac Uradech and Aife found itself almost within the walls of Alt Clota's legendary fortress. When they made it into Dun Breatann they were to move as silently as possible, killing any sentries before lighting a torch on the summit to signal their successful ingress into the fortress, and then opening the gates to the rest of Drest's army.

Brude wished he had worn a damn tunic now, for the end of his cock was stinging like crazy where it had scraped on the fallen rocks they'd been forced to climb over, but he wasn't about to admit that to Aife. He liked her, but she was a full head taller than him and he already felt like the men saw her as the real leader of their group. He'd never admit she was right, although it did seem foolish to be wandering along in the gloom without a stitch on now – he could have worn something and discarded it before they left the tunnel to start the attack after all.

Oh well. The pain between his legs would be a small price to pay for the success of this night's work – if a small cut in his foreskin was the only injury he suffered before Dun Breatann fell it would be a miracle. Gods, even if his cock fell off it would be worth the fame and glory he'd earn for being the one to open the gates to Drest! Although he fervently hoped that wouldn't happen, for there were many women within Dun Breatann and he hoped to make at least one of them his slave.

"Hold the lamp up, man," Aife scolded from close behind. "And stop daydreaming – we can hardly see where we're going here."

"Are you stupid?" Brude demanded. "It's hard to get lost within a tunnel that only goes in a straight line!"

"We don't want to trip over any more of this rubble," the woman replied, kicking aside a stone, and the rest of the warband muttered agreement. Although most of the way had been smooth and only the tallest of them had had to crouch to avoid hitting their heads on the ceiling, there were places where sections of the walls had fallen in, making the footing treacherous. Not forgetting the places where they'd had to crawl on their bellies through narrow openings, scraping their torsos, arms, legs and everything else. The thought of the entire tunnel, with the monolithic weight of Dun Breatann, collapsing on them had also never been far from their minds. All these trials were only compounded by the darkness, so Brude raised his arm, allowing the light from his oil lamp to cast welcome, flickering shadows ahead of them.

One other man carried a lamp, but he was in the middle of the group. Brude did not envy those at the rear of the column, with the inky darkness behind them. It was easy to allow your imagination to run wild in a place like this, seeing shapes moving in the corner of your eye, or hearing footsteps or whispered voices behind you when you knew no-one could possibly be there.

Although he feared a fight with no mortal man or woman, Brude knew the dark places of the earth harboured things that couldn't be harmed with a sword or hammer.

He wasn't the only one in the party who was thinking of such things.

"This reminds me of the tale of the Hairy Hand," someone behind him muttered fearfully. "Remember? The fairy tunnels that were made for them by the gigantic hand? A flute player went into the ones at Smoo Cave with his dog, and the dog came back out with all its hair torn off, but the flute player was never seen again and his music can still be heard sometimes when—"

"That's enough," Aife growled, turning to glare at the storyteller. "We've enough to concentrate on, without you making us think about spirits and demons and giant hairy hands chasing us."

The man shrugged petulantly and they continued moving in silence, the sense of claustrophobia growing within them with every passing moment.

Eventually, after they'd been walking and crawling for what seemed like hours, there was a distinct change in the air. A cool breeze came from the gloom ahead, carrying with it the unmistakable scent of water and, most welcomingly, fresh air.

"We're nearly there," Brude said, halting and turning to look at his followers. They were all deadly fighters – skilled with their chosen weapons and veterans of dozens of battles. They had walked with death all their lives and welcomed this opportunity to carry Damnonii heads back to their homes in Pictland. Brude didn't need to give them a speech. They knew their jobs.

He nodded, smiling grimly, and, loosening his sword within its sheath, moved forward again, a little slower now, more warily, for they really had no idea where this tunnel would bring them out. The fact it was a secret, even to the men and women of Alt Clota apart from the druid, Bellicus, suggested the entrance inside the fortress was well hidden, but, even so, Brude was wary.

He knew the Damnonii druid to some extent, having been one of the men guarding King Drest during his meetings in the cell with Bellicus. The thought of the giant, shaven-headed warrior being on the other side of the tunnel when the Pictish warband came through was not a particularly pleasant one. There were easier foes to face, Brude thought, and, although it would bring a man great renown to take down the fabled Bellicus, the most important thing right now was not personal glory, it was opening the gates to the rest of Drest's army.

"Wait." The line halted behind him again as they appeared to have reached a dead end.

"Did we miss a doorway or something?" Aife asked, looking around in confusion before fastening an accusatory stare on Brude. "So much for not getting lost in a straight tunnel."

He didn't bother to reply but crouched down and held his oil lamp close to the wall that barred their way, then he grinned and ran his hands across the stones. Dust fell away from the joins and he rose to his feet, inspecting the blocks closely until, near the top, he reached out and worked one of them free.

"This seems far too easy," Aife muttered sceptically as Brude handed her the lamp and removed more stones to reveal a gaping hole that would allow them to pass through one at a time into…what? The darkness in the chamber beyond was complete, so she subsided into silence, allowing her captain time to finish his task.

When the hole was big enough Brude took the oil lamp back and held it out into the room ahead.

"Oh, shit," he said, shoulders slumping, and Aife, along with the others, crowded forward to try and see what lay before them.

The light was too dim to make everything out properly, and the man with the second lamp passed it ahead, illuminating the black chamber on the other side of the false wall. Even with the doubled illumination it took them all some moments to look around and understand what they were seeing.

"This must be the well," Aife said, understanding Brude's disappointed oath.

"Indeed," he replied, but he'd had a few seconds longer to examine this new chamber and stepped forward now, holding the lamp out further. The water was unfathomably deep, doubtless being fed from an underground source far, far below. "You still glad you wore armour?" he said, smiling ruefully back at Aife.

She gazed down, imagining her death if she was to fall in. Not the strongest of swimmers anyway, the weight of the chain mail would drag her down and…She shuddered and turned her eyes back to the smooth, damp walls around the water.

"There's a ledge," one of the men said, pointing to the left, and Brude nodded, tracing the path of the ledge all the way around to an even darker section of the chamber on the other side of the water. Their lights did not penetrate that far.

"And there's the way out," he said. "That must be where the people come to collect water. And where we get out of here."

"Who's going first?" someone asked, and there was fear in the voice. Understandable, Brude thought. These warriors had been hand-picked for their fighting prowess and penchant for violence, not for their skills as swimmers.

"I'll go," Brude said. He knew how to swim, and the opportunity to prove his bravery while Aife remained silent was too good to pass up. He handed the lamp to the young woman again and, sucking in a deep breath to calm his nerves, inched his way forward, one slow step at a time, hands questing for something to hold onto.

"There's a rope," he said with relief, tugging it to make sure it was secure. It was. The druid must have kept it maintained against the damp. "Come on," he urged. "Follow me, one at a time so the rope isn't overburdened."

"What about the lamps?"

"Leave them there. We'll need their light to help us reach the other side, but not once we're out of here."

"What if there's a locked gate ahead?" Aife persisted. "Or some other obstruction we need to see to get past?"

"Then someone will have to come back for a lamp," Brude hissed, irritably. "Unless you want to try and climb around here, holding onto the rope with only one hand."

And so they began to make their way around the wall, palms slick with sweat despite the cold from the deep, stagnant water beside them and their nakedness, until they were all on the other side, grinning at one another in the faint light.

Brude went on alone into the dark tunnel, sword now drawn although its blade reflected no light for it had been smeared with soot, as had all of their weapons. Moments later he came back to them and his face was set and deadly serious.

"There's a gate, but it was easy to unlock."

"Never mind the gate," one of the men asked. "What's on the other side of it?"

"Glory," Brude replied with a lupine grin. "Draw your weapons. There's torches, braziers and sentries on guard, but only a handful as far as I could tell. Everyone else is tucked up in their beds. Aife?"

"I know what to do," she said, the whites of her eyes seeming strangely bright in the darkness. Brude would head up to the summit and signal Drest on the plain below with a lighted torch, while it would be Aife's job to lead the men down the main staircase, dispatching any who got in their way, and then open the gates for their compatriots outside.

"Within the next hour," Brude said. "There'll be dozens of Damnonii dead, their women and wealth will be ours, and Dun Breatann will belong to the Picts. Let's move, and may the gods of war be with us."

With that, he led them out of the tunnel and into the benighted fortress.

CHAPTER TWENTY-TWO

King Drest paced backwards and forwards, fidgeting with his fingertips, touching the pommel of his sword, and occasionally glancing up at the walls of Dun Breatann before muttering to himself. This had been going on for the past couple of hours and it was beginning to wear on the warriors around him, although they didn't say anything. Who told a king how to act after all?

The one man apparently not worried at all was the old druid, Qunavo, who stroked his long white beard and watched Drest's wanderings with some amusement.

"They should have been inside by now," the king growled. Again.

"Give them time," Qunavo said, blue eyes appearing lighter than ever in the pale moonlight. "They must move carefully to avoid being detected."

"Are the men ready to move, Lutrin?" the king demanded, ignoring the druid's reassurances.

The tall, one-eyed guard captain stifled a groan but Qunavo could hear the irritation in the man's voice as he replied. "Aye, lord. As soon as the gates are open, we'll be through them. Don't worry."

It was essentially the same response he'd given Drest the last couple of times the king had asked the question since night fell. By the gods, everyone could see the Pictish soldiers standing ready to move, despite the gloom.

Ria had often told Qunavo that she feared Drest was too weak to rule a united nation of kingdoms, and his anxious behaviour tonight lent weight to her arguments. But Drest was the man in charge for now, and replacing him would set back Qunavo's plans too much so, here they were.

"Fill it," Qunavo commanded, holding his empty wine cup in the air for a servant to fill. Although the rest of the warband stood, or crouched on their haunches, alert and ready to move, the druid sat on a folding camp chair, with his feet on another, rather enjoying the evening. His drink was refilled and the servant—a slave-girl in fact, taken during a raid on a southern land the previous summer—faded back into the shadows.

He sipped the wine, enjoying the powerful scent and slightly dry flavour, and stared at the fortress they had besieged. The air was still and calm and the scent of woodsmoke drifted down from the homes on the great rock above, while the barking of a dog could be heard every now and again. Things were peaceful just now, but tonight Dun Breatann would fall and Drest would take control of all Queen Narina's lands. That would leave only Dalriadan and Votadini territory to be taken and, with the wealth that Alt Clota's trading networks and mines would bring, soon the dream of uniting all the tribes north of Antoninus's Wall would become a reality.

Qunavo hoped that success would spur Drest, fire his ambition and see their army pushing even further south, to smash the Selgovae and, eventually, who knew where it would lead? His one-time protégé, Bellicus, had cautioned them against the threat of the warlord, Hengist, but they would deal with the Saxons when the time was right.

First, Qunavo wanted control of all the northern tribes, but not merely for the wealth and power it would bring – his ultimate aim was to destroy Christianity and bring the Old Ways back to the prominence they deserved. Surely then his brother druids would have to bestow on him the title he'd secretly coveted for years: Merlin.

For the moment, however, Dun Breatann's capture, and the subjugation of its people, was a vital stepping-stone for the Pictish druid's plans.

"Lord King!"

Lutrin was gazing up at the towering rock ahead of them, its massive bulk seeming like a gaping void against the lighter night sky behind it, and Drest spun at the guard captain's voice.

"They've done it!"

High above them, near the top of the flatter of the twin peaks, a single torch could be seen, its orange flame a mere ember in the night. This was the signal Drest had been waiting so anxiously for all evening.

"Prepare yourselves men," the king called out. "Ready your weapons and be ready to move. The gates will be open any second now."

Although his soldiers were already alert the sounds of weapons being drawn and feet shifting mingled with low murmurs as many of the warband offered prayers to their gods that this night's work would be a success.

And how could it be anything else? Drest thought moments later, smiling with satisfaction as there was a sound of wood grinding against wood and then, miraculously, the massive outer gates of Dun Breatann opened wide.

"Time to kill!" Drest roared, hammering the pommel of his sword against his shield as he gazed joyously along the line of his warriors. "Charge!"

Qunavo never moved from his seat as the Pictish ranks thundered past. He sipped his wine, already a little drunk, and waited happily for the sounds of battle to begin, wondering what they should call a land united under himself and Drest.

* * *

The first clash of armies coming together in a battle was always a shock to the senses: The smells of sweat, fear, and the strong drink many of the warriors imbibed to take away the edge of their terror, along with the piss that soaked the breeches of those who still found the prospect of violent death too traumatic to cope with; the sounds of weapons meeting flesh and bone and the screams, whimpers and war cries that went along with them; the agony as a spear tore through one's torso, or a sling shattered the front of your skull; the taste of blood, bile and tears; the fierce, animal joy as you carved a gaping wound in the neck of a man you'd never met before and knew nothing about…

This particular battle for Dun Breatann was missing some of those experiences. It was not really a battle, in truth, more of a slaughter.

As Drest led his men through the gates, grinning in triumph, there was a shout from atop the second gate just ahead. These gates were rapidly being pulled shut, much to the Picts' surprise. Their shock was compounded when, in response to the cry Drest had just heard, there was a flurry of snapping sounds, and whirring, before the arrows, slingshot and javelins of the Damnonii hammered into the bewildered Picts.

Miraculously, Drest was unharmed, but he was too stunned to react until he heard the defending commander order his men to repeat their missile attack.

"Retreat! We must retreat!" The king had no idea who was calling out, it was too hard to make sense of a single voice amongst the myriad agonized sounds of the dying, but he knew it would be suicide to run back towards Qunavo. Instead, he fell on the ground and used the corpse of one of his own men as a shield. The man wasn't dead yet, however.

"Help me, my lord," the warrior sobbed. "Please, help me."

Horrified, Drest gazed into the man's single eye, realising it was his captain, Lutrin, he held, before the body jerked, and then jerked again, as two separate missiles slammed into him.

He was dead now.

It didn't take long before the courtyard became eerily quiet, as those who'd followed Drest through the open gates were all lying dead or injured, while the rest of the army, seeing their fellows cut down, had turned back, fleeing into the night. But Drest still didn't move. He didn't know what to do. Should he run, and risk being shot down? Or should he stay, and throw himself on the mercy of the Damnonii queen?

How had their plan failed? Had Ria betrayed them? Surely not. Drest knew the druidess held little love for him, thinking him weak and unambitious, but she loved Qunavo dearly. That thought set his mind on a different track.

Had Qunavo and Ria been working together to…He realised his thoughts made no sense and tried to think calmly and rationally, which was almost impossible given the circumstances. It didn't matter right now why his plan had failed. All that mattered was surviving the next few hours.

He decided to try and crawl past the bodies of his men, using them as cover, hoping the night would hide him until he could stand up and make a run for it. The alternative, being taken by the Damnonii, would probably be just as fatal as an arrow in the back, but his death would be slower and considerably more painful. There would be no mercy for him, he was sure of that. Bellicus would make sure he suffered.

As he began to move, though, he heard the second set of gates, the locked ones, being unbarred. The Damnonii were coming out to loot the dead and finish off any survivors. Drest crawled faster, but the constant fear of a missile streaking out of the dark and into his flesh stopped him from running. Not yet—he would be safe soon enough, if he just kept moving, slowly and steadily.

There were others of his warband still alive, and those who could still move were copying him, either dragging themselves across the ground or lurching on injured legs towards the outer gates, but the warriors on the walls continued peppering their arrows onto the would-be escapees and Drest realised he was one of the few not yet cut down.

He was sobbing, convinced the way out was not getting any closer, wondering just how many of his brave Pictish soldiers had died that night. And now he heard the footsteps of men running out from the fortress, the harsh, clipped tones of an officer guiding them to capture any living nobles who might fetch a ransom.

Who would pay a ransom for Drest? Qunavo?

The king got to his feet and began to run.

"Get him!" The officer's shout rang across the courtyard but it was unnecessary, for there were already three Damnonii running towards the fleeing man, and they were all younger and faster than he was.

Drest spun as he heard the first of them come close, sending his sword out in a desperate, wild arc. He felt it strike something but didn't stop to see how much damage he'd done, running as hard as he could now, finally just a short distance from the gates.

He was going to make it!

The brief moment of elation was blasted from him as something struck his shoulder. It wasn't a mortal blow, but it was enough to put him off balance and send him sprawling. He used his hands to push himself up instantly and move on again, but his legs were kicked away and he spun, landing on his back with a tortured, despairing cry.

"Bastard's cut my arm wide open," a voice said, before a boot smashed into the side of his head.

"Look at his clothes," said a second man, whose face, like the first's, was shrouded in shadow, the moon being behind both of them. "This is a nobleman."

"He's a dead man," shouted the warrior with the injured arm, and another kick hammered into Drest, this time in his ribs. Then another, and another.

From somewhere far away, the Pictish king thought he could hear Bellicus laughing before the pain grew too much and he felt no more.

CHAPTER TWENTY-THREE

Narina was grinning from ear to ear, walking around her soldiers, congratulating them, thanking them for their service, and promising riches to all who'd helped vanquish their Pictish besiegers that night. This victory had raised her standing with the men for they believed now that she was blessed by the gods and, as she passed amongst them, they loudly proclaimed their loyalty to her with ale, mead and anything else they could find.

Bellicus, on the other hand, was grim and quiet. He was as glad as anyone in Dun Breatann to lift the siege and restore their freedom, but the way he'd been fooled was galling. The knowledge that so many people would hear of his naivety only added to his black mood.

"What's the matter with you, lad?" Duro demanded. He too was smiling and enjoying their victory—indeed Bellicus had not seen his friend without a mug of ale in his hand since the 'battle' was over—and he didn't seem to understand why the druid wasn't joining in whole-heartedly with the celebrations.

"I'm supposed to be a wise man. One of the gods' messengers here on this mortal plane of existence. Yet I was taken in by the oldest trick there is." He shook his head angrily. "It's embarrassing."

"You may have the ear of the gods," Duro replied seriously. "But you're human yourself, and Ria would have twisted most young men around her little finger. She was beautiful and charming, and you had much in common with her, given your upbringing. There's nothing to be ashamed of."

"I trained for years, Duro," the druid said, still angry and ashamed at himself for not seeing through Ria's scheme. "I was taught how to read people. To tell whether they were being truthful or not. I should have known what she was doing."

The centurion shook his head and took a drink from his mug, spilling much of the ale down his face. "Listen," he said. "Ria was given the same training. More in fact, since she remained on Iova with your tutors when you left to come here."

"She learned better than me then," Bellicus retorted.

"Maybe," Duro admitted. "But I'd say the only reason she successfully tricked you was through no fault of yours. The gods made us the way we are, Bel. They made us think with this," he pointed between his legs. "Rather than with our heads. Forget it, my friend. It's over with now, and all is well. Use this as another lesson and move on."

The druid had to admit Duro had a point. It wasn't pleasant to admit one's own failings, but it was certainly true that men, even the cleverest, could be easily manipulated by a pretty woman with a full figure. Aye, he should have been above such a simple ploy, but it was still shameful how eagerly he'd taken Ria into his home. His bed! His heart?

"Is there any sign of her?" he asked. "Have you heard?"

Duro shook his head. "No. Either she's found an excellent hiding place, or she somehow managed to escape. Over the wall perhaps."

Bellicus narrowed his eyes thoughtfully, then slapped his friend on the arm and pushed his way through the men and women gathered within the great hall. Cai followed him, of course, but the centurion merely watched him go, perhaps expecting him to go and brood for a while over his lost woman.

The druid hurried past his house though, and down the main staircase until he reached the section of wall that ran along the western side of Dun Breatann's great rock. Guards were stationed here, as usual, to make sure there was no further trouble, and they eyed him curiously as he moved past, face grim in the light from the few braziers that were spaced along the walkway. None dared question him and he barely even registered their presence as he made his way to the spot where he and Ria had made love just the day before.

The spot where the wall had been built a few feet higher than everywhere else.

He saw the rope immediately, tied around the timbers that formed the wall and, with a sinking feeling in his stomach, he looked over, down to the river's shore below. This was far from the highest section of the fortress's walls, but even so, if someone fell from here they would not survive, and it would take strong muscles, and even stronger nerves to climb safely down to the ground using such a slim length of rope.

Despite her duplicity, and the pain it caused him, not to mention the death and destruction it might have brought to the people of Alt Clota, Bellicus did not wish to see Ria's body smashed on the ground beneath him.

If she *had* escaped, why hadn't she warned Drest that their scheme had failed? Bellicus assumed that there wouldn't have been enough time for it, given how fast events were moving at that point, and, on top of that, Ria would probably have been glad to be rid of the unambitious king once and for all.

His eyes traced the line of the rope down, all the way, until at last the druid let out a breath in relief. There was no sign of her.

The druidess had escaped and, since there had been no sign of Qunavo amongst the dead or captured Picts, it seemed her mentor had also managed to get away. The thought was bittersweet for Bellicus. They had caused a lot of trouble between them, and, had their plan succeeded, the occupants of Dun Breatann would all be enslaved or food for the crows right now. On top of that, if they were able to make it back to Dunnottar they would be free to weave more trouble together. Drest's successor would look to them for advice and legitimacy in his, or her, claim to the throne which would surely lead to more grief for the surrounding lands.

Yet, as he untied the rope to make sure no-one could climb up it from outside and then made his way back up to the great hall, Bellicus tried to take something positive from Ria and Qunavo's continued existence. Had they both been killed this night it would have left an opening for those among the Picts who followed the new Christian religion to step in. Drest had wanted to take control of all the lands in this northern part of Britannia, but at least he adhered to the old ways.

If both the Dalriadans and the Picts crowned Christian kings it would surely only be a matter of time before Bellicus and his fellow druids became nothing but a memory. No, it had to be one of his primary tasks to keep their old ways alive.

He heard much singing and laughing as he returned to the central section of the fortress and he was glad. Dun Breatann still belonged to the Damnonii, and, with the destruction of the Pictish army, they were in the strongest position Bellicus could remember. He wondered how Narina would proceed from here: Would she wish to consolidate and allow her people to enjoy the peace that must now follow Drest's defeat? Or would she take advantage of the weakened Dalriadans and Picts? Was she that ambitious?

And what of the Saxons and Duro's desire to return south with a warband to join Arthur and the Merlin?

The centurion saw him returning and seemed relieved, no doubt glad the druid had decided to join the celebrations instead of lying alone in his house.

"Here," Duro said, thrusting a mug of ale into his hands. "Drink, my friend. You deserve it."

Bellicus drank, downing the liquid in two long draughts before smiling and accepting another mug from one of the laughing warriors crowding all around.

Tonight, they would simply enjoy their stunning victory. There would be enough time in the coming days to advise Narina on what they should do next. Before that there would be drinking, and, if Drest was still alive, perhaps a chance for Duro to gain some revenge for his stolen fingers...

* * *

When Bellicus awoke the next day, it was late. At first, he forgot what had happened the previous evening, but then it all came flooding back along with the headache he'd earned during the victory celebrations. Feeling slightly sick, he lay on his straw-filled mattress for a while, glad the closed shutters kept out most of the late-morning sunlight. They also kept out the fresh air though, and the stench of stale sweat and beer-breath hung heavily around him. Duro was still snoring on the far side of the room but Cai was awake by the door, staring at him. A wry smile tugged at the corners of the druid's mouth and the dog padded across to lick his master's face and have his ears ruffled.

"You'll not run away and leave me, will you, boy?" Bellicus muttered, struck once again by the betrayal and subsequent departure of Ria but glad to have his two most loyal friends still by his side.

Wincing, he pushed himself up onto his feet and walked to the door, pulling back the bolt and opening it wide to let Cai out. The dog needed no persuasion, ambling away and lifting his leg against the tree that stood directly across from the house. Bellicus looked around blearily, breathing in the fresh air and watching the folk of Dun Breatann going about their daily business. Anyone would think there hadn't been a battle here just a few hours earlier, as women moved hither and thither carrying water and clothes for washing, shouting hello and enquiring after one another's families, while the smell of meat roasting drifted on the wind towards him from the great hall.

Turning back inside he left the door ajar for Cai to return when he felt like it, and to get rid of the pungent smell within. A cup of water eased his dry mouth although the jug had been lying since the day before and he almost went outside to refill it from the nearby spring. Almost. No, that could wait for later, when the tight band of pain around his skull eased.

Still, the queen would send for him soon enough, to discuss how they should proceed in the coming weeks and he had no desire to appear in her presence stinking and hungover.

"Wake up!" he called, disturbing Duro in mid-snore as he threw off his dark robe—which he'd slept in, naturally—and poured some of the water into a wooden basin. Adding a little dried lavender which had come on a ship from Gaul during the winter, he washed his face and upper body, feeling like a new man when he was finished. Then, as Duro rolled onto his side, facing the wall and muttering to himself, Bellicus opened the long wooden chest which he used to store his clothes.

Shoving aside the ceremonial white cloak he only wore for certain religious occasions he took out his other hooded, dark robe, and a red linen shirt with gold thread embroidered around the lower hem, and put them on.

"Very handsome. The red really enhances your bloodshot eyes."

Bellicus laughed and filled another cup with water, handing it to the centurion. "You don't look so fresh yourself, old friend. Here, get this down you and have a wash – Narina will be coming for us soon. How's your hand?"

Duro made a fist and nodded. "Feels all right. How long do you think it'll take for the fingers to grow back?"

Bellicus grinned and turned away as Cai came bounding back into the house, moving from one man to the other, nuzzling them, tail creating a great draught and almost catching Duro in the face. The centurion had learned from bitter experience how painful that could be, and pulled his blanket up, laughing, which only made Cai even more excited.

The sunlight was obscured then and Bellicus looked to see a figure filling the doorway. Cai barked, but it was a welcoming sound, not a warning or a challenge.

"Good afternoon you three," said the man, sarcastically, before shaking his head at Bellicus's invitation to come in for some bread and cheese. "I've had something already," he said. "I just came to tell you that the queen wants to see you both at midday, if you could be ready."

Duro got up and set about washing himself as Bellicus had done before him. "Did many of the Picts survive?" he asked, cupping water in his hands and splashing it onto his face. "Drest?"

Gavo nodded. "Aye, a few are still alive, including Drest. But I'll let you get cleaned up. We'll discuss what's to be done with the prisoners in a while. It's a great day to be alive, lads. Well, unless you're a Pict!" With a grin, the guard captain disappeared.

Duro finished washing, then took out his own fresh clothes and dressed in silence. Since he'd been sharing Bellicus's house for a while he had a chest of his own, where he stored spare clothing along with his legionary helmet and armour.

The druid could see emotions warring within his friend. It would be a strange experience to meet the Pictish king again, after what the bastard had done to them, particularly the centurion.

"Have you any thoughts on what we should do next?"

Duro frowned. "In what way?" he asked, pulling on his boots and securing the laces tightly.

"Well, if Narina wants to send a warband north-east to take Dunnottar, or west to Dalriada – do you think we should volunteer to go? Or are you still set on us leading men down to fight the Saxons with Arthur?"

The centurion probed a tooth with his tongue, dislodging a piece of gristle, and stood up. "I haven't thought about it," he replied. "Eventually I want to make Horsa pay for what he did to Alatucca but...For now, I'm happy to go where you lead. If that means returning to Dunnottar and smashing the painted bastards up there, that's fine with me." He put on his clean tunic—an off-white, long-sleeved garment with purple designs embroidered on the cuffs and around the hem which came down to the knees—and smiled. "Do you think the queen will have food?"

"I think there'll be a veritable feast laid out for us," Bellicus said, placing his dirty clothes in the middle of the floor as Duro did the same. "Come on. We'll go and see."

They went outside, squinting in the light although clouds had covered the sun by now. Bellicus looked up, wincing, and saw a sparrowhawk hovering overhead, searching for prey amongst the long grass and bushes that grew on the steep rock the fortress was built upon. "Looks like it'll rain soon," he said, hurrying towards the great hall.

By the well there was a wooden shelter with a thatched roof, where Dun Breatann's servants cleaned clothes in a big vat of urine collected from all the fortress's inhabitants. As they passed, Duro called out to one of them. "Aine. We have things for washing, if you could…"

The woman glanced up from the child's blanket she was scrubbing and, wiping her forehead, called out in reply, promising it would be done.

"Thank you!" Duro waved, turning back to Bellicus as they neared the hall. "I like this tunic well enough, but it's a bit fancy. I feel kind of…out of place wearing it."

The druid nodded. "I know how you feel. I'll be glad to get into my plain old robe again too, but we should look like noblemen for this meeting at least." He stopped and faced Duro seriously before unlatching the door and heading inside. "I don't know how Narina plans to do this, but we should be prepared to see Drest."

The centurion's jaw was set, and it twitched now as if he was grinding his teeth, but he merely nodded grimly. He did not have his sword as no weapons were allowed during an audience with the queen, or Bellicus felt sure his friend would have grasped the hilt.

They went in, nodding to the pair of guards who were stationed by the door within the hall. The men eyed them up and down, seeing no weapons—apart from the druid's ubiquitous staff, which was permitted—and smiling warmly. Everyone within Dun Breatann was in a good mood today, despite the preponderance of hangovers.

"Good to see you, gentlemen." Queen Narina was already at the high table and she gestured for the newcomers to take their usual seats, with Bellicus at her right hand, and Duro to his right, which they did. Gavo and Gerallt were on the left.

"Morning," Gerallt said, then he sniffed and smirked at Gavo. "What's that? Are you two brave warriors wearing lavender?"

"No jokes, please," Bellicus replied, pouring himself a small cup of ale from a mug that was set on the table before them. "Trust me, lavender is much preferable to how Duro smelled when he woke up this morning."

The centurion looked affronted but didn't join in with a retort of his own, a sign perhaps of how the coming meeting with King Drest was weighing on his mind.

"I've also invited Ysfael of the Votadini to join us," Narina said, stroking Cai's head as he crawled beneath the table, sniffing at everyone before returning to his master and settling down with his eyes closed. "Since we're hoping he'll lead his men wherever we ask him, I thought it only courteous to let him be part of this discussion. Agreed?"

The advisors all nodded. Ysfael was respected well enough by them all, although Bellicus hadn't really had a chance to get to know him much.

"He'll be here any moment," Narina went on. "So, if there's anything you wish to discuss without him, now is the time."

"How many casualties did we take last night?" Duro asked.

"Only one man was badly injured," Gerallt said. "And even that could have been avoided if the fool had been more careful."

"One of the dying Picts managed to slash his foot through to the bone," Gavo reported. "He should survive unless the wound is infected. Maybe you…"

Bellicus nodded as the captain peered along the table at him. "Of course, I'll check on him when we're finished here. That's quite the victory for us, eh? How many of Drest's people did we kill?"

"Thirty-seven dead," Gerallt reported. "Twelve captured and now held within the prison until we decide what to do with them. The rest escaped, although we've sent riders after them."

"How is Drest?"

"He is well, centurion," Narina said, and there was something in her tone that seemed off to Bellicus. A harshness that suggested…what?

The doors opened again and Ysfael of the Votadini came in, striding confidently past the guards and up to the raised dais. He knelt and bowed respectfully to the queen.

"Take a seat, my lord," Narina said. "Please don't take it as a slight that your chair is not up here on the dais but—"

"Of course," Ysfael said, raising his hand and smiling as he sat at the bench nearest the high table. "This will suit me very well, lady, especially with all this here." He reached out and lifted a piece of roast beef from the trencher before him. There was also ale, wine, cheese, bread, and smoked fish although it was clear from Ysfael's toned, muscular frame he did not usually overindulge in his food or drink. "I appreciate your including me in this council of war."

Gerallt, Gavo, and Narina seemed pleased by the young man's respectful words and bearing and he seemed genuine enough to Bellicus, so although he'd heard murmurs about Ysfael's arrogance, he decided to trust their judgement.

"I assume we'll be ransoming the Pictish nobles," said the druid. "And executing Drest."

"After I've had a few moments alone with him," Duro growled and Bellicus noticed Narina rubbing her fingers together, fidgeting rather uncharacteristically.

"Well, that's what we're here to decide," Gavo said.

"What is there to decide?" Bellicus asked, nonplussed.

"I believe Drest may be worth keeping alive," Narina said, staring at Bellicus and Duro almost defiantly. "Not in terms of being paid a ransom for him, but in terms of controlling his lands."

"That whoreson imprisoned me and Duro, cut off his fingers, tore out his nails, and brought an army to our gates on more than one occasion," Bellicus said, voice rising with every point he made. "If it hadn't been for the will of the gods every one of us would likely be dead by Drest's command right now."

"This is all true, Bel," said Ysfael and the druid's head whipped round as he stared at this outsider who was only supposed to be here as a gesture. "But think about it," the Votadini warrior went on, licking meat juice from his fingers. "If we kill Drest – what then? We already have the Dalriadans fighting amongst themselves to take control of those lands in the west. If Drest is removed, the same thing will happen with the Picts. And what happens when one of their chieftains takes the throne?"

"We've crushed their army," Duro snapped. "Who cares about their hypothetical next king?"

"Drest was a good administrator," Narina said softly but firmly. "A fine logistician, who ran his lands well, drawing what wealth he could from them, and keeping the peace there. But he was a poor warrior, and an even worse commander."

Bellicus shrugged. "So we always thought, but look how close he came to seizing control of Alt Clota last night."

Gerallt waved a hand dismissively. "Pah. A stronger king would have taken this place years ago. Drest was content to sit in Dunnottar counting his wealth when, given how many warriors he could call on, he might have become High King of all these northern lands. He lacked ambition."

"And when he finally discovered it," Gavo put in. "He made an arse of it!"

"Qunavo is still free," Ysfael said. "And Ria too, of course, as you know." There was a glint in his eyes, a hint of mockery that deeply irritated Bellicus but he held his tongue as the young man continued. "They will find a strong man to take Drest's place. And the next time a Pictish army marches on Dun Breatann, or against my father in Dun Edin for that matter, there will be no mistakes. They are simply too wealthy, and have too many men at their disposal, druid. The one thing they've lacked in recent years is an ambitious, capable leader."

Narina nodded in agreement with Cunedda's son. "Keeping Drest on his throne will be to our advantage, I think that much is clear."

Bellicus relaxed into his high-backed chair, looking up at the high vaulted ceiling and rolling his head from side to side to work out the kinks his poor night's sleep had left. They were correct, he knew, as much as the idea of letting Drest live galled him. What Narina seemed to be proposing made sense.

"You're not going along with this are you?" Duro demanded, and Bellicus, pained by the hurt in his friend's voice, met his gaze apologetically. "I can't believe what I'm hearing," the centurion went on, angrily getting to his feet which made the two guards at the doors quite uneasy.

"Calm yourself, Duro," Narina commanded, momentarily mollifying the former legionary although his silence was perhaps driven more by his old habit of following his superiors' orders than anything else. "I understand how you feel. Drest's behaviour was unacceptable, given the high status of yourself and Bellicus, but I will remind you: I am queen here. You are all invited," she looked at the men gathered about before returning her eyes to Duro, "to offer advice. But I will decide how we proceed. Is that clear?"

Duro's face had become an unreadable mask as she spoke and Bellicus was shocked. He had never seen his friend behave like this before, not even when he'd discovered his wife's body in Luguvalium. The druid was always able to read Duro's emotions from his body language and facial expressions – now, though, Bellicus couldn't tell whether his friend was about to cry, or attack everyone in the great hall.

Duro had been a Roman centurion. He knew how to fight and, given his ordeal at Drest's hands along with Alatucca's horrific manner of passing just a few months ago, the turmoil that must be going on behind Duro's hooded eyes frightened Bellicus.

"I have nothing to offer this discussion, my lady," the centurion said, his voice held calm with a clear effort. "I am no politician. I am, was, a rank and file soldier. By your leave, I will wait outside until you are finished."

Narina sighed, and she too looked visibly upset by what was happening, but she nodded and watched in silence as Duro strode towards the doors. They were opened by the guards who seemed visibly relieved that he was going. He turned back once more, however, and addressed the high table. "Where are the captured weapons?" he asked. "The ones taken from the captured or killed Picts I mean."

Gavo pointed up to the right vaguely. "Store-room beside the garrison. You know it?"

"I do. My spatha was taken from me by one of the bastards. I assume I can take it back if I find it?"

"Of course," Narina replied, and Gavo bowed his head then went away, leaving an awkward silence behind him.

"He won't do anything stupid will he?" Gerallt asked at length, and Bellicus shook his head.

"I don't think so. Like he said, he's a soldier – he was trained to obey orders, even ones he doesn't like or agree with. Although . . ." He looked at the doors thoughtfully, as if he could see through them and track his friend's movements outside. "It seems clear everything that happened from the moment me and Duro were captured by the Picts was orchestrated by my old mentor, Qunavo."

"The druid?" Ysfael asked in confusion. "I've heard the story about your…ordeal in Dunnottar, my lord. I thought Qunavo hadn't even been there during it all."

"So we were told," Bellicus admitted. "But he was surely behind the scenes, directing Drest. The things he did to us, particularly to Duro, were designed to break our spirit. To push us to the very brink of madness. The starvation, the constant darkness, the physical violence, the mental torture. Qunavo knows better than anyone how to manipulate a man."

"Including you," Narina muttered.

"Aye," Bellicus agreed. "Ria was part of the plan. She made us trust her, so, when we reached Alt Clota and found our way into Dun Breatann—to safety—blocked, I was willing to use the secret tunnel to escape Drest's warriors. I let my friendship with Duro cloud my judgement, and it almost led to Alt Clota's doom."

"That all sounds rather far-fetched," Ysfael said, and the others in the room seemed to agree, although they respected Bellicus too much to say so. "It seems more like a series of unhappy, unconnected events to me. How did they know you two would ride after them in the first place?"

"They didn't," Bellicus said. "But once they captured us, Qunavo would have started looking for a way to exploit the situation. His was the hand that guided us back from Dunnottar with Ria, and into the secret tunnel. There had been rumours of its existence for many generations, and Qunavo would have known that if anyone could lead him to it, it would be me. Thinking on it now, that explains why we were able to escape relatively easily from Dunottar."

"Easily?" Gavo said, head tilted rather like a puzzled dog. "I thought you were nearly cut down by one of their horsemen, and then almost killed at the shelter they burned down."

Bellicus nodded. He'd wondered about that himself, but it made sense to him now. "Qunavo couldn't just let us walk free, it would have raised our suspicions. So they sent men after us, probably some of their lesser fighters, and then simply hoped Duro and me would be able to defeat them."

Again, Ysfael made a dismissive sound, and Bellicus's eyes narrowed. He was growing tired of the brash outsider now. "Do not doubt me when I tell you Qunavo is one of the most brilliant men I've ever met, and also one of the most ruthless. It shames me to admit it, but I was manipulated by him and Ria and…here we are. Their plan very nearly worked, as incredible as it might seem to you."

"What does this have to do with Duro's current mood?" Narina asked.

"Duro has suffered much in recent months," Bellicus said, turning back to her. "And the things they did to him in Dunnottar, he may never get over them. I believe seeing Drest pay for his actions might have gone some way to healing Duro's mental sickness. Now, though…I don't know how he'll react, and I don't think even he knows. He is not himself."

"The man was a Roman officer," Ysfael sniffed. "We have all suffered much in our lives. What makes Duro so special? If everyone became moon-touched when something bad happened—"

"Are you not listening to me?" the druid demanded, and the simmering rage in his voice made everyone wince. "Qunavo, the most senior druid north of Hadrianus's Wall, was behind the things that happened to Duro in Dunnottar's dungeon. This was no mere battlefield injury, or terrors of war. He was methodically tortured by a master of his craft."

Everyone liked the centurion for he was an honourable, pleasant companion, and they did not enjoy hearing Bellicus's words. Narina took a sip of her drink and blew out a breath before speaking into the silence. "We will all do what we can to help Duro," she promised. "You, Bel, are a druid so perhaps you can figure out how to reverse Qunavo's efforts and heal the scars he left on our friend. It will have to wait, however. For now, we are here to discuss what our plans will be moving forward."

"I say we take our men west and seize Dunadd," Gavo said. "Many of the people there were sick of Loarn mac Eirc's rule before he died, and they'll be happy to have a strong ruler taking control again. Taking Dalriada back would make us much more powerful."

Gerallt nodded. "I agree. A lot of those lands, especially the nearest settlements like Arachar and Tairbert, were ours not so long ago anyway, before the Dalriadans came across the sea from Hibernia and took them over. The folk there will fall back in with us easily enough, I'm certain, as we saw during the first of Drest's recent sieges, when so many of them came to fight with you, my lady."

"Is it worth the trouble?" Bellicus asked. "Holding Dunadd will be an easy matter, assuming we can take it. We don't even know who controls it now after all. But even if we take it without a single casualty, what then? More Dalriadans are coming in their ships every day, settling the lands all around Dunadd. I doubt it would be possible to hold that region without gathering a huge army and driving the newcomers back across the sea."

"A huge army you don't have," Ysfael said. "I think we must learn to live with the Dalriadans. They are not going away."

"That's easy for you to say," Gavo retorted. "Your people are far away in the east, with Alt Clota acting as a buffer."

"Correct," the Votadini noble conceded. "But still, who do we fear most? Dalriadans or Saxons?"

That brought a return to the thoughtful silence of earlier, as the spectre of Horsa and Hengist and their dangerous hordes seemed to loom across the great hall.

"He's right," Bellicus said. "I suggest we fortify and rebuild our defences on our western borders, to keep out the Dalriadans. Hopefully it will be a long time before they find a new king and cause us any more trouble. In the meantime, as we originally decided what seems a lifetime ago now, I will lead Ysfael and his men, along with a force of our own Damnonii warriors, south, to join the warlord Arthur and the Merlin."

This seemed acceptable to Narina and her two captains, but the druid wasn't quite finished speaking.

"We still have the Votadini to think about though," he said to the queen. "Aye, they've agreed to an alliance with us for now, and Cunedda even sent his son to aid us." He looked at Ysfael now. "But we will need something to bind our peoples together. A royal marriage."

Narina stared at the druid and he was surprised at what he saw in her eyes, but she turned her head before he could decide whether it was anger or something else.

"I agree," she said. "I've been thinking about it for a while, and that's why I think Ysfael and I should be wed."

No-one said anything to her suggestion and when she looked at Bellicus he held his expression neutral, glad that Gavo had forewarned him of this.

"Well?" the queen demanded, and her frosty tone told Bellicus everything he needed to know. This idea might have been in her head for a while, indeed, Ysfael's smug expression suggested this had been his proposal originally, but Narina only decided to go ahead with it when Bel returned from his weeks in captivity with Ria on his arm.

Why were people driven so easily by their emotions?

"My lady," he said, holding his voice as neutral as possible. "When I suggested a marriage, I meant Catia might be betrothed to Ysfael. Not you."

"Catia is a child," Narina replied, and again, Bellicus could read more from her tone than her few words. The idea of her daughter leaving Alt Clota, after her ordeal with the Saxons, was anathema to Narina. He shook his head, saddened by the baggage they had all been forced to carry in recent times. It seemed more trouble than was fair had been visited on Alt Clota by the gods over the past year or two.

"Children are often betrothed," Gerallt noted, a little sheepishly for he could tell the queen was unhappy about something, even if he didn't know what. "I must admit, this seems a sudden decision, my lady. Perhaps we should have talked about this before—"

"Who I choose to marry is up to me," Narina stated flatly. "I don't need men to give me permission."

"That's not what he meant," Gavo said and Bellicus feared another argument was about to break out.

"You can rest assured," Ysfael said smoothly "I'll be a good husband to Queen Narina."

"Let's all have a rest for now," the druid said irritably, ignoring the young lord and getting to his feet with a gesture for Cai to follow suit. "As you say, lady, you are queen and it is your lot to guide Alt Clota. We are here to advise you, though, and perhaps it would be wise to allow us some time to think over your suggestion. If you marry Ysfael, there will still be the question of Drest and how to keep him in check if we let him return to Dunnottar."

"We have his daughter," Narina said, surprising Bellicus again, for he hadn't been aware of this fact. He didn't even know Drest had a daughter. "A bastard," the queen said, noting his bemusement. "But a young warrior-woman of apparent high standing amongst the Picts. She will be held here as a hostage, to make sure Drest doesn't break the alliance."

Bellicus looked at Gavo and Gerallt, who nodded slightly. They had known about this girl's capture at least. He cursed himself for drinking so much the night before and sleeping so late. It seemed he was at a disadvantage now, being drip-fed information without time to properly digest it.

"I'll go and check on Duro," he said. "And I will think on all this. Perhaps the rest of you can do the same, until I return in a short while. My lady? Is that acceptable to you?"

His tone was as cold as hers had been and she nodded. "It is. Don't be too long, druid. The sooner we agree on all this, the sooner we can begin moving forward."

Bellicus gave a shallow bow and, with Cai hot on his heels, went out into the rain which was sheeting down by now. Both he and Cai were quickly drenched although Bellicus took little notice.

Gods! Narina was moving far too quickly for his liking. These were far-reaching decisions – choices that would reverberate around Alt Clota for years to come. They should be ruminated upon, with conclusions only made after much discussion and thought. He still wasn't sure how he felt about the idea of Narina marrying Ysfael. He didn't want her to do it, that was certain, but *why not*? Did he want her himself? Aye, at times he did and, in another life he'd have asked her to wed him, but that was out of the question just now so perhaps he was merely jealous of Ysfael, who would gain power and status and the hand of a wonderful, inspiring woman.

He headed for his home, head whirling but, as he reached the front door, he remembered Duro and his fears for the centurion resurfaced. Would Duro even still be here, or would he have decided, in his anger, to simply return to his old home in Luguvalium? Would he do something even more reckless, like try to kill Drest within Dun Breatann's prison?

He pushed open the door and looked inside, anxiety making a heavy weight within his belly. Duro was there though, staring at him stonily.

Thank Sulis.

"You found your spatha," Bellicus said, closing the door behind him and walking across to the hearth, rubbing his hands as the heat quickly made the rain on his robe turn to steam. Cai shook himself vigorously, sending droplets flying about the room before he sat down next to the fire, raising his head and sniffing at the meaty scent from the cauldron hanging over the flames.

"Aye," Duro agreed, patting the pommel of his old sword. "I found it under a pile of weapons in the store-room Gavo mentioned." He didn't look as pleased to be reunited with the spatha as Bellicus would have expected, and this was confirmed a moment later as Duro went on. "It doesn't feel the same. I've grown used to the other one – the one Ria gave me."

"We'll get you another spatha," Bellicus promised. "Or have one made to your specifications. You've earned it."

They were silent for a time, and then the druid said softly, "I'm sorry, Duro. I wanted to see Drest pay for what he did to us too."

"It's not your fault," the centurion shrugged, getting up and coming across to stir the broth. He might be upset but it seemed he still had his appetite. "I've decided though. I won't fight another battle for Narina or the Damnonii. They are not my people, and she is not my queen. It's time for us to part at last, my friend."

CHAPTER TWENTY-FOUR

The idea of being separated from Duro tore at Bellicus then. They'd become fast friends since rescuing Catia from Horsa and been through so much together since then. It had seemed to the druid like they would always be friends. "You're going back to Luguvalium?" he asked.

Duro shook his head. "No. I couldn't just return to that life, baking cakes and pastries all day, every day. That life is gone."

"What then?"

"Arthur. My fight is with the men who murdered my wife. I'll ride south and offer my services to Arthur, if he'll have me. We've said it often enough, to ourselves and others over the months: If they're not stopped, the Saxons will overrun us all." He shook his head grimly. "I can't stand by, baking bread, while Horsa ravages these lands."

They looked at one another and it seemed there were no more words to be said, but then, turning away to begin packing his things into a sack, Duro asked in a gruff voice. "Will you come with me?"

Again, the thought of parting from his friend struck at Bellicus like a dagger in the guts. Although they'd only known one another for a relatively short period of time, and there was a fifteen-year gap in their ages, a bond had formed between them. There was almost a telepathic connection when they fought side by side which was usually only experienced by brothers, and in daily life they were in accord in most things meaning arguments were so rare they were practically non-existent.

Bellicus was Druid of Dun Breatann though. This was his home. He shook his head sadly. "I'm afraid not."

The centurion grunted but did not turn round to face him, apparently continuing to pack his things although the task must surely be completed already since he didn't have that many possessions.

"Once things are stabilised here," Bellicus said. "And Narina is safe on the throne, with no more invaders to worry about…" That day seemed so far away it was almost inconceivable, but the druid carried on. "Then I will lead our warband south, to join you and Arthur against the Saxons."

Cai opened his mouth to yawn, finishing with a soft whine. Even the dog could sense the unhappiness in the room and he eyed Bellicus balefully, as if commanding the druid not to split up their fellowship.

"You're not leaving today?"

Duro shook his head. "No. I'll need to decide the best way to go. I'm not really ready for such a long ride, not after Drest's treatment." He stared at the bandage on his hand in disgust. "So perhaps I should take a walk down to the docks and see if I can find passage on one of the ships. At least for some of the journey."

"A sensible idea," Bellicus said. "You could wait for a few weeks, until your strength—"

Duro shook his head. He'd made his decision and wanted to see it through as soon as possible.

"All right," the druid said, walking towards the door. "Eat some of your broth; build yourself back up. I'll check your wounds again later. For now, I want to simply walk and think on what Narina's proposing before I head back to the great hall. I'll see you later."

Cai followed as he went out into the rain once more, drawing his hood up and latching the door behind him before heading down the main stairway. Once at the bottom, the guards let him out through the gates and he walked across to the river's shore. There, the dog wandered, sniffing, and splashing in the Clota happily as Bellicus gazed at the far bank, skimming the occasional stone and trying to gather his thoughts as the spattering rain made a multitude of circular ripples on the water's surface.

This was not how he had expected things to end up. In a few weeks, Duro would be gone and Narina would be married to Ysfael. The Picts would be neutered, the Votadini would be allies, and only the Dalriadans would be left to threaten Alt Clota, meaning Bellicus would probably be sent with Gavo or Gerallt to make sure the fiery warriors from across the western sea did not cause any trouble.

Was this truly how Bellicus wanted to fulfil his duties as a druid? On the one hand it made sense, as the Dalriadans were mostly Christians nowadays, so they threatened his existence in more ways than one yet…He had greater ambitions surely? Bigger dreams than merely keeping a few warlords from raiding Alt Clota's borders.

Sighing, he looked up at the sky as the rain stopped and the dark clouds parted, noticing how far the sun had moved since he first stepped out of the great hall for a rest and muttered an oath. "Cai! Come on, lad, let's go." At a run, he made his way back through the gatehouse, ignoring the curious looks from the guards, and back up the stairs to the central part of Dun Breatann. The muscles in his legs were burning by the time he came to the hall, a sad indictment on his drop in fitness after his time in captivity, but he'd kept the queen and the rest waiting long enough so he burst in, drawing in gulps of air.

"You're back," Narina observed caustically. "At last."

"My lady," he said, striding to his chair by her side and dropping into it with an apologetic smile. "I lost track of the time."

"Here," she said, filling his ale mug and pushing it across the table to him. "It looks like you could do with a drink. Are you all right?"

"Aye, lady," he nodded, taking the drink gladly and taking a sip. "Just need to rebuild my weakened muscles." Only then did he notice Ysfael was no longer seated by himself at the table in front of the raised dais. Another man sat there, and Bellicus felt his grip tighten on the ale mug with so much force the vessel might have split apart if he hadn't slammed it down on the table.

Drest flinched at the violence of the movement, as did Gavo and Gerallt. Narina had seen it coming though, and she laid a hand on the druid's arm now.

"You." Bellicus stood up, the queen's fingers falling away as he did so, and then he stepped around the table and down from the dais.

"Bel," Gavo muttered, but the druid ignored him, walking towards the beaten Pictish king and towering over him threateningly.

"The last time we met, I was in your dungeon, and you'd been chopping off my friend's fingers." He slammed his great hand onto Drest's, pinning it to the table as he leaned down and stared into the frightened king's eyes. "It seems our roles are reversed."

Drest swallowed and turned pleading eyes towards Narina.

"Bellicus," she said, softly but firmly. "Take your seat by my side again. Please."

The druid continued to stare into Drest's eyes, and when the king tried to pull his hand away Bellicus held it firmly in place. Even in his weakened condition he was much too powerful for Drest to overcome.

"Druid, sit down," the queen said, exasperated now." We've much to discuss and you've kept us waiting long enough already."

"Whatever happens here today," Bellicus hissed, his gaze seeming to hold Drest fixed in an almost hypnotic trance and the king grimaced as his hand was crushed further down into the tabletop. "At some point, I shall repay you for what you did to Duro and me. By Taranis, you can count on it."

He held his stance for another long moment before finally stepping back and retaking his place at Narina's side.

"Your daughter led the warband that came through our not-so secret tunnel," the queen stated, watching Drest's face. The Pictish king tried to hide his thoughts but anguish was in his eyes which any parent could understand.

"How do you know that?" he asked in a gruff voice, undoubtedly intended to mask any tell-tale emotions.

"One of your noblemen told us," Narina replied. "He was quite happy to tell us whatever we wanted to know in hopes of saving his own skin."

"Did it?" Drest demanded with a curl of his lip.

"Aye," Gavo smiled. "We wouldn't kill someone who might fetch a decent ransom."

"I will, if I get my hands on the loose-tongued son of a whore," Drest muttered but Narina went on, ignoring his grumbling.

"Your daughter is alive," she said and, for the first time since the king had been brought into the hall, his eyes lit-up hopefully. "Your nobleman told us the girl is a bastard, the daughter of some peasant in Pictland, but, despite that, you have a soft spot for her, and bestowed high status upon her thanks to her abilities as a warrior."

"She's a hardy fighter," Drest admitted proudly. "I'm surprised she allowed you to take her alive."

"Well, for now she'll be doing no more fighting," Narina told him. "From now on she will be our prisoner here in Dun Breatann."

The king frowned, but said nothing, instead watching Narina thoughtfully as he tried to make sense of what was happening and wondering why he hadn't been executed already. Part of him wished he was dealing with Coroticus, for this new queen was, in some ways, much more formidable than her dead husband.

"With that out of the way," Narina said grimly. "Let's get down to the real business."

"Business?" Drest asked hoarsely. "What business?"

Narina clasped her hands and leaned forward, placing her elbows on the table in front of her and smiling coldly at the Pictish captive as she said, "The business of my ruling the Northern Throne, of course, as High Queen."

* * *

It was dark in the cell, but not as dark as it had been in the tunnel that had brought her here. Aife closed her eyes and leaned back against the wall, trying to remember the previous night's events.

It had all happened so fast, yet, as her companions were dying beside her it seemed to last a lifetime.

They'd come out of the tunnel, weapons ready, blood pounding in their veins with the excitement and glory of their mission. Aife had come second in line, behind Brude mac Uradech, following his lead as he crept up the steps that led out of the well and onto the central, flat section of Dun Breatann.

She had seen, in the dim light, houses and a large structure that could only be the Alt Clotan fortress's great hall. Behind them was the high, western peak, towering over them, a massive black void, while in front was the lower, eastern peak.

Her eyes had taken all this in as she waited for the rest of their warband to come up the steps from the well, so she had her bearings and knew exactly where to go next. She would lead the men down the main staircase to the gates, while Brude would run up the lower of the two peaks, quickly light the torch and wave it to Drest waiting below. The whole thing would be over soon and the fortress, along with Alt Clota, would belong to the Picts.

"Taranis be with you," Brude said, teeth glinting in the darkness as he smiled encouragingly at Aife before he ran, crouching low and keeping to the shadows, up the western slope. She watched him go, the pack that contained the torch and items to set it alight bouncing against his back. When he was out of sight she turned to her men.

"Ready, lads? Remember, be as silent as possible, we don't want the alarm raised before the gates are opened."

Brude was out of sight now so Aife began moving, along the path that led away from the great hall. Before she moved a dozen steps, however, a shout came from the darkness and then the unmistakeable, terrifying snap of bowstrings being released in unison. As she spun to see where their enemies were hiding, she saw her kinsmen dying, their naked, painted flesh offering no resistance to the barbed missiles that tore into them.

Then something, presumably another arrow, had cannoned against her head and the night, already dark, had become infinitely more so.

She'd woken up in this cell and quickly realised the iron gate could not be forced or jemmied open – not with bare hands anyway. Her weapons were gone, as was her armour, and her head ached, although she seemed to be otherwise uninjured.

A torch or some other light source, a rushlight perhaps, was burning along the corridor and she had been able to see a guard there. He'd noticed her moving and stared at her but said nothing and she had sat down on the filthy floor in despair, head spinning, knowing her father's army must be destroyed. Her own future looked bleak, but she had vomited and then passed out again before she could dwell too much on her fate.

When she awoke once more her stomach felt empty, but her head had stopped spinning and she felt strangely *alive*. The earlier despair had passed, for now at least, and she wanted only to find out what had happened to the rest of the army and figure out a way to escape from this cell.

As she sat there, listening to the muffled, familiar sounds of a busy fortress beginning its day, she felt a strange, prickling sensation and glanced up, shocked to see an enormous man staring at her through the gate. How he'd managed to approach without her noticing was beyond her comprehension.

She licked dry lips and hoped her voice wouldn't betray her anxiety as she got to her feet. "You're the druid."

Bellicus looked at the young woman standing in the flickering shadows of the cell before him, sizing her up. She was tall, rather more so than most women, and athletically built. Her gaze was confident, not cowed at all by her status as a prisoner as she waited for him to reply to her comment.

"Aye," he said. "And you're Drest's daughter, Aife."

Her chin came up immediately, almost defiantly, and Bellicus guessed she was somewhat touchy about her position within the Pictish hierarchy.

"I am one of his bastards," she agreed. "And, despite my youth, also one of his commanders."

The giant mystic nodded to the guard, who approached and unbolted the iron gate. "Come with me," Bellicus said. "I would talk with you somewhere more pleasant."

Aife eyed him suspiciously but she did not refuse his invitation for the cells were damp and cold and she longed to feel fresh air on her face again. It felt like she'd been cooped up for an age although it had been less than a day. Of course, the fact that she knew her kinsmen had been so terribly routed, her father's dreams of conquest in tatters, made her captivity even more difficult to endure.

Bellicus saw her eyes examining him, noting his sword and the bulge in his trouser leg where he kept a dagger hidden, but he felt no need to warn her against doing anything rash. She was an impressive young woman, and one he wouldn't particularly want to face in a fight, but her bearing was placid enough. He did not think she would attempt to escape.

Not yet anyway.

The guard led the way to the exit, Aife following and the druid bringing up the rear. As they walked the guard's flickering torch gave off smoke which made Bellicus squint but, even so, he could see from the way Aife moved that she was lithe and supple. A born warrior.

Narina's plan to hold her in Dun Breatann as a hostage began to seem less sensible than it had when they discussed it in the great hall. Such a woman as Aife would be unlikely to accept being a captive of her enemies without causing trouble or, at the very least, attempting to escape. A hostage like that could be more trouble than they were worth, especially if they were harmed or even killed while in their captors' care.

However, that one flicker of defiance when he'd mentioned her being Drest's daughter might, he thought, give him something to work with. There had been something behind that little flicker and he suspected it could be key to Aife being a model prisoner. She would never be called that of course – officially, she would be an honoured guest of Queen Narina and the people of Alt Clota.

This chance to meet Aife would, Bellicus hoped, give him an idea of how she'd adapt to her new life. If she accepted the reality and saw herself as a guest, all would be well. He feared the young woman would rebel against the enforced captivity though.

"Wait." He held up a hand, stopping both Aife and the guard in their tracks and then he stared into the cell nearest the prison's exit. Six or seven men sat on the floor, sullen and bloodied, but, despite the bruising on one older warrior's face, Bellicus had recognised him. Indeed, with his bald head, straggly grey beard, and scarred forehead, the man was hard to miss. "Gartnaith. We meet again."

"Bellicus, my lord!" The man scrambled across to the cell gate, wide-eyed but much more respectful than he'd been when the druid last saw him. "Well met, druid. Have you come to set us free?"

Bellicus laughed at that, long and hard, the sound echoing menacingly around the gloomy prison. He thought back to their last meeting, when Gartnaith had so arrogantly escorted him and Duro through Drest's army, where the king had then ordered their beating and capture. The tables had turned now, and the druid thought about killing the sour-faced old prick on the spot. He shook his head though, laughter gone at last. "No, I'll not set you free, Gartnaith." He leaned close to the bars that separated them and stared coldly into the Pictish chieftain's eyes. "But I might come back to visit you later. When I do, I promise you'll wish you'd died in the battle last night."

Gartnaith paled which made the blue and yellow bruises on his skin stand out even more lividly, but Bellicus turned away and nodded to Aife who was watching him with a mixture of amusement and uncertainty.

"Go ahead, lady," he said, and they moved on again, reaching the prison door and allowing the guard to pull it open for them.

"As easy as that?" Aife asked. "I just walk out? No shackles?"

Bellicus shook his head. "I don't think there's any need for them. Oh," he smiled broadly, charmingly. "I'm certain you could put up quite a fight if you wanted to try and escape but there's no point. The only way out of here is through the gates at the bottom of the main stairs, and there's guards all over the place."

They stepped through the doorway and went up the stairs leaving Gartnaith and his frightened comrades behind. It was late afternoon by now, and heavy grey clouds threatened to empty their contents across the land again but, even so, the brightness made Aife screw up her eyes. She soon adapted however, and breathed the fresh air gratefully as she looked around, taking in the people working in this central section of the fortress. She didn't even attempt to hide it when she looked at the walls, clearly searching for possible ways to get out and back on the road to Dunnottar.

"You would need a very long rope to climb down from here," Bellicus said, still smiling, and the honesty in his words and expression seemed to make the girl warm to him. Her face remained grim, impassive, but she looked at him from glittering hazel eyes and there was amusement there as well as the earlier suspicion.

They walked up the slope towards the eastern summit, eventually coming to a section of wall that afforded fine views across the lands to the north, including the village of Dun Buic. On a day like this everything looked so calm and serene, with wispy cooking fires and tiny figures and wagons moving slowly here and there, that it was easy to lose oneself in simply watching the passage of life. A sparrowhawk hovered overhead, harassed by angry crows, but it evaded them with languorous ease.

"How did you know we were coming through the tunnel?" Aife asked, breaking the silence and leaning her arms on the wall to look out across the land she had fully expected her father would be ruling by this time today.

Bellicus took up a position beside her, a small smile on his stubbled face. "Qunavo and Ria thought they had the perfect plan, eh?"

"Aye," the warrior-woman said. "We all did to be fair. I've seen men fall apart before once Ria starts to charm them. I felt sure she'd do the same to you, or at least the centurion." Aife seemed amused by the druidess's manipulation of weak men, although she frowned now as she looked at Bellicus. "I assume your own training as a druid made you immune to Ria's ways."

For some reason the thought of lying, of agreeing with her flattering assessment of his mental strength, didn't appeal to Bellicus. He found it easy to talk to this Pictish girl, a princess of a sort in her own right, even if she wasn't officially recognised as such by Drest.

"No, she had me ensnared," he admitted ruefully. "Almost as firmly as that fly in the web there."

Aife looked down, watching a little spider racing across its gossamer threads to begin the task of cocooning the hapless midge that had fluttered into its web. "Thankfully, Duro is more experienced than I am. He's a bit older after all, and gained much useful wisdom in his extra years." Although he found himself trusting this stranger, he did not tell her of Catia's part in the thwarting of Ria's plan. Did not tell her that the young girl had suspected Ria's duplicity and warned Duro about it – for some reason it seemed like that information should not be imparted to Aife, who was, and would remain a prisoner here in Dun Breatann for the foreseeable future.

"I'm a little embarrassed to admit that even my dog saw through your druidess's scheme," he said, raising his chin towards Cai who was lying on the grass beside them. "He didn't seem to like Ria very much. I assumed he was simply jealous that someone other than him was getting so much attention." He put out his hand as the mastiff stood up and licked Bellicus's palm, rumbling in his great chest as the druid ruffled his ears and the fur on his broad back. "I should have known better."

"I wouldn't want him as an enemy," Aife smiled, but she showed no fear of Cai, instead reaching out slowly to stroke the dog beneath his chin.

"Don't worry, he likes you," Bellicus said, watching with a look of loving pride as Cai ambled off and began rolling on his back, biting at some invisible enemy in the air, tongue lolling and heavy tail swishing from side to side.

They gazed back out across Alt Clota as a cloud passed away from the sun and warm, golden light flowed across the land from east to west, chasing a great shadow before it that even the highest hill couldn't slow.

"So, you started to suspect Ria. That doesn't explain how you knew we'd be coming through the tunnel though. Where is she anyway?" Aife looked horrified as she went on. "You didn't kill her, did you? I know you thought my father was going to execute you, but that was just part of Qunavo's plan, there was never any real intention to do away with you."

"Of course not," Bellicus growled. "They simply wanted to frighten us by threatening our lives and chopping off Duro's fingers."

Aife shrugged. "This is war," she said. "Bad things happen to good people sometimes. You would not have been killed though. Not a druid." Again, she met his gaze. "Your previous king killed one of our druids before. I heard all about that."

"Aye," Bellicus nodded. "And that was one of the things that started this war in the first place. Coroticus, as you know, is no longer ruler of Alt Clota, and no, we do not kill druids. Ria escaped."

Aife smiled in admiration at her tribeswoman's fortitude. "Good. You may not agree, but she's a loyal friend and I'm glad to know she lives still."

Bellicus frowned at her words, but didn't tell Aife that Ria's loyalty to her friends would soon be forgotten if it suited the druidess better to betray them. What would he know anyway? Ria had played him like a lute, making him sing her tune as if he was nothing more than a lustful youngster.

"Did you torture her before she escaped," Aife asked. "Is that how you knew our plans?"

"Oh no," the druid said. "Duro went to Queen Narina with his suspicions. He'd been wondering about Ria's claim that your army numbered in the hundreds. It seemed unbelievable, and he began to suspect she'd exaggerated in order to keep us cooped up inside the fortress, too fearful of riding out when we had so few men ourselves."

Aife shook her head dolefully. "My father should have killed the centurion."

"Aye, he should have," Bellicus said. "But he didn't, and Narina sent out two scouts. They climbed down ropes and slipped around to the back of your da's army. It wasn't long before they returned and confirmed Duro's suspicions: Drest only had forty or so men with him, yet he was outside our gates as if ready to attack. It made no sense." His face became grim now. "I was in my bed when all this was going on."

"With Ria."

He looked sidelong at her but ignored the remark and its lascivious undertones. "Narina sent for me then and, leaving Ria in my house, I went to the great hall and was told about the scouts' findings. It was then that I remembered Ria had apparently 'lost' a fine, white-handled dagger during our flight from the Pictish scouts. I realised I'd last seen it just before we entered the secret tunnel and that's when I knew Duro, and Catia, and Cai, had all been right to suspect Ria." He shrugged and blew away a dandelion clock that was floating close to his face. "We set up the ambush outside the well, stopping your little warband before they could carry out their mission although we let your torchbearer light his signal before he was dispatched. And then, we simply opened the outer gates and slaughtered your army when they came through into our killing ground."

Aife bowed her head sadly, remembering the others of her group who had come through that inky black tunnel with her. "I told them to wear armour," she muttered.

"That's the only reason you survived our attack," Bellicus told her. "An arrow must have ricocheted off your helmet and knocked you out cold. When you woke up, the battle was over and, since you were well dressed, it was assumed you were a noblewoman and might fetch a ransom. So, your fine armour actually saved your life twice over." He smiled at her. "I must admit, we were shocked to discover your true identity."

"What of Ria?" she asked, frowning at his enjoyment of the Picts' defeat.

He looked up to watch the crows still screeching and attempting to drive away the sparrowhawk overhead. "Narina sent guards to arrest her before we even set up our ambush at the tunnel, but she must have spotted them gathering and suspected her scheme had been found out. By the time they reached my house, Ria was gone. Over the wall."

"You don't seem bothered," the warrior-woman said. "Her magic lingers on within you, eh?"

"Perhaps," he shrugged. "But I always liked her. Part of me is glad she escaped, although I've no doubt she'll come back to haunt me again one day. Honestly..." He paused, as if weighing his words, and the wisdom of sharing them with this stranger, before going on. "I'm embarrassed how easily she fooled me. I'm supposed to be a druid. Men say I have the gift of foresight and believe I'm in touch with the gods and yet...I was completely taken in by Ria."

"It's natural to see the best in people," Aife said. "And you'd been through a lot. You needed hope, and Ria offered it to you."

Bellicus nodded and smiled gratefully at the young woman. "Perhaps. It's all turned out for the best in the end anyway. Well...Maybe not for you, but Narina won't be unkind to you while you're staying in Dun Breatann."

"Can I see the battlefield?" Aife asked suddenly, as if not yet ready to accept her fate. "I mean, the place where my father and his men were attacked. I'd like to pay my respects to the shades of my dead kinsmen."

The druid nodded. "Of course. Come on. Don't try to escape when we get to the gates, though, or I'll set Cai on you."

She shuddered but realised he was joking. Or at least, she hoped he was. Cai watched her from bright eyes however, and even if she *had* harboured thoughts of escape, they evaporated now.

"What are you going to do with us?" she asked as they walked down the slope towards the great hall once again, passing the well and the dried blood of her kinsmen that still stained the path there. "Me, my father, the rest of those you took hostage, I mean."

"What do you think we'll do?" he replied. "What would Drest do if the roles were reversed?"

They looked at one another and Aife decided there was no point in lying. The druid was no fool.

"Kill the queen and ransom the rest, most likely."

"Would you do the same, if you were in charge?"

Aife smiled coyly. "I'm only a young girl," she said. "I don't know how these things work."

"A young girl who was ready to cut down the men and women in this fortress," he retorted, and her smirk disappeared.

"Like I said," she replied, ignoring the admiring stare of a Damnonii guardsmen. "Things happen during war. But, to answer your question, I honestly don't know what I would do if I was in your queen's position." Her jocularity faded completely as they came to the main staircase and began to move down it. "May I see my father before he is…executed?"

Bellicus didn't reply and they went down the stairs in silence. When they reached the inner gates, he made a gesture and the guards quickly removed the heavy bars holding them shut, then pulled them open just enough to let the pair walk through. They would be opened all the time during the coming days but, for now, Narina had ordered them to remain shut until they were certain all the Pictish soldiers had fled north.

"Here," the druid said, nodding to the flat ground outside the gatehouse. "Is where your fellows died. You may spend some time here, alone, if you would like. I'll take Cai to the river – he enjoys swimming in the water."

"Thank you," the girl said sadly, and the weight of the previous night's momentous events showed clearly on her face.

"Come and get me when you're ready," he said kindly. "And we'll find something to eat and drink and talk some more." He headed towards the next, outer, set of gates—these were lying open—and called back over his shoulder as he went. "As for your father: Narina has decided he's to be spared and allowed to go home. You will remain here as our hostage, however, to make sure he doesn't come back with another army."

He disappeared through the gates with the dog, but Aife didn't call out or even know what to say. For now, she was just happy that the Alt Clotans weren't going to kill her and her father for it meant there was still a chance for her to follow Ria, over the wall and back to Dunnottar.

* * *

The next day a boat came along the Clota and Duro, who was at the docks to seek passage south, immediately recognised the little vessel, and the man sailing in it. "Maedoc! Well met, my friend," the centurion shouted, striding out into the waters lapping against the pebble-strewn beach and helping the man drag his boat ashore. "What brings you here?"

Maedoc hailed from Auchalic, a small settlement to the west that had been part of Loarn mac Eirc's territory in Dalriada until recently. With the king's death, the people had chosen to pledge allegiance to Queen Narina, returning once more to their original status as part of the Damnonii tribe. Duro had spent some time in Auchalic along with Bellicus when they escaped Loarn's deadly wrath the previous year and Maedoc had been the one who brought them safely back to Alt Clota in his boat.[3]

"I bear bad tidings, I'm afraid," the sailor said as they made sure his vessel was secure and wouldn't be drawn off when the tide came in. "Can you take me to the queen?" He looked anxious at the thought of meeting Narina, then said, swallowing nervously, "Or even just Bel. He can pass on my message, can't he?"

---

[3] See _Song of the Centurion_

Duro laughed. "Of course he could but, you do realise Bel is just as important a person as Queen Narina? Even more so in some ways. Come." He led the sailor along the beach towards the gates of Dun Breatann. "What's so pressing that you had to come all the way here anyway?"

Maedoc shook his head and his features were pinched, tense. "I fear my settlement is about to be wiped from the face of the world, Duro."

CHAPTER TWENTY-FIVE

"An army?" Gavo groaned when Duro had brought Maedoc to the great hall and the queen and her advisors were gathered to hear his news. "Not another bloody army. By the gods, are we ever to be left alone? Just a few weeks' peace would be nice!"

"How big is this army?" Narina asked kindly. Although she was as irritated as her captain by the news from the western edge of Alt Clota's borders, she could see the messenger was nervous and sought to put him at his ease.

Maedoc bowed his head and stared at the hall's rush-strewn floor. "We're not sure, my lady," he admitted. "Probably not that big – maybe fifteen or twenty men? But, if they're skilled warriors that's more than we can deal with in Auchalic. They've already taken control of some of the settlements closest to us, and any who tried to stand against them were cut down. Their leader is a chieftain from over the sea, claims to be some kinsman of Loarn mac Eirc and the rightful king of Dalriada."

"Do you know his name?" Gavo asked, but the messenger shook his head.

Narina smiled at him. "Thank you, Maedoc. You may sit there and refresh yourself while we discuss your news."

The man gratefully took his place at the table the queen had gestured towards and sipped the ale that a servant set out for him. There was cold, salted beef and some bread, but his stomach was turning too much to eat just then so he sipped the ale instead.

"Twenty men," Gerallt muttered. "Even if that's an accurate figure, it should be easy enough to put them down."

"Twenty men a week ago," Bellicus cautioned. "Could have risen to double that number by now, if men from the villages this chieftain is taking control of are joining his warband."

"Or half of the twenty might have been killed by the villagers they've been attacking," Gerallt said.

Narina sighed. "Whatever their numbers, we have a duty to do something about it. The headman, Galchobhar, and the other people of Auchalic joined us back when Drest's first siege was in place. They, along with others from those lands, came here with Gavo and me to fight on our side. I'll not abandon them now."

Bellicus nodded. "I agree," he said. "Galchobhar's a loyal friend and we must help him and his people. It's going to be hard to maintain our hold over all those villages going forward, however. This is just the first in what will likely be a continuous, ongoing threat to our new borders."

"That's something we'll need to look at," said Narina. "Perhaps setting up a warband that will patrol those areas continuously. Gavo, Gerallt, you two can start to think how best to do this. Maybe cavalry would be useful, so they can quickly travel where they're needed?"

Gerallt nodded enthusiastically. "Aye. And we could rotate them, so men do a month as part of the unit then return home while another goes to take their place." Clearly his mind had begun to work out the logistics of such an operation already but this was all for the future. Maedoc and his settlement still needed help now, before this new Dalriadan chieftain arrived.

Duro, although wanting no part of Alt Clotan troubles anymore, had stayed in the great hall when he brought Maedoc, purely because the nervous sailor had asked him to, being a friendly face that he at least knew. Bellicus looked at the centurion now, hopefully.

"If the queen wills it, I'll lead a warband to Auchalic today," he said. "What do you say, Duro, old friend? One last adventure, for old times' sake?"

"He's hardly fit enough for a fight like that," Narina protested, adding, "and neither are you, Bel," before the druid looked at her, shaking his head.

"I grow stronger with every day," he said. "And Duro won't need to fight, just advise. He was a centurion after all – who better do we have for a task like this?"

All eyes turned to Duro, who was frowning and touching his bandaged hand absently.

"Come on," Bellicus cajoled. "You, me, and Cai. One last battle before you head off to join Arthur."

Duro rolled his eyes. "I suppose someone will have to keep you out of trouble," he said, and Bellicus grinned.

"That's settled then," Narina said, getting to her feet. "Bel: you and Duro make ready to leave while Maedoc finishes his meal. Gerallt and Gavo, come with me and we'll see about gathering the men that'll travel to Auchalic with them." She headed for the doors, eager to get things moving now that the talking was over but, as she reached the centurion she stopped and laid a hand on his shoulder. "Thank you, Duro," she said earnestly. "You've served Alt Clota, and me, well. I'm truly sorry I can't properly repay Drest for what he did to you, but you have my thanks for everything you've done for us. I'll forever be indebted to you."

The centurion nodded but didn't reply and soon only he, Bellicus and Maedoc were left in the hall.

"Well," he growled to the druid at last. "What are we sitting here for? We've things to do before we leave. Let's move, soldier."

* * *

"I was supposed to be finding a ship to take me south," Duro said, standing in the prow of Maedoc's boat as it scudded across the water on a westward course. "Yet here I am, malnourished and exhausted, about to fight a chieftain whose name we don't even know, in a land I never thought I'd set foot in again."

"And you love it," Bellicus grinned, slapping his friend on the back and glorying in the fine spray that was cast backwards every time the boat crested a wave and dipped down into the river again.

It hadn't taken long for Gavo and Gerallt to choose twenty men from the garrison to join them on this journey. While the warriors were gathering their weapons along with provisions of meat and drink and carrying them down to the docks, Narina had commanded two of her captains to prepare their ships and, by early afternoon they were underway.

The lead ship, the *Milwr Môr*, was captained by Cistumucus, who Bellicus knew to be a competent and experienced sailor. The second vessel was helmed by a small, stocky man named Judocus, and Maedoc had tethered his own small boat to this, being towed along by the larger, faster ship, which allowed him to raise his sail, lie back, and simply enjoy the journey.

"Do you think twenty men will be enough for this?" Duro asked seriously.

"Aye," the druid replied confidently. "Twenty-two, counting us, plus however many join us in Auchalic. The Dalriadans are disjointed and working in small groups to try and grab whatever territory they can from us, and one another. It's the age-old story." He stared into the middle distance as if in a daydream. "If all the different noblemen and petty warlords joined together under a high-king they might seize control of Alt Clota but with Loarn's demise they've returned to their old, feuding ways. At least, I imagine that's what's happening. It usually is."

"We'll find out soon enough," Duro said, turning away and walking a little unsteadily across the deck to his pack where he sat down and took out some cheese. Bellicus had told him the crumbly yellow food, an Alt Clotan specialty, would be good for putting meat back onto his bones and, since the centurion loved cheese, he'd made sure Dun Breatann's stores were raided to put as much of it into his pack as possible.

Cai remained by his master's side, although he padded across to the centurion once, hoping for some scraps, and wandered off when none were forthcoming. The rest of the men on the ships were similarly lounging around: eating, sharpening weapons, crafting arrows, playing tafl, and chatting amongst themselves about the coming battle. Although they had just won a famous, crushing victory over Drest's Picts, none of the Damnonii warriors had actually done any real fighting – they'd simply rained arrows down on their enemy and slaughtered or captured the few who survived the missiles. Now they were looking forward to raising sword and shield and testing themselves against the men from across the sea, winning booty and renown in the process.

Also in their ship was the Votadini hothead, Eburus, who had asked Bellicus, uncharacteristically politely, if he might come along with them on their mission. Since his martial skills were not in question, and the people of Dun Breatann were growing rather tired of his brash personality, the druid agreed.

The young man was telling a tale about an adventure he'd had while out with his friends raiding cattle from a neighbouring tribe and Bellicus watched as he spoke. Eburus gestured with his hands a lot, and directed questions such as, "D'ye know what I mean?" to specific people every so often, calling them by name and staring at them with a grin on his face, inviting them to laugh along and become invested in his story. Bellicus realised that, for all his bluster and posturing, the Votadini champion was quite immature and desperately in need of validation. He wanted people to respect him. To like him.

Of course, those traits—in combination with Eburus's size, strength and love of strong ale—made for a volatile relationship with everyone around him. Like a dam that developed a weak point within its structure, it would only be a matter of time before it burst, and a devastating torrent was unleashed on everything nearby.

Many people would get hurt if that happened with Eburus, unless someone took the young man under their wing and gave him the tutelage he so clearly needed. Although Bellicus was only a few years older, he had the benefit of a druid's training behind him and, for some reason, he rather liked the brash young warrior.

His tale of a raid gone wrong ended and, tellingly, his own laughter was the loudest. Bellicus noted the men in the audience smiling politely, even warily, but their looks to one another and out across the glistening Clota, made it obvious they wished Eburus would be silent for a time. He was only just getting started however, as he opened his mouth and began another tale, this time about an encounter he'd had with a neighbour's wife.

"Eburus," the druid called to him, still standing in the ship's prow. The Votadini glanced around, still smiling like a daft boy, and Bellicus waved him across. Eburus's eyes narrowed for a moment, before he grinned at his relieved audience and walked towards the head of the vessel to stand before the druid.

"How have you liked your time in Dun Breatann?" Bellicus asked in a friendly tone, trying to set the wary young man at his ease. Neither of them had forgotten that first meeting, when the druid had confused Eburus and ultimately embarrassed him by putting him flat on his back. To help relax him, Bellicus offered his ale-skin and sat down on the deck, nodding at Eburus to do the same.

"Don't mind if I do," the pony-tailed warrior grinned, accepting the drink and slumping down next to Bellicus with the stopper already out and the spout raised to his lips. "How have I liked it in Alt Clota?" he said, wiping his mouth with the back of a hand. "Not much. It's been boring, apart from that first battle with the Picts. I enjoyed that. Killed four of them myself, at least."

"It's not as much fun being in a fortress that's besieged though, eh?"

"Aye, you can say that again," Eburus said, shaking his head and passing the ale-skin back to Bellicus. "I was getting to the stage where I thought it might be best just to climb out of the gatehouse and attack Drest's army by myself. It wears on a man's nerves being cooped up, y'know?"

The druid nodded, imagining how much worse it must have been for those unfortunate enough to be stuck with Eburus all day, listening to his banter and boasting.

"I was impressed when you asked to come along on this mission," Bellicus said, truthfully. "This is not your fight, after all. It's Alt Clota's borders we're sailing to protect."

"We're allies now," the Votadini champion said. "Besides, I hate Dalriadans more than I hate you Damnonii bastards."

They both laughed at that and the conversation moved on to lighter topics, from the druid's dog to seasickness and how being tall meant some people always saw you as a target. By the end of it, the ale-skin was empty and Eburus was quite at ease with the druid. They may not be fast friends yet, but a start had certainly been made in that direction.

"I'm going to speak with Cistumucus," Bellicus said as it neared mid-afternoon and he knew if he didn't get up and move around the deck he'd fall asleep. Reaching down, he grasped Eburus's hand, helping him up and they stood looking at one another with a newfound camaraderie.

"Thanks for the ale, druid," said the Votadini champion, eyes twinkling from more than just the drink. "I'll grant you Alt Clotans one thing: You know how to brew a good drop of ale."

"We do," Bellicus agreed. "And we'll share even more of it together, you and me, once we kick the Dalriadans' arses back over the sea to Hibernia."

Nodding, Eburus grinned and turned to walk back to the companions he'd been sitting with at the start of the journey, but Bellicus softly called his name and, when he turned round, the druid said in a low tone. "If you ever need someone to talk to, you know where I am." He thought about saying more but decided against it. Too many people were around, and, at this early stage in their friendship it would be easy to say something that might be misconstrued as a criticism or even challenge, ruining the foundations Bellicus had laid over the past hour or so.

Eburus looked a little surprised by the druid's words and pondered them for a moment before finally nodding gravely and walking carefully back to the other men.

Rather more steadily, for he'd hardly touched the ale in his skin, allowing the young Votadini the lion's share, Bellicus headed to the stern where Cistumucus tended the steering oar.

"Are we stopping for the night soon?"

"Aye," the captain said, shading his eyes with his hand as he looked along the coastline they were passing. "We've had a decent wind and made good time. We're halfway there so…" He looked at the sun, gauging how long they had before it dipped below the horizon, picturing in his mind's eye where might be a decent place to drop the sea anchor, or if they could put ashore for the night. Usually, these lands would be safe but, given their mission and the threat of Dalriadan raiders, it would probably be best to spend the night on the Clota. The men wouldn't like that much, not being used to sleeping on something that moved after all, but better that than an axe in the skull. "We'll sail on for another hour perhaps, then you can decide what we do for the night, lord."

They had passed a small number of other vessels during the day—traders or fishermen—with no sign of invaders, which was only to be expected. The Dalriadans would surely want to take control of the territory nearest to Dunadd, and work outwards from there; but there was always a chance a particularly aggressive, or ambitious chieftain, would head straight for the likes of Carden Ros, deep in the heartland of

Alt Clota, in the hopes of finding the people there unprepared for an attack.

When the time came to stop for the night, however, Bellicus decided it was safe enough to camp on land. Cistumucus chose a spot that had a good view of the terrain around it, so they wouldn't be sneaked up on during the night, and sentries were posted to make doubly sure. It would take a sizeable force to best the Damnonii warband anyway, given its size. Bellicus told the two captains to keep their ships ready to be pushed back into the water though, just in case. He had no desire to lose his men before they even reached Auchalic.

When tents had been erected, cooking fires lit, water collected from a narrow burn beside the camp, and everyone settled in for the evening, Bellicus and Duro sat watching the sun go down. The warriors continued their pastimes from the day's journey—dice, knucklebones, tafl and even some raucous arm-wrestling. What surprised the druid and his centurion friend was Eburus's choice of activity.

The Votadini champion spent some time exercising, warming up his muscles a short distance away from the main group of men. When he was ready, he then took his sword and practised manoeuvres with it, both defensive and offensive. Clearly, he took his skills seriously and hadn't become his tribe's best fighter at such a young age by dint of raw, natural talent.

"I'm glad he's on our side," Bellicus said admiringly. "He's got the size and strength to make him a naturally great fighter without much effort, but he chooses to hone his skills instead of relaxing with the rest of the warband."

Duro wasn't as appreciative. "The man's an arsehole," he growled, munching another piece of cheese.

Bellicus laughed. "It's always good to hear your blunt opinion, but I think you're wrong." He continued to watch as Eburus moved with practiced ease from one position to another, his footwork flawless, eyes hard, face set and determined. "He's just a young man looking for his place in the world. He thinks he has to impress those around him all the time and it makes him loud and brash and that comes across as arrogance."

"It comes across as arrogance," Duro said. "Because that's what it is. And when he starts on the ale, he becomes even more insufferable."

Bellicus didn't argue for it wasn't really important who was right. They would both be glad to have Eburus with them if they came up against Dalriadan raiders, and that was what mattered.

Eventually, the Votadini completed his workout and quickly washed the sweat from his face and limbs in the nearby burn before finding a space around the fire and a mug of ale.

"Here we go," Duro muttered, rolling his eyes and heading for his tent. "I'm going to try and get to sleep now, before his loud boasting keeps me up until dawn. Wake me when it's my turn for sentry duty."

The druid shook his head. "No need. You're still recovering, and I'd say you've earned the right to enjoy a full night's uninterrupted rest. We both have – commanders' privilege. Make the most of it, my friend."

Duro looked uncomfortable at the idea of not taking his turn on watch, and Bellicus shared the sentiment, but their warband was large enough that everyone would get plenty of rest and their mission would be best served if both centurion and druid returned to full fitness as soon as possible.

They woke early the next morning, glad to see the men already tearing down the camp.

By the time the sun appeared on the horizon the ships were on their way once more.

CHAPTER TWENTY-SIX

"Shit, we're too late!" The smoke rising from Auchalic was thick and black and came not from cooking fires, but from homes burning. Duro slammed his hand on the prow of the *Milwr Môr* and called out an even stronger oath as Cistumucus ordered the oars be put into the water that they might reach land quicker.

The men did as they were commanded and soon both ships were racing towards the shore. Bellicus gazed at the village they'd come all this way to save and felt sick to his stomach. The people of Auchalic had been good to him and Duro, particularly the headman, Galchobhar, and the thought of raiders butchering them was hard to take. From one battlefield to another in the space of just a couple of days. By the gods, would the people of Britannia ever stop killing one another?

"They're still there," he muttered, squinting against the sunshine as he watched figures moving about the settlement. "They're still there!" He turned to the men rowing and urged them on. "We might be too late to save the villagers' lives, but we can still avenge Auchalic's destruction for the Dalriadans are still there."

Their approach had been spotted by now, and the soldiers plundering the village were forming up into a line, preparing for this new threat.

"Put in here, Cistumucus," Bellicus ordered. "We must get ashore as soon as possible, or they'll cut us down with their javelins when we're getting off the ships."

The captain nodded and shoved his steering oar, bringing the *Milwr Môr* into a tighter turn than before as Bellicus waved at Judocus in the second ship to follow suit.

It was just as well the druid had commanded this move for the Dalriadans had indeed started moving towards them, lined up with shields ready and, although they didn't appear to have javelins, they had spears which would undoubtedly have been launched at Bellicus's men if they could have been caught disembarking from their ships.

"Tight formation," Duro bellowed, strapping on his crested helmet as the *Milwr Môr* scraped onto the beach and the warriors jumped out into the water. "Shields locked together! How many do you see, Bel?"

The druid counted perhaps sixteen oncoming Dalriadans and he relayed this information to the centurion who he was happy to cede command of this larger section of the warband to. This was exactly what a Roman officer trained for after all. Duro cursed, knowing the enemy force was large enough to make this a hard-fought battle which might go either way.

Bellicus lifted Cai from the ship and they ran to join the men from the second vessel which had just reached the shore. He ordered the men to form a similar shield wall to Duro's group, although he led them off to the right, creating a gap between his and the centurion's men. Two targets would be much harder for the Dalriadans to deal with than one.

The invaders came on until Bellicus could see their faces, and the man who led them. He was a flame-haired warrior of average height, but with enormous shoulders and a cruel grin beneath his beard that suggested he'd been enjoying himself before the arrival of the two ships disturbed his activities.

"What are ye after, lads?" the Dalriadan called out, taking in the centurion's helmet and armour and addressing Duro after an initial moment of surprise at the out of place dress. "I'm Dubhslaine of Cell Dara; you've probably heard of me. We're a little bit busy here just now, but we'll be done soon enough and then ye can be about your business."

Bellicus stepped ahead of his men and pointed his eagle-topped staff at the man. "We're here on behalf of Queen Narina of Alt Clota, you grinning fool, and no – we've never heard of you before. These are Alt Clotan lands you're burning, so I think it only fair that you make good the damage." He swept his staff around, including all of the Dalriadan soldiers in its arc as he went on. "I am Bellicus,

Druid of Dun Breatann, and by Dis, we'll nourish the ground of Auchalic with your lifeblood, and then I'll take your souls for my own."

Some of the enemy warriors blanched at this curse, but not the leader. He grinned even wider and drew out a cross that had been hidden beneath his chainmail. "You may not have heard of me, Bellicus, but I've heard about you. Your old gods have no power over us, druid, for we follow Christ."

"You follow nothing but your own desire for blood and power, you whoreson." Bellicus looked up at the sky and roared, "Taranis! Guide our blades and accept these Dalriadan worms as a sacrifice." He nodded towards Duro and the centurion—who was, unusually for him, at the rear of the shield wall—ordered the advance.

"This way," the druid said to his men, and they moved up further to the right, looking to flank the Dalriadans, Cai staying tight by Bellicus's side.

The intention was clear, and Dubhslaine eyed the two approaching groups warily. He was outnumbered and had very little chance of winning this fight with the way things were progressing. His men knew it too, with some of them looking back over their shoulders, apparently checking if the way was clear should they decide to flee.

"Wait," the Dalriadan called, his grin fading. "There's no point in all of us dying here. Why not just let us be on our way, Bellicus? We'll take only what we've already gathered, and leave the rest for you."

"What about the people you've murdered?" Bellicus demanded. "Do you think I would just let you wander off with your stolen wealth while the blood of good Damnonii men and women stain the ground here?"

Dubhslaine shook his head, waving a hand dismissively at burning buildings. "These folk were Dalriadans until a few months ago – they have no loyalty to your queen, they follow whoever they're told to. Are you going to see your warriors cut down to avenge the deaths of such people? Besides, we hardly killed anyone – they saw us coming and ran away, the cowards."

That lifted Bellicus, although he had no way of knowing how true it was. Still, if Galchobhar and the rest of the villagers had survived the raid, that was good news. The settlement may be burning, but if the inhabitants still lived, they could rebuild.

"You see, druid?" Dubhslaine said, grin returning to his face. "There would be no shame in avoiding a battle with us over this shit hole. We'll just be on our way and never return here again, since, as you say, Queen Narina has claimed the land as her own."

"Maedoc."

The sailor was at the very front of the men with Bellicus and he called out now. "Aye, lord?"

"Does it sound like the Dalriadan is telling the truth? Would Galchobhar have taken the people to safety? Or stood and fought?"

Maedoc patted his leg with the long knife he carried, as if he could hardly contain his desire to attack the men who'd set alight to his home. "Aye, he might have led them away. There'd have been lookouts after all since we knew the Dalriadans were in the area, so their coming would probably have been noted."

"You see?" Dubhslaine called, overhearing the exchange despite being fifty yards away with the sounds of the village burning behind him, and the gulls crying out overhead for the fighting to start that they might fill their bellies with man-flesh. "There's no dishonour in allowing us to retreat. Let your men return home to their families, druid, to fight another enemy, another day."

Bellicus looked across to Duro, who nodded. He might not be kin to any of the men he was leading, but he still valued their lives. "Let them go," the centurion advised. "Then we can set about dousing the fires before they spread further. A few of the buildings may yet be saved if we move quickly."

Some, including Maedoc and the Votadini, Eburus, cursed at the idea of missing out on a chance to repay the Dalriadans for their destruction, but it was the druid who had the final say, and he valued Duro's counsel over all others.

"You can go, Dubhslaine," Bellicus shouted, "but be warned: Henceforth, these lands will be patrolled by a warband more than four times the size of yours." He was exaggerating wildly, but he wanted any other Dalriadan invaders to think twice before attacking these lands again. "We've recently smashed the Picts and allied with the Votadini so Narina is now High Queen of all the lands the Romans knew as Caledonia. Tell the rest of your people to stay away from Alt Clota's borders, for the next time there's an attack like this we'll not be so merciful."

The Dalriadan nodded and the cruel sneer on his face, the triumphant smile, almost made Bellicus change his mind and order the attack. The enemy warriors began to edge backwards however, in response to their chieftain's laughing command, and the druid grudgingly let them go.

"This isn't right, my lord," Maedoc said, and his voice was heavy with frustration. "They should die for what they've done to Auchalic."

"They should," Bellicus agreed. "But my men shouldn't, and, unfortunately, an unacceptable number of them would lose their lives if we were to engage with the Dalriadans in battle."

"Maybe not," called out Eburus, raising his sword to point into the burning settlement. "Look there."

Bellicus squinted, trying to see through the thick smoke and embers that swirled about in the breeze.

"What is it?" Duro demanded. "More Dalriadans?"

Figures appeared between the flaming buildings, but it was not more invaders. Front and centre was Galchobhar, and he carried a sword purposefully while the others with him—a dozen at least—also carried weapons ranging from pitchforks to carpenters' hammers.

"It looks like we're going to have a fight after all," Bellicus called to Duro and, although he wasn't happy about it, the sight of Galchobhar – alive – pleased him greatly.

"Yaaaassss!" shouted Eburus, clattering the blade of his sword against his shield yet somehow retaining his discipline and standing in the line until the centurion ordered the advance.

Dubhslaine looked back at Bellicus, his arrogant sneer gone, replaced with panic. "You swore we could walk away, druid!" he cried, but it was too late.

"Charge!" roared Galchobhar, his face black with soot and rage. "Make the bastards pay for what they've done to our homes!"

Dubhslaine could see the time for talk was over and decided to make a break for it. "Back!" he called to his men, "Smash through the villagers and run!" This was the obvious course of action, for the other direction only led to the river and the Damnonii warbands. His force outnumbered Galchobhar's by two-to-one however, so, desperately, the Dalriadans ran towards the men and women of Auchalic.

With their shields, spears, and armour, Duro could see only one outcome for the villagers, who were clad only in their everyday, working clothes, and carried makeshift weapons for the most part. There would be a terrible slaughter, and then the Dalriadans would be through and running. They might even have horses waiting nearby, and their escape would be complete.

"Loose spears!" commanded the centurion, jogging along behind his charging men. "Loose them. Now!"

Bellicus could see what his friend was trying to do, and repeated the instruction to his own men, urging them to make their throws count.

The Dalriadans were too far away to be met with sword and shield, but the volley of spears tore through the air much faster than any man could run and, although some fell short, or wide, of their targets, others slammed home in the tight formation of Dalriadan raiders. Screaming in agony, more than half of Dubhslaine's men were cut down before the rest clashed with the villagers.

Bellicus, still not fully recovered from his tribulations in Dunnottar, hung back, Cai at his side, as the fighting continued and more cries of pain and fear filled the air, along with blood and phlegm and the smell of piss as men lost control of their bodies. Still the Dalriadans clung to their plan and two managed to smash through the line of Auchalic defenders, racing away without backward glances. The rest were pushed back, forced into a fight for their lives as Galchobhar and his fellows slashed and thrust at them with a brutality born of outrage.

Cai barked furiously at the fighting before him, the hackles on his back raised, but Bellicus held him by the scruff of his neck, muttering reassuring words to him as one of the villagers was chopped down, and then another.

And then, at last Eburus arrived, hacking down into the shoulder of a Dalriadan before reversing his cut and slicing the hamstrings of a second. The rest of Duro's force now joined the fight, and Bellicus's men came in at the side, and for a few moments the carnage continued in a strange near-silence.

From his left there came a cry of alarm and he turned, blood running cold as he saw Duro all alone, facing six approaching figures. More Dalriadans! The druid started to run, not yet ordering Cai ahead, but he knew he was too far away to help the centurion. The enemy warriors must have been looting the houses on the eastern side of the village and slipped unseen down towards the beach using the undergrowth there as cover.

Six against one, and Duro weakened after his ordeal with the Picts. The odds were too great and Bellicus roared an oath to Taranis as he ran, begging the thunder god for aid. It seemed this group of Dalriadans had realised there would be no escape on land for their gestures to one another made it clear that they planned to cut down the centurion and then steal the nearest Damnonii ship.

Duro had his spatha drawn and he met the first opponent's attack with a parry that put the Dalriadan off guard but there was no way for the centurion to capitalise on the opening as the next enemy was already upon him.

"Erebus!" The druid called and the Votadini champion turned to see Duro in trouble but he too was in the middle of a fight for his life and had to concentrate on the battle raging before him.

There was nothing for it – Cai was the only one who could move fast enough to help Duro. There was no need for the druid to give the command though, for, as if reading his thoughts, the dog was already streaking ahead of him.

The centurion was down on one knee but, mercifully, all six of the Dalriadans weren't coming for him. Three had broken off and were running towards the *Milwr Môr,* but there were still far too many for Duro to deal with. Gods, Bellicus knew even one would be too much for him in his current state.

A blade took him in the side and, roaring in agony, he dropped onto his back on the rocky beach as the three Dalriadans encircled him. There was no triumph on their faces for they knew they still had much to do if they were to escape, and they came for the downed centurion who had just enough energy to bat aside the first of their thrusts.

Tears blurred Bellicus's vision as he tripped on a boulder. This was all his fault. The centurion was supposed to be sailing south just now, safe and well, but Bellicus had persuaded him to come here to Auchalic for one more battle. It had been selfish and now Duro would die and probably Cai too, for, despite his strength, the dog's unarmoured hide was no match for a steel blade.

The loyal hound had reached Duro now and, as a Dalriadan stepped forward to plunge his sword into the centurion's groin Cai slammed into him, teeth sinking into the man's sword arm, crushing and fixed in place as the Dalriadan fell onto the ground, screaming in shock and pain.

To Bellicus's surprise, Duro somehow managed to stand up again, making the most of his enemies' confusion as Cai let go of his opponent's arm and attacked the face instead.

The Dalriadans saw this and gaped in horror, but they were seasoned warriors and attacked Duro again. Their companions were at the *Milwr Môr* now and their escape was still possible.

From out of nowhere, a spear streaked through the air and tore into one of the Dalriadan's with terrific force, punching easily through his armour and throwing him a yard sideways. Still running as fast as he could on the rocky beach Bellicus saw Erebus nodding in satisfaction and the druid grinned at the young warrior's prodigious throw.

And then he was at Duro's side and the final Dalriadan decided he'd had enough, sprinting after his friends at the Damnonii boat.

"Cai!"

The dog left the mangled neck of the man he'd killed, looking up at his master with eyes shining malevolently, maw reddened horribly. Bellicus pointed and the sight of the Dalriadan running away sparked his instinct to hunt and, once again, the dog sprinted across the beach. It was only a moment before he caught up with the fleeing warrior and nipped at his churning legs. Screaming, the man fell as the teeth dug into his calf and he fell across a pile of seaweed and rocks, sword spinning out of his hand. He was sobbing in terror for he'd seen what Cai had done to his comrade and he lashed out with his palm but Bellicus called the dog back.

Relief flooded the Dalriadan's face as the druid approached, murmuring soft words to the blood-stained hound but Bellicus was no angel of mercy. His sword, Melltgwyn, licked out and took the man in the heart but the druid continued on, towards the boat.

Aboard the *Milwr Môr,* Cistumucus had seen the raiders approaching and the first of them who placed his hands on the hull to push it into the water found himself missing a few fingers as the Dalriadan sailor's sword hacked down, severing the digits with a thump.

The other two heard their companion cry out and knew they must deal with Cistumucus before they could escape but if they thought he would be any easier to deal with than any of the other Damnonii warriors they were quickly disabused of the notion. He harried them with his sword until, at last, knowing time was running out, they decided to try and climb on board at the same time.

The first's skull was caved in by Cistumucus's blade, while the second was halfway over the keel when Cai's jaws clamped onto his backside and dragged him back onto land. Bellicus stamped down on his sword arm as he made to get back up, and then Melltgwyn finished it. The third man, the one who'd had his fingers severed, was running away, gripping his mutilated hand, stumbling and muttering to himself in shock.

He was no threat, so the druid let him go, nodding up at Cistumucus who waved in salute and then Bellicus headed back towards Duro and the main battle, keeping Cai close to his side and stroking the dog's side lovingly as he walked. Had there ever been a more loyal companion? Bel doubted it.

As they reached the village the druid could see that the two Dalriadans who had managed to break through the line of villagers were small specks in the distance by now, and their kinsmen were nothing but tattered, mangled corpses. The battle was over.

Galchobhar hacked away at Dubhslaine's tattered body, making it a terrible mess of blood and gore before exhaustion finally forced him to stop. Tears streamed down his face and he muttered, "Bastards," to himself, over and over.

"Are there more of them nearby?" Bellicus asked one of the other, calmer villagers. The man shook his head but didn't reply, perhaps because his jaw was shaking uncontrollably from the shock of the fight.

"All right," Duro said in a surprisingly calm yet firm voice, gesturing to those men who'd been part of his group. "Help the villagers put out the fires. Buckets, water, you all know what to do. Get to it." As they moved away, the centurion looked at Bellicus. "Are we going after the two who escaped?"

"No," the druid shook his head. "They can tell their countrymen what happened to them. Maybe it'll deter any other warlords from raiding these lands for a while. Until we can get that border force together anyway."

"Go and help the others with the fires then," Duro ordered, and the rest of their warband hurried to do his bidding, joined by more of the villagers – women, children and older folk, returning from where they'd been hiding in the nearby landscape.

Bellicus clasped his friend by the arm. "You fought well considering you're so weak right now," he said. "But I need to check the wound in your side. Take your armour off."

"What wound?" the centurion asked, frowning and looking down at his ribs.

To the druid's surprise, Duro's breastplate was completely intact. He'd thought one of the Dalriadans had stabbed the centurion, probably fatally, but his friend was smiling at him knowingly. "Roman armour, Bel," he said blithely. "The best."

Surprised but greatly relieved, Bellicus shared Duro's smile and then went to deal with the aftermath of the battle. "Galchobhar." The headman was standing, looking at the dying settlement and shaking his head sadly. He didn't seem to hear the druid, who repeated his name, touching him lightly on the shoulder. "Did many of your people die, Galchobhar?"

With a heavy sigh, the blood-stained villager came back to the present and met Bellicus's eyes. "No. Only those," he said, gesturing with his head to four bodies on the ground, "who were killed when we stood against the Dalriadans just now."

Puzzled, for he'd looked on as Galchobhar had hacked the raiders to pieces with terrible fury, as if a great many of his kinsmen had died, Bellicus smiled consolingly. "That's good news then. You were luckier than most settlements who came up against these raiders from what I hear."

"Lucky?" The headman demanded, pointing at the little feasting hall that had granted welcome shelter to the druid and Duro just a few months earlier. "Four of my people—good men and women—are dead, and our village is destroyed, druid. I'd hardly call that lucky."

Duro opened his mouth to rebuke the headman, but Bellicus held him back, shaking his head and asking him to go and help the villagers. Now was not the time for an argument.

"Our lookouts warned us of their approach," Galchobhar was saying, still apparently in shock at the scene of destruction before them. "But there were too many for us to fight, so, rather than throwing away my peoples' lives, I ordered them to run and hide in the woods."

"You did the right thing," Bellicus said firmly. "Your hall, and your homes, can be rebuilt."

"Can they?" Galchobhar demanded, eyes blazing as brightly as the flames that were consuming the thatched roof of the hovel directly behind them.

"Of course they can," the druid replied. "Queen Narina will send supplies and waive your taxes until Auchalic is rebuilt." He grasped Galchobhar by the arms and stared down at him. "Material goods are easily replaced. A human life, once snuffed out, is over until the next incarnation and only the gods can say when or how that will come about. You showed good leadership in sacrificing the buildings instead of your people. Now you must continue to lead them well, instead of standing here complaining."

For a moment it seemed like Galchobhar would lash out at the giant druid, but the battle fever was already leaving him and, thankfully, he looked away, shoulders dropping as the weight of responsibility settled upon him.

"We'll help you douse the fires and clear the rubble," Bellicus said. "Come on, your people need to see you. This is something you'll overcome and be stronger for once it's all over. Trust me, I've seen it before. Thank the gods you weren't caught unawares or Auchalic would be nothing but a memory now."

Galchobhar nodded, comforted by the druid's words, and breathed deeply, filling his lungs and drawing his shoulders back again, steeling himself for the work ahead. "You're right. Of course you are." He even managed a smile as he headed purposefully towards the middle of the village, where the fires were still burning the brightest. "Come on then, my lord. Grab a bucket and help me save my village!"

CHAPTER TWENTY-SEVEN

Aife looked at the queen of Alt Clota, trying to get some idea of what Narina might be like. The Pictish warrior-woman was no longer being held in the prison, having been given a room in one of the roundhouses near the top of the fortress. She'd been allocated a young girl to act as a maid, and her quarters were pleasant enough, but she was most definitely a prisoner. If she wanted to go for a walk, she had to ask permission from the guards that would be posted on her door night and day.

It was not an ideal situation but Aife accepted her lot for now. She might have been dead after all and the fact that the queen had deigned to visit her at all was, hopefully, a good sign.

"I hope you're comfortable enough," Narina said, but, although she spoke politely, she did not smile. "I don't want to make your time here unpleasant, Aife, but I can't ignore the fact that you tried to sneak into my fortress in the hopes of murdering me and my people."

Aife nodded. "That's only to be expected," she said. The thought of standing up crossed her mind, for she would tower over the queen and it might reverse their roles a little – give Aife more of an advantage. But she dismissed the idea when she saw Narina's light green eyes watching her and realised it would take much more than that to intimidate the queen.

"Is there anything else we can do?"

Aife shrugged. "Not really. I like to stay strong and fit so, if I might be allowed to run, swim in the river on warm days, spar with some of your men, that kind of thing, I'd be grateful. Other than that, I don't need much."

Narina sat on the low bed beside Aife, which surprised the Pict. Either the queen did not fear her at all, which was galling, or she trusted Aife, which could be seen as foolish. Aife did not believe Narina was a fool, and instinctively wanted to be worthy of the older woman's trust.

She smiled, thinking back to the giant druid Bellicus's complaints about being easily manipulated by Ria and wondering if this Queen Narina had similar powers. She would find out in time, no doubt.

"Of course, you may exercise," Narina said, returning the Pictish woman's smile. "In time—when you've proven yourself trustworthy and not attempted to kill anyone, or escape—you'll be given more freedom to roam. I've no intention of keeping you cooped up like an animal, but you must earn my trust, and the trust of everyone in Dun Breatann."

Aife remained silent. She was at the beginning of what might prove to be a very long stay within the walls of this towering fortress and had no intentions of making any promises before she had a chance to fully understand how her life was going to be here.

"Your father and some of his men have left," Narina told her. "The rest of them, apart from one or two who I'll be holding here as hostages the same as you, will go once their ransom has been paid."

They looked at one another and, despite their differences, Aife felt like she might be friends with this young queen. It would not stop her trying to escape, of course, but, for now, there was no point in being antagonistic for it would merely make things difficult for herself. She would play the part of the docile captive for a week, or a month, or however long it took to lull the folk of Alt Clota into a false sense of security, and then she'd steal a horse or a boat, and make her way back to Dunnottar.

"You are thinking of escaping," Narina said, and her tone remained friendly, but her eyes were hard. "I can understand that. You're a warrior, after all, and a good one, I have no doubt. But you can't defeat everyone in Dun Breatann. Oh, you could take me prisoner and threaten to kill me, but how far do you think you'd get?" She reached out and patted Aife's hand, almost in a motherly gesture although Narina was only a few years older. "You'll be happy enough here, don't make things harder than they need to be." She stood up and walked to the door. "I plan on making the lands here in the north of Britannia a force to be reckoned with, no matter what it takes. I would like us to be friends, you and me, but if you get in my way you will regret it, Aife."

The Pictish warrior-woman stared at her defiantly but she could see there was no point in making threats or bold boasts. Narina was not a woman to be easily cowed or put off when she was set on a path, that much was obvious even from this short meeting.

"Alt Clota is a beautiful place," the queen said in a friendlier tone, lifting the latch on the door and letting a sliver of sunlight stream in. "There will be much to keep you occupied – things a warrior will enjoy, if you allow yourself. You may even grow to like it here. I hope so." She smiled and left, the sound of the bolt on the outside being slotted back into place confirming her departure.

Aife stood up and went to look out one of the small windows that afforded a view of the Clota. It was not big enough to climb through, and the wooden walls were much too sturdy to break apart without some kind of tool, but she was grateful that she could look outside and see the sun and the boats on the river, and the gulls that wheeled in the sky overhead.

She breathed deeply of the fresh, clean air and thought about her future, and the future of all these lands. She was not particularly close to her father, Drest, and, as she grew into a strong adult herself, she had come to realise he was not the strongest of kings. He was not a bad ruler, but unambitious and fonder of hunting animals than battling enemies.

To Aife it seemed like things were changing. For generations her people had been left alone, being too far in the northern wilderness to make it worthwhile for the Romans or anyone else to seek to conquer them. But the world appeared to be growing smaller and more dangerous, and the idea of one strong ruler to oversee everything north of the Roman walls appealed to her.

As to the question of who the best person for the job would be, Aife could understand why many people thought Drest was not the answer. Perhaps it wasn't a High King the land needed – it was a High Queen.

And given the outcome of the recent battle, it seemed like the gods had given their blessing to Narina. Maybe Aife would too, one day. For now, though, she would bide her time until the chance to escape presented itself, for she was still a Pict, and the Damnonii were still her enemies.

* * *

Cistumucus, captain of the *Milwr Môr,* was surprised when, two days later, as Auchalic's rebuilding was well underway, Bellicus told him they were not going home to Dun Breatann just yet. First, they would sail further west, and see if any other settlements needed their help.

Their journey didn't last much longer though, for they found the rest of the coastal villages had also been torched by Dalriadan raiders—whether Dubhslaine's men or not, they had no way of knowing—but, unlike Auchalic, those settlements were beyond help. The people were all dead or scattered, their valuables stolen, livestock taken or senselessly slaughtered and left out in the sun to rot, while the buildings were simply blackened shells.

"What now?" Duro asked when they'd come across the fourth scorched village and the sight of murdered men, women, and children had—horribly—become less shocking. "Do we take the men and march inland to find the Dalriadans responsible for these outrages?"

Bellicus had thought about it but decided they should return to Dun Breatann and deliver their news to the queen. "No," he said. "We're too close to Dalriadan lands and don't have the numbers to stand against a proper army. Our men are tired, and we were only supposed to be going to Auchalic anyway. We'll discuss what we've seen with Narina, Gavo and Gerallt, then decide what's to be done." He stared at the burnt-out buildings and then commanded the men to build a funeral pyre before they sailed for home.

It was no simple task to build a fire big enough to deal with the bodies of so many people and the men were glad to set sail for Dun Breatann that afternoon. They had come on this mission to fight raiders – none had expected to witness so many ruined settlements, or to build funeral pyres for so many sad corpses. Even the most grizzled of the warriors was sick of the smell of burning flesh and the greasy, black smoke that they left behind whenever they moved on.

Eburus too had grown more and more subdued as the days passed, his loud jesting and boasting slowly replaced by quiet introspection and silence. He helped with their grim work as much as anyone but appeared a different man by the time the sails were unfurled and the ships pushed back into the Clota for the journey home.

"Here," Bellicus said to the young Votadini champion as the wind mercifully cleared the smoke from the air and drove them ever further away from the devastated settlements.

Eburus looked up from where he sat, alone, on the deck and gazed blankly at the ale skin in the druid's hand.

"I don't normally encourage people to drink excessively," Bellicus told him. "But sometimes it's good to forget the things you've seen, even just for a short time. Take it, my friend, you've earned it."

Wordlessly, Eburus grasped the skin and un-stoppered it, taking a small sip, staring out at the landscape passing so serenely by before taking a longer, deeper draught and handing it back to the druid who shook his head.

"You can finish it if you like, there's plenty more on board. Ale was one thing the men made sure they loaded before we set sail from Dun Breatann." He took a seat beside the Votadini warrior, Cai lying down beside his master and resting his head on Bellicus's thigh. Duro also came over with a drink of his own and sat on the other side of Eburus.

"I must admit," the centurion said, patting the younger man on the leg and raising his ale skin in salute to him. "You've been a better companion than I expected on this trip, and you have my thanks for saving my life. That was quite the spear throw!" He became deadly serious as he went on. "Try not to let the things we've seen over the past few days bear you down, lad. War is terrible, but the sun always rises after even the darkest of nights."

Bellicus was surprised to hear the veteran soldier offering this advice, given his recent mental anguish. Perhaps counselling Eburus would be good for both of them. He smiled. Life was never dull.

"I'm the Champion of my people," Eburus said. "But that's because I beat the best of our warriors in single combat. Honestly, I've only been in a handful of real battles and they…" He shook his head and took another swallow of ale. "They were nothing like what we saw in those villages. Children killed, by the gods! For what? Pregnant women murdered…" His voice trailed off and there was a haunted look in his eyes that Bellicus knew all too well. He imagined he himself had a similar expression the first time he saw such wanton, vicious brutality.

"That sort of thing is why your king allowed you, and the rest of your kinsmen, to join us," Bellicus said. "Trust me, the Saxons will do what those Dalriadans did, but on a much bigger scale, unless we stop them."

"Will Narina still be sending that warband to join Arthur?" Duro asked. "Things have changed since we came up with that plan. I can see her changing her mind and, rather than looking south, using the warriors she has to strengthen her own borders and consolidate her position."

The druid shook his head slowly. "I don't know. *We* may call her High Queen, but that would mean a proper, lasting peace with the Votadini and Picts. Even if the kings agree to it in public, behind closed doors they may still seek to claw back whatever lands or power they can. As it's always been."

"I didn't join you to fight Dalriadans," Eburus growled. "I mean, I did, for this journey. But that was just because I was bored." He fell silent momentarily, peering at his ale skin thoughtfully, as if he'd rather be bored than have witnessed all the senseless death and brutality of the past few days. "Cunedda won't sanction us staying in Alt Clota just to strengthen your own borders. We have enough troubles of our own, what with Picts, Saxons, Jutes and all the rest of the scum that washes ashore on our beaches."

"Perhaps," Bellicus shrugged. "Maybe Cunedda will be happy to leave your warband in Alt Clota if his son marries Narina though. Who knows what such a union would bring?"

"What of you, Bel?" Duro asked. "Will you take command of the border force?"

"Not me," the druid replied, wriggling out of his dark robe as the sun appeared from behind a cloud and the temperature became stifling again, despite the ever-present spray that permeated the air. "It's an important job, but it'll be carried out by one of the junior officers I imagine. I don't know what Narina will expect of me going forward." He genuinely didn't have a clue what his life would be like in the coming years if Narina married Ysfael, and Duro left Alt Clota to return south. It was not a pleasant thought and, although druids were fabled for having the gift of foresight, Bellicus thought it probably for the best that he couldn't see through the mists of time at that point. It all seemed quite bleak.

The three men, and Cai, relaxed in thoughtful silence for a long time then, lost in the gentle motion of the ship and the hypnotic sound of the water as the *Milwr Môr* slid easily through it. If only life could be as peaceful all the time! Although not one of them would be happy for long if that was the case, Bellicus knew. Well, apart from Cai maybe.

But Narina was, as much as anyone could be at this point, High Queen, and the thought of spending the coming months and years dealing with petty raids from the surrounding tribes until, at last, one or more of them built up the strength and togetherness to besiege Dun Breatann yet again was a depressing one. Especially if he had to watch another man be with Narina and act as a father to Catia.

"I'm coming with you," he said, nodding his head as a wide grin formed on his stubbled face.

"Me?" said Eburus, frowning as he rose to his feet somewhat unsteadily. "I'm only going for a piss, but all right."

"Not you, you stupid bastard," Bellicus laughed, shoving the Votadini away towards an empty section of deck where he could empty his bladder over the side without it blowing back onto the men on board. "Duro."

The centurion was smiling too now but he still wasn't quite sure what was being said. "You'll come south with me? To Arthur?"

"And the Merlin. Aye."

"What about Alt Clota, and Narina?"

"They're in the best position they've been in for many long years and they can do without me, for a time at least, now that Koriosis is there to help. We can't lose sight of the Saxon threat, old friend. Horsa and Hengist will come for us eventually, and if we don't curb their expansion now, they'll be unstoppable by the time they're at Dun Breatann's gates."

"If you're both going," Eburus called over his shoulder as his stream of urine disappeared into the Clota. "I may as well come too."

"It's settled then," Duro shouted, getting to his feet and grasping Bellicus by the arm in the old warrior's grip as Cai watched them with a bemused expression. The relief on the centurion's face was obvious, for he'd been dreading their parting just as much as the druid. "The four of us together, lads. The Saxons won't know what's hit 'em!"

Author's Note

The Northern Throne was written, mostly, during the 2020 lockdown. It was a very strange and frightening time, being confined to our own houses, not allowed to go anywhere and, without planning it, or even realising it at first, my feelings of being imprisoned made their way into the novel. I think, when Bellicus finally escaped and made it back to his beloved Dun Breatann we could all share—if only in a little way—his relief at finally returning to normality. Most of us would have felt the same when lockdown finally eased, and we could see friends and family, go to the pub, or visit a favourite beauty spot again.

Lockdown is hopefully over for good now but, for Bellicus and friends, there's plenty more trials to be faced. I haven't written down a detailed plan for the next book but the Saxons—Hengist and Horsa—are clearly the main threat to the Britons so we're going to see a lot more of them, along with Arthur and Merlin. I hope you'll join me for their coming adventures.

Before I begin work on that book, however, my standalone Roman slave novel, *Lucia*, which has been available exclusively from Audible until now, will come out this October on Kindle and paperback. Then I plan on writing another Forest Lord mystery to follow on from 2019's *Faces of Darkness*, so look out for all that and please *stay safe*.

If you enjoyed *The Northern Throne* please leave a review on Amazon, it really is a HUGE help and greatly appreciated.

Steven A. McKay,
Old Kilpatrick,
July 18th, 2020

Acknowledgements

Thanks to my beta readers, Bernadette McDade and Robin Carter, and to my editor, Richenda Todd. I think between us we made *TNT* a decent read.

Printed in Great Britain
by Amazon